The
Arabian Nights
Murder

John Dickson Carr Mysteries:

The
Arabian Nights
Murder

John Dickson Carr

PERENNIAL LIBRARY

Harper & Row, Publishers, New York
Grand Rapids, Philadelphia, St. Louis, San Francisco
London, Singapore, Sydney, Toyko

A hardcover edition of this book was originally published in 1936 by Harper & Row, Publishers.

THE ARABIAN NIGHTS MURDER. Copyright © 1936 by John Dickson Carr. Copyright renewed © 1964 by John Dickson Carr. All rights reserved. Printed in the United States of America. No part of this book may be used or reproduced in any manner whatsoever without written permission except in the case of brief quotations embodied in critical articles and reviews. For information address Harper & Row, Publishers, Inc., 10 East 53rd Street, New York, N.Y. 10022.

First PERENNIAL LIBRARY edition published 1989.

LIBRARY OF CONGRESS CATALOG CARD NUMBER 88-45957

ISBN 0-06-080981-7

89 90 91 92 93 WB/OPM 10 9 8 7 6 5 4 3 2 1

"You swear by the Beard of the Prophet. Then could not the teller of tales make us a curious story even out of a beard?"

—Arabian Nights' Entertainment

"I hesitated; and at length a single word, uttered distinctly but slowly, and as if breathlessly spoken, fell upon my ear; it was, *'Whiskers!'*"

—Life of the Rev. R. H. Barham

Contents

PART III: THE SCOTSMAN IN THE ARABIAN NIGHTS: STATEMENT OF SUPERINTENDENT DAVID HADLEY

The
Arabian Nights
Murder

Prologue

Four men sat round a circular table in the big library at Number 1 Adelphi Terrace. In the course of only a few years, a good many queer and startling exhibits have been placed on that table under the drop-lamp for Dr. Fell's inspection. There was, for instance, the clockwork toy dancer, that little tin figure whose gyrations provided the clue in the Weatherby Grange affair; or the six blue coins which hanged Paulton of Regent Street. But the table has seldom seen a more incongruous collection of articles than were placed there on this night. They were the exhibits in that case which has come to be known as the Arabian Nights murder. There were half a dozen of them, beginning with a cookery-book and ending with two pairs of false whiskers.

The strong lamp over the table had rather the effect of a spotlight. There was no other light in the room except that of the fire, which had been built up for (if necessary) an all-night sitting. Enthroned in his largest chair, presiding over a side table replete with cigars and spirits, Dr. Gideon Fell sat beaming. The doctor was in the most exuberant good health after four months in the south of France. He had gone to Cannes, it may be remembered, over the Giraud poisoning case in which the two English girls had got themselves entangled; a bad business. Afterwards he had idled along the Côte d'Azur, partly to cure his asthma but chiefly from a healthy natural laziness. Now his face was redder than ever under the droplamp. His small eyes twinkled behind eyeglasses on the broad black ribbon; chuckles animated his several chins and ran down over the bulges of his waistcoat; and his vast presence seemed to overflow the room like the Ghost of the Christmas Present. One hand rested on his cane, the other held a rich cigar with which he pointed to the exhibits on the table.

"Yes, I am interested," he admitted, with a wheeze of pleasure. "I am willing to listen all night to any case which can somehow combine a cookery-book and two pairs of false whiskers. One pair is white, I note, and the other black. But I say, Hadley, what about these other exhibits?" He pointed. "They seem almost as bad. That curved blade I can understand; it looks deadly enough. But what about these photographs? This one looks like a set of tracks. And *this* one—well, it looks like a photograph of an Eastern stall or bazaar, with a big black splash on the wall just over the door. Hey?"

"Quite so. That," said Superintendent Hadley, gravely, "was where somebody threw coal at the wall."

Dr. Fell stopped with his cigar half-way to his mouth. He inclined his head a little on one side, so

2

that his big mop of grey-streaked hair tumbled over one ear.

"Threw coal at the wall?" he repeated. "Why?"

Divisional-Inspector Carruthers interposed with a gloomy air. "Yes, sir. It's very important, unless the superintendent's reconstruction is altogether wrong. And, in connection with that mark, your attention is respectfully directed to this black false moustache. You see that it had spirit-gum on it to begin with, which is more important still . . ."

"Be quiet, will you?" roared Sir Herbert Armstrong, that eminent business man whose talents had now made him Assistant-Commissioner of the Metropolitan Police. "Can't you see you're gettin' it all tangled up? You be quiet, both of you, and let *me* explain. Now! Fell, we're in a nasty situation, and as a last resort we're going to put it up to you. It's so crazy that nobody else will understand it."

"You overwhelm me," said Dr. Fell. "Go on."

He looked round the table at his three guests. Each was a contrast for the telling or even the thinking of a story, though each had been produced by that Britain whose corners were drawn together round the table.

John Carruthers, the Irishman, was Divisional-Detective-Inspector at Vine Street. He was of the new type of police-officer: not more than thirty-five, a university honours-man for scholarship as well as athletics, well-mannered, with a strong and sometimes erratic imagination. He had learned sharply to curb this imagination, though the curbing often made him a little self-conscious. His only un-Irish trait was a sometimes uncomfortable ability to see the other person's point of view. Otherwise you saw a long, sombre, humorous face, with a pipe dangling from one corner of

3

his mouth and dark brows drawn together over ironical eyes.

Sir Herbert Armstrong, with his bald head and his hard stoutness, was unfathomably English. He might have sat as a model for that Dr. Bull whose name alone remains of his personality. Loyal, sentimental, cynical, genial, garrulous, hot-headed and stubborn, he disliked his own virtues but was very proud of his prejudices. He possessed an explosive but completely harmless temper, which (behind his back) had gained him throughout mysterious channels in the Force the regrettable nickname of Donald Duck. Finally, he was always a good friend, as at least one person in the Arabian Nights case could testify.

The third of the trio, Superintendent David Hadley, came originally from north of the Tweed. He was Dr. Fell's best friend, and the doctor knew him as well as anybody; but, Dr. Fell often admitted, you never knew where you were with him. Cautious, even-tempered, and logical on the surface, he could be alternately slow and brilliant, alternately stolid and erratic. That calm stolidity of his—it is still told how he walked alone into the most odorous thieves' kitchen east of Poplar, arrested Myers and Bailey with a dummy gun, and calmly walked them out ahead of him with his back turned to every knuckle-duster in the place—that stolidity covered a streak of touchiness which was quick to take offence at any slight, even when none had been intended. He disliked scandal, was a great family man, and had possibly a too-great sense of dignity. Though he would have denied it angrily, he had perhaps a stronger imagination than either of the others. Finally, he was never known to turn down anybody in serious trouble, friend of his or not.

Dr. Fell looked round the group and wondered.

"You listen to me," Sir Herbert Armstrong went on, whacking the table. "This business at the Wade Museum has got to be thrashed out. You're sure you haven't seen an English newspaper in four months, and don't know *anything* about it? Right! All the better! Here's every record verbatim, in these files. We have here the three people who handled the business through all its stages, up to the point where it was triumphantly crowned with failure..."

"Failure?" said Hadley. "I shouldn't go so far as to say that."

"Well, legal failure, anyhow. It's like this: Carruthers here had the first blast of the lunacy, the murder and the situation which nobody on earth seemed able to explain. Then I took over, and we got an explanation of the situation—which still made howling nonsense of the murder. Then Hadley took over, and we got an explanation of the murder—which still made howling nonsense of everything else. This damned case is a kind of chrysalis, which opens layer by layer, with a successive explanation on each layer, and under it the word 'Stung.' Coal-dust!" said Armstrong bitterly. "Coal-dust!"

Dr. Fell looked a little dazed.

"It's a fool's game," pursued Armstrong, querulously, "but we're going to go over this mess of nonsense again. You've got to sit on the flying carpet whether you like it or not. Each of us is going to tell his story in turn and supply the explanation of the previous man's problem. At the end of it, you've got to suggest what in blazes we're going to do about it. That is, if you can see anything: which I doubt. All right, Carruthers. Hop to it."

Carruthers seemed uneasy. He reached for the pile

of blue-bound typewritten sheets at Hadley's elbow, and his sombre and humorous eye moved round the group. Then a grin appeared behind the waggling pipe in his mouth.

"I'm afraid I bungled the thing badly," he said. "However, sir, I do not seem to have got into undue trouble over it, so I am a little easier in my mind. Thus spoke the taleteller from his seat by the bazaars. I suggest that you fill up your glass and hold tight to your hat, sir, for here we go.

"My first intimation that something was wrong—"

Part I

The Irishman in the Arabian Nights:
Statement of Detective-Inspector
John Carruthers

1

The Disappearing Whiskers

My first intimation that something was wrong came from Sergeant Hoskins—a uniformed sergeant, it must be remembered—and even then it was difficult to see in the business anything more than a lunatic capering on a wall. Still, though we get cases of hilarity at Vine Street, especially when the white ties are making a night of it, the perpetrators seldom wear long white whiskers.

I met Hoskins at just eleven-fifteen on the night of Friday, June 14th. I had been late at the station, and still had work to do; so I was going out for coffee and a sandwich at a coffee-stall in Panton Street before I went back to work. When I looked out into the Haymarket for a breather under the lights, I almost ran into Hoskins. He is one of the old-fashioned type; heavy and magisterial, with a Napoleonic moustache, and I had never seen him so jarred out of his calm.

He was breathing hard; he drew me over into the shadow, and said, "'*Ere!*"

"Sir," said Hoskins, "I've been seeing what they call rags for twenty-five years, but I never saw a rag like this. And him with long white whiskers, too, even if they was false! I'll whisker him!" said Hoskins malevolently. "'Ere!" He pointed to his neck. I could see above the collar the long and deep scratches of nails. "You know the Wade Museum, sir? In Cleveland Row?"

Like most people, I had heard of the Wade Museum. I had always thought vaguely that I must drop in there one day, though I had never done it. Our division had strict orders to keep an eye on it; not only from Wade himself, but from quarters high up in the Force. I suppose you must have heard of old Geoffrey Wade, even if you know him only as an immense bank-balance. That would not please him, however. Though I had never seen him, I had heard him described as fiery, eccentric, and "the greatest showman on earth." Also, I knew that he owned some property in St. James's, including a block of flats in Pall Mall Place.

About ten years ago he endowed a small private museum (open to the public) of which he himself acted as curator. It was an Asiatic or Oriental museum, I had always understood, though I remember reading an article somewhere which said that there were also some good exhibits of early English coaches: a hotch-potch after the old man's heart. The museum is in Cleveland Row, across the square from St. James's Palace. But it is tucked away towards the eastern end of the street, among those gloomy little squares and buildings which seem to have been deserted since the eighteenth century. You will not find it a very lively neighbourhood

10

even in daytime—there are too many echoes—and at night you can give it any queer colours your imagination likes.

Consequently, when Hoskins mentioned the place, I was interested. I told him to stop breathing brimstone and tell me what had happened.

"I was going round the beats," says Hoskins, drawing himself up, "and walking west along Cleveland Row. Time about eleven, sir. I was going on to my next point—Pall Mall beat—to pass the constable there. And I was passing the Wade Museum. You've seen the place, sir?"

I had passed it a few times, and retained some recollection of a two-storeyed stone house fronting the street, with a narrow strip of high wall at either side. Also, it had high bronze doors, circled in a frieze of what may or may not have been an Arabic inscription: that was how you came to notice the place. Both Hoskins and I came off the official high-horse; I'm afraid I can never ride it for very long.

"So I thinks to myself," pursued Hoskins, with a hoarsely confidential air, "I thinks to myself I'll try the doors, and make sure Barton hasn't overlooked nothing. Well, sir, the doors were tight-locked. So I flashed me lamp about, without thinking anything, you see, sir; I flashed it up—" He stopped. "Well, I got a turn and no mistake. For there 'e was up there, sitting on the wall. A tall, thin, oldish man in a top-hat and a frock-coat. And he had long white whiskers."

I studied Hoskins. I didn't know whether to laugh, or what to do; and, if I had not known him better, I would have sworn this was some sort of elaborate leg-pull. But the man was malignantly serious.

"Yes, sir, I mean it! Sitting on the wall. I put me light on him; naturally I was a bit staggered—at his

11

age, and with the hat stuck on the side of his head, and a bit smashed, like—but I called out, "'Ullo! What are *you* doing up there?' Then I got a dekko at the chap's eyes, and I'm bound to admit——"

"You're too sensitive, sergeant."

"All right, sir, you may laugh," said Hoskins darkly, and with an ominous nod, "but you didn't see him. He'd got on big shell-rimmed glasses. He was glaring at me like as if he was crazy. That long face, and them unnatural whiskers, and them long thin spidery legs hanging down over the wall. . . . All of a sudden he jumped. *Bing!* like that. I thought he was going to jump on me. Ever see a church-warden, sir, passing the collection plate round? He looked like that, only mad. He fell all in a heap, but he got up. And then he said to me, *'You killed him, and you'll hang for it, my fine impostor. I saw you in the coach.'* And with that he came at me with both hands."

Now, Hoskins was not drunk (he was breathing hard in my face, so I could tell that); nor was he capable of imagining this monstrosity.

"The Old Man of the Mountain, probably," I said. "What then?"

Hoskins was apologetic. "I 'ad to paste him one, finally, sir. He was a wildcat, for all his old looks, and it was the only thing I could do. Well, I got him under the jaw to make it easy, and down he went. Then I discovered the queerest part—his whiskers were false. So help me, sir, that's true. They was fastened on with some kind of gum, and they'd come loose in the row. I couldn't get a good look at his face, because he'd kicked my lamp to blazes trying to kick me, and it was a bit dark in that part of the street."

Despite himself, a grin began to steal over Hoskins' face.

"Well, sir, I thought to myself, 'Lummy, but *'ere's* a rum business if you like!' "Ere I am (I thought) stranded with what you might call a venerable-looking old bloke, wearing a pair of false whiskers and laid out flat as a door-mat not a hundred yards from Pall Mall!' Eh? Made me feel a bit of a fool, I can tell you. The only thing I could do was call the Black Maria. I remembered I was to see Constable Jameson, on the rounds, in Pall Mall just then. So I thinks to myself I'll get Jameson to stand guard over the chap while I telephone. Well, sir, I propped 'im up in the gutter, with his head on the kerb-stone so he wouldn't get a rush of blood there and perhaps make 'im crazier. Off I walked, and I hadn't gone no more than a couple of dozen feet, when I looked back—just to make sure 'e was all right. . . ."

"And was he?"

"No, sir, he was not all right," Hoskins answered solemnly. "He was gone."

"Gone? You mean he got up and made a dash for it?"

"No, sir. He was dead to the world; that I'll kiss the Book on! I mean he was vanished. Pfft!" said Hoskins, with a strong effort of imagination and a broad tense wave of his hand. "That's as true as I'm telling you, sir." He drew himself up with dignity; something was evidently rankling. "You're an intelligent gentleman, sir, and I know you'll believe me. Constable Jameson, *'e* wouldn't believe it, and what does he do but try to make a game of his superior officer? 'Gone?' he says. 'Was 'e now? Carried off by the ruddy fairies, I suppose,' 'e says. 'False whiskers!' Jameson says. 'False whiskers me eye! Perhaps 'e 'ad roller-skates and a green parasol as well. Better not tell that story when you get back to the station, my lad.'—But I am telling it, because that's my duty, and I stick to it! What's more, there was nowhere that chap could have vanished *to.*" Hoskins conquered his smouldering wrath, after a few deep breaths. "Look at it, sir. 'Ere the chap was, lying as you might say in the middle of the street, and feet away from any door. What's more, it was so quiet I'd certainly have heard anybody who came near; I'd have seen anybody, because the street wasn't as dark as that, and I'd swear I'd gone no more than thirty feet away. But I saw nothing, I 'eard nothing, and in the course of ten seconds that chap was—pfft! If that ain't straight out of Maskylene Mysteries, sir, I dunno what is. Gone! Vanished where he couldn've vanished from, and that I'll take a Bible oath. But what bothers me is just this: things being what they are, what am I going to Do?"

I told him to go back to the station and cool off while I had a cup of coffee. Much as I should have liked to treat this situation seriously, and find in it some deadly significance which should help me to pull off my first *coup* in the West End, it was impossible to devote solemn thought to the Problem of the Disappearing Whiskers without feeling a worse fool than Sergeant Hoskins. Like Sergeant Hoskins, what the devil was I to do? On the other hand, unless Hoskins had been the victim of a complicated practical joke, it was no use denying that the thing had an unpleasantly queer look as well as a comic look. Though I kept pounding him with questions, Hoskins still swore that it was impossible for Whiskers to have been carried off in any way whatsoever, without his either seeing or hearing it done; and he was equally positive the man had been unconscious. There was only one thing to be done at the moment: I went to get my coffee.

And when I came back, now even more worried as to what the damned business *might* mean, there were already developments. Sergeant Hoskins met me at the door; he was off duty and had changed into plain clothes, but he lingered with repressed glee, jerking his thumb towards the saturnine countenance of P. C. Jameson behind him.

"Bit of luck, this, sir," he announced. "Jameson's had his whirl on the roundabout now."

"You mean Whiskers has appeared again?"

The saturnine Jameson saluted. He seemed uneasy. "No, sir, it isn't the same chap. It's somebody else who started kicking up a row at the Wade Museum not five minutes after the sergeant had gone. But when I ran into this fellow—*he* wanted to fight too." He glowered. "I thought you might like to talk to him. I haven't charged him, but I can do it in case you want to hold him for any reason: he tried to take a whack at me with his cane, the bleeder. I just asked him to step along quietly for a word with you. He's in your office now."

"What happened?"

"Well, sir," said Jameson, shifting a little, "I was going on with my beat—past that museum—when I saw this fellow standing outside with his back to me; he seemed to be running his hands over the bronze doors. Very fashionable young gentleman in evening-kit; hefty-built; sort of movie-actorish damn-your-eyes air about him. I called out and asked what he was doing. He said, 'I'm trying to get in; isn't that fairly obvious?' I said, 'I suppose you know that's a museum, sir?' He said, 'Yes, that's why I want to get in. There's a bell up here somewhere; come and help me find it.' Well, I pointed out that the museum was closed, there weren't any light, and hadn't he better move along home. He turned around, furious, and says, 'If it's any odds to you, I was invited to a private view; now I'm

15

not going to move along and what do you intend to do about it?' I said," Jameson puffed out his cheeks, "I might have to assist him. Then he says—it's the first time I ever heard it outside the movies—he says, 'Why, curse your impudence' (just like that), and up he whirls this stick of his and tried to take a cut at me. . . ."

"Seems to be in the air, sort of," the sergeant commented gloomily, scratching his moustache. "Hanged if I understand it; do you, sir?"

"Go on, Jameson."

"I got hold of his stick and I asked him gently, of course, if he'd mind stepping along to the station to be asked a few questions by the inspector. He changed a good deal. He got quiet. Questions about what?— that's what he wanted to know. I said, 'About a disappearance.' I thought he looked very queer; but he didn't raise any fuss, as I expected he would, and walked along asking me question after question. I didn't say anything, sir. He's in your office now."

Jameson, as you know, had gone beyond his duty; but the whole business was beginning to sound so weird that I was glad he had. I went down the corridor to my office and opened the door.

Now you will hear tonight various interpretations of the characters of these people we have to deal with. I can only give you mine. The man who had been sitting in my swivel-chair and who got up as though he were momentarily uncertain how to treat me, was impressive enough: especially in my dingy office. For a second there was something so vaguely familiar about him that I could have sworn I had met him before. This ghostly feeling persisted until I realised what it was. The man before me was the typical hero of a thousand novelettes. He was the novelette-hero miraculously come to life and toned down to credibility by his own careful efforts. (Also, he knew it.) For instance, he was tall, he was broad-shouldered; he had those hard and craggy good looks favoured of the women novelists, with light-blue eyes under tangled brows and dark, heavy hair cut short; he was even, I swear, sunburned. Set down any list of *clichés*, including the perfect evening-clothes, and the general air of one who has fought tigers: you will not go wrong on any of them. But most of all it was his air. Carried a little farther towards absurdity, you could almost imagine him saying, "Ho, varlet!" with a flicking wave of his wrist—but you had an uncomfortable idea that the varlet would jump to attention. What saved him from looking like a stiff-backed prig was a very genuine charm of manner, as though under this exterior there was an honest brag and bounce and excitability which he tried to repress. So those light eyes studied me out of the craggy sunburnt face (he was about twenty-eight); so I got an impression that under the stiffness he was weighing something, and was shaking with some strong mental excitement. Then he made a kind of salute with his stick, evidently deciding on hearty friendliness, and showed strong teeth when he smiled.

"Good evening, inspector," he said. His voice was exactly what you would expect; supply more *clichés*. He looked round with an air of casual humour. "I'm bound to warn you I've been in police-stations before, and some rather unpleasant gaols as well. But never before without knowing quite well why I was there."

I adopted his own attitude. "Well, sir, we've got a very decent gaol here," I said, "in case you want to increase your experience. Sit down, please. Smoke?"

He sat down again in my chair, and accepted a cigarette. He was leaning a little forward, his hands folded

17

on his stick, studying me with such glowering intentness under the tangled brows that he seemed almost cross-eyed. But the smile reappeared again, and he waited for me to strike him a match.

"I couldn't help thinking," he went on, with complete assurance when I did strike the match, "that your policeman had gone a little off his head. Naturally I accompanied him—you see I am fond of adventures, and I was curious to see what would happen." (A sort of bluff whimsicality.) "London's a dull place, inspector. But I am still in doubt as to what I have been and gone and done." He hesitated. "Robert said something about a 'disappearance.'"

"Yes. Just a little matter, Mr.——?"

"Mannering," he said. "Gregory Mannering."

"Your address, Mr. Mannering?"

"The Edwardian House, Bury Street."

"Your profession, Mr. Mannering?"

"Oh, say—a soldier of fortune."

Despite his deprecating and captivating bluffness, I thought this struck a very sour note; but I let it pass. He went on:

"Let's thrash this out, inspector. Maybe *you* can give me an answer, for I certainly can't. Look here: this afternoon I got an invitation—a personal invitation—to come round to the Wade Museum at eleven o'clock tonight . . ."

"I see. You know Mr. Geoffrey Wade, then?"

"As a matter of fact, I've never met him. But I imagine I shall get to know him pretty well, since I happen to be his prospective son-in-law. Miss Miriam Wade and I——"

"I see."

"What the devil do you mean, 'I see'?" he demanded, very quietly.

My ordinary stop-gap words had made his brows come down like a V and given him that suspicious half-cross-eyed look when he stared you straight in the face; but he conquered it and laughed. "Sorry, inspector. I admit I'm a bit annoyed. When I got there and found the blasted place dark, and not a sign of life anywhere—But I don't see how Miriam could have mistaken the date. She phoned me this afternoon. There was to be quite a distinguished gathering, including Illingworth of Edinburgh—the Asiatic scholar —you may have heard of him; he's the clergyman who's always addressing meetings. . . . And, since I have had some slight experience in the East, Miriam thought—" His mood changed. "By God, why am I telling you all this? Why all these questions, anyhow? In case you don't know it——"

"Just one more question, Mr. Mannering, to get things straightened out," I said soothingly. "What was this gathering at the museum to do?"

"I can't tell you that, I'm afraid. It's a discovery of the museum's; something private. In a manner of speaking, we were going to rob a grave. . . . Do you believe in ghosts, inspector?"

Again we were friendly, in one of this man's bewildering changes of mood.

"That's a difficult question, Mr. Mannering. But one of my sergeants was on the point of believing in ghosts tonight; that, really, was why you were brought here. Do ghosts wear false whiskers?" I looked at him, and was suddenly startled. "This particular ghost was lying very quietly, and then he disappeared right under the sergeant's eyes; he was moved. But the ghost made a certain accusation . . ."

I was rambling on with this true nonsense, trying to conceal the fact that I must be making a fool of myself, and wondering why Mannering had lowered his head and slid down in the chair a little. He lowered his head slowly, as though he were thinking; but the chair creaked back, and I saw that the head was now wagging limply to one side. His silver-headed stick rolled round his fingers, hesitated against his knee, and bumped to the floor. The cigarette fell after it. I called out to him, so sharply that I heard someone come running in the corridor outside.

When I wrenched his shoulders back, I saw that Mr. Gregory Mannering had fainted dead away.

2

"Haroun Al Raschid's Missus"

I hauled Mannering's great weight across to a bench, rolled him on it and called for water. His pulse was thin; by the way he was breathing I suspected that even so vigorous a specimen had a weak heart. Sergeant Hoskins, who came in after a hurried knock, stared from Mannering to the hat, stick, and cigarette on the floor. He picked up the cigarette.

"'Ere!" said Hoskins violently, studying the cigarette rather than the man on the bench. "Then there *is* something funny about that museum——"

"There is," I said. "And we have stepped into the middle of it; only God knows what it is. I'm going over there to find out. Stay here with him, and see if you can revive him. Take down anything he says. I mentioned your friend Whiskers, and he fell over in a faint. . . . Is there any way I can get into the museum at this hour? Night-watchman on the premises, or somebody like that?"

"Yessir. There's old Pruen. Museum's open in the evening, three nights a week, seven to ten; fad of the old gentleman's, d'ye see, sir. Pruen acts as attendant during the three hours, and later 'e's night-watchman. But you can't make him 'ear from the front. If you want to knock him up, go round to the back—Palmer Yard way."

Palmer Yard, I remembered, was an alley opening off St. James's Street, and running parallel with Cleveland Row at the rear. Hoskins admitted that he had not thought of routing out Pruen, on the grounds that he did not connect such carryings-on *with* so respectable an institution as the Wade Museum. But, it occurred to me as I put a flashlight in my pocket and went out to start up my car, it was now possible to treat the Problem of the Disappearing Whiskers with some degree of seriousness.

Now common sense said that there was only one way by which an unconscious man can suddenly vanish from the middle of an empty street. It was not a dignified way, it was even a gloriously comic way; but why should we expect crime to be dignified? You see that I was already thinking of it as a crime, even if I thought of it as lunacy. When I joined the Force eleven years ago the first thing I was ordered to get rid of was a sense of humour; and for anyone who comes from the County Down I have done the best I can on such short notice.

I drove down the Haymarket and along a deserted Pall Mall. There is not in London so lonely-looking a place as the foot of St. James's Street at that hour of the night. It was bright moonlight, and the gilt clock over the palace gate said five minutes past midnight. Towards the west Cleveland Row looked heavy and shadowy. I did not go round to the back, as Hoskins

22

had suggested. I parked my car directly in front of the museum, got out, and searched the dark pavement with my flashlight. Over near the edge of the kerb I saw what Hoskins with his smashed lamp had missed: a circular opening in the pavement, loosely fitted with an iron cover.

In other words, the disappearing lunatic must have been whisked down a coal-hole.

Don't laugh, gentlemen. You didn't see the confounded thing as I did, in the middle of a dark square beyond human life, with those bronze doors of the museum grinning directly opposite. Whiskers had slid back into the coal-hole like a genie back into his bottle. I turned my light on the museum. It was a heavy building of about eighty feet frontage on the street, rather squat with its two storeys of polished stone blocks. The lower windows were blocked out with stone, the upper ones covered with iron grilles after the French fashion. Half a dozen broad and shallow steps led up to the front doors; there was a hood over the doors, supported by two stone pillars, and inside the bronze winked under my light with a clutter of Arabic characters. No more fantastic house out of the *Arabian Nights* was ever tucked away into a London street. About six feet of high wall stretched on either side. Beyond the wall on the right I thought I could make out the top of a tree; it was probably only a London plane tree, but your fancy could easily transform it into something more exotic.

I went back to the coal-hole, lifted the iron cover, and turned my flashlight down. The coal-slide had been moved away. In the dead of summer there was very little coal below, and it was a comparatively short drop. I did what the situation seemed to call for. I let myself down—chinned on the edge, so that I could pull the cover nearly closed again in case some choleric colonel should be returning home late and step into it—and then I let go.

There were boxes and packing-cases below. My feet nearly touched them as I hung. They had evidently been shoved into the coal-cellar at random, but they formed a kind of platform on which somebody had doubtless stood to pull Whiskers through. Moreover, the door of the coal-cellar stood open into the rest of the cellar: it had a heavy padlock hanging open from the hasp, with the key still stuck in it. I happened to kick over a box, which made a hellish booming noise, and jumped out into the bigger part of the cellar.

The place was damp, warm and stuffy. My light moved over white-washed walls; the floor was stacked with more packing cases, and almost carpeted with shavings and excelsior. Towards the far end there was a dead furnace stretching out asbestos-covered pipes: the whole cellar, I should have judged, was about a hundred feet long. Just beyond the furnace, three flap-windows were set high in the rear wall. At the left of the furnace was a big coal-bin, a kind of high wooden-walled pen with its door towards the front of the cellar, and still containing an excavated hill of coal. I was looking everywhere for Whiskers, expecting to find Lord knows what; and I even looked in there. But there was no sign of him. Nevertheless, my uneasy sensation increased. *Something* was here, if not the man himself. In putting out my hand to avoid bumping my head on a furnace pipe, I found a hanging electric-bulb; and the bulb was still warm. There was a draught from somewhere, and I could have sworn I heard somebody walking.

Towards the right there was a flight of concrete steps. The cellar ran far beyond them in that direction; they were built up like a monument against a board partition which cut off this rather narrow segment from bigger storage-vaults beyond. These steps faced back in the direction from which I had come. I went up, with my light off but ready. At the top there was a fireproof steel door, painted to represent wood, and equipped with one of those compressed-air valves to prevent the door from slamming. I eased open the knob. The valve made a noise like *whish;* an abrupt sound which made me stop half-way through the aperture. . . .

Ahead of me was what looked in the gloom like a big hall with a marble floor. And in the middle of it somebody was dancing.

That is a literal fact. I could hear the echoes of that unholy tap-dance clicking and tumbling hollowly. Looking towards the front of the museum, the bigger part of the hall was now on my left; I could see the balustrade of a white marble staircase. Up ahead showed the gleam of an electric lantern, a little glow in a gulf. It was motionless. It made ghostly the white marble floor, and threw a barred wheel of light round the object on which it was resting—an oblong box, about seven feet long by three feet high, whose new nail-heads glimmered. Round it, in capering shadows, tapped and clicked and cavorted a little human figure. It was all the more grotesque because the little man wore the neat blue uniform and brass buttons of an attendant; and the patent-leather peak on his neat blue cap shone as he wagged his head. He executed a last shuffle. His glee ended in asthmatic breathlessness. He kicked the box, and the booming echoes tumbled under the roof. When he spoke it was only a whisper.

"Haroun al Raschid's missus!" he said rather tenderly. "Ho, ho, *ho!* Spirit, I call it! Spirit!"

Now I am telling you in sober fact what I saw and heard, but could not credit. It was exactly like one of those moving-picture animated cartoons in which inanimate objects suddenly come to life after dark; and nothing, I've felt, could be more inanimate than a museum attendant. But his nasal voice was real. After a couple of wheezy chuckles, he settled his uniform primly, took a flat bottle from his pocket, shook it, and put back his head to drink.

I switched on my flashlight.

The beam across the hall caught his Adam's apple bobbing up and down in a red, wrinkled neck like a turkey's. His arm jerked down as he peered at me. As he blinked he seemed surprised but not at all alarmed.

"Is that—" he said; and then in a different voice, "Who's there?"

"I'm a police-officer. Come over here."

Sane values settled in again. Something stiffened him; something drew over him a shell of querulousness and defiance; he shrank and he glared, but still he was not at all alarmed. There was even a remnant of his glee. Picking up the lantern, he came shuffling over, muttering, moving his neck from side to side. I saw a bony framework of a face, the wrinkled skin in reddish blotches that extended to more than the tip of his long nose; a squeezed-looking face, with spectacles down on the nose, and squeezed-looking eyes that glared up at me as he set his head almost on one shoulder to look up. He ruffled himself.

"Oh, you are, are yer?" he enquired, with elaborate sarcasm. Then he wagged his head, as though at a dark suspicion confirmed, and had to clear his throat. "And may I ask what's the game, breaking and entering like that? Where did you *come* from? May I ask what's the GAME?"

"Save that," I said. "What's been going on here to-night?"

"Here?" he demanded, as though I had changed the subject after speaking of some other place. "Here? Nothing. Unless the unprintable mummies has got out of their obscene cases—and I haven't seen 'em—why, nothing."

"Your name is Pruen, isn't it? All right. Do you want to be had up on a kidnapping charge? If not, what's happened to the tall old man with the shell-rimmed glasses"—my gorge rose at saying false whiskers—"who was here about an hour ago? What have you done with him?"

He made a noise of incredulity, not unmixed with hoarse mirth. His defiance seemed to relax as he stared at me.

"You're loopy, old cock," said Mr. Pruen simply. "Look here, you haven't been round to the Dog and Duck, now, have you? 'Tall old man with'—oh, I say now, draw it mild! 'Ere, after all! I tell you what, old cock: you just get along home and sleep it off like a good——"

I put my hand on his shoulder. The fact that I wondered myself whether I might not be loopy made me want to wring his scrawny neck.

"Very well, we'll make it a murder charge then," I said. "In any case, you'll just step round to the station with me. . . ."

He collapsed, his voice going up shrilly. "'Ere, now,

I say—stop a bit! No offence. . . ."

"What happened here tonight?"

"Nothing! There's been nobody here since I shut up at ten o'clock!" (The worst of it was that this sounded like the truth.)

"There was to be a private view, or something like that, here tonight at eleven—wasn't there?"

Light seemed to break over him. "Oh, that! *That!* Why didn't you say so?" He became aggressive. "Yes, there was to have been one; but there wasn't. It was called off. ('Ere, I say, leggo; I've apologised; no offence; there!) Yes, they was to view some things, and Dr. Illingworth himself was to be here to see 'em, that's how important it was. Only at the last moment today Mr. Wade—that's the old gentleman—and *ain't* you going to ruddy well catch it from *him!*—that's the old gentleman, not young Mr. Wade—he had to go out of town. So it was called off this afternoon. That's all. Nobody's been here at all."

"Maybe. Just the same, let's have the lights on and take a look round."

"With pleasure," chortled Pruen. He looked at me. "Just man to man, though, and between ourselves, what did you think happened here? Anybody make a complaint?" As I hesitated he pounced triumphantly. "No, they didn't. Eh? Well, then! Are you paid to go about breaking and entering when nobody's made a complaint?"

"Are you paid," I said, "to dance round boxes in the middle of the night? What's in that box?"

"There's nothing in that box," he declared, with a solemnly gleeful wag of his head. "I know you're bound to suspect there's a dead man in it, but there ain't even a dead woman in it. That's just the joke: there's nothing in that box! Eh?"

Before I could make head or tail of this he had shuffled off in the darkness, swinging his lantern. He disappeared on the other side of the staircase. There was a series of clicks, and a line of soft light ran round the cornice of the ceiling. Concealed bulbs lit up the hall with a soft glow like moonlight.

The place did not grow less eerie for being illuminated. It was a very broad and high hall, floored throughout in marble, and with two lines of marble pillars—spaced about ten feet apart—going to the front doors. About it was that naked air which comes to public display-rooms. At the rear, in a direct line with the front doors, a broad marble staircase ascended to branch into two open galleries which evidently formed the first floor. The roof of the whole was in glazed tiles of chequered green and white: the colours, I later learned in the course of picking up much curious information about this place, of the mosque-domes at Baghdad.

In the side-walls were four open archways, two on either side; and over them I read in thin gilt lettering, "Persian Gallery," "Egyptian Gallery," "Gallery of the Bazaars," "Gallery of the Eight Paradises." Aside from these, and the big bronze gates at the front, there were three more doors. One—the door by which I had entered—was at the left of the staircase as you faced it. Another, exactly similar, was at the right of the staircase. The third was nearly at the extreme rear of the right-hand side-wall (as you faced the staircase); it had in gilt lettering, "Curator. Private," and was nearest the archway marked "Gallery of the Eight Paradises."

But it was at the exhibits in this hall, though there were few enough of them, that I looked. The right-hand sidewall—still facing towards the rear—was hung with great carpets, of a pattern which so haunted the eye that you found yourself twitching round constantly to look at them. I am not quite certain how to describe this. It was not merely their richness or their intricacy, or the drugged images they brought to the surface of the mind (as a matter of fact, they were mostly patterns like layers of flowers strewn on the ground), but it was their languid and living quality. They increased the eerie unreality of this place. Down the middle of the hall ran flat, glass-covered cases containing weapons; your eye moved instinctively from carpets to knives.

It was a relief to look towards the left-hand wall, between the line of pillars and the wall itself. Here was an exhibit which should have been incongruous, and yet for some reason was not: the coaches or carriages. There were five of them, looming huge and ugly in the moonlight glow. That nearest to me, at the front, was a low, gaudily painted, unwieldy, open box, whose placard read, "Built by Guilliam Boonen, coachman to Queen Elizabeth, and the first to introduce coaches into England, *circa* 1564. The traces are of leather, to indicate royalty, but the body is not yet suspended on straps." . . . I looked on. There was a seventeenth-century glass coach, a gilt-gingerbread French carriage with the Bourbon arms in red and green, and a Dickensian mail-coach whose door-panel bore the lettering, "The Ipswich Telegraph." Finally, in the middle was a gigantic equipage painted black and hooded closely in black leather, having only small glass windows like peepholes, and set on arched springs a good five feet off the floor.

I walked up and down, my footsteps echoing, and was roused by a sarcastic voice.

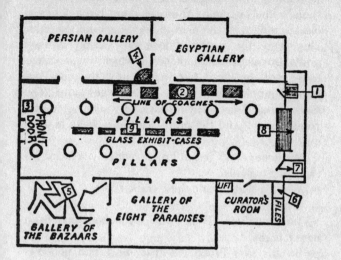

1. Stairs from cellar leading up to door into museum.
2. Carriage where body was found.
3. Where Pruen sat.
4. Circular iron staircase leading to floor above.
5. Wall with coal-dust marks.
6. Lavatory with window open into backyard.
7. Door to passage leading to rear door of museum.
8. Main staircase, going to floor above.
9. Glass case from which dagger was taken.

"All present and correct?" enquired Pruen. The wrinkled eyelids opened and shut in his wrinkled face. He cocked his cap at a sharp angle, and put his hands on his hips. "No kidnapped victims? No dead bodies? I say now! No traces at all——"

He broke off sharply, for I had gone to the front

31

again near the bronze doors, and I had seen traces of something. Stretching out about half a dozen feet, in a straight line beginning from the door, ran a series of black smudges on the marble floor. I got out my light. They were the marks of feet; not sharply defined prints, but angles and blotches in which you saw clear traces that somebody had walked in at this door and gone about two yards before the smudges faded. The mark of half a heel was distinct; so was the side of a pointed shoe. And the prints had been made in coal-dust.

"Whatcher GOT?" cried Pruen suddenly. I heard his clattering footfalls.

"Who," I said, "made these tracks?"

"What tracks?"

"You see them. Didn't you say nobody has been here tonight?"

"Ba-ah," says Pruen, "is that all? I said nobody's been 'ere after the museum closed at ten, that's all. How should I know? There was dozens of people 'ere earlier—don't you smile—dozens! We're popular, we are!"

"Where's your position when you're on duty? I mean, where do you stand or sit?"

He pointed to a chair at the left of the bronze doors as you faced the rear. It commanded a view down the hall of the right-hand side of the coaches, and also more than half of the door by which I had come upstairs.

"You sat there. Didn't you see anybody make these tracks?"

"No, I didn't."

"And you can explain, I suppose, how somebody walked in off the street with the soles of his shoes covered in coal-dust?"

Something flickered behind those flimsy little spectacles of his, as though he were nervous but determined. His lower lip came out.

"Now I ask you, I just ask you, whether that's my business? That's yours. Foot-marks: I ask you!" His voice grew high. "Maybe the corpse you're looking for walked in there when it was alive, eh? And maybe I took a knife and stuck him, eh? And then I shoved him away in one of them coaches, or maybe in a stall in the Gallery of Bazaars, or maybe in the Eight Paradises, or up in the Arabian Gallery upstairs. . . . Whatcher up to now?"

Something rose up in my throat. I walked down— rather quickly—past the line of coaches, leaving Pruen fluttering and flapping in the background. It was the middle equipage which held me: that enormous black-hooded carriage with its secret windows and its polished brass door-handles. A placard hanging on the door-handle read, "English travelling-carriage, early nineteenth century, built for tour on the Continent. It was used to ensure complete privacy."

Pruen's voice followed me: "Gorn!" he jeered. "Watch out when you touch it, old cock. There's a dead man inside! There's a great big bloody corpse lying just in——"

Then his voice rose in a kind of bubbling screech.

I reached up high and wrenched open the door-handle. Something pitched out head foremost, almost in my face. It seemed to jump like the opening of a jack-in-the-box, and I saw its eyes. It went past my shoulder; its shoes caught on the step of the carriage; it went sideways, and landed on the marble floor with a sodden flap.

The body of a tall man was lying flat on its back, arms and legs partly spread-eagled like a gingerbread

33

figure, and with it had fallen a brown-bound book from one hand. The man was as lifeless as gingerbread. He wore a long dark topcoat; and on the left side of his chest this coat was pushed up in a curiously tent-like fashion. When I drew that side of the coat away, I saw the white handle of the knife sticking up from a sodden shirt. But that was not what drew and fixed my eyes, not that or the top-hat that had been jammed down on his head.

As a height of the nightmare, the dead man was wearing false whiskers: a curt and draggling beard that had nearly come loose from his chin. But the false whiskers were *black*.

3

The Body In The Museum

I submit, gentlemen, that there are times when the rational brain has *no* coherent thought: when it can only file and absorb every visual detail before the eyes, in a paralysis of common sense. If that sounds too metaphysical or (in the case of a copper) like too much plain damned nonsense, I can tell you that you didn't stand over that grotesque thing in false whiskers in the Wade Museum at twenty-five minutes past midnight.

I noted the time while I examined every detail. The victim seemed to be between thirty-five and forty years old, although he had been made up to resemble a much older man. Even the false beard had careful tinges of grey. His face was distinctly handsome in spite of a slight roundness; it was of a satirical boldness even in death. His top-hat, decrepit but carefully brushed, was jammed down on dark hair. The brown eyes were wide open, the nose was high-bridged, and the skin had been very faintly swarthy. He wore a (real) black moustache. Under cheeks and chin still glistening with spirit-gum, the black whiskers hung by a patch about the size of a sixpence along the angle of his left jaw. The mouth hung open. He had been dead, so far as I could judge, not less than one hour and not more than two hours.

The topcoat was old like the hat, and frayed at the sleeves, but carefully tended. Putting on my gloves, I opened the coat again. Round the collar of the topcoat and going down inside the coat itself, ran a length of black ribbon terminating in a pair of eyeglasses. He wore evening clothes, also old, and with one button missing from the waistcoat; his linen was worn, with the exception of a new collar rather too large for him. From his chest—at a point higher than the heart, although by the look of him he must have died instantaneously—a heavy ivory handle projected about five inches in the blood. I looked over at his outflung right hand, and at the book which had tumbled from his fingers when he fell. It was bound in rubbed calf-skin, lying flat open with the pages twisted together, and it suggested even uglier secrets to be read into this puzzle.

I picked it up and opened it. It was a cookery-book.

Gentlemen, lunacy could go no further. The title was *Mrs. Eldridge's Manual of Home Recipes*, and the first item I encountered was a little lecture on the proper way of preparing mutton-broth.

I put the book down reverently; then I got a hand up and hoisted myself to the high step of the carriage for a look inside. My flashlight showed that the interior was swept and dusted. With black leather upholstery and a clean wooden floor, it showed no trace even of its late occupant. He must have been propped forward in a kneeling position, his cheek against the door, and his head down so that he could not possibly be seen from the outside. Some blood-stains on the floor: nothing else.

The first point I had to establish added even to the present chaos. This was the identity of the dead man. Now, unless two staggering mistakes had been made, the man with the knife in his chest could not possibly be the man who had assaulted Sergeant Hoskins outside the museum at a little past eleven o'clock. He was tall, yes. He was on the thin side, yes. It might be possible to confuse a frock-coat, of the old-fashioned type affected by Victorian statesmen, with an ordinary topcoat like this one. But it seemed impossible to confuse a white beard with a black one, and eyeglasses on a ribbon with large shell-rimmed spectacles: Hoskins could not have been so *completely* wrong on the two most important points of the description. Unless, of course, for some fantastic reason somebody had made a complete change.

I jumped down and scraped at the soles of the dead man's shoes. They had a thickish coating of coal-dust.

But the inception of a case is not the time to think; not even to think of that insane yell of White-Whiskers—to Hoskins, of all people—"You killed him, and you'll hang for it, my fine impostor. I saw you in the coach." For the moment, that matter must be dropped. I turned round to Pruen.

"You were quite right," I said. "There was a dead man inside."

He stood some distance away, wiping the back of one hand across his mouth, holding the flat bottle of gin against his chest with the other hand, peering at me out of rheumy eyes. For a second I thought he was going to start crying. But he spoke very quietly.

"I didn't know it," he said. "So help me, God, I didn't know it."

The hoarse voice seemed to come from far away. I took the bottle out of his hand and drew him forward. He was shaking badly.

"Do you still insist you were the only one in the place tonight?" I said. "If so, of course it'll be a murder charge after all."

A pause. "I can't help it, sir. I still tell you—that is—I—yes, I was alone. . . ."

"Come here; closer. Do you know this man?"

He twitched his head away, with such unexpected quickness that he masked his expression. "Him? Never saw him before. No. Looks like a dago."

"Look at the handle of that knife. Ever see that before?"

Pruen turned round and looked me in the eye, with the same watery doggedness. "Yes. Yes, I'm telling you straight, I've seen that knife a thousand times. Because it comes from here, that's why I've seen it, so make the MOST of it! 'Ere, I'll prove it to you!" he cried, as though I had doubted him, and plucked at my arm before he jabbed his finger towards the cases down the middle of the hall. "It comes from that case. It's what they call a '*khanjar*'—a Persian dagger, it is. Did you know that? Hah! I bet you didn't! A *khanjar* it is, that the carpet-spreaders carry. It's curved. A *khanjar*, gone from that case, which is used—" His voice had taken on the familiar habitual sing-song of someone repeating a set speech, and he blinked when he realised what he was saying; blinked, shuddered, and checked himself.

"So you know it was gone?"

Another pause. "Me? No. I mean to say I know it now."

"We'll talk about that after I do some telephoning. Is there a phone here? Good. By the way, do you still say that Mr. Geoffrey Wade is out of town?"

He still said so, violently. In charge of the museum while the owner was away, he told me, was a Mr. Ronald Holmes. Mr. Holmes lived not far away, in a service-flat in Pall Mall Place, and Pruen suggested with almost ghoulish eagerness that I should get in touch with him immediately. Gabbling, he led me across to the door marked "Curator." But when he pressed a wall-switch beside the door, he jumped a little at what he saw in the room, and I could have sworn it was as new to him as to me.

Although there were no more bodies, something of a rather violent nature had evidently taken place here. It was a big, comfortable room, richly carpeted after the Kurdistan fashion. There were two desks, one a big mahogany flat-top in the middle of the room, the other a business-like looking typewriter-desk in a corner surrounded by filing cabinets. The chairs were of red leather, the walls a sort of Moorish fretwork against which framed photographs looked outlandish. On the mahogany desk a small book lay open beside an ash-tray filled with cigarette-stubs.

But first you were conscious of the draught in the room. In the left-hand wall, towards the rear, was an open door giving on a small lavatory. A window high in the rear wall of the lavatory, over the wash-bowl, stood open. I looked round. On the carpet in front of the mahogany desk lay smashed the fragments of a small portable mirror. A little rug, of the occasional sort spread out on carpets, was twisted up awry. But that was not all.

To the right of the door by which I had entered, an electric lift had been built into the wall. The double-doors of the lift, each with a little glass window backed in wire, stood partly open. One of the windows had been smashed, obviously from inside. Splattered glass lay on the floor, along with a hatchet and a placard which had been hung on the outside of the lift doors, reading "OUT OF ORDER." I noticed that there was an iron latch across the lift doors outside, so that they could be fastened from outside as well as inside. It looked as though somebody had been imprisoned in the lift, and had taken summary action about getting out.

I pushed the doors open. A little light filtered through a long screen of ventilator-holes high in the wall of the lift towards the main hall. An overturned wooden box lay inside; otherwise it was empty.

"I keep telling you I don't know nothing about it," said Pruen helplessly. "I haven't been in this place to-night. That there lift has been out of order for a week; there don't nobody seem able to fix it, and God knows *I* can't. The old man's been cutting up rough about it as it is, becos 'e swears somebody put it out of commission deliberately, which ain't true, but it should 'a' been done becos 'e *won't* look sharp when he uses it, and nearly decapitated hisself twice; but when he sees that mess—ow!"

"The old man? You mean Mr. Wade? By the way, what does he look like?"

He stared at me. "Look like? 'E's a fine-looking man, Mr. Wade is, even if he is on the smallish side. Fiery. Great showman; ha! Fine big white moustache; regular martinet. Yes, and Important!—two years 'e's just spent in Persia, excavating after them caliphs' palace, with full permission, hand and seal of the Government itself. Yes. And—" He stopped, glared, and grew querulous. "Why do you want to know all that?

Why don't you telephone? There's the phone, on the desk, right under your nose. Why don't you use it?"

The vague idea that had been bothering me—namely, that it might have been the fiery Mr. Wade himself who had donned a pair of white false whiskers and gone capering round his own museum—seemed to be eliminated by this description of "smallish side." I rang up Vine Street, explained the situation to Hoskins, and told him to send round the photographer, finger-print man, and police-surgeon. After a stunned interval Hoskins spoke with an air of triumphant discovery.

"That chap Mannering, sir. . . ."

"Bring him round with you. You didn't let him go, did you?"

"No, sir. Oh, I'll bring him round, right enough!" whispered Hoskins. "What's more, I've got the evidence. A note fell out of his pocket, sir. It proves there was murder meant. You'll see. Murder and conspiracy——"

For Pruen's benefit I repeated, "Note that proves conspiracy—" and hung up the receiver with a decisive slap. "That seems to settle it," I told Pruen. "You don't need to talk now unless you want to before I take you away. We've got the story. So there was a conspiracy, was there, and you murdered him?"

"*No!* Who said that? Who said it?"

"Why deny it? An explanation was found in a note in Gregory Mannering's pocket."

His mood changed; the name seemed genuinely to bewilder him.

"Mannering—?" he muttered, and blinked his eyes. "Go on! Mannering! Why, 'e'd be the very last person, the very last . . ."

I held up my hand sharply for silence, for we both

41

heard footsteps. The rear window in the lavatory was wide open, and the sounds seemed to come from outside. I told Pruen that if he made a noise of any kind he would not like the consequences. Then I went into the lavatory, climbed up on the wash-bowl, and peered out of the window.

Behind the museum there was a grass-paved yard and a high wall whose iron-grilled gate opened on the alley called Palmer Yard. Somebody was unlocking that gate and coming in. The moon was still high; I could make out the figure of a woman. Closing the gate behind her, she came rather quickly up the walk. She saw my head silhouetted in the window and evidently expected to find somebody there, for she waved her hand.

"You stay here," I said to Pruen, "and if there's a peep out of you—How do you get to the back of this place?"

He did not seem at all anxious to let out a peep. To get to the back door, he explained, you went out into the hall and then through the door at the right of the stairway. It opened on a short passage going past his own living-quarters, and then to the back door. I went out into the hall, followed his directions, and was in the short dark passage just as the woman opened the rear door. I could see her silhouetted against the moonlight as she reached up to grope after a hanging electric light. Then the light went on.

There, gentlemen, was a *woman*. I have seen girls more beautiful in a classic way, but never any with an allure that so reached out and took hold of you. You could feel her presence. For a second I saw her motionless under the dazzle and shadow of the light, one arm upraised as she stood on tiptoe, and her eyes blinking to adjust themselves to the glow. She wore a dark wrap thrown back over her shoulders, and under it an evening-gown of dull scarlet cut low at the breast. She was not tall; nor was she exactly plump. I am not more explicit, gentlemen, and I draw my sketch with a light and gentlemanly pencil, because I have since become more than casually acquainted with her. But, as I say, she conveyed an impression of plumpness. She had that heavy dark hair which seems to reflect the light around it; she had long, very luminous dark eyes under lids that looked waxy; she had a pink mouth and a small neck. The eyes seemed strained, and she was undoubtedly nervous. But despite this strain it was the intense vitality of the girl—a kind of jovial, smiling, rollicking intensity—which made her as vivid as the scarlet dress in that passage. The light bulb swayed over her head, moving her in and out of shadow. She looked down the passage at me, staring.

"I say, Ronald," she began excitedly, "I saw your light in there, but I didn't think you'd be here. I thought you'd gone over to your flat; I was just going there. Is anything wr—?" She stopped abruptly. "*Who's that?* Who's there? What do you want?"

"Madam," I said, "without seeming unduly curious, I want to find out what in blazes is going on in this madhouse. Who are you?"

"I'm Miriam Wade. Who are *you?*"

At my reply she opened her eyes wide, and then edged closer to get a better look. But perplexity was as dominant as fear in those dark eyes.

"A police-officer," she repeated. "Whatever do you want here? What's happened?"

"Murder."

At first she did not understand; I might have said, "Parking over the twenty-minute limit." When Miriam Wade did understand she began to laugh, a sound

43

which gradually became hysterical as she studied me. Her clasped hands went up to her teeth, and then to her cheeks.

"You're joking. . . ."

"No."

"You mean—dead? Who's dead? Surely not——?"

"That's what I want to know, Miss Wade. Will you come in and see if you can identify him?"

She was searching my face, as she might have searched a book for a line escaped; it was disturbing intensity under those long black lashes, and there was always in it a quality of glazed watchfulness.

"Of course I will," she said at length, with an effort. "I still think you don't mean it, but I will. I'd like to—I mean, I've never seen a—I say, will it be very awful? Can't you tell me anything? Who brought you here?"

I guided her out into the hall. Before I could point it out, she saw the One Exhibit lying with its head towards us. Of only one thing could I be certain when she jerked back: that it was not what she expected to see. Then she nerved herself, straightening out her arms at her sides. She walked forward, looked at the face, and stopped. Bending down suddenly, as though to go on her knees, she checked herself; her face, brilliantly lovely under that moonlight glow, was as expressionless as the shuttered hood of the carriage from which the dead man had fallen. Expressionless, and for some reason subtly *mature*. Something changed and shifted there, as though at a sort of silent cry; something hardened, and yet for a moment I thought her eyes were filmed with tears. It lasted only for that brief time.

She got up stiffly, and said in a quiet voice: "No, I don't know him. Do I have to look at it any more?"

What the devil is logic? I think it was the vague gigolo appearance of the man on the floor, something dashing in his dead jeer or his frayed evening-clothes, which made me tell her what I did.

"Don't lie," I said. "It will make things a whole lot harder for me if you lie."

She almost smiled, shakily. Her hands were moving up and down the sides of her dress. "You're rather nice," she said. "But I'm not lying. He reminds me of somebody—that's all. For God's sake, tell me what happened! How did he get here? What happened? That knife—" She pointed, roused as she saw it, and her voice went shrill: "It's the one Sam——"

"The one Sam——?"

Without seeming to hear me, she turned and looked at the long, somehow ugly-looking packing-case which lay where Pruen had danced around it. But she had the question well in mind. When she turned back to me she had an almost horrible coquettishness which did not move the mask-like expression of her eyes, or subdue the sharp rise and fall of her breast.

"I say, you mustn't mind me. If you drag me in to look at corpses, you can't expect me to be very coherent, can you? Honestly, I didn't mean anything. Sam —Sam Baxter, that's a friend of mine—he admired that knife. It was in one of the cases here, or some-where. Sam always wanted to buy the dagger from my father, to hang on the wall of his room, and he said it had a p-pretty ugly and sinister——"

"Steady, Miss Wade. Come away from it now." I took her arm and led her down towards the staircase. "Why did you come to the museum tonight?"

"I didn't! I mean Ronald Holmes—that's my father's assistant—Ronald was giving a little party tonight at his flat, and I was going over there. And when I'm

45

anywhere near this neighbourhood I always park my car in Palmer Alley, because that saves leaving it out in the street and having some policeman come along and say—Anyway, I parked it there, and then I saw your light here. So I thought Ronald must have been detained. . . ."

At each word she uttered she was going farther away from the dead man, and I was following, as though I were trailing her. Now she was beyond the pillars on the right-hand side of the hall. She reached out and touched a tall Persian carpet on the wall behind her; its twisted richness loomed behind her as she backed against it, and her thin, wiry hands stroked its surface, as though it gave her assurance.

"You were going to a party at Mr. Holmes's flat," I repeated. "But wasn't your *fiancé* going along?"

A pause, and I had to prompt. "You are engaged to a Mr. Gregory Mannering, I understand?"

"Well—yes, sort of unofficially." She ran through that rapidly and in a slurred voice, as though it were of no importance; but her eyes were creeping over towards the dead man again, and they had a startled look. "Greg! I say, what has Greg got to do with this? He hasn't seen—that, has he?"

"I rather think he has. . . . Look here, Miss Wade, I'm not trying to bulldoze you, or spring mysterious secrets." It was unwise, but I told her exactly what had happened that night. She seemed to be searching wildly in her own thoughts, as a woman might ransack cupboards, and once I could have sworn I heard her say, *"Cellar window."* But I went on: "The point is this. I made some rambling statements, which none of us could understand, about a man in false whiskers disappearing—and your *fiancé* went over in a clean faint. Can you understand this?"

But she did not even seem to be interested in this.

"Policeman," she was saying this time, "your policeman saw a man in white—I say, why is the word 'whiskers' so horribly *funny?*—a man in white whiskers, who accused him of being a murderer?" Her voice trailed off; for some reason she was cooler than she had been before, and her mind came back to my previous question. "Fainted? Oh, that! You don't understand. Greg fainting because he—if you only knew him, you'd know how comic that is! Greg's served in the Spanish Civil Guard, and he was attached to the Foreign Legion as a spy among the Arabs when they were having all those troubles somewhere, and he's had a wonderful time. . . . But you see it's his heart; he has to take digitalin tablets. That's why he's had to give it up. If he's had strong exertion, or if he gets worked up—you said he had a row with the policeman, didn't you?—something goes wrong. Only last week he carried a trunk upstairs on his back, because Ronald Holmes bet him nobody was strong enough to do it alone, and he had an attack afterwards. He's awfully strong; he carried it up two whole flights of stairs before he missed a step and let it slip: only it was filled with some kind of old porcelain, and father was furious. Greg fainting because somebody said something to him! That's absurd. You understand, don't you?"

"But how did he come to misunderstand about tonight? He was here banging on the door, you know, and insisting that there was to be some sort of meeting at the museum. . . ."

She looked me in the eye. "He couldn't have got my message, that's all. I telephoned to his place early this evening; he was out, but they said he'd be in in a few minutes, and they promised to give him my message. I said the meeting had been called off, and to come

47

round to Ronald's flat in Pall Mall Place instead...."

"Who was to have been present at this meeting?"

"Just my father—you see, I wanted him to meet Greg in nice congenial surroundings; they've never actually met face to face; Greg doesn't even know my brother...." She was throwing out a screen of words, desperately, but I let her talk because I hoped there might be something revealing under that breathless tirade. "What was I saying? Oh, yes. Just my father, and Greg, and Ronald, and Dr. Illingworth—that's the Scotch preacher, you know, who's so terribly moral but is very much interested in the *Thousand and One Nights*...."

"The *Thousand and One Nights?*"

"Yes. You know. Ali Baba and Aladdin, and all those people. Only, and this is what infuriates me, from what my father says he's not just interested in them as stories. He doesn't even know they're stories; he tries to trace their historical origin, or something. I remember trying to read an article of his in the *Journal Asiatique*, about that Arabian Nights story of the men transformed into fish—white, blue, yellow or red fish, you remember, according to whether they were Moslems, Christians, Jews or Magians. Dr. Illingworth went on about this representing the colours of the turbans which Mohammed Somebody of Egypt commanded his Moslem, Christian, and Jewish subjects to wear in the year 1301. I'm not quite sure what it was, but it was something terribly learned and dull, I know."

She was gripping her fingers together, trying to assume an air of ease, but very anxious to divert me from some subject. What subject?

"And what was it," I said, "that they were going to examine tonight, before your father had to go away?"

"Examine?"

"Yes. It wasn't to be just a social gathering, I understood. In fact, Mr. Mannering told me, 'We are going to rob a grave,' and he asked me whether I believed in ghosts."

Somebody hammered sharply on the big bronze doors, with a booming echo which made her jump. But I saw fear in her eyes now, while the hollow knocking echoed through the museum; and it was my last question which had brought it there.

4

"There Has Got To Be A Corpse"

I hurried down and pushed back the bolts on the big
doors. Hoskins, his moustache bristling, entered as
though he expected to find a body on the threshold.
With him came Dr. Marsden, the divisional-surgeon,
Crosby, the finger-print man, Rogers, the photographer, and two constables. After warning them to look
out for the coal-dust smudges, and telling Rogers to
photograph these marks, I gave them the usual instructions. P. C. Martin remained at the door, and P.
C. Collins set out for a (probably useless) search of the
premises. Rogers and Crosby went immediately to
work round the dead man, for I could not even examine the victim's pockets until the routine work had
been finished.

Hoskins drew me aside.

"I've got 'is Lordship—I mean Mr. Mannering—
outside in the car," he told me in a confidential rum-
ble. "Shall I 'ave Jameson bring him in now?"

"Stop a bit. What did he say when he revived?"

The sergeant seemed puzzled. "Told me about his weak 'eart, and showed me a little bottle of tablets. But as to being scared, sir—why, he's done a complete change of front. When I told him about old White-Whiskers and what White-Whiskers done to me——"

"You told him that?"

"I 'ad to, sir! Wasn't no way out of it, when a man asks why he's being detained. . . . Well, sir, did it upset him? No! He laughed. He laughed and laughed." Hoskins scowled. "Seemed as though that faint took a whole lot off his mind. Then, when you telephoned about the murder and the man in black whiskers, he was all interested and excited, but no more of what you might call scared than I was. 'E kept putting in his oar and telling us about a Thug murder in Iraq or somewhere, that he'd 'elped the police investigate, though," said Hoskins, closing one eye confidentially, "just between ourselves, *I* think he's a bleedin' liar. You see, sir, we've got him to rights, with that note. . . . Shall I have Jameson bring him in now?"

"First we've got to settle something. Come down here and tell me if this man is the same one who tried to strangle you outside the museum."

Hoskins lumbered down eagerly. Catching sight of Miriam Wade, who was still leaning against the tapestry and to whom I made a reassuring sign, the sergeant whistled. When I told him who she was, it was clear from his expression that he considered it very sinister. Then he looked at the body.

"No, sir," he announced, after a squinted stare, "that is NOT the same man."

"You're sure of that?"

"Absolutely positive, sir! Look here! This 'ere chap's got a roundish sort of face, and what you'd call a Jew-

51

ish nose. The old man who jumped down off that wall——"

"Look here, you're certain he was old?"

Hoskins puffed out his cheeks. "N-no, sir, not like swearing it, you understand. I've been thinking about that, now you ask it. But this I do know. He'd got a long, thin face like a horse, and a flattish sort of nose. Not like this chap at all. I'll take my oath they're not the same." He became brisk. "Orders, sir? I'm not on duty, but since in a manner of speaking I walked into this business——"

Well, that seemed to settle it. There had been two people in false whiskers wandering about the place. What I could not decide was whether this made the business better or worse; worse, probably. It presented lurid visions of a club of false-whiskered men meeting in an Oriental museum at the dark of the moon. This wouldn't do. . . .

"Let me see that note," I said.

Hoskins produced it with tender care. It was a sheet of ordinary notepaper, folded twice into a square pressed very flat, and along one side very grimy. I unfolded it. Prosaically typewritten, and casually headed "Wednesday," were the following rather unusual words.

DEAR G.,

There has got to be a corpse—a *real* corpse. The means of death doesn't matter, but there has got to be a corpse. I'll manage the murder—that ivory-handled *khanjar* will do the trick, or strangling if it seems preferred *(there followed a couple of words blotted out with x's, and the note ended)*.

I tried to adjust my wits to this. Sergeant Hoskins read my thought.

"Sort of off-handed bloke, ain't 'e, sir?" he enquired. "Murder—whiff!—'meet you at Lyons for tea'—just like that. Eh?"

I said: "Damn it, Hoskins, there's something wrong with this. Did you ever read anything that sounded less like a murderer crying to heaven for blood?"

Hoskins reflected. "Well, sir, I can't say I know exactly 'ow a murderer *does* cry to heaven for blood. It does sound as though he ought to take it more to 'eart, like. But I'm bound to admit it sounds ugly to me."

"Where did you find this?"

"It dropped out of Mr. Mannering's overcoat pocket when I was lifting his arms up and down to wake him up. I didn't say anything about it to 'im; I thought I'd leave that job up to you. I say, though: What's a ivory-handled *khanjar*?"

"There has got to be a corpse—a real corpse." That line was ugly enough, anyhow. With Hoskins following, I walked along the line of the glass-topped cases down the middle of the hall, and looked for the case from which the dagger had been taken. It was easy enough to find. In the third case from the front, labelled "Modern Persian," the dark blue velvet had an empty indentation of a curved dagger-shape about ten inches long. The case was closed, and showed no sign of a hinge; how, I wondered as I had often wondered in museums, were these glass boxes opened? I put on my gloves and went over it carefully. In the wooden support at one side there was a tiny lock, without a key. Evidently the whole side opened like a door, but it was locked now. Therefore, presumably, whoever removed that dagger had possessed a key: which led directly to the Wades or their associates. "There has got to be a corpse—a real corpse." So murder had been only a little item in some fantastic programme?

Of course, the most immediate person to whom this evidence led was old Pruen. That was the difficulty. I did not believe, and if I had been serving on a jury would not have believed, that Pruen knew anything whatever about the murder.

"We've got to get to work," I said to Hoskins. "I want you to get hold of your friend Pruen, the care-taker you told me about; he's down in the curator's room. Take him somewhere else—I'll need that room for other witnesses—and pound him about anything that happened tonight. Ask him about this dagger, when he knew it was gone, and anything about it. You see that packing-case over there? Find out why Pruen was doing a dance round that tonight, and what he meant by talking about 'Haroun al Raschid's missus.'"

Hoskins not unreasonably wanted to know who Haroun al Raschid was, and what this had to do with his missus. So far as I could hazily remember, Haroun had been a Caliph of Baghdad in about the eighth century, the famous figure of the *Arabian Nights* who liked to seek adventure in disguise. Somebody had once told me that "Harùn er Raschid," translated, meant "Aaron the Orthodox"—which seemed rather a come-down. You might suppose that he had a wife: at least, there was an obvious lead here. Mannering had spoken of a find made by the museum, a secret affair, and said that in a manner of speaking they were going to rob a grave. Was it possible that Geoffrey Wade (whom Pruen had described as "excavating after them caliphs' palace") had discovered, or thought he had discovered, the coffin of Haroun al Raschid's wife? Add to this, however, Pruen's gleeful statement that there was nothing in the box. And, when you have added it, try to imagine how it fits in beside a false-whiskered corpse with a cookery-book in one hand. . . .

I mentioned the new possibility to Hoskins, who stared over at the big packing-case. He lowered his voice.

"You mean, sir," he enquired, "one of those mummies? The kind that get up and walk about in the films?"

I pointed out that the caliphs had been Moslems, and had a coffin burial the same as anybody else, which seemed to reassure Hoskins. He regarded mummies with a very suspicious eye; his broad general view, in the expression of the music-hall song, was that they were dead but they wouldn't lie down.

"So long," said Hoskins, "as it ain't mummies—What do you want me to do, sir? Disinter it, if that's the word?"

"Yes, if Pruen won't talk. There's a hatchet in the curator's room. If you don't get anything out of Pruen, break it open; carefully. What we want is somebody who knows all about this place. . . ."

"Well, sir, even if old Mr. Wade's away, there must be somebody in charge. Couldn't you ring him up?"

Ronald Holmes. But there was a better idea than ringing him up. Ronald Holmes, who according to Miriam Wade was at that moment giving a party at which those connected with the museum would probably be present. And he lived not five minutes' walk away, in Pall Mall Place. If I took ten minutes off and went over there now before news of this business came to them, it might bring results.

"You take charge," I said to Hoskins. "I shouldn't be gone long, and I'll bring Holmes back with me. If we get any witnesses, this place is big enough to keep them in separate compartments. Meantime, we'll put the girl down in the curator's room, in charge of Martin. We don't want her communicating with anybody; keep Mannering away from her, even if he kicks up a row. Meantime——"

"Where's the lady?" demanded Hoskins abruptly.

We both whirled round. The line of Persian carpets along the wall was deserted; I had a sudden feeling of being at the wheel of a car gone out of control. She could not have run towards the front; there was P. C. Martin standing solidly at the bronze doors. I hurried down the hall towards the curator's room. The door was closed, but I could faintly hear a voice speaking indistinguishable words inside. To Pruen? The words could not be heard through that steel-bound door, but just over my head beside it were the ventilator-holes to the lift-shaft on the other side of the wall.

I pushed the door open quickly, and was just in time to catch half a dozen clear words.

But again the whole business looked queer and unreasonable. Miriam Wade sat behind the mahogany desk, bending over the telephone. The words I heard were, "Whitehall double-o, double-6. I want to speak to Harriet Kirkton." But she had put a handkerchief over the mouthpiece of the telephone—evidently further to disguise her voice, for she was speaking with a wabbly contralto deepness which contrasted with her usual tones. When she saw me, she snapped the receiver back on the hook and stood up with her face blazing.

"Yo—!" she cried, and gasped. "You—hateful—damned—oooo! Snooping! Snooping. . . ."

"Now, now," I said. The temptation was always to say, "Now, now" to this rollicking piece, who looked now like Messalina in an imperious temper, but destroyed the effect by her choice of words. "You were

56

making a phone-call. Why don't you go on?"

"It's none of your business why I don't."

"Under the circumstances, I've got to ask you who you were telephoning to."

"You heard it, didn't you? To Harriet. She's one of my best friends. She came home on the boat with me. She——"

"Yes, but do you usually disguise your voice when you call up your best friends? Look here, Miss Wade; this wouldn't be a time you would choose for playing jokes——"

I thought she was going to pick up the bronze ashtray and whang it at my head. Instead she conquered the impulse, pressing her hands to her full breast; and she told me, in what was doubtless intended to be a tone of cold contempt, explicitly what I could go and do.

"Whitehall double-o, double-6," I said. "Whose number is that? I can find out from the exchange, you know."

"It's Ronald Holmes's flat. You don't believe me, do you?" (I had picked up the telephone directory.) "You *wouldn't*. But that's what it is." Her eyes filmed over. "I say, have you got to keep me here? Do you think it's pleasant for me, with that—thing out there, and everything else? Won't you let me go, or let me call somebody? Won't you let me get my brother?"

"Where is your brother?"

"At Ronald's flat."

The question, as to why she didn't ask for her brother instead of this Harriet Kirkton, if she wanted to speak to him, was so obvious that I did not even ask it. But she had been telling the truth about the number: Ronald Holmes, Prince-Regent Court, Pall Mall Place, was listed as Whitehall 0066. Putting

57

down the book, I realised for the first time that Pruen was not in the room; but she anticipated it, with a bitter and lofty composure.

"He's in the lavatory," explained Miss Wade. "I asked him to go in there while I made my call. All right Raffles, old chap! You can come out now."

Sullen but embarrassed, Pruen opened the door and defiantly shuffled out. His attitude toward the girl, from the one look he gave her, was close to adoration; and he seemed to be seeking an excuse to round on anybody who spoke to him. I beckoned to Hoskins and P. C. Martin in the doorway.

"Take charge, Martin, stay in here and look after Miss Wade until I come back. That telephone is out of order, got it?" The girl had sat down grimly in a red leather chair, and I turned to her. "Now take it easy for a few minutes, if you don't mind. Your brother is being communicated with, and we'll get him here; then everything will be all right. I'll be back shortly."

I heard her swearing when I went out, in a way which my aunt and uncle in Belfast would strongly have deprecated. On my way out I stopped at the centre of activity round the travelling-carriage. Rogers had finished photographing the position of the body, but Crosby was still at work after fingerprints, and Dr. Marsden was making a thorough examination. The dagger had been withdrawn from the wound. Crosby held it out on a handkerchief: a vicious-looking curved blade a little under ten inches long, sharpened on both edges and with a needle-point. They had wiped it off.

"Plenty of prints on this, sir," Crosby reported, pointing at the ivory handle. "But smudged up and overlaid, as though several people had touched it. I'll enlarge it and see if I can get anything clear. Some clear prints inside this cab. . . . Here's something else.

The fellow's name seems to be 'Raymond Penderel.' These two visiting-cards were sticking out of his waist-coat pocket, and the same name's printed in his hat."

He held out two blood-stained cards, on which "Raymond Penderel" had been stamped by one of those street-corner card-makers who set type while you wait. I looked at the taciturn Dr. Marsden, who grunted.

"Not much to tell you," said Marsden. "That knife did for him: straight to the heart; died instantly." He got up stiffly. "Time of death—um. What time did you find him? Twelve-twenty-five. So. It's now not quite a quarter past one. I'd say he died between ten-thirty and eleven-thirty, though you can give some leeway." He hesitated. "Look here, Carruthers, it's not exactly in my line, but I'll give you a tip. See the shape of that blade? Very few people without medical knowledge could have calculated exactly where it would have reached the heart. A stab like that was either a devil of a big accident, or else the murderer knew just where to strike."

I knelt down and went through the dead man's pockets. They were empty except for sevenpence in coppers, a packet of ten cigarettes, and a frayed news-paper cutting. The cutting was from some sort of gossip-column; it had been near the top of the page, and the date of the paper appeared as "—AY 11," a little over a month ago. It read:

> Returned to England today, from rigours of climate in Iraq, Miss MIRIAM WADE. Young, beautiful, unconventional, a terror to hostesses. Before departure eighteen months ago, ru-moured engaged to "SAM" BAXTER, son of LORD ABBSLEY, once whoopee-artist (see this column

9/5/31) but now rising star at British legation, Cairo. Expected next week, father GEOFFREY WADE, student and collector, whose long moustaches bristle at scholarly gatherings. Believes that traces of the Caliphs' Palace at Baghdad can be——

The cutting, which I folded up and put in my notebook along with that ugly note found on Mannering, did not make clear whether the whoopee-artist was Lord Abbsley or his son; but we could take it as the latter. It was still another link. But of Raymond Penderel, who he was or where he lived, there was no trace in the clothes. The dress-suit smelt of camphor, as though it had been long put away in mothballs, and the inside pocket bore the label, "Gaudien, English tailor, 27 Boulevard Malesherbes, Paris." That was all.

Leaving Rogers and Crosby with instructions to look for traces in that mess round the lift in the curator's room, I went out to find Ronald Holmes. Outside, in a police car parked at the kerb, Gregory Mannering argued violently with P. C. Jameson; I hurried past, not wishing to become involved in it, and struck east along Pall Mall. The whole town seemed deserted, under the empty shimmer on the pavements, and the distant honk of a horn sounded as though it were close at hand. Pall Mall Place is a little court and lane opening off the street under a deep tunnel of an archway. I found the archway, and found beyond a dark huddle of buildings in which a tall narrow block of flats glowed with the neon sign "Prince-Regent Court." Inside was a long narrow hall, with the cage of an automatic lift at the end. There was no hall-porter in sight, but a sleepy youngster in buttons yawned at a telephone switchboard and prepared to go off duty. It would not do to announce myself yet.

"Party," I said, "still going on at Mr. Holmes's?"

"Yes, sir," said buttons, with a dispirited attempt at military smartness. He reached for the cord to plug in. "Name?"

I used a coin with effect. "Wait a minute! Don't announce me. I'm going to hammer on the door and say I'm a police-officer. I'll go on up; it's D, isn't it?"

He grinned obediently. He said that it was E, and I would hear it. Stepping into the lift, I stopped with a by-the-way air.

"How long have they been up there?"

"All evening," answered buttons. "Since nine o'clock, anyway. Mind that step, sir."

When the creaking lift swayed upstairs and stopped, I did hear it. I was in a dim little corridor, painted green, and just big enough to turn round in. From beyond a door at the far end proceeded the faint but hearty strains of a mouth-organ, supported by muffled voices singing with slow religious fervour in the dim religious light. Solemnly the faint harmony rang. Thus:

> We are Fred Karno's ar-my,
> The rag-time in-fan-treEEEE,
> We cannot fight, we cannot march,
>   What God damn use are weEEE?
> And when we get—

I hammered loudly with the knocker; so loudly that those inside evidently thought it was somebody coming to protest about the noise, for the singing stopped as though it had been choked off. There were rustlings, the sound of a door closing and footsteps. The door was opened by a thin man with a glass in his hand.

"I'm looking," I began, "for Mr. Ronald Holmes. . . ."

"I'm your man," he said. "What is it?"

He stood sideways so that the light fell into the hall. He was wearing large shell-rimmed spectacles.

5

Keys To The Dagger-Case

I followed him as he backed into the room. It was a small room, empty and tidy, and not the scene of the concert. From beyond a closed door opposite came a sound of laughter, with a few thoughtful experimental notes on the mouth-organ. The only light here was from a big yellow-shaded lamp, which threw its own reflection in a polished table-top and illuminated the side of my host's face.

His eyebrows were a little raised in mild curiosity; nothing more. He was of middle size, and lean, with a slight stoop. His yellowish, wiry-curling hair was cropped close to a long head. Mild blue eyes looked at me behind the spectacles; he had a long, thin, sharp-featured face with a rather apologetic look about it. He wore a dark lounge suit, and a hard collar with a rumpled dark tie. His age might have been in the early thirties; but, as he turned his head against the light, I saw thin lines etched in a forehead glistening with heat. Although he was not drunk, he looked as though he had taken a few. Clearing his throat, he shifted, looked down at the glass in his hands, shook it in long fingers, and looked up again. His courteous voice had an odd note between apology and determination.

"Yes?" he prompted. "Is anything wrong? Look here, don't I know you? It seems to me we've met——"

From behind the door came a woman's voice. It began in an ordinary tone, and then suddenly soared up at the end in a sort of querulous but happy yowl. "Is that you, Rinkey?" it called. "Rinkey, you ass! I say, is that youooou?" There followed the noise of a woman kicking her heels rapidly, for emphasis, against hollow wood.

"Be quiet in there!" Holmes unexpectedly roared, twitching his head round. "It's not Rinkey." He turned back again, with quiet expectancy.

"Yes? As I say, your face looks familiar, but——"

"I don't think we've met before, Mr. Holmes. I am Detective-Inspector Carruthers, and I have come to ask you what took place at the Wade Museum to-night."

During a space in which you might have counted ten, Holmes stood motionless with his head silhouetted against the light.

"Excuse me for just one moment," he said briefly.

The man was so quick that I had not even time to open my mouth before he had put down the glass, gone smoothly to the inner door, opened it, and disappeared inside. I had a short glimpse of a smoke-filled room and a woman's long legs on a couch. I heard his voice saying something, not more than half a dozen words, inside; then he was out again with the door closed.

"They make so much noise," he explained, apologetically, "that we can't hear each other think. Now, then, inspector. I don't think I quite understand you. You've come to ask *me* what—" He stopped. "Good God, what is it? Not a burglary?"

"No. Nothing has been stolen."

"Or—you mean a fire?"

"No."

Holmes got a handkerchief out of his breast pocket and carefully mopped his face. Those mild eyes seemed to be studying me over and under and around the handkerchief. Then he smiled.

"Well, it's a great load off my mind, of course," he said, "but I still don't understand. Er—will you take a whiskey and soda, inspector?"

"Thank you, sir," I said. I badly needed one.

Still talking, he carried his own glass to a sideboard, pulled out another, and splashed a good three fingers of whiskey into each. "We still seem to be talking at cross purposes," he continued, clearing his throat. "So far as I know, nothing happened at the museum tonight, unless Mr. Wade came back unexpectedly. I haven't been there. I—hang it all, don't be so mysterious. What did happen?"

"Murder," I said.

He had just started to press the handle of the soda-siphon, and he missed the glass altogether. The soda hissed and splashed across the oak sideboard; he had his handkerchief out instantly, and seemed to pounce as he mopped at it before turning round. When he did turn round, there was a little corkscrew vein showing in relief against his temple.

"Clumsy," he muttered. "That's impossi—Are you joking, or trying to—? Look here, who was murdered? What's this all about?"

"A man named Raymond Penderel. He was stabbed tonight with an ivory-handled dagger from one of the cases at the museum. I found his body in that big closed travelling-carriage in the hall."

Holmes drew one shuddering breath, and then became composed. His eyes were as mild as ever, but they were bewildered. It was then that I noticed, on the wall over the sideboard, a framed photograph. It was that of a man in a woodland scene, wearing a robe; and this man had very elaborate white whiskers. Wherever you looked in this case, there were whiskers: with me they had grown to a nightmare and an obsession.

"Penderel," Holmes was repeating, in what I could have sworn was genuine perplexity. "Raymond Penderel! The name means absolutely nothing. How the devil did it happen? What was he doing there, anyway? And who killed him; or don't you know that?"

"We don't know the answers to any of these questions, Mr. Holmes. But you may be able to help us. About the dagger this man was killed with. . . ."

At the mention of the dagger, for the first time Holmes's eyes wavered a little. "It's a curved blade with an ivory handle, called, according to Pruen, a *khanjar*. . . ."

"Pruen!" exclaimed Holmes, as though he had forgotten something. "Er—yes, of course. What does Pruen have to do with this? What did he say?"

"He denied that anybody had been at the museum tonight except himself. So, of course, it looks bad for him." I let that sink in. "Now, about the dagger. Who has a key to those cases in the main hall?"

"I have. But if it was stolen——"

"Anybody else have a key?"

"Well, Mr. Wade, of course. But——"

"The dagger was not stolen. It was taken out of the case by somebody who had a key, and the case locked up again."

Holmes's voice was very quiet. As though mechanically, he picked up the two glasses off the sideboard. I made a gesture of refusal now, because you can't drink with a man you have plunged into an accusation like this; but he said in a tone of curt sanity, "Don't be a fool!" and went on in the same low voice. "Then there must have been a duplicate key. I can only tell you that *I* didn't do it, and I never heard of anybody called Raymond Penderel in my life. My friends and I have been here all evening——"

"By the way, who is here with you?"

"Jerry Wade, Mr. Wade's son; a friend of ours named Baxter; and Miss Kirkton. I don't suppose you would know them. We've been expecting Miss Wade and a friend of hers named Mannering——"

"Is anybody else here?"

"Not now. There were others, but they've gone. Look here, will you let me call Jerry Wade in here?"

I looked over towards the closed door of the other room. It was suspiciously quiet now, as it had been ever since Holmes made that brief excursion. At one point the woman's voice had tried to strike up "Barnacle Bill the Sailor," but at the first soaring note there were sounds indicating that she had been fiercely shushed.

"Excuse me for a moment," I said to Holmes. I went over to the door, knocked, and opened it.

After the first startled silence it seemed by the variety of sounds that I had got into a parrot-house. It was a room almost as small as the other, similarly lighted, and blue with smoke. On a couch facing the door there sat curled up a thin, long-legged blonde, who was winking and blinking happily, holding up straight a cocktail-glass with her elbow propped on the arm of the couch. She had one of those spiritual, soulful faces such as you see in pre-Raphaelite paintings, very pink and white and china-blue-eyed; also, she had a habit of leaning forward suddenly, as though the devil had given her a push.

Standing behind a forest of bottles on the table was a stoutening young man with fiery red hair and ultra-correct evening-clothes. He had a cigarette hanging from one corner of his mouth, and was blinking to keep the smoke out of one eye while he studied a sticky cocktail-shaker in his hand. At my entrance he whirled round, stared, and then tried to adjust a mask of stony dignity: which was somewhat marred by the fact that somebody had taken a long red ribbon off a chocolate-box and pinned it slantwise across his chest with safety-pins. Also, he was frightened.

The third figure sat in a low chair polishing a mouth-organ. I can only describe him as a young man with an old man's face. Though he could not have been past the late twenties, he had one of those faces cut up into lines by equal grinning and equal poring over books; aside from our friend Dr. Fell's, I think it was the most good-humoured face I have ever seen. He looked excitable, and seemed to gesticulate even when he did not move a hand. A small man in an old tweed coat, with black hair cut German fashion, he rolled back in his chair and waved his hand affably.

A silence, and then the parrot-house came to life. Harriet Kirkton threw back her head with an air of pleased inspiration, and opened her mouth to an extent that showed pre-Raphaelite tonsils as she soared into song. It seemed to split the roof.

"Who's that kno-cking at my door?
Who's that knoaa-king at my door?
Who's that KNOOA-king at my door?"
Said the fair young maayy-den.

The red-haired young man drew himself up and
began in a whiskey-baritone: "I say, this is most un-
warrantable to come crashing in here. . . ."

The old-young man put out his hand levelly, with a
gloomy air as though he were going to mesmerise me.
"'Thou can'st never say I did it,'" he declared in deep
tones. "'Shake not thy gory locks at me.' 'And Eugene
Aram walked between with gyves upon his wrists.'
'Oh, Sammy, Sammy, vy woren't there a alleybi?'"
Then he blew an emphatic blast on the mouth-organ,
grinned, and added in a natural tone: "Good evening,
old chap. Sit down. Have a drink. How are all the false
whiskers at Scotland Yard?"

Into this babble fell Holmes's quiet, even, edged
voice. He said:

"For Christ's sake, shut that row."

It was as actual as a real deluge of ice-water; I have
never heard any group grow so instantly quiet. The
old-young man quietly put down the mouth-organ beside his chair and looked up.

"Whu-ho!" he said, after a pause. "I say, what's this,
Ron? You sound as though you were trying to keep
from exploding."

"Sorry to break in on you like this," I told them,
"but this is important. Does anyone here know a man
named Raymond Penderel?"

Red-hair looked completely blank. The little man
opened his mouth, then reconsidered, and shut it
again, though he did not look as though his speech
would be enlightening. But Harriet Kirkton did know

69

the name: of that I am sure. She seemed a little less tipsy. Although she did not move, and still sat with her arm stuck stiffly upwards from its elbow-rest, I could see under the lamp-light beside her the white places on her nails where her fingers were gripping the stem of the glass. But it was not yet time to spring the mine I was thinking about.

"Nobody?" I prompted.

Nobody spoke, and I had a weird feeling that bridges were being burnt in that silence. Holmes's voice, now deprecating again, struck in:

"Inspector Carruthers tells me that this man Penderel has been murdered. Don't interrupt. He was stabbed tonight in the museum—correct me if I am wrong, inspector—with an ivory-handled knife out of one of the cases." Holmes spaced his words carefully. "I have told him that we have all been here tonight, from nine o'clock on, but he still seems to think——"

"Murder—" repeated Red-hair, and rubbed a hand shakily over his face. He had been tolerably drunk; but this seemed to rouse him like the smash of a motor-wreck. It was a curious gesture he made over his face, as though he were trying to rub something off, or find something there. Burnt reddish by the sun, his features were dissipated but good. His brown eyes grew sharper behind their glaze. "Murder! Good God, this is awful! You mean murdered right in the museum? When? When did it happen?"

He began to knock his knuckles against the table. But Holmes's smooth voice took up the sentence as before.

"—but he still seems to think we are a sinister lot. Oh, yes; allow me. Miss Kirkton, this is Inspector Carruthers. Mr. Baxter," he nodded towards Red-hair, who was muttering something about ivory knives.

"And Mr. Wade—junior." The man with the old-young face bowed in friendly irony, and Holmes pursued: "So try to talk sense when you're questioned, or we may be in for trouble even though we seem to have what is called a corporate alibi."

"Of course we have," said Harriet Kirkton, and laughed shakily. "What on earth have *we* got to do with it?"

Young Wade waved his hand for silence. His goblin-like eyes were puckered.

"There has come into this mouldering mind," he announced, with a slow elaborateness of speech which contrasted with his excited movements, "the itch to examine a puzzle which makes absolutely no sense whatever. Shut up, curse ye!" He picked up the mouth-organ and blew a long blast to emphasise this. After glaring at Sam Baxter he turned back to me. "Now then. The first question——"

"Yes, but look here, Gaffer," interposed Baxter, "*I* asked a question, and the inspector was going to answer it. When was he killed?"

"He was killed," I said slowly, "between ten-thirty and eleven-thirty."

"You mean P.M.?" demanded Baxter, with a kind of ghoulish hope.

"I mean P.M."

There was a pause. Baxter sat down. I was in no hurry to ask them questions, because what they said without prompting was more revealing. Young Jerry Wade, whom they called Gaffer, seemed to sense this; and under his amiable casualness he was even more worried than Holmes. For he was clearly getting an idea; as he moved the mouth-organ back and forth against his teeth, softly, I saw the idea begin to glitter and grow behind his eyes.

"Inspector," he said abruptly, "who was this man Penderel, and what does he look like?"

"We don't know who he was. There were no papers or marks of identification on him except a couple of visiting-cards. In fact, nothing in his pockets but a newspaper-cutting dealing with Miss Miriam Wade. . . ."

"*Hell*—!" said Miss Kirkton.

Baxter looked up, his eyes hard. "Wind's blowing from that quarter, is it?" enquired the whiskey-baritone, in a smoother—what you might almost call a diplomatic—tone. It was grotesque in contrast to the Chocolate-box ribbon pinned across his shirt. "Sorry, inspector. Carry on."

"As for a description of him: he's about six feet tall, roundish face, hooked nose, olive complexion, black hair and moustache. Does that mean anything to anybody?"

To the three men, at least, it quite plainly did not; or so it seemed to me. The light faded out of Wade's look, and he blinked. But my next remark produced very definite results. "And when I saw him last with the dagger through his chest," I went on, "he was wearing a pair of black false whiskers——"

Wade hopped up. "Black whiskers!" he yelped. "Did you say *black* whiskers?"

"Yes. In point of fact," I said, "you were expecting them to be white whiskers, weren't you?"

The other caught himself up. "My dear inspector, he answered, with an antediluvian grin, "I tell you solemnly that I was uninhibited by whiskers. My mind was whiskerless. I never even thought of them. But you put such stress on the 'black' that I seemed to see us all going to the gallows because of some ominous meaning there." (This little goblin had more imagination than the rest; and, I thought, he would make an expert liar if he turned his hand to it.) "A corpse in false whiskers! Was there anything else?"

"For the moment, let's have a little talk about whiskers," I suggested. It was time to attack now. "This case is a nightmare, and we might as well have some sense out of it. . . . For instance, Mr. Holmes, you've got in your outside room—up over the sideboard—a photograph of somebody wearing a robe and white whiskers. It's an amateur dramatic-society picture of some sort. Who is it?"

Holmes opened his mouth, hesitated, and glanced across the room. It was Jerry Wade who answered.

"Oh, that?" he said in an offhand way. "That's me."

6

The Inseparables At Home

"You're quite right," pursued Wade. "That's an O.U.D.S. picture, and you see me in my celebrated role of King Lear. It doesn't surprise you, does it? Kindly examine this desiccated map of mine, and it won't. People tell me I look younger every day.... Why are you so interested in it? You're not chasing any whiskers, are you?"

"I am doing just that. Let's have fair play. I'll tell you what has been found out, and you will give me any help you can." I looked round the group; at the mention of the black whiskers, Harriet Kirkton's expression had become as blank as any of the others. Even Holmes had lost his air of polite defiance and frankly stared. I went on: "The story is so wild and woolly that *somebody* must possess a reasonable clue to it, even if it's an innocent clue.

"At a few minutes past eleven tonight, a station-sergeant from Vine Street was passing the Wade

Museum. A tall man in a frock-coat, shell-rimmed glasses, and with white false whiskers gummed to his cheeks, came roaring over the wall. He yelled to the sergeant: 'You killed him, and you'll hang for it, my fine impostor. I saw you in the coach.' Then he ran at the sergeant like a lunatic, and tried to strangle him. The sergeant had to knock him out to keep him quiet. Then, when the sergeant went for assistance, the unconscious man—apparently—disappeared from the middle of an empty street."

About that group now was an uneasy air of tensity. Harriet Kirkton began to laugh uncontrollably, and pressed her hands to her mouth while the china-blue eyes stared at me.

"I never heard of any pixies in that part of St. James's," young Wade observed thoughtfully. "But then I may be wrong. Go on."

"Some minutes later a rather self-important young gentleman came along, began hammering at the door of an empty museum, and cutting up such a row that he was taken to the station. He gave his name as Gregory Mannering, and said that he was engaged to Miss Miriam Wade." (Baxter's face looked ugly at this point, but Holmes only nodded and Wade remained grave.) "He also said that he had been invited to what he called a private view at the museum tonight, given by Mr. Geoffrey Wade for a certain Dr. Illingworth of Edinburgh. . . ."

"So that's why Mannering didn't turn up here," observed Holmes. "At the police-station, eh?" He eyed the ceiling with an air of dreamy pleasure. "Well, inspector, it's easily explained why there was nobody there. A message was left for Mannering at his flat. You see——"

"Yes," I said, "there have been explanations of that

already. I understand Mr. Wade had to go away unex-pectedly. . . ."

Baxter sat up. "How did you know that?" he asked sharply. "Did Mannering say so?"

"Just one minute. Is that true, Mr. Holmes?"

"Quite true, although it wasn't exactly unexpected. It was like this. Mr. Wade has only recently come back from Iraq. He had been out there for two years, doing some research work with Morel of Lyons on the plain westward of the Tigris, outside Baghdad. This is the site of the old city of the caliphs, you understand; modern Baghdad is on the east. Unfortunately some of the ruins are being cleared off, and a large part of the place was a burying ground, so there was some diffi-culty with the authorities about excavating. In the course of two years he has made a good many discov-eries, most of which have been shipped back to me here. One of them was to have followed him by the boat, and to have arrived here early this week. It is of some bulk; a fragment of Saracenic brickwork from a tower very much like the *Bab-el-Tilsim*, and contain-ing an inscription which—But I don't want to divert you with all this——"

"You're not diverting me. Go on."

Holmes looked at me curiously. In his mild eyes there was something like fanaticism when he talked about bricks, provided they were Persian bricks. He hesitated, cleared his throat, and continued:

"Well, that's it. The shipment, as I say, was sup-posed to have arrived in England on Tuesday. Then we had word that the boat was delayed, and would not be here until Saturday. Today we heard that it would dock this afternoon. So nothing would do but that Mr. Wade must go down to Southampton himself to see the crate ashore—part of it is tile, you see, and fragile—and

76

then to bring it to London himself. He said that the meeting tonight could easily be postponed until Saturday or Sunday."

"I see. Now a few personal details. When did Mr. Wade return to England?"

"About three weeks ago. I think it was the twentieth of May."

"And Miss Miriam Wade arrived a week earlier than that, round about the eleventh?"

Baxter got up again. He reached heavily after a bottle of Scotch, splashed a good measure into a cocktail-glass, and pointed the glass at me. "What's the game?" he asked. "This is damned funny police procedure, if you ask me. What's Miriam got to do with this? She's been at home all tonight. What's Miriam got to do with a beggar in false whiskers that none of us ever heard of?"

They were all staring hard at me, and I turned it off for the moment.

"It was not so much about Miss Wade," I said, "as about Mr. Mannering." It would mean wary walking here, for I did not want to bring her into it yet. "Like this. Mr. Mannering is engaged to her; but so far as I could gather he hasn't met either her father or her brother. How does that happen?"

The bright, shrewd little eyes of Gaffer Wade were fixed on me behind the mouth-organ. He spoke with a kind of pounce.

"Aha! Deduction. Got it. You're thinking that the heavy father and the grim-lipped brother are trying to break off this hodious match, which flourishes in secret over garden walks. 'Curse you, sir, never shall your base blood mingle with the serious plasma of old Jeff Wade!' Horseradish, inspector. I repeat firmly—horseradish. I rather think the shoe's on the other

77

foot." He wrinkled his forehead. "The straight fact of the matter is that Mannering's the only one in the lot of us who can be called well-born. Somebody who knew his family was talking to my old man. From what I hear of Mannering, he's the world's most decorated liar, but he really did have ancestors in the Crusades. I can readily believe it, because I know now who originated all those whoppers about riding into battle and murdering three hundred Saracens with one swing of your sword. The Mannering touch can be darkly seen. . . . No, I think my old man was rather pleased at the idea, and Lord knows *I* don't mind. . . ."

Baxter made a gurgling noise.

"Take it easy, Sam," said Jerry Wade quietly. "I'm on your side, old son, but the wench has got to make up her own mind. To continue, inspector, the old man's not meeting him was pure accident. You see——"

"Oh, be quiet, you—you overgrown gnome!" cried Harriet Kirkton suddenly. Wade flushed a little; that, I saw, had struck deep and hurt. There was a silence, while Wade sat back and the girl hesitated, herself flushing.

"I'm s-sorry, Gaffer," she went on. "I didn't mean— only, I say, you *do* babble so!" She turned to me. "Miriam met him on the boat coming back; I was with her. I can't quite make up my mind about him, really. Then, as soon as we got to England, Miriam was sent to visit an aunt in Norfolk for two weeks——"

"Sent," I prompted, a little too sharply.

"Well, one does go to see aunts sometimes," interposed Jerry Wade, with an air of reasonableness. (There was always that buckler waiting to be thrust between.) He grinned. "I know it's an incredible motive to put in a detective story, but there it is."

"Just a minute, sir. . . . What did you mean, 'sent,' Miss Kirkton?"

"I didn't mean anything! It's a perfectly natural phrase, isn't it? Good Lord, what would I mean? Her father thought that before he got back she might stay with her aunt—her mother's dead, you see—and there was the aunt waiting at the dock so she couldn't skip out of it. And I went along." The sublimely innocent face was turned up with an expression which Burne-Jones would have liked to paint. "But you were asking about Greg Mannering, weren't you? Well, he called up there to see her. And then, when she came back here after two weeks, Greg was going to call on the old man in his best style—that's at Miriam's house, in Hyde Park Gardens—only he got there too early in the afternoon. So he was showing off, juggling a trunk full of old pottery or something, and it slipped and he busted it to blazes." It was as though a light of devilment had been turned on in her face; she opened her eyes wide and beamed. "Oh, I say, it was an AWFUL mess! So we thought we'd better get him out of the house and not come back until the old man cooled off. Afterwards she telephoned him that——"

The girl stopped, rubbed her forehead, and remembered something. Again her expression altered, this time to fear.

"Where's Miriam?" she demanded, with shrill abruptness. As I did not answer she pointed her finger. "Where's Miriam? Listen, you chaps. You remember—a little while ago—Ronald said a woman telephoned here for me—and in a disguised voice— and then rang off all of a sudden? Who was it? What's happened to Miriam? Why are you asking all these questions about her?"

I looked at them and laughed.

"You always seem to want to lead the subject back to Miss Wade," I told them, "when my idea is to get on with Mannering. Listen! It's no good denying that we have evidence which proves he was probably entangled with this business tonight."

That stopped them. There was a silence, which I felt (and this was bad) to be nevertheless a silence of muddled wits and complete incredulity. Ronald Holmes walked slowly into the room from the door behind me, as though to take charge of the situation. He sat down on the arm of a chair, juggled the glass in his hand, and looked at the waggling toe of his shoe.

"Evidence," he stated rather than asked. "What evidence?"

"I'll answer that by first asking you about what your 'private view' tonight, before you called it off, was to be. It's true, isn't it, that you were going to open the coffin of Haroun al Raschid's wife?"

"Oh, Lord—!" groaned Baxter, and Holmes stopped him. The latter seemed staggered, but he spoke quietly.

"No, it is not true. Where the devil, may I ask, did you get such an idea as that? From Mannering?"

"Partly. To begin with, he said you were going to 'rob a grave.'"

"Easy, Gaffer. . . ." Holmes looked at the ceiling. "Now why? *Why* did he tell you that? No, I'm not wandering; it's the abstract problem that interests me. The coffin of Haroun al Raschid's wife!"

"Never mind the abstract problem for a moment. You say it's not true. Think it over, Mr. Holmes."

He turned round with a pale smile of such scepticism that he seemed to be making a face. "Let's both think it over," he suggested. "Tell me: do you know anything about Baghdad?"

"No."

"The tomb of Harùn er Raschid's favourite wife, Zobeide—I presume that's the one you mean—is in the burying-ground of the Old Town, not far from the tomb of Sheik Maaruf. It is one of the chief monuments of Baghdad; it was built well over a thousand years ago, and it has been jealously restored by several Moslem rulers. Nobody has ever seen the coffin of Zobeide. A direct view is seldom permitted by Moslems; witness the tomb of Mahomet at Medina, where visitors must look through palings to see even the outer tomb of the prophet. Nobody knows any more about Zobeide than that she was put into a leaden coffin encircling a golden one. And the idea that anybody could—No, no, no!"

He shook his head in a more lively way.

"Imagine somebody stealing the coffin of Nelson out of St. Paul's, or the coffin of any public person from any public monument. That would be lurid enough, but it would be mild compared to the desecration—Lord! A Moslem shrine! It has nothing to do with ancient Egypt, you know; it's a living religion. Add to that the complete impossibility of robbing such a tomb. . . ." He spread out his hands and shrugged. Although there was a twinkle behind his spectacles, I thought that his manner was a little more emphatic than was necessary when he glanced at the others and added: "Of course it's absurd. What puzzles me is how Mannering got such an idea."

"I wish it had been true, though," observed Baxter, with gloomy enjoyment. That last heavy drink had brightened his look considerably. He sat back with his hands in his pockets, eyeing the bottle. "It'd make things ruddy exciting, if you ask me. I remember that tomb; brick place with a cone up on top. The old man showed it to me himself when I flew over from Cairo. Much better than mucking about with——"

"With what?" I demanded. "If it wasn't a coffin, then what *were* you going to examine?"

Holmes looked whimsically at the others. "Ever hear of Antoine Galland, inspector?"

"No."

"And yet everybody in the world has heard of what he did. He translated the *Thousand and One Nights* out of the Arabic into French between 1704 and 1712, and translations of the French came to us. Mr. Wade is particularly interested in the *Arabian Nights* because he shares the view that they were taken directly from the Persian *Hézar Afsáne*, or *Thousand Tales*, though the treatment is Arabian throughout. So, when he had the opportunity of buying the first two hundred manuscript sheets of Galland's original translation, together with the notes and interpolations——"

"Just a minute," I said, "do you mean that what this party was to have gathered for was just to look at some manuscript sheets?"

At this point, I regret to say, it was borne in upon me that I, who have always considered myself a sober and rational person, was honestly enjoying this lunacy of tonight, and that Holmes's explanation was disappointing. Holmes seemed surprised as he glanced round.

"Yes, of course. That was why Dr. Illingworth was to have been there. *With* notes and interpolations, you understand. . . ."

"And is that all?"

Jerry Wade, who had been looking across with a bright and steady expression of interest, leaned forward. "Shake hands, inspector," he urged. "I feel exactly the same way. Under your buff blue beats the soul (so to speak) of a kid reading *Treasure Island*. I sympathise with you, sink me if I don't, at being roused from your dreams of coffins; and if this blighter had any sense of——"

"I have a sense of propriety, anyhow," said Holmes. His voice was so cold that I was jarred back to common sense. "Don't forget that after all there's been a murder, a real murder, committed." He turned back to me with a worried expression. "Is that *all?* you were asking. Why, man, don't you understand. . . . Galland's manuscript sheets!" He made a vague gesture, as though I had asked him, "What is civilisation?" or some question too big to be answered. "The flood of historical light it will throw——"

"Historical light be blowed," observed Jerry Wade. "I will not be crushed. 'A murder has been committed.' All right. But it's not common sense for Inspector Carruthers to look on us with a sinister eye just because we're not all cut up and melancholy about the death of somebody we never heard of. I'm going to take the forthright human view that this thing is interesting; it's the *Arabian Nights* come to life. Your trouble is that you aren't interested in stories at all. You're only interested in a roaring good story of how a sultan murdered six wives because it throws a flood of light on the marriage customs at Basra under Hassan the Hose-mender in 1401. Now I've picked up a smattering of information from you and the old man, just so that I could talk about it and help Rinkey Butler write a detective story. But deep down in my soul all I really know about Asiatics consists in a splendid idea that they wear funny clothes, talk about Allah, and run around murdering people for pinching sacred relics. Which is enough. I don't know a Persian Moslem from an Indian Hindu. But I do know that the goblins will git me if I don't look out, which is the secret of an exciting life."

"Steady, Mr. Wade," I interposed, as he began excitedly hopping in his chair and pointing his finger at Holmes. "Does that mean you're not—connected with the museum, then?"

Holmes smiled. "It does. The Gaffer's only occupation is reading; book after book of good-for-nothing lore. That's what produces his attitude—the psychologists would call it a defence-mechanism. He would like to imagine a world where all commonplace things had gone just a little crazy: where vicars were seen climbing the rain-spouts of their churches, and the Lord Mayor of London unexpectedly said, 'No' when the royal procession wanted to go past Temple Bar. Bosh! I've told him a hundred times that a thing is not necessarily more interesting simply because it is exhibited upside-down. And the plain fact is, Gaffer, that that's not the real world."

"Isn't it?" I said. "I'd be inclined to agree with Mr. Wade."

After a pause Harriet Kirkton turned on me with nervous and puzzled exasperation. "Oh, *won't* you tell us what you want with us?" she cried. "Why are you spinning this out, and—and—I don't know, but it's very funny somewhere, and—*why?*"

I said: "Because, miss, it's possible that one of you is lying. As for queer conduct, a vicar climbing a rain-spout isn't any more out of the way than a museum-attendant dancing round a packing-case and singing about Haroun al Raschid's wife. Or a corpse with a cookery-book in one hand. Are you sure you haven't anything to tell me now?"

"No!"

I gave the facts briefly. There were some mutterings

and table-poundings from Baxter. But it was the mention of the cookery-book which seemed most to put them off balance. Holmes, still repressed but with a look of waxy fury about his face, turned towards Jerry Wade.

"If I didn't know—" he said, and swallowed. "This sounds like your insane work. A cookery-book! I'm almost inclined to believe you had something to do with it after all."

"Take it easy, Ron," said Baxter, with unexpected and sharp authority. He craned his neck round. "But look here, Gaffer. I mean to say—you didn't, did you? —after all——"

"Believe it or not, I don't know anything about it," answered Jerry Wade simply. (He seemed very uneasy nevertheless.) "A cookery-book isn't quite picturesque enough for my style. Oh, Lord help us, a—! Something's got to be done about this. Keep off me, will you, while I try to think? I don't suppose the fellow was a dago chef of some kind?"

"Well, if he was," grunted Baxter, "he'd hardly be carrying round Mrs. Somebody's book of home recipes, would he? I mean, he wouldn't get many hints on how to prepare *Soufflé à la Carmagnole*, or any of those fancy things, and that's all they seem to know about. Unless it's a cryptogram or a cipher or something of that sort. I mean to say 'Steak and onions': 'Fly at once; all is discovered.' It might be a dashed good way of——"

Holmes was on his feet.

"Are you people drunk," he said with pale calmness, "or does it naturally occur to you to act like kids, or haven't you got it through your heads that this is serious?"

"We're as scared as hell," Jerry Wade replied, just as

calmly, "if you want to know the truth. Got any more cards up your sleeve, inspector? If we haven't come to the end of the business where clergymen climb rainspouts and——"

He stopped, looking at the door, and everybody else followed his glance. I was standing well to one side, and at the moment the new-comer did not see me. For there was poked into the room the helmet of a policeman.

He was a large police-constable, with white arm bands for point duty, and he glared at the occupants of the room.

"Has anybody got three-and-sixpence?" he demanded. "I need it for cabfare. *Cré nom de nom d'un petit chou-fleur rogue!*—what a night! There's bad trouble brewing, so stop goggling and dig up three-and-a-tanner, can't you?"

7

The Policeman Who Kicked His Helmet

Before he saw me, or before I could deal with this, the new-comer very gravely removed his helmet, held it poised like a football, and kicked it across the room. It narrowly missed the lamp, hit the wall, and rolled back almost at my feet. Harriet Kirkton got up with a scream.

"Get out of here, you fool!" she cried. "There's a real——"

The new-comer swung round. I saw the numerals on his collar and understood. He was a powerful young fellow with a round amiable face, now dull with sweat and worry. He was going bald under loose strands of black hair, some trailing down on his forehead. The white arm band was always brushing across the forehead; there were wrinkles of worry at the corners of his eyelids, under which pale-grey eyes looked out without their ordinary sleepiness, and the corners of his loose-lipped amiable mouth were turned down. He looked capable, lazy, and somehow dangerous. But he was welcome. The sight of him had given me the solution to at least one part of this nightmare, and I knew now how to fit together a few of the pieces that were most puzzling. When he saw me he hesitated, took a quick glance round, and drew himself up in an obvious attempt to adjust his face like a mask. It entailed drawing in his chin and bending on me a kind of gloomy leer; had it been carried a little farther, he would have been on the point of thrusting his thumbs into the armholes of an imaginary waistcoat.

"Now then!" he began gruffly, in a different voice. "Now then——"

"That's pretty rotten," I said. "I'm from Vine Street myself. What's your division?"

He remained motionless, breathing hard. "Yes," he answered, without relevancy. "Yes, of course. You see——"

"There's no such number as ZX105. Who are you, and where did you get the uniform, and why are you masquerading?"

"Gimme a cigarette, somebody," requested the other, half over his shoulder. His arm made motions in the air. "What's up, officer? Just a joke, that's all. Butler's my name—Richard Butler. I'm quite a respectable citizen, in a way." He tried to smile, uneasily. "What's all the row about? No harm in going to a fancy-dress party."

"A fancy-dress party where?"

"For God's sake, Rinkey, be careful," gabbled Harriet Kirkton, almost hopping up and down on the couch in an agony of indecision. "He's been telling us all about a murder that's supposed to have been committed at the museum; and we've told him we don't know anything about it and weren't near the museum, but he still thinks——"

"Oh," said Butler, and remained staring at my shoulder.

"A fancy-dress party where?"

"Eh? Oh, well, just some friends—" He hesitated again, and his face darkened. "Here, what the devil's the idea of looking at me as though I'd killed somebody? Why hop all over *me* as soon as I walk in?"

"I'll tell you in a moment, sir, if you'll come along. I was just leaving here, and if you'll come along with me to the Wade Museum for a few minutes——"

"Oh," repeated Butler in the same heavy voice. He was moving his shoulders slowly under the tunic. "And suppose I won't come?"

"You don't have to go, you know," Holmes interposed coolly. "If I ring up Mr. Wade's solicitor——"

"Well, sir, Mr. Butler's pretty heavy," I said, "but I think he could be taken along, and I should just have to risk trouble with your solicitor. Also," I looked at Holmes and Jerry Wade, "I'd like you two gentlemen to go with us." The parrot-house began to screech. "Listen here, you damned young fools! Be quiet, and listen a minute. I can't pick all of you up and carry you there, but why make an unnecessary row? Common curiosity ought to make you do the most you can to help; and if you don't do it the authorities are going to cut up rough—to say nothing of what old Mr. Wade will say."

It was a lucky touch about the old man. Holmes stopped, passed his hand across his hair, and nodded gravely. Jerry Wade, with an air of gloomy reminiscence, breathed into the mouth-organ a bar or two of "For He's a Jolly Good Fellow." And Butler, still swabbing his forehead with his sleeve, let out a shout of laughter; he seemed imbued with a feverish mirth, behind which I thought I could see in his eyes the shift and twisting of a nimble brain on a duel of some kind. Those pale-grey eyes acquired a prominence and fixity of their own, though his manner was pleasant.

"Right you are, old son," he agreed. "I don't know what this alleged murder is, or why I have become so important all of a sudden. But I'll go along quietly, provided somebody gives me three-and-six to pay off that cab. The driver's still waiting downstairs, and the hall-porter's off duty, so there was nobody to pay——"

"Rinkey!" cried the girl, "don't you realise he's going to question that driver? Don't you see it's why he wants to get you downstairs?"

"Oh, is that all?" Butler enquired, with a broad gesture. "I want him to question the driver; maybe I can shunt the bill off on him. Here, pass me a quick one before I go, will you?"

"We'll all go," declared Baxter, with an air of inspiration, as though somebody had suggested a party. "We'll all go, and present a united front."

I stopped this with some difficulty; I wanted neither Baxter nor the girl along, and I was getting mad. My three charges (Butler having retrieved his helmet and downed a stiff drink) were got out ahead. In silence we went downstairs, eyeing each other with that curiously blank stare which people assume when they are jammed up together face to face in lifts. The taxi-driver—a cadaverous man with a bent back and a red nose—had been taking no chances; he was waiting below-stairs in the hall. While Wade was paying him off, I got busy.

"Where did you pick up this fare?"

"So he ain't a copper," said the driver, with the air of

a proud suspicion verified, "and *you* are. I know. Haha. Orkney Hotel, Kensington High Street."

"How long ago?"

"'Bout twenty minutes."

"He came out of the hotel?"

"No. Outside on the pavement, walking along. What's up, sir?"

I looked at Butler, whose bland face had a look of satisfied innocence. "No, I wasn't at the hotel," he said. "Listen, driver, Sir Robert Peel here doesn't believe I was at a fancy-dress party. Enlighten him, will you?"

The driver was deferential. "Easy enough for him to 'a' been, Sir Robert," he told me. "There was a fancy-dress ball two or three doors off, at the Pennington, only it let out a bit earlier. Basket-weavers association or something. . . ."

This was one in the eye for the theory I was developing, but I felt more and more convinced that the theory must be right. Though I questioned the driver further, nothing developed, and I let him go with his name and number for reference. We resumed our march, with Wade and Holmes some paces to the rear so that I could question Butler.

Pall Mall has seen few queerer processions. These three were under a bad nerve-strain, which manifested itself in the wrong way. It may have been in some degree the partial verification of what Butler had said; but I think it was mostly the fact that for the first time in their lives they were approaching a real murdered man—a staring ugly business, where blood was not the red ink of the stage or the ectoplasm of the stories—which shocked home to them and produced a nervous revulsion of shaky jocularity. Jerry Wade still had his mouth-organ; he gave a rendition of "The Animals Walked in Two by Two," and I found that we were keeping step like soldiers to tunes offered as comments. Although the correct Holmes offered no remarks which did not befit his black tie and his brushed bowler hat, he laughed with witless enthusiasm, at the others' remarks. Grotesque hilarity went down that rigid dun-coloured street under a setting moon, because it was to end in the contemplation of death; and it became very unfunny when Butler suddenly leaned over and roared "Boo!" in the ear of a stout old gentleman just coming down the steps of his club.

"Having a good time?" I enquired, when I had contrived to shut the noise off. "Let's have it now. I suppose you're going to say you were attending the basket-weavers' Ball? Why?"

"I was. There was a beautiful blonde basket-weaver—" He saw my expression and stopped. Something shrewd and elusive was gathering again in his face; prepared for the duel, even desperately prepared. "Now listen, inspector, you've been a pretty good sort for a sleuth, and I'll tell you the truth. I did go to the basket-weavers' ball—it was a motor manufacturing company, as a matter of fact—and, incidentally, there *was* a good-looking blonde who said she'd meet me somewhere tomorrow. But I went to the thing for a while chiefly as an excuse."

"Excuse?"

"Yes. Here's the game: I do adventure stories, any kind of lurid excitement, for the American pulps— pulp magazines, that is—with occasional assistance from Gaffer Wade. The museum's invaluable for material about the Curse of Kali, or maybe it's somebody else. But what I wanted to do was to test out this business of whether there really was excitement and colour floating about the streets. Now I ask you, what better chance would a man have to bump into the bright eyes of danger than to put on a policeman's uniform and saunter through the——"

He was growing inspired with his own ideas, which I could have sworn had struck him only in the last few minutes, and with the play of his fine voice. When he turned round to look at me, there was something consciously hypnotic in his stare; something which, despite his broad-lipped smile, struck me in that moonlit street as blank and creepy.

"All this," I said, "amounts to the statement that you weren't at the Wade Museum tonight?"

He was pulled up short. "At——? Eh? No. No, I wasn't."

"Can you prove where you were?"

"Might be a bit difficult. Masks at the ball—and then wandering the streets—might produce the blonde, though," he muttered, as though to himself. "Damn it, if it comes to that, can you prove I was at the museum? What's going on here, anyhow? I don't even know what it is I have to explain. Sam Baxter was gabbling some hazy stuff about a man named Penderel who was killed with an ivory-handled dagger, but I don't know anything about it. Can you prove I *was* there?"

"Possibly. You were seen, you know."

He stopped now in a physical sense, turning round with a big swing of his shoulders, but I pushed him on so that the others should not overtake us. Behind us the mouth-organ hummed that we were sailing on Moonlight Bay, but Butler's face was in horrible contrast to it.

"Seen?" he repeated. "That's a dirty lie. Who said I was seen? Who saw me?"

"A man in white false whiskers. He came out the back of the museum and climbed up on the wall. Now listen! He saw my station-sergeant, who has the same build as you, and looks something like you except for his moustache. This man saw the sergeant, in dim light, trying the doors of the museum. He said: 'You killed him, and you'll hang for it, *my fine impostor*. I saw you in the coach.' He didn't mean the sergeant; he mistook the sergeant for somebody else.... Who could it have been?"

Butler, walking very slowly and staring ahead of him, said a curious thing. He said:

"Have you told the others about this?"

"No."

"And where is this witness in the false whiskers?"

"He disappeared."

"Do you know who he is?"

"Not yet."

Butler looked round with an air of wild and boisterous congratulation. "Excellent, inspector! True to type, shrewdly guessed, and—thin as tissue-paper. It won't do. You couldn't hold anybody on a charge like that. What does it amount to? You have a noble and spotless witness (whom you can't produce, by the way) with a taste for wearing false whiskers, climbing walls, and leaping at police-sergeants. On some meaningless words spoken by this—to put it mildly—eccentric character, you single out of eight million people one person who that night happens to be going to a fancy-dress party, and can prove that he was. (The other fellow seems to have been wearing fancy-dress as well, but let that pass.) This therefore establishes that I killed a man I never heard of, in a place where I couldn't have been. Can any reputable witness, who was not a phantom and who was on the scene and who can be produced, say that I was at the museum? There's old Pruen, for instance, with twenty years' service with the Wade family behind him, and ten years in the museum. What does he say? Does he say I was at the museum tonight?"

"Well, just at the moment——"

Butler regarded me deprecatingly, with a shake of his head. He went on: "Honestly, my boy, it won't wash. You may think privately that I was there. I wasn't; but we're not discussing that. I say you may think privately I was there, but can you prove it? Would you have the nerve to go before a magistrate with the evidence you've got? Why, man," he was firing up with fresh eloquence, "think of your case as it stands! You claim I stabbed this unknown man and chucked his body into a carriage in the hall——"

"Do I? Nothing was said about the carriage in the hall. How did you know that?"

His cool gaze did not waver. "Oh, well, I'm convinced I heard Sam or the Gaffer say something about it during the babble back there. Are you going to take me up on such crazy evidence, I ask you?"

"When the whole case is crazy, the evidence is bound to be crazy too. Here we are."

The big bronze doors of the museum were not quite closed, and a line of light slanted down on the pavement. The upper windows glowed; there was a look of savage activity about the place in that drowsy neighbourhood. But one thing I saw with a good deal of inward profanity: the police-car, in which P. C. Jameson had been sitting with Mannering, was now empty. The blunder had been mine for leaving the place, but there would be trouble if, contrary to my instructions, Mannering had been allowed to speak to Miriam Wade. First I had to deal with half a dozen newspaper men and camera men round the doors; I promised them a story shortly for, if no information were forthcoming about the dead man's identity, we should have to broadcast an appeal. Butler passed unnoticed as a genuine constable, but several flash-bulb snapshots were taken of Wade and Holmes, the former being nervously complacent and the latter furious.

Hoskins, with P. C. Collins behind him, was waiting just inside. The sergeant stared when he saw Butler, who gave him a smart salute. But there was an end of that defiant jocularity. In that subdued place where there were too many echoes, the artificial moonlight was more suggestive than the real; the twisted colours of the tapestries stood out against white walls; the line of coaches waited, and so did the dead man still sprawled on his back. Jerry Wade's face looked a little wild, and Holmes took off his hat. They began to talk in whispers. After giving instructions that they were to be taken to look at the body, and then put together in some other room with P. C. Collins along to see that their talk did not become too interesting, I drew Hoskins aside.

"Where's Mannering?"

Hoskins hesitated. "Well, sir I thought——"

"You mean you left him in the same room with Miss Wade?"

The sergeant's face changed. "But I thought, sir, now where was the 'arm?" he demanded. "You thought yourself she didn't have nothing to do with it. And she asked me—started crying like—no 'arm in it, except to her maybe, if the chap's a murderer; and, anyway, Martin was there most of the time. They're still down in that curator's room." Although he did not move his arms, he seemed to convey a flapping motion. "Listen, sir! I've been pounding away trying to get something out o' Pruen, as you specially instructed me——"

"Never mind now. Did you get anything out of him?"

"No, sir, 'fraid not. 'E won't say anything! Just, 'I don't know,' or 'Never 'eard of it,' even when you ask him his own name, and keeps telling me 'ow Mr. Wade'll take the stripes off my arm. But we did find one or two things. . . ."

"Yes?"

Hoskins checked off the points on his fingers. "First, that packing-case. I opened it, as you told me. There was something inside, right enough. A thing like a coffin, very old looking you might call it, and made of lead; they'd got it packed in sawdust. Somebody'd put sealing-wax on the line where you open it. I didn't tamper no more, sir; I thought you might want to do it yourself."

It was difficult to say whether this was verification of what I had thought, or still another hard one in the eye. For some little time I had been expecting that there would be nothing in that case: that it was a part of some hoax or hoodwinking to explain Pruen's evil glee. The mild voice of Holmes sounded again, his smooth explanation that only a fool would ever think that there might be a coffin of the sort I expected; and yet about Holmes there was a false atmosphere. He was lying—or somebody was lying—and Pruen had been dancing round a real coffin in this lunatic museum.

"Anything else?" I said.

"Yessir!" nodded Hoskins. "Coal-dust! Coal! Come with me."

When you faced the rear of the museum, as I have explained, there were in the right-hand side-wall beyond the line of pillars two open archways, marked in gilt letters, "Gallery of the Eight Paradises" and "Gallery of the Bazaars." The first, a name which had caught my eye and which I meant to investigate, was towards the rear. The second was at the front, not far from the bronze front doors. Hoskins led me over to the arch, ten feet wide but so high that its breadth looked less. Lights had been switched on inside, for an effect which was like stepping out of London into the East or, if you were more prosaic-minded, into the underground gallery of a waxworks without any wax figures.

The long room had been fitted up to represent a street intersected by other crooked streets, and roofed over with a fretwork of branches and twigs. It seemed to be a full-sized reconstruction of an Eastern bazaar, skilfully lighted so that you saw it in a twilight through the branches, for the thing I most remember is that woven pattern of shadows. Against walls of burnt brick coloured a yellowish-red, but subdued now to dusk, the shops and stalls made caverns behind a forest of curtains realistically grimy. There was too much of it to describe. I remember a stall of weapons, a stall of beads, and a stall of gleaming brass and pottery outside which stood one of those big glass water-pipes called hookahs, with a cushion behind it as though the smoker had just got up to go inside. Over it the pattern of shadows made it look thin and secret; you felt that the vast noise of the place had only stopped just before you stepped into the street. It was a good illusion, so good that I automatically glanced over my shoulder at the line of coaches in the hall.

"Rummy place, ain't it?" considered Hoskins, scratching his chin. "If they 'ad to kill that chap somewhere, I wonder they didn't do his business right in this shop-window. I was thinking about my kids; they'd think it was a rare place to play 'ide-and-seek if I took 'em in this shop. Now, sir! Collins went all over the place. Nothing! Nothing out of the way, I mean—except that."

He pointed high at a jutting of the wall where the imitation street curved close to us. Over a crooked awning outside the brass-and-pottery stall, the yellowish-red wall had a black splash like a star. It was coaldust. The awning was spattered with it, among gleaming particles of coal. More bits littered the floor before it, broken off a big lump of coal whose remnant lay near the hookah. Hoskins enquired:

"See it? There! From what it looks like, somebody stood down near where we are now, and 'e takes a big lump of coal, and 'e ups and chucks it *bang* at the wall over this boudoir. Eh? Now, why? Why does somebody stand chucking coal up at a wall? What does the chap aim *at*? There's nothing up there, and nobody at all could climb up without bringing the 'ole shop down. You don't suppose they was 'aving a playful fight with coal all over the place, do you, sir? I didn't know what it meant, but Collins saw it and I thought I'd better show you. Right 'ere the chap must have stood," argued Hoskins, who liked to make things shiningly clear by repetition, "and *bang!* up goes a piece of coal right against that wall——"

"Yes, I understand that. Did you ask Pruen about it?"

"Pruen don't know anything about coal. So 'e says. About any coal."

I reflected. "Sergeant, there is, or God knows there ought to be, a reasonable explanation which will fit all these things together. Why anybody should stand chucking coal at a wall I don't know any more than you do. As you say, he couldn't have been throwing it at anybody; nobody could get up there without disturbing the whole bazaar. . . . You didn't find anything else, did you?"

"Hoyessir!" declared the sergeant, with an evil grin, and nodded violently. "Come this way now."

We went out into the hall again. Round the body of the unknown the group consisting of Wade, Holmes, Butler, and Collins had begun to break up; the first three were edging away. Holmes looked sickish, Wade determinedly cynical, and Butler expressionless.

"Never saw him before," Jerry Wade cried down the room, his voice booming back in such unexpected echoes that he jumped. Then his voice quavered when he went on in a parody of cheerfulness: "What do you want with us now? All reasonable requests willingly complied with. Ron wants to go to the curator's room and make sure everything's in order, if you've got no objection."

Despite their protests I sent them to the room labelled "Persian Gallery," in charge of Collins. Holmes was brushing at the sleeves of his coat and again talking about a solicitor. Although I had been afraid that the sound of young Wade's voice might have brought Miriam and Mannering trumpeting out of the curator's room, evidently P. C. Martin in charge was controlling matters. Then Hoskins beckoned me down to the glass case from which the dagger had been taken.

"Now, sir. Look there. You remember, you wanted Rogers to go over this case for finger-prints? Right! And the little door at the side of the case was locked. But Collins knows a thing or two about locks, so when Rogers thinks there might be prints inside on that little door, then Collins goes to work and picks it neat as you please with a bent pin. See?"

He bent over asthmatically and waggled the little wooden flap back and forth. Then he reached inside, with the air of a conjuror, but kept his hand there.

"So we opened it. I looked inside—like this—and I saw what we couldn't see before, because it's pretty dark itself and against that dark velvet. Eh? But there it was! There it was, lying all neat and snug just inside this 'ere little door, lying all neat and snug and arranged on the velvet like as if it was to be shown. And it's this."

He withdrew his hand quickly bent back as though to enjoy a commendation, and held out in his palm a black moustache.

8

Zobeide's Coffin Is Empty

"So," I reflected, and juggled the new exhibit in my hand, "we now have an addition to our hirsute collection. Somebody removed the dagger from the case, and substituted the false moustache. Any idea about this, sergeant?"

"N-no, sir. Except one thing that I could deduce," Hoskins replied with modest grimness. "That moustache don't belong to *him*." He jerked his thumb towards the dead man. "First point, he's got a real one. Second point even if 'e hadn't, this moustache was made for a different kind of make-up; see it? This chap Penderel's whiskers are kind of greyish-streaked in little bits to make him look oldish, and it's fine 'air—real 'air. This little thing is dead black, and it's cheap; sort of moustache kids get for sixpence at a shop as a Guy Fawkes's dress-up."

"So we get still a third person decked out in—h'm."

"Looks like it, sir; now don't it? People chucking

coal at walls!" exploded Hoskins, who for some reason seemed to consider this the most darkly mysterious part of the whole affair. "And putting in false moustaches where daggers was! Well. What do we do now?"

I ascertained that the van had been sent for, to take the body to the mortuary until it should be identified. There might be some means of identification in the dead man's linen; I ordered that his clothes should be kept, as well as the false whiskers and the eyeglasses. The separate classification of finger-prints, I learned, could be had in the morning; little enough time for me to make a full report, since it seemed very probable that the Yard would take the case out of my hands. So I added the moustache to my collection of exhibits, and drew again out of the envelope that folded, tight-pressed, grimy sheet of note-paper on which was typed the message found in Gregory Mannering's pocket. I read it again.

DEAR G.,

There has got to be a corpse—a *real* corpse. The means of death doesn't matter, but there has got to be a corpse. I'll manage the murder—that ivory-handled *khanjar* will do the trick, or strangling if it seems preferred——

It was time to spring this on Mannering, who should now have worked himself into a state sufficiently nervous for my purpose. This might be the key to the whole case, with Mannering figuring as incidental villain; and yet I doubted it. If anybody had asked me why, I could have given no reason that would have been upheld in a court of law, and yet I doubted it. Now, then, what could be deduced from the thing?

The note was written on an ordinary grade of good

note-paper, with an ordinary black-ink ribbon, and on an ordinary typewriter which had no peculiarities visible to the naked eye except a slight slur in the tail of the comma. It had been presumably written by somebody used to a typewriter, for the typing was very clean-cut and without those bumping hesitations visible in the copy of the novice. Moreover, to judge by the casual reference to the ivory-handled *khanjar*, it had been written by somebody thoroughly familiar with this museum: which narrowed the field. As for the grimy side of the note—I looked again, and it seemed to me probable that the grime was coal-dust. That blasted stuff was becoming as omnipresent as whiskers. I rubbed some of it off on a leaf from my note-book, which I put away for analysis. But, if it did turn out to be coal-dust like the heavy smudges at the front door of the museum and the splatterings round that stall in the "Gallery of the Bazaars," what then? The note had been found in Mannering's overcoat pocket. . . .

And then, gentlemen, at last (at long last) there banged through my thick skull one plain fact, so obvious from the very beginning that it should not have been obscured even by a whole clothes-line hung with whiskers. And it was this: the note could not have been written to Gregory Mannering.

It could not have been written to Gregory Mannering, for the not-very-complicated reason that it was unfinished. It broke off in the middle, and had its last half-line crossed out in the middle. If you are writing a note to somebody, you may from one cause or another omit your signature. But you do not stop suddenly in mid-flight half-way across the sheet, and then shove the note into an envelope and send it off. As a matter of fact, this letter was not even folded to fit an envelope. It had been folded into a square, sharp-creased and flat as though there had been pressure against it. . . .

In short, the writer of this note had done what many another careless correspondent has done when there is no wastebasket at hand. The first few lines he wrote had not been to his liking, or he had decided not to write, so he had broken off. Then, to get the thing out of the way, he had folded it up and thrust it into the inside breast-pocket of his coat, where there were other papers to press it flat. Mannering, then, had never received that note; but had he *written* the note? It had been found on him, but I did not think it probable that he had written it either.

To begin with, it had been found in his overcoat pocket, and stuffed in loosely enough to tumble out. You do not sit down to a typewriter in your overcoat— it was an evening-coat, in addition—and, even in the unlikely event that you do stuff unfinished notes into the pocket of an evening-coat, you do not first get them pressed flat in some other pocket, pull them out, get them smeared with coal-dust, and thrust them in loosely enough to protrude. It began to look as though Mannering had neither received nor written that note. It began to look as though he had picked it up somewhere, and hurriedly put it into his pocket. The note was dated "Wednesday," which meant that it might have been picked up at any time during two days—or on any day following a dozen previous Wednesdays, for all I knew—and, despite my hypnotized willingness to see coal-dust everywhere, it could have been picked up anywhere in broad London just as well as in the neighbourhood of this museum.

Although all this was based on supposition, nevertheless the figure of Mannering as a sinister villain began to collapse and run together like heated wax. *Now* I found myself unreasonably getting mad because I had not pitched into Mannering before I discovered this; it took the edge off my enthusiasm. In case something should happen before it cooled altogether, I stumped down to the curator's room.

There were four people there, who looked up in various moods at the swishing of the door. In one corner sat Pruen, huddled with a drawing-portfolio on his bony knees, and with disgruntled flips turning over the cards for a game of patience. Just behind him towered P. C. Martin, glancing casually over Pruen's shoulder with the expression of one just about to advise playing the black nine on the red ten. But at the far side of the big mahogany desk, half risen with her hands gripping the arms of the chair, Miriam Wade regarded the door with a smeary look of past tears whose anger was not altogether for me. . . .

For Mannering, then? There had been some sort of row or emotional explosion here, one of those silent explosions which show traces in the air. The waves of it reached me when Mannering disturbed the air by turning round; he had been standing erect, with his back partly turned to her and his arms folded, staring darkly at a wall-safe across the room with an expression rather like a Byronic burglar. There showed again the dark hair, the rugged face with its tangled brows. Framed in Moorish surroundings which were somewhat more exotic than a police-station, he now looked genuinely impressive. His grim smile turned slowly round.

"Ah, inspector," he greeted me, with a Satanic richness and suavity. "We were beginning to think you had deserted us and gone home."

Pruen stopped with a card poised in the air. His thin voice cracked.

"Thank God you're back," he croaked. "You ain't much, but at least you're a 'uman being. Maybe you can make The Sheik over there shut 'is row. He's been upsettin' Miss Miriam——"

She cried, "Pruen!" and he subsided as though he had been shot, dropping and muttering in the chair. Then she turned a flushed lovely face towards Mannering, with the tears still on her eyelashes, and an expression of uneasy contrition. Some people have all the luck.

"Honestly, Greg, I didn't mean what I said. I was so upset, and this horrible business of being kept here," she looked venomously at me, "that I've been half out of my mind——"

"Try to forget it, my dear," said Mannering. "Both of us were upset." He patted her hand. "I will deal with the inspector."

"Miss Wade," I told her, "your brother is here now, out in the other room, with Mr. Holmes and Mr. Butler. If you'd like to go to them, they're waiting. They don't know you're here. Pruen, you'd better go along too."

She flew out of the room with an alacrity which seemed to strike Mannering with double bitterness. He stood clenching and unclenching his hands; then he sat down beside the desk. I whispered to Hoskins at the door as the girl and Pruen left: "Withdraw Collins out of that room. Let 'em talk, but listen."

Then, dismissing Martin as well, I turned back to Mannering with my note-book. Mannering did not seem to notice. He sat slumped in the chair, in an attitude suddenly so unstudied and bitter that the cross-eyed look had returned almost to the extent of a deformity. There was a change in the atmosphere; a lowering of pressure or vitality, somehow. He sat brushing his thumb across the forefingers of clenched fists, and shifting a little. When he spoke, the words were thrown out abruptly, as though he were striking a blow.

"What's the matter with me?" he demanded.

"Matter?"

"Yes, you know what I mean. I'm a human being. I don't care about any of the swine. . . . I've never cared for what they thought in my life, come to think of it—until this leaky value here," he pressed his chest under the heart, "started cutting capers. I can't do any of the things I used to do without even thinking of them. I try to do some little thing—then something goes *crack*, and you know what happens. It's looking like such a damned silly ass that I hate," he said through stiff jaws, in a low voice but so violently that his face went red. "My God, if there's anything in this world I hate, anything at all, it's looking like an ass. . . ."

Unwillingly I found myself rather liking the man. "Don't you suppose," I said, "that if you didn't think so much about it, and forget——"

"Think about it! Think about it! Ask a man to walk into a room and refrain from looking at the walls. Ask him to go to the theatre and keep his eyes off the stage. You're always in the forefront of your own eye; or at least I am. . . . And, up to a little while ago, I always thought that was quite right. I liked to be in the forefront of my own eye," he told me, with completely unconscious arrogance, "because it was right, and I could no more look like a fool than—But something changed—all of a sudden—and now I have to keep driving at it, and talking, and talking. . . . Look here, I've done things; I've really done them and I wouldn't want to talk about them except that something makes me, and the stuff sounds like such bilge when I tell it that I sound like a fool to myself. Do you undersand me? So I have to insult people. Come to think of it, I'd have insulted them in the old days— genuinely, because I have a rather low opinion of them," he stated this as a serene fact, quite unruffled, "but now it's deliberate. I thought of it particularly in connection with that crowd of Miriam's——"

"Do you know them?"

"I know Holmes and the Kirkton girl, that's all. I said I had no wish to meet the others," he spoke in a cool voice, "because they didn't particularly interest me. I remember that Miriam had a photograph of this fellow Sam Baxter—one of those enlarged coloured photographs; she likes childish things—and I drew an exact scientific parallel, detail by detail, between that and one of the red apes of the Malay Peninsula."

"Very scientific, no doubt."

He considered. "Well, it was stretched a little farther than the facts, of course. But, when Miriam went on to tell me how Baxter, after not more than eight months at the legation in Cairo, could speak Arabic like a native, I dealt with that in the exact way it deserved." His smile was replaced by the puzzled bitterness again. "Why don't I want to meet them? Why? I could out-face them, I could—But because I made a ruddy ass of myself with a trunk full of pottery—and then fainted like a schoolgirl—!"

He jumped up from his chair.

"It's no good. I'll have to fight it out alone. I'm telling you this partly to get it off my chest and partly to explain why I made such a fool of myself in your office tonight. I don't know what happened to me, unless it was the row with your constable. I simply dropped over: why should I, when you mentioned a white-cfwhiskered man assaulting your sergeant? Why? *I* don't know. But I don't know anything about what happened in this place tonight, and I certainly never saw the dead man before."

Having got this off his chest, he drew a long breath; and I felt that he was adjusting his role again, going back under the grease-paint to lower or strut in the character of soldier of fortune. Again there was that subtle change in the atmosphere. By the way he smiled, by the contemptuously airy expression and gesture he assumed, it was plain that he was about to make some remark like, "Away with those vapours! Richard's himself again!" But I had to head him off.

"If you don't know anything about it," I said, "where did you get this note?"

I put it on the desk. He scowled and stared a little (it was as though he braced himself) but he did not seem at all alarmed. After staring at the note for a moment, he looked up.

"So you did pick it up at the police-station," he stated quietly. "I thought I must have lost it there. If you must know the truth, I got it in Holmes's flat."

He looked me straight in the eye without moving.

"In Holmes's flat. . . . When?"

"Tonight, just before I came to the museum."

"But I thought you said you didn't know the gathering at the museum had been called off? If you went to Holmes's flat—when was it?——"

"At about twenty minutes to eleven."

"Well, then, didn't the rest of them tell you that the gathering had been called off?"

"No, they did not," Mannering replied evenly. "You see, there was nobody there."

To cover up the possibilities of this, and to arrange

110

my attack in some sort of form, I walked round the desk, read the note again, and put it down. "Right," I said. "Let's hear what happened."

"As I told you, I was to be at the museum at eleven tonight. Miriam and her brother were to have been at some sort of dinner, and were to have come on to the museum from there; I was not escorting her. But I thought I might as well go to the museum with somebody, to—not to seem like an outsider." He shut his teeth hard. "Holmes was the only one I knew. So, as I say, I dropped in at Prince-Regent Court about twenty minutes to eleven. The boy at the switchboard said there was a party going on upstairs, and didn't want to let me go up. But I showed him his place, of course, and went up."

He hesitated.

"Nobody answered my knock up there, and there was no sound of anybody inside. The door was on the latch, and I went inside. The flat was empty, but I could not understand why, after the boy's statement. In a little back sitting-room there was a coal fire burning; recently made up. That note was lying open in the dirt on the hearth close to the fire. Open—not as it is now, although it was creased. I—" His jaws were tightening and he had gone a sullen red in the face, though he spoke like a sleep-walker. "I picked it up and read it. Then I put it in my pocket."

"Why?"

"There is a reason, but I am not going to tell you what it is." (He was on the edge of an outburst; the black brows were again drawn down like a V, and blind blue eyes stared witlessly under them. His voice had become thick.) "There is a reason, which is none of your business."

"Do you have any objection to all the others knowing about this?"

"Not in the least."

I went to the door, opened it, and spoke to Martin outside. "Get all the others and bring them in here. Just before you bring them in, get Collins, and—you know that big packing-case, with the lead coffin inside that the sergeant opened?—well, haul it in here."

While Mannering remained standing upright, silent and with his eyes fixed on the open lift doors across the room, I did what should have been done before. In one corner of the ornate room, as I have mentioned, there was a typewriter-desk of folding pattern. I hauled the machine upright; it was a Remington 12 of the standard pattern, with red-and-black ribbon. On a sheet of paper from the drawer of the desk I typed a couple of lines. There was the same slur in the tail of the comma. Barring coincidences, and subject to expert examination, the note Mannering found in Holmes's flat had been written on this machine.

The typewriter with the paper still in the carriage I left up for effect while Martin and Collins, trailing spilled sawdust, trundled in the packing-case. Its lid had been removed, and from a sawdust bed rose the curvilinear back of a leaden box something under six feet long. The lead was far gone in corrosion; but, by brushing off sawdust, I thought I could make out Arabic characters carved into the lid. Along the line where the lid fitted on the coffin, there were modern seals of red wax.

Collins handed me a hatchet and a chisel just as the door opened again. Miriam came in first, her glance going immediately to Mannering. After her came Jerry Wade, then Holmes, then Pruen, then Butler with his police helmet still cocked at an angle. But it was the only sign of any facetiousness, for they all looked steadily at Mannering; with such concentration, in fact, that they did not even notice the packing-case until Jerry Wade stumbled over it.

"What the devil's this thing?" he demanded, and his homely, querulous voice seemed to ease a tension. Somehow that wizened little goblin—in appearance more outlandish than anybody else—still seemed the most human figure in the room. "Many's the time I have barked my shanks over funny-looking junk in this place, but what in the name of Allah is *that?*"

"We're going to find out," I said. "It may or may not be Haroun al Raschid's wife. By the way——"

It was Miriam who eagerly made the introduction of Mannering to Wade and Butler, smiling between them as though she hoped everything would be all right. Although Mannering had seemed genial enough earlier that night in my office, he did not extend his hand.

"Oh, yes, of course," he said. "I think I've heard of you both. But Miriam didn't tell me Mr. Butler was a policeman."

I beckoned to Collins and Martin, who went to work on the lead box with chisel and hatchet. They had only to cut the wax seals and pry off the lid. The noise of the chisel seemed to rouse Holmes, whose gaze had gone roving round the room; to the wall-safe immediately, then to the typewriter and back again.

"I fail to see the point of this," he observed rather shrilly, indicating the box. "Why have you got this out? It is not new; it has been in the Arabian exhibits upstairs for years, and it is nothing but an Arabian silver-chest. There is nothing inside it. What wild idea have you got into your head now, inspector?—Er, by the way, I should like to know who has been fooling about with my typewriter?"

"Got it, sir," said P. C. Collins. "Shall we hoist the lid? It's on hinges on the other side."

"Hoist away," I said, and got ready.

The group fell silent, though I saw them exchange glances, and their expressions were baffling: they looked as though they themselves did not know what attitude to take. For a couple of seconds, as the two constables strained at the lid, there was no noise but a harsh creak and rasp. And my own mind was full of cloudy ideas, as though the worst thing we could find in that box would not be Persian dust or even another corpse, but merely a pair of false whiskers. Then the lid reared up, with a jarring screech which was now mingled with the noise of Pruen's mirth.

There was nothing in the box. It was lined inside with steel, and there was nothing in it; not even London dust from London air. It was clean.

"All right, boys," I said. The lid fell with a crash.

"I told 'im there wasn't nothing in it," Pruen's voice rose up with a hoarse chuckle. "Haroun al Raschid's missus, 'e says! I told him there wasn't nothing in it."

Holmes's pale smile met me as I looked up. "That seems to settle the matter, doesn't it?" he asked. "Alas for Zobeide! But I can assure you you will never find her inside an Arabian silver-chest. Are you willing to believe me now?"

"Not necessarily about everything," I said, and took the note out of my pocket to unfold it slowly. "Did you write this?"

"Did I write what?"

"'Dear G., There has got to be a corpse—a *real* corpse. The means of death doesn't matter, but there has got to be a corpse. I'll manage the murder—that ivory-handled *khanjar* will do the trick, or strangling if it seems preferred.' Look at it! Did you write that?"

"Certainly not," said Holmes, and went oily white behind the big lenses of his spectacles. "What the devil are you talking about? Don't try to intimidate me, my friend! What ridiculous idea——"

"It was written on your typewriter over there. Do you deny that?"

"My dear sir, I neither affirm nor deny it. I don't know. *I* didn't write it. I never saw it before."

Holmes took a short step backwards. His pleasant, poised, deprecating face was fixed like the mild blue eyes.

"Hold on a bit, inspector!" said Jerry Wade, jumping a little. "Hang it, if——"

"You shut up, Gaffer," interrupted Holmes, in an agony of quickness, but still coolly, "and let me handle this. You say it was found in my flat. Found by whom?"

"By Mr. Mannering. And there's something else. You say that you, and all the rest of your party, were in your flat all evening from nine o'clock on?"

"Certainly."

"But Mr. Mannering went there at twenty minutes to eleven, and there was nobody at home. Nobody whatever."

Out of a motionless group by the door, which had now become a united front in more ways than one, lumbered Richard Butler. He had stuck his helmet on the back of his head, supported by the chin-strap: a grotesque effect over a round heavy face where the sleepy greyish eyes were a little squeezed up. He had his hands in his pockets, and he walked slowly up to Mannering.

"You spying swine," he said quite calmly.

Mannering looked at him.

"I choose you for this," said Mannering, "because you're the biggest."

As I say, Butler had his hands in his pockets, but even with them out of his pockets I question whether he would have had time to guard. Mannering must have been about five times quicker than a rattlesnake, because nobody actually saw the thing happen. Afterwards Collins told me that his fist must have travelled up only twelve inches. But we were not conscious of that: only of the fact that something seemed to explode inside Mannering like a bomb. When I saw his face for a second past Butler's shoulder it was a maniac's face; and I heard only a flat, bony sort of noise. Then Butler, without a sound and as quietly as though he did it of his own free will, slid forward, down on his knees, and folded together on the rich carpet.

In silence I heard Mannering's breath whistling, and nobody moved.

"That was the proper thing to do, I admit," said Jerry Wade's voice, in the middle of that void, "but does it prove you any less an ass?"

For a second I thought Mannering was going to turn on him, and I was ready to break the man's arm if he tried it. But Mannering, still breathing thinly and white under his tan, picked up hat and stick from the desk.

"Sorry to put witnesses out of commission, inspector," he announced in a normal tone, "but he'll be around in five minutes. Is there anything else you want of me?"

"Thanks," I said, "but that will be quite enough for one evening. All right. You can go along home."

Which, gentlemen (said Detective-Inspector Carruthers in conclusion), almost ends my official connection with the case. The result of my notes you will hear carried out by better men, but I have been instructed to give you full details of the inception of this crime; together with my own descriptions and impressions of the characters in the affair. Some of them are prejudices, and may be corrected by those who follow me. My facts are alone to be considered; and I got no further facts out of the group of people, though I questioned them until four o'clock in the morning. They kept their united front.

Any theories of mine have no place here, because at ten o'clock on the following morning the whole case was turned upside down. In turning upside down, it explained every bit of the previous nonsense which had been puzzling me—but, unfortunately, it substituted more nonsense instead.

I didn't go home to my place in Brixton that night. I got a few hours' sleep at the station, and then went to work on my report. The classification took some time; I was just completing it when Superintendent Hadley phoned through and told me I was wanted in the Assistant Commissioner's office at the Yard. When I got to his office a little before ten o'clock, I found Sir Herbert Armstrong walking up and down the room alternately chuckling and swearing over a letter. That letter put the cap on the whole staggering business. Here is a copy of it. It is dated, "Orkney Hotel, Kensington, 1 A.M., Saturday, June 15," and is addressed to Sir Herbert personally. The handwriting shows rather an excited frame of mind. It reads:—

SIR,

It is with a profound reluctance not untinged with apprehension, no less than a sense of the deepest shame, that I write these lines. But I have searched my heart, and I know that my duty compels it. In the course of twenty years' humble (but I trust, not unhelpful) service as pastor of the John Knox Presbyterian Church of Edinburgh, I have become embroiled in at least a few situations which might be called painful or embarrassing. (You may recall my difference of opinion with the Moderator, in the columns of the *Protestant Churchman,* touching the question of whether the collection-plate should not be passed from right to left, instead of from left to right; a controversy which was, I fear, at times allowed to become acrimonious.) Nor am I, I hope, in any sense a narrow-minded man. I see no harm in card-playing or the healthful relaxation of dancing, and observation convinces me that the depravity of church socials has been much over-estimated. Even if I had ever been disposed to adopt provincial views, still my extensive travels in the East, entailing as they did a contact with men and manners of other lands, would (so to speak) have broadened my eye.

I write this to demonstrate that I am not without practical experience or liberal views. But never in my wildest dreams have I imagined that I, a minister of the Church of Scotland, should ever—of my own volition—affix to my face a pair of white false whiskers; that I should leave a building through the means of egress afforded by a lavatory window, descending thence with the assistance of a rainspout; that I should climb upon a wall; that I should murderously assault a police-constable who, I am now sensible, had done no harm; and, finally, that I should make my exit from this lamentable scene by means of a coal-hole. These things I need scarcely add, were not done for amusement; nor can I ever plead that I was under the influence of drink, drugs, or a hypnotic spell.

But this was not all, or I fear I should never have been constrained to speak. Let me be brief: I saw a crime committed, and, regardless of the consequences to myself if these other details become public, I *must* speak. If you will permit me to pay my respects to you this morning at eleven-thirty precisely, you will incur at once my deepest obligation and my deepest humiliation.
Yours faithfully,
WILLIAM AUGUSTUS ILLINGWORTH.

Part II

The Englishman in the
Arabian Nights: Statement of
Assistant-Commissioner
Sir Herbert Armstrong

9

At The Bronze Doors: How Dr. Illingworth Played Ali Baba

Well, boys, when my secretary put that letter on my desk at nine o'clock on Saturday morning, I was flabbergasted. Yes, my fatheads, flabbergasted. But what got under my skin as much as anything else was the way the fellow wouldn't come to the point. If there's anything I like to see, it's somebody who goes straight to the heart of things. There's nothing in the world that ought to be dawdled over, except perhaps a good dinner with the right kind of Burgundy—haa! Don't let 'em tell you it's not good for the waistline; what's wrong with girth, if it's solid flesh? Look at mine. Hard as iron. What the hell was I saying? Stop diverting me. Oh, yes: now there's you, Carruthers—trouble with you is, you've got too many of the instincts of a gentleman ever to get anywhere. Now *I* haven't. That's why I can organise a police department or a milk-churn company, or whatever it is, and they all know if they don't get down and dust gravel I'll dance on their graves. Straight to the point. Treat 'em rough. Grr! That's me.

So, as I say, at nine o'clock on Saturday morning my secretary walked in and hissed in my ear. . . . That's a habit he's got. I've been intending to sack that fellow for five years, and, what's more, I think he's the chap who had the infernal cheek to start calling me Donald Duck behind my back. He put the letter on my desk, and looked solemn, and I read it.

I said: "Who's this Illingworth?"

Then he knitted his forehead, and scratched the back of his hairline, and finally said, "I should say he was a Scotchman, sir."

I said, "I know damn well he's a Scotchman. But what I was asking you was, who *is* he? Do you know anything about him? Where's the *Who's Who?* Besides, what's all this about false whiskers? Nonsense! Clergymen don't wear false whiskers."

"Well, sir, this one did," he pointed out. "Maybe it's a part of the ritual in Scotland. Anyway, what do you mean to do about it? I thought I might tell you about this morning's report. There was a man, not yet identified, murdered last night in the Wade Museum. Superintendent Hadley thinks this may have something to do with it."

He gave me the first skimpy details, and I was so flabbergasted that for a few minutes I didn't even bother to contradict him. D'ya see, I've known old Jeff Wade since long before he made his money; we were born in the same village in Somerset. He was always a great chap for ruins—he'd rather revel in a ruin than in a public-house—but he wasn't so deliberately foggy and scholarly as he encourages himself to be nowadays. I remember Jeff Wade on the road between High Littleton and Bristol (six inches deep in dust, that road was), wearing a checked suit and a bowler hat with a curly brim, and trying to ride a penny-farthing bicycle six feet high in the saddle. He would stagger all over the road like a man on stilts; off he'd go about every dozen yards, and once he landed on his own hat, but he always climbed on again. That was Jeff Wade. There was a farmer leaning over a fence, who evidently thought it was some kind of self-immolation, and said, "What's thee doing, Mr. Wade?" Jeff said, "I've smashed my blinking tile but, by God, I'll reach Bristol tonight if I smash my blinking so-and-so." And he did—I don't mean he smashed it, but that he got there. Even then he cultivated those big moustaches like sabres that stuck out at the sides of his face; he was a short stocky chap. Then he went north and made millions out of linen or trousers or the like. Queer thing about Jeff Wade, how he always hated foreigners; particularly dark-skinned foreigners. It's only right that his chief interest now should be Persian or Egyptian ruins, though I suppose he considers it's all right if the foreigners are dead: we English usually do, but not until then. Still, I always remember Jeff reeling about that road in a cloud of dust, with the farmer leaning over the fence, and the apple-trees in bloom around.

Popkins, my secretary, said: "Forget the apple-trees. This is a murder case. Let's go straight to the point, sir. What do you want me to do?"

After I had ticked him off properly, I called for all the available reports and sent out after Carruthers to give me the story. When I had heard the gist of it (and the important point of it stuck out plainly, as I'll show you in a second), I was worried. Devilish worried. What we wanted was this Dr. William Augustus Illingworth to give his version of a nightmare that I wouldn't have believed if it didn't concern Jeff Wade. So I shoved aside all other business, and smoked cigars and waited for Dr. Illingworth. Exactly at eleven-thirty, just on the stroke of Big Ben, a couple of constables brought him into my private office like a criminal, and he looked round as wildly as though they were taking him to be hanged.

I don't know what I had been expecting, but he was homely enough in both senses to reassure me and make me mad at the same time. He was tall, lean and bony— like an over-grown kipper; there was even something of a kipper in his fishy eyes—but when he got a grip on himself he looked at me with real dignity. I mean that. He had a long, leathery kind of face, and a habit of tucking his chin back into his collar when he began to talk, so that the wrinkles went up to his ears. Also a habit of looking down hard at the floor when he opened his mouth, and looking back up again quickly so as not to miss the point. Out of his pocket came a pair of shell-rimmed reading-glasses; his hands shook when he put the glasses on, and they made his nose look longer than ever. He was wearing a rusty dark suit, carried a soft hat under his arm, and had greyish hair combed a little crooked. Of course I'd already had the man looked up; he was just what he pretended to be. In addition I formed the impression now (and I'm not often mistaken, my fatheads) of a stiff, well-mannered, kindly, foggy dodderer who was capable of suddenly doing a great unexpected sprint after his duty, and landing in the soup. I can't think of anything else, except that he stood a good deal straighter than a Grenadier Guard, and must have worn number eleven boots.

"Sir Herbert Armstrong?" says he, in a harsh voice that gave me a jump.

"Sit down," I said. "Take it easy."

Down he went in a chair as though he'd been shot, and I jumped again.

"Dammit, don't do that!" I said. "Take it easy. Now then. To the point."

He put his hat carefully on the floor, drew in his chin, opened the cavern, and started to speak all in a rush. *Whiz!*—like that. I couldn't pull out of my own memory the string of sentences he used, so I'm quoting the whole business from the record of the shorthand man.

"I note, Sir Herbert, that you have received my communication," says he. "I trust that I was forgiven, and *am* forgiven, for a pardonably over-wrought state of mind, which may have caused some misapprehension of my meaning to have been conveyed to you through the medium of my letter. But I—er—I confess with a feeling of relief that I do not see—as yet—any sign of your producing—manacles or leg-irons . . ."

"No," I said, "I'm an assistant-police-commissioner, not a blacksmith. Have a cigar."

He took the cigar, bit off the end delicately, and went on.

"To resume the thread of my discourse, Sir Herbert. While I do not retract, or wish to retract, any of the statements in my communication of last night, I wish earnestly to disabuse your mind of any belief that the crime to which I made reference had any application to—in a word, that *I* committed it. Although I have always attempted to cultivate the practice of incisive thinking and writing, I fear that in my disordered state of last night I may erroneously have conveyed to you the impression—I beg your pardon!"

He broke off at the right time. First, you see, he had taken a box of matches out of his pocket; and in trying to get one out, he had yanked the box apart and sent a shower of matches into my face. *That* was all right. Then he had picked up one and struck it to light my cigar. Where he said, "I beg your pardon!" was where his fingers shook so much that he softly dropped the lighted match down between my shirt and waistcoat. He said it was extraordinary how he came to do it, and I agreed. The things I also said while I pounded at my chest should never have been said in front of a clergyman. For a minute I was so wild that I was going to have him chucked out, but I got a grip on myself and only gave him a cold look.

"Dr. Illingworth," I said, when I could get my breath, "Dr. Illingworth, I have told you that I am not a blacksmith. Adopting your own conversational style, I may say that neither am I a goddam skyrocket. This is a match. Look at it. It is a useful article, applied to the proper surfaces, but my person is definitely not one of them. Now *I* will light *your* cigar, if you can be trusted with a cigar. Then, police-regulations or no police-regulations, you are going to have a drink. You need one."

"Thank you," he answered. "While I do not, of course, share the national weakness, and am myself a zealous worker in the cause of temperance, nevertheless, *true* temperance—in short, yes."

I poured him out a man-sized one, neat; he swallowed it without winking, and with an absolutely expressionless face.

"That was very refreshing," said Dr. Illingworth, gravely dropping the glass into the waste-paper-basket, "and it will fortify me in telling what must, alas, be told. Secondly, Sir Herbert, I thank you for an informality of manner which does much to place me at my ease under perturbing circumstances: circumstances which, I see with agitation, will have no soothing effect on the elders of the John Knox Presbyterian Church. However, I

128

must not digress on such matters, however painful. While journeying in the train from Edinburgh, I beguiled my leisure time (most of the journey being devoted to the composition of my address to the United Presbyterian Sunday Schools, which was to have been delivered in London this evening); I beguiled my leisure time, I say, by perusing a police hand-book entitled *The Dagger of Doom*, kindly lent to me by a commercial traveller in the same compartment. My pastoral duties, no less than my researches into the history of past civilisations, have left me little time for reading which deals with the living world about us; but I may say that I found the account moving, even enthralling, and that it was a revelation which made a profound impression upon me. Indeed, I was appalled by the villainy of the central character, whose identity was not revealed until—No, Sir Herbert, despite your remarks, I do *not* digress. What I wished to say was this: if I learned nothing else of your methods from *The Dagger of Doom*, I have learned that nothing must be kept back or omitted, howsoever insignificant it may seem. While recounting my story I shall endeavour to bear this in mind, so far as is consistent with that legal terseness you require."

Gents, I was on the point of an apoplectic stroke, but this courteous old jackass looked so much like a martyr that I only gave a sign to the shorthand reporter. He cleared his throat a couple of times and took a pull at the cigar before he flew off again.

"My name is William Augustus Illingworth," he announced all of a sudden, like a ghost at a séance. "I am the minister of the John Knox Presbyterian Church of Edinburgh, as was my late father before me; I reside at the manse of that church, together with Mrs. Illingworth and my son Ian, who is studying for the ministry. On the evening of Thursday, June 13th (the day,

I may remark, before yesterday), I arrived in London, and was driven from King's Cross Station to the Orkney Hotel in Kensington High Street. My reason for coming to London was partly, as I have already indicated, to address a meeting of the United Presbyterian Sunday Schools at the Albert Hall; but my eager anticipation of this journey sprang from another, and I fear more selfish, motive.

"For some considerable time I have been most interested in endeavouring to trace the sources and development of those interesting historical documents regrettably popularised and therefore often deprived of significance, known as the *Thousand and One Nights*. A certain esteemed scholar, by name Mr. Geoffrey Wade, had been so fortunate as recently to acquire two hundred manuscript sheets of the first translation——"

"Wait a minute," I said. "Let me state this part of it, and we'll see if we can't hit a bull's-eye first shot. You were invited to the Wade museum last night for an examination of a manuscript by a man called Antoine Galland, and a general chin-wagging. Is that correct?"

He wasn't surprised; not a bit of it. I think he'd got the idea that I must have deduced it, and he shovelled out about three bushels of words which meant yes.

I said: "Do you know Jeff Wade? I mean, do you know him personally?"

It appeared that he didn't. They had held a long correspondence, paid a lot of compliments to each other, and decided to meet at the first opportunity: the gathering at the museum had been arranged by letter before Illingworth left Edinburgh.

"And," proceeds Illingworth, showing more animation in his wooden face as he got towards the meat of the story, "it was with considerable disappointment that yesterday at noon precisely, I received at my hotel a telephone communication from Mr. Ronald Holmes, Mr. Wade's assistant and associate. Expressing his deepest regrets, he explained that Mr. Wade had been unexpectedly called out of town, and was therefore under the unfortunate necessity of postponing our meeting until a more suitable time. I have said that I was disappointed, but I cannot truthfully say that I was surprised. From time to time I have received information (from mutual friends who were, I trusted, exaggerating) that Mr. Wade was a gentleman of strong and decided, but capricious, mind; that some might even call him eccentric. Indeed, I have it upon reliable authority that, when one of his views was questioned during his reading of an original paper to the Middle Asiatic Society of Great Britain, Mr. Wade designated his interrupter with the distressing term of 'pipsqueak,' and was even understood to intimate that the chairman, Sir Humphrey Ballinger-Gore, had a face like a prune.

"Therefore it was again without astonishment that—at five o'clock yesterday afternoon—I found that he had altered his plans for the second time. On returning to my hotel from a stimulating two hours passed in the South Kensington Museum (which I for one do not find nearly so frivolous an institution as some would have us believe), I was given a telegram from Mr. Wade, handed in at Southampton a short time before. Here it is."

He laid on my desk a telegram which said:

> FIND I CAN GET BACK EARLY WE NEEDN'T CALL
> IT OFF AFTER ALL MEET ME MUSEUM TEN-THIRTY
> TONIGHT GEOFFREY WADE

"In the light of subsequent events," pursued the doctor, nodding at the telegram, "I have endeavoured to deduce something of importance from an examination of that document, in accordance with certain admirable suggestions gleaned from *The Dagger of Doom*. I have carefully held the paper up to the light to look for the watermark. However, since I am uncertain as to precisely what a 'watermark' may be, I fear I must have escaped any sinister meaning which its presence or absence might denote.

"But allow me to proceed. Although I confess to having been a trifle impatient with Mr. Wade for his second change of mind, and for his somewhat cavalier treatment of my time, nevertheless I was not at all unwilling to go. I dressed myself with some care, and took with me a volume which seldom leaves my person—the very rare Arabic first edition of the first one hundred *'Nights,'* published, as you are aware, at Calcutta in 1814—to show Mr. Wade. I had been promising him this treat for some time."

He took carefully out of his coat pocket a big leather-bound book, and laid it on the desk beside the telegram as another exhibit.

"To proceed," says he. (He was getting pretty excited now.) "At roughly twenty minutes past ten I entered a taxicab outside my hotel, and was driven to the Wade Museum, which I reached at precisely ten-thirty-five—or twenty-five minutes to eleven. This I can establish beyond question, since while I was in the course of paying the cabman, my watch became in some inconceivable fashion entangled with my fingers or with the loose silver in my pocket and dropped upon the pavement. It ceased to function, and indeed I have not succeeded in putting it in motion yet."

Out came the watch, which was put down on the desk beside the telegram and the book. It was as though we had started playing strip-poker.

"For a moment, I confess," continued the old boy, tucking in his chin, "I could not resist the temptation to linger at the portals of this edifice and to lose myself in musing contemplation of the magnificent bronze doors: faithful reproductions of those doors which, we are told, adorned the entrance of the *Hasht Bihisht*, or Eight Paradises, of Shah Abbas the Great. Thus I might have stood a while lost in contemplation, having struck perhaps a match or two to aid me in examining the Iranian inscription there; until I was rudely awakened by the ribald comments of two passers-by in the street, who appeared to labour under the impression that I had just returned from a neighbouring public-house called The Dog and Duck, and was in no condition accurately to find the keyhole.

"These aspersions I treated with silent dignity and, when the passers-by had passed by (so to phrase it) I rang the bell as I had been instructed to do. The doors were opened, and by the lights inside I saw that the person who opened them must be the same man of whom Mr. Wade had sometimes spoken: a faithful servitor of many years' standing, who acted as night-attendant and night-watchman. His name, I believe, is Pruen."

"So-ho!" I said. "Then he was there after all."

The old boy didn't seem to hear me. Instead he fixed on me such a steady look that I began to have an uneasy conscience.

"There then ensued," he said, "what I can only describe as the first and lightest of the extraordinary happenings which were to befall inside those accursed doors. In a word—Pruen laughed in my face."

I said: "He what?"

"He laughed," declared Illingworth, and nodded

gravely, "in my face. After first beckoning me inside, with some parade of secrecy, he examined me with concentration and then emitted what I can only describe as an explosive chuckle which seemed to distend his face in a forward direction. He then said the following words, in an argot which I shall not attempt to reproduce. He said, 'Hullo! And who are *you*?'

"I was not unnaturally nettled at this surprising and unseemly behavior, and my reply was delivered in a tone of some acerbity:

"'I am Dr. William Augustus Illingworth, my good man,' I informed him, 'and I believe that Mr. Wade is expecting me. Will you have the goodness to take me to him?'

"To my complete astonishment his mirth not only failed to subside, but grew to an alarming extent. He appeared to creak with it, doubling up with his hands folded over his stomach, rocking from side to side in a mysterious fashion, but producing very little noise.

"'Oh, you're a one, you are,' he then informed me, after a series of gasps and a wiping of watery eyes. 'I can't see why you're not a success on the halls, for the life of me, I can't.' (This phrase 'on the halls,' I have subsequently learned, has reference to performers on the music-hall stage, such as singers, bicycle-riders, acrobats, and the like; it seemed completely incomprehensible when applied to a minister of the gospel.) 'You're the most convincing thing *I* ever saw,' added this astonishing old man, 'and you'll help the murder no end.'

"And with this, Sir Herbert, in the midst of an excruciating chuckle, he extended a long forefinger and prodded me in the ribs."

10

The Opening Of Enchantment: How Dr. Illingworth Played Aladdin

"For the moment I could come to no other conclusion than that the man was drunk, although there was no evidence of this state apart from his extraordinary behaviour. I thereupon looked round the hall in which I found myself, hoping to find Mr. Wade ready to greet me. I was indeed impressed by the noble proportions and pillared grandeur of my surroundings, softly illuminated by a whitish glow from the cornices of the ceiling, which imparted an aspect of ghostly moonlight not unpleasing to one of musing temperament. It lent a strange colour even to the face of the small old man, dressed in a species of blue uniform, who was capering at my side. Whereupon he addressed to me the following words:

"'You'll want to go along and see the boss. You're late as it is—er—old cock.' I am endeavouring, Sir

Herbert, to be precise. 'But you will be forgiven, and you'll even get payment in advance if you ask for it, on the strength of *that* get-up.'

"Now I can assure you, sir, that there was nothing in the least singular about my top-hat or my frock-coat (which were of an ordinary and even of a severe pattern); consequently I became convinced that this must be lunacy or misunderstanding. When my informant added, 'Curator's room—straight down, turn to your right, first door; he's in there now,' I was compelled to speak.

"'For some reason,' I said, 'you appear to doubt that I am Dr. Illingworth. Since you doubt it, here is my card. Since you doubt it, pray look at this first edition of the first hundred *Nights* which I am bringing for the inspection of Mr. Wade. If this is a genuine misunderstanding I shall be happy to excuse you; if it is merely an unwarranted impertinence on your part, I shall make that fact clear to Mr. Wade.'

"I had observed, throughout my speech, a certain doubtful and wavering change come into his expression; and although he spoke no audible words, his mouth opened. However, deciding that I could find my way unaided to the curator's room, I continued on with as great a dignity as I could assume—until I was arrested by the sight of a thing still more singular.

"Although you are doubtless familiar with the inside of Wade Museum, I may explain that in the wall towards one's right hand, as one takes up a position immediately facing the rear, there is some twenty-odd feet along from the front doors a large archway inscribed, 'Gallery of the Bazaars.' This is an amusing but (from an archaeological or historical point of view) completely unimportant reconstruction of a bazaar or street of merchandise in an Eastern city. The representation, I may say, is tolerably accurate; and it has been given a theatrical reality by means of lighting, which produces a scene of dappled shadows thrown upon a fantastic street. As I glanced in that direction I was given pause not only by a fleeting illusion that I looked upon a street in Ispahan towards twilight, but also by the human figure which I saw standing there.

"In the middle of the street, standing motionless under a lattice-work of shadows and looking at me, I distinctly saw a Persian nobleman in his native costume.

"Sir, I am not in the least disordered as I tell you this, and I can assure you upon my solemn word that I am speaking the truth. I was, of course, most arrested by his clothing. He wore the customary high sheepskin hat; his tunic was of blue embroidered silk, and worn very long, which—together with the white-shirt —indicated wealth or quality. The *zirjamah* or trousers were of white cotton, but the most conspicuous mark of rank was the belt of black varnished leather, which instead of showing a brass clasp as in the case of the ordinary courtier, had the nobleman's clasp in a great round ornament of cut rubies. Of the face, which was in shadow, I could distinguish only the olive complexion showing up by contrast the whites of the eyes. Such an apparition against such a background conveyed to me the momentary belief that it might be a wax figure, set up to lend an air of verisimilitude to this display. But it was not so, a fact of which I had ample proof. It was a commonplace test, but in those circumstances producing an effect which I can only describe as horribly uncanny—*viz.*, the man was opening and shutting his eyes.

"I believe that I can be described as a thoughtful rather than as a fanciful man. For the curious state of

137

mind into which I found myself falling, I can offer as an excuse only the incongruity of such a sight at such time. But this irrational feeling (I blush to acknowledge it), that through some crack in the Cosmos I might myself have strayed into one of the *'Nights'* and that the blue-uniformed attendant might be a dark Shahrazád pointing to other adventures, was dispelled not only by my religious principles, but by my strong common sense. This common sense told me the obvious explanation. Was anything more natural than that Mr. Wade, with his doubtless wide circle of friends in Persia and Iraq, should have contracted the acquaintance of a nobleman there, and that this gentleman should have been invited here in turn to make *my* acquaintance? Certainly not. I therefore determined, with the greatest formality, to address him. For this purpose I chose the pure Arabic rather than the (I use the term in no invidious sense) bastard 'New Persian' which Arabic has corrupted out of its former purity.

"I therefore lifted my hand in a salutation. *'Masa el-khair,'* I greeted him, *'es-salâmu 'alaikoom es-salâm. Inshâ allâh tekoon fee ghâyit as-sahhah.'* To which he gravely replied: *'Wa 'alaikoom es-salâm. Ana b'khair el-hamd lillâh.'*

"His voice had a grave and deep quality, and he spoke with an incomparable dignity, but he seemed exceedingly surprised that I should be able to address him in this tongue. Another fact which I noticed with interest was that the intonation of his Arabic was Egyptian rather than Persian. For example, when I continued, *'El kâ'ât kwyee-seen—'* I beg your pardon, Sir Herbert, but did you speak?" broke off Dr. Illingworth. "In the excitement of my recital I fear I forgot myself. Did you speak?"

Having been listening to this fellow Illingworth bur-

138

ble on for so long, you can bet I did speak.

"WHOA!" I said. "It's a fine imitation of somebody up on top of a mosque, but stop calling the faithful to prayer and tell me what that was all about in English."

Believe it or not, he looked surprised.

"Excuse me. Yes, of course. It was merely a customary form of greeting which the scrupulous foreigner will not neglect. After bidding him good evening, I said, 'Peace be unto you! I hope you are quite well.' To which he answered, also in the formal manner, 'And upon you be peace. I am quite well, thank God.' Shall I continue? Thank you.

"I was about to pursue my questionings further when he cut them short, imperatively but with great courtesy by pointing down in the direction of the curator's door to which I had been at first directed. Although feeling that there was still some deep mystery here, I continued on my way—adding a few graceful remarks over my shoulder, and concluding in English if he should care to address me in that language—and I was just past the middle of the hall when I perceived the next of this night's wonders. This was a beautiful young woman wearing a dark crimson-coloured dress with whose technical name I am not familiar. . . .

"You appear to give a convulsive start, Sir Herbert, at the mention of this young woman. I shall make myself quite clear, since this fact may be of the utmost importance. As one faces the rear of the museum there is directly in the centre a large staircase of white marble. In the rear wall on either side of this staircase there is a door: a door to the left and a door to the right. It was the door towards the left which I then perceived to open. Out of it came the young lady in the red frock, a dark-haired young lady with what I should describe as a great deal of winsome charm. Of all those who had greeted me at the museum so far, each had in different degrees exhibited surprise; but this young lady, though she also appeared surprised, seemed in such an abstracted frame of mind that she paid me scant attention. Instead she turned and ran up the marble staircase to the galleries above, whence she disappeared from view. I may remark that—from some point upstairs, whose exact location I could not identify—there proceeded a noise very similar to that produced by someone driving nails into wood.

"But I had no time to muse over this. Some distance over to my right, as I now stood at the foot of the staircase, the door marked 'Curator' was flung open; and at last—with, I may say, an inexpressible sense of relief—I saw my host.

"Although I had never seen a photograph of Mr. Wade, those who knew him personally had dwelt on two points of physical description: his short stature and his long white moustaches. I was prepared for the short stature (which I saw), and for the long moustaches (which I saw), but I was not prepared for the luxuriant white whiskers which descended to his chest and lent him an impressive, even venerable, aspect. His white hair and white whiskers framed a face somewhat withered by age, but with two exceedingly sharp dark eyes surveying me from head to foot. Indeed, in poise and dignity as he faced me, he reminded me of the figure of King Lear as portrayed by Sir Henry Irving many years ago. What was my complete stupefaction when I saw this distinguished gentleman thoughtfully draw from the pocket of his coat a mouth-organ—yes, Sir Herbert, a mouth-organ—put it to his lips, and in a meditative fashion proceed to perform that exercise which is called, I believe, 'running the scale.'

140

"At the mention of the mouth-organ, Sir Herbert, I again perceive that you give a violent start. Unless I am mistaken, you also uttered the word '*Jerry*.' What that may portend I can guess, since I have been informed that Scotland Yard possesses a list of all desperate criminals together with their peculiarities, for reference in case of a crime. It is probable that you can instantly lay your finger on this man's identity due to his betraying weakness for playing the mouth-organ while engaged in burglary or murder, just as Dr. Chianti in *The Dagger of Doom* (it afterwards flashed upon me) played the trombone. But, unfortunately, it did not at the moment occur to me that I had penetrated into a den of desperate criminals. Alas, sir, having been informed of Mr. Wade's slight eccentricity, I assumed that his *penchant* for the mouth-organ was one of those lighter relaxations often indulged in by men of strongly studious mind—just as my friend, Dr. MacTavish of the University, a scholarly and otherwise exemplary gentleman, has a deplorable habit of going to the cinematograph performances and laughing uproariously when someone is struck in the face with a custard pie. So, therefore, I showed no surprise even when my host addressed me with some violence.

"'You're late,' he said, and pointed the mouth-organ at me. 'Why do you want to dawdle about here talking? We've got work to do. You're late, curse it, and we've only got half an hour. Come in here. Hurry!'

"His manner had changed to an agony of excitement, which seemed to me unnecessary and even ill-mannered, and he went into the curator's room ahead of me with a surprising agility in one of his years.

"'I am exceedingly sorry, Mr. Wade,' I told him, with some curtness, 'if my slight unpunctuality has caused you any inconvenience. I confess I had hoped that our first meeting might be in a more amicable spirit.'

"With the same agility, and muttering to himself, he crossed the room and sat down behind a large flat-topped desk. I observed spread out on this desk a small book, and beside it an ash-tray filled with the ends of cigarettes, on the edge of which ash-tray a cigarette was still smouldering. After picking up this cigarette and inserting it in his mouth, to the imminent peril of his formidable moustaches, he ran his finger down a page of the book.

"'Yes, yes,' he said, 'I didn't mean to be short with you, but this business must go off smoothly.' Not then, Sir Herbert, did the ominous sound of that word 'business' penetrate into my consciousness; for my host, fixing me with an eye grown suddenly stern and terrible, exclaimed the following words in Arabic: '*Yâ onbâshee irga' ente bi'd-deurtena 'l wa kool li'l-yoozbâshee hiknadâr el-imdâ-diyah yegee henâ bi'lghâr!*' Which, unless my ears were completely deceiving me, meant, 'Gallop back, corporal, and tell the captain in command of the support to come up at the trot!'

"I could only stare at him.

"'My dear sir,' I said, 'you appear to be under some abstruse apprehension. I am not a military man, and I have never——'

"'Wrong page,' said this extraordinary man, abruptly. He turned over, puffing furiously at his cigarette. 'These damn grammars,' excuse me, Sir Herbert, but I must be precise however painful it is, 'these damn grammars are no good. Dismount, and open fire! Mount and reform, and cover the left flank of No. 2 squadron! *That* won't do. Very spirited and rousing stuff, of course, but a bit difficult to introduce

142

smoothly into the ordinary social conversation. Ah, here we are!' After muttering to himself for a moment, he again fixed me with a penetrating glance, and enquired in the Arabic: 'Tell me, friend, do you know the shop of Hassan the goldsmith near the police-station, which was robbed last night?—Answer in English.'

"For a second I thought I could discern a glimmer of light. 'Is it because you have been robbed, Mr. Wade,' I asked, 'that you find yourself in this agitated frame of mind? If so, I can readily understand it. The shop of Hassan the goldsmith in which city?'

"'Never mind which city,' declared my host somewhat testily. 'The point is, did you understand what I said? Excellent. Anyway Sam tested you out—Sam Baxter is impersonating the Persian nob with the music-hall hat, the one you spoke to as you came in, and Sam's supposed to be a whiz at gargling Arabic. Consequently, I can assure you in all solemnity that everything is quite okey-doke with me.'

"I have exercised a constant effort, Sir Herbert, to quote from memory exactly the amazing and uncouth concatenation of words which poured with horrifying jocularity from the lips of this venerable scholar. It was almost as though an Old Testament patriarch were suddenly to begin dancing a jig. But all previous sensations of awe and trepidation were flooded out of my mind by the next speech of my host, who arose majestically from his chair and struck the desk a blow with his fist.

"'It's all right except for one thing,' he cried. 'Where are your whiskers?'

"'Whiskers?' said I, unable to believe my ears.

"'Hang it all, you've got to have whiskers!' he cried, in what I can only describe as an agony of angry reasonableness. 'Who ever heard of an Asiatic scholar without whiskers? Why, there's an old boy at the British Museum who's got 'em clear down to his knees. I can assure you with my hand on my heart, Laughton, my boy, that you never saw such a beaver outside the Whipsnade Zoo.'

"'But I do not possess whiskers.'

"'I know,' agreed my host patiently. 'That's what I'm complaining about. But you've got to have whiskers. Here,' he added with an air of inspiration, 'here— have mine!'

"In a few moments more, Sir Herbert, I had come to the end of my blindness with regard to what was transpiring in this evil place. Just then, however, I noted with a paralysis of mental and emotional faculties that my host had begun to explore with his fingers the region of his jaw. He walked across the room and opened the door of what I perceived to be a small lavatory attached to it. With the assistance of a mirror on a shelf over the wash-bowl, he carefully detached the whiskers (which had been affixed with some liquid adhesive substance) from his cheeks and jaws.

"'Sit still just where you are,' he proceeded, 'and I'll tack 'em on you. Quite easy to moisten the stuff again and they're the best whiskers a theatrical costumier could supply; guaranteed to deceive Sherlock Holmes himself.... As a matter of fact, I should never have decided to wear these at all, and I was against the idea myself. As you understand, I am to play the part of the old man—Jeff himself—in the business tonight, because naturally I look a good deal like him. But Rinkey Butler is always for overdoing everything, and just in case the victim should spot me as being younger than I ought to look, he insisted on turning me into an embryonic Santa Claus. (I say, this is a dashed good wig, isn't it?) You take the whiskers, but I'll keep the moustaches. You won't really need any moustache. Of course you're an experienced hand, and I don't need to warn you, whatever you do, to keep your face straight and refrain from smiling when the murderer is going to strike. Here, I want to get these whiskers on you before the others come down. They're upstairs preparing the coffin now.'

"I sat frozen with horror. I admit that, sir, without a trace of shame. For the first time the full import of these proceedings began to penetrate my mind, and I realised what I should have realised long ago, since there was an almost precisely similar situation in *The Dagger of Doom*. Without the least sacrilegious intention, I say firmly that I shall always regard as a manifestation of Providence the moment when that police hand-book was placed within my reach. Of the specific details of this conspiracy I could not yet be sure, but so much was clear: this museum was in the hands of a gang of desperadoes, who had taken advantage of Mr. Wade's absence to have their leader impersonate him (a favourite stratagem, I remembered, of the terrible Dr. Chianti). Not only was the museum to be robbed, but presumably some outsider was to be lured into the trap and killed; either for reasons connected with the gang—such as that he had betrayed them—or for articles of value he might carry with him—such as diamonds and rubies. For an instant I sickened with the thought that *I* might have been the intended victim and the prize my 1814 Calcutta first edition, which I still clutched to my breast.

"But a brief reflection convinced me that this would not be so. Quite evidently I had been mistaken for some desperate villain with many aliases—for my host, in the hideously jocular way which froze the blood in my veins, referred to me on three separate

145

occasions under the names of Charles Laughton, Wallace Beery and George Arliss—and it was an irony of ironies that I, *I*, was in the nefarious business to play the part of an Asiatic scholar.

"What, therefore was I to do? In a situation fraught with extreme peril, should I attempt to make my escape with one wild dash through these cut-throats, and alarm the Flying Squad? You will perceive that such a course would have been useless. And more! Sir Herbert, I say this in a shame mingled with obscure pride: in that time of craven fear there rose within me a sensation to which hitherto I had been a stranger. I found my pulses beating with some wild strain of hitherto-forgotten Highland blood, which awoke and rioted in the hour of danger. Should I tamely allow Mr. Wade to be robbed and some inoffensive stranger butchered by these villains? No! By heaven, No!" roared Dr. Illingworth, suddenly getting up from his chair and sweeping his arm round like a jib-boom in a heavy sea. There was a framed picture of my wife standing on the desk, and his arm sent it flying clear across the room. He was so excited that he didn't even apologise, but he got a grip on himself and lowered his voice. "Very well. I could watch. I would wait. I would pretend to *be* this infamous Asiatic scholar. Much as my own strong feelings bewildered and alarmed me, I would ply the leader with crafty questions until I had elicited the full details of the plot—exactly as your Scotland Yard man did in *The Dagger of Doom*—and meantime I would set my wits to work to devise some means by which they could be frustrated.

"Although I have gone to some length in describing my mental state, all this was the thought of a moment. The leader, with his fiendish chuckle, was stepping across the room (his shaven chin under the great

146

moustaches lent him an appearance even more evil) and preparing to affix the false whiskers on me. Though every fibre of my being shuddered at that touch, I held myself rigid and made no complaint. This monster who could leeringly advise me not to smile when murder was done, this monster should find his match in me! I even went to the length of admiring my appearance in the detachable mirror from the lavatory, which he placed on the desk. Then, nerving myself with terrible effort for the ordeal, I lowered my voice to a creaky whisper.

"'Who are we going to bump off, boss?' enquired, to his eternal shame, the pastor of the John Knox Presbyterian Church of Edinburgh."

11

The Terrible Mr. Gable: How Dr. Illingworth Played William Wallace

Boys, at this point in the craziest recital I'd ever listened to, I had to give old Illingworth another drink. He needed it. And, by George, I admired him!—it even seemed to me that the shorthand reporter was smothering an impulse to cheer. Jerry Wade and his gang had been up to some sort of fool stunt, of course. But Illingworth didn't know that. He thought he'd gone and walked straight in among The League of the Clutching Oyster. So? He was the foggiest and most impractical old gent who ever staggered out of a pulpit; but when it came to scratch he showed the guts and the sporting instincts of an old Scotch chief defending the pass at What's-its-name. After a little while, when he'd been panting and feeling his chin as though the whiskers were still there, he cleared his throat and went on.

"As I said these last words, I thought I detected a curious expression on the face of the leader, as though he had observed a change in my own demeanour. Indeed, catching sight of my own whiskered countenance in the mirror facing me as I sat by the desk, I observed that I had counterfeited on my face the semblance of a hideous leer—which, seen by the congregation of the John Knox Church would, I am convinced, have terrified the occupants of the first three pews out of their wits.

"'Well, you're the rummiest sort of bloke I ever met,' he declared, looking at me in an odd and uncanny fashion. 'Now look here: we've only got a few more minutes. The others will be downstairs with the coffin, and then we'll go over our final instructions, Mr.—by the way, what is your name, really?'

"'Wallace Beery,' I replied, choosing one of the aliases at random.

"This, Sir Herbert, appeared to inspire him with a species of hopeless and terrifying wrath; I perceived that he had wished me, in the phrase of the police hand-book, to 'come clean' with my authentic cognomen, and he was aware that I had not done so. Every mark of evil passions was stamped upon his face as he began to strike the desk with his fist.

"'Yes, of course,' said he, 'and I am Clark Gable. Look here, does a theatrical agency usually send out people with such a perverted sense of humour as you've got? I don't know what to make of you. You've got a face like a church-warden—you look as though you really ought to *be* Dr. Illingworth. . . .'

"The effect of this name demoralised my wits, as you can readily understand, but after the first sickening sensation I was firm enough to ask:

"'What do you mean?'

"'I say you look as though you really ought to be Dr. William Augustus Illingworth, the man you're to impersonate in the business tonight,' replied Dr. Gable. A terrible suspicion appeared to strike him. 'Good Lord, don't tell me Rinkey Butler or Ronald Holmes —Rinkey was to see you, wasn't he, this afternoon?— don't tell me he didn't tell you what you were to do?'

"You can picture my state of mind then, even aside from contemplating the audacity of bringing my name, *my* name, into this deviltry; for now it seemed that I was required to impersonate myself. But this knowledge lent me coolness and strength for the guile I must now exercise.

"'I am thoroughly acquainted with the details of my role, mug.' I informed him. (The criminals in the hand-book are described as frequently employing the term 'mug,' and I felt that it would lend an air of verisimilitude to my speech.) 'But suppose, for the sake of clearness, we enumerate the various events, mug; eh, what? For example, who is the victim?'

"Dr. Gable lowered his head as though to cool it.

"'Well, they recommended you,' he observed, in an offhand tone, 'and I suppose they know their business. Anyway, they said you were half Persian yourself, and knew all about ancient monuments and manuscripts and whatnot. You see, you'll have to be in the forefront doing most of the talking; that's why one of us couldn't do it—and Sam Baxter's part, the threat and the stabbing and so on, will be very brief.

"'Now listen. The victim of the business is a man named Gregory Mannering, and we're going to give him a little test of the nerve he brags so much about.'

"'Is he a member of your gang?'

"'I'm willing to bet he won't be much longer,' answered Dr. Gable, with another of his fiendish expres-

sions. 'I haven't got anything against him, but Sam
Baxter and Rinkey Butler and Ron Holmes are wild—
he said Sam looked like an ape, and couldn't speak
Arabic any more than an ape, and the things he said
about the others will not bear repeating even in our
company, though he's never even *met* any of us except
Ron. That's why they can play their parts, and so can
I, without detection. We are going to see whether that
dauntless courage of his (which he declared in one account sustained him when he was stealing the Kali
ruby from the idol, pursued by a swarm of maddened
priests) will sustain him when Sam, in the role of Persian Nemesis, is bending over him with the ivory-
handled knife to cut out his liver.'

"So there was a double motive, both hatred and
plunder. 'And you will get the ruby, of course?' I said,
with a leer I shudder to remember.

"He shook with laughter. 'Oh, without a doubt,' he
declared, and this fiend of the pit winked. 'Oh, without a doubt we'll find the ruby sewed up in a little
chamois bag under his hat. . . . But it isn't anything in
connexion with that ruby that we've used as an excuse
to lure him here. That wouldn't do, and might make
him suspicious.'

"'Ah, yes,' I said, seeing the cunning reason of this.
'Of course.'

"'He has been told that old Jeff—that's me—has
secretly stolen from the mausoleum at Iraq the coffin
of Zobeide, the favourite wife of Haroun al Raschid. . . .'

"'But, my dear Dr. Gable!' I expostulated, 'surely it
is obvious, mug, that—'

"'Just a minute. Now Miriam didn't want to lure
him into this (Miriam is my sister) because she's engaged to him, but Sam and Rinkey challenged her to

such an extent that she agreed to—put him on the spot, as it were, to see what he could endure.' (If I had not read *The Dagger of Doom,* Sir Herbert, such perfidy of a woman to her lover would have been beyond my comprehension, but the beautiful half-caste Wonna Sen did a precisely similar thing in the torture-chamber of Dr. Chianti. But, think of it!) 'Here is the plan,' pursued the relentless Dr. Gable. 'He is to come here at eleven o'clock or a little past—it's nearly time now. He knows that a Dr. Illingworth was to have been here to see the old man—that's you—because it's been in the newspapers, and everything will look just right. Ron Holmes will play his part as my associate, which will also look right. Miriam will be there as herself, along with Harriet Kirkton. Sam Baxter (as Abú 'Obaid of Táif, prince of the House of Mihrán; we pinched his costume out of the Persian Gallery) and Rinkey Butler (as the policeman) will lie doggo until the proper time.

"'As the coffin of Zobeide, we're using an Arabian silver-chest; never mind the discrepancy; it's the only thing we could find. Of course all the silver has been removed from it long ago. . . .'

"'Of course,' I said sardonically, but with rising fury.

"'And the story is that there is a curse on that coffin. . . . Actually what the old man and this fogy Illingworth were really going to examine was some asinine manuscript, but Mannering doesn't know that. . . . There is a curse on that coffin. This, my lad, is where you give your lecture. Whosoever touches the coffin and disturbs the sacred bones therein enshrined,' said Dr. Gable, in a deep rolling voice and with a reptilian stare which convinced me I was dealing with a maniac, 'shall first have his hands and feet cut off. Then his face shall be mutilated with the

Ninety-four Tortures. . . . It's all Rinkey Butler's plot, carefully worked out by him and each of us with his part assigned. You think you can put it across?'

"'By heaven, what I have in mind shall be put across!'

"'All right, then. Who will open the coffin? I hesitate. So do you. Atmosphere all worked up. The dauntless Mr. Mannering offers to brave the curse. Soft lights and music,' cried my host, who was striding rapidly round the desk and waving his hands in the air. 'The Gallery of the Eight Paradises. The noise of a chisel and hammer. Then the coffin. The lid is touched—hah! Suddenly *you*—and this is where your experience as an actor will come in—you change. You spring into the group. From your pocket you whip out a pistol. This pistol.'

"From his own pocket he took out an automatic pistol of black and incredibly lethal-looking design, which he thrust into my hands.

"'Then suddenly revealing yourself for what you are, "Stand back!" you cry, "stand back, infidels and blasphemers! By the soul of my dead mother"—you really are half Persian, aren't you?—"by the star-lanterns of holy Iraq and the great wind of the desert, I swore an oath that whosoever touched," etc.; you know your lines. "Is it well, O Prince?" you say. And in comes Sam Baxter. Hah! It's all atmosphere. "It is well," says he. "Let the impious mocker be seized. . . ."'

"Something of his own wildness, I can only imagine, must have communicated itself to me. I experienced a constriction in the throat as well as a violent beating of the heart which portended ill for a man of my age; but I felt within me a reckless emotion of triumph, for this miscreant—ecstatic in murder with his wizened face and his long moustaches—this miscreant, like Dr.

Chianti, had made his mistake. He had put into my hands the loaded revolver which, at the proper time, should be his undoing.

"'When the policeman comes in—of course he's one of us,' he went on, 'you'll shoot him. We'll have an inside room, and nobody will be able to hear the shot. So——'

"He paused, looking over my shoulder. And again, Sir Herbert, I can only offer my humble thanks to that Providence which seems beneficently to have guided me from the start. As I may have mentioned, there was propped up on the desk facing me a portable mirror, by whose reflection I was now enabled to see the door behind. That door had opened by stealth to an extent of perhaps five inches. Framed in the aperture I saw the face of a young man peering surreptitiously at me and evidently attempting by silent gestures to attract the eye of Dr. Gable. He was a young man whose outward semblance would not customarily have betrayed what lurked within: a non-brutal and even pleasant face to the outward eye, having light hair and large shell-rimmed spectacles similar to my own, but labouring under some strain of hideous doubt or perplexity. As I looked, the pantomime was played out behind my back. Lifting his forefinger he pointed it at me with motions resembling the wagging of a duck's head. Then he lifted his shoulders in a broad shrugging gesture, and, opening his eyes to their widest extent, slowly shook his head.

"I was discovered.

"By what means my real identity had been discovered I could not know, but the sickening truth was out. Dr. Gable had said that his confederates were upstairs preparing the coffin; and now they would have descended, to muster about the door for my apprehension. Even at this point I would not—sir, I *could* not—despair, although I experienced a resumption of those physical symptoms I have described, and there was a curious blur before my eyes.

"Stealthily I looked round the room. Of means of entrance or exit in the room there were three. One was the door to the hall, outside which Dr. Gable's gunmen would be assembling. One was a lift in the wall immediately behind me; but the heavy doors of this lift were fast closed, and upon them was hung a placard reading, 'OUT OF ORDER.' Finally, in the lavatory towards my left I had observed a window high up over the wash-bowl: which, if the worst indeed came to the worst, afforded a practicable method of escape. But was I prepared to flee my Bannockburn and, craven-hearted, fly from the field of honour, especially (if I may say so) by any such unregal and indeed socially-unmentionable means as a lavatory window? No! While I looked round that room, seeing my mood reflected in the rich colours of the carpet, there flashed through my brain as an inspiration those noble and stirring lines which you may remember:

> Scots, wha hae wi' Wallace bled,
> Scots, wham Bruce has often led,
> Welcome to your gory bed,
>   Or to victory——!

"And as Wallace would have done, so now did I. I remember placing the Calcutta first edition carefully in my pocket, putting my top-hat on my head and tightening it down. My most important feeling was that Dr. Gable's gunmen must not be allowed to penetrate through that hall door, lest they should prove too many for me; and, if I could cut them off now, the leader would be in my power.

"Then, Sir Herbert, I sprang.

"Leaping up, with one sweep of my arm I knocked the mirror from the desk—even as now I again sweep off *your* desk the picture of your good lady you have replaced there—THUS!" (Bang!) "Not, Sir Herbert, because there was any practical result to be gained by so doing, but because in my exalted emotional state it seemed imperative to knock something off somewhere. In two bounds I was at the door, before Dr. Gable's minions could pour through; I slammed the door in the face of the young man in spectacles, turned the key in the lock, and with a cool smile turned to face Dr. Gable with my pistol levelled at his heart, even as Wallace might have done.

"Dr. Gable said: 'Here, here, here, I say! What does all this mean?'

"Some wild power within seemed prompting me to a glory of words that had never entered my head before, though I retained an icy calm.

"'It means, Dr. Gable,' I said, 'that the game is up! I am Detective Inspector Wallace Beery of Scotland Yard, and I arrest you for the attempted murder of Gregory Mannering! Throw up your hands!'

"The human mind is irrational. Even in that hour of peril, even with those white whiskers spreading from my face and with my hat pressed upon my head at an angle more acute than is seemly in a clergyman, I could not help wondering—with a sudden thrill of pride—what the members of the Tuesday Evening Ladies' Aid Society would think of the pastor if they saw him now. Even more triumphant was my feeling when I beheld the frog-like expression which overspread the lineaments of Dr. Gable, whose eyes seemed to grow as large as spectacle-lenses, and stared over the great white moustaches with an admixture of what was probably fear and guilt.

"He said:

"'Look here, old chap, have you gone off your onion?'

"'These subterfuges will avail you nothing, Dr. Gable,' I told him sternly. 'When you are installed in a cell, you will have the opportunity to reflect on the providential design that frustrated your plot. Take a step in any direction, or make one sound, and I blow out your brains!'

"'Mad as a hatter!' cried Dr. Gable, flourishing his fist wildly in the air. 'That gun's only loaded with blanks, you ass. Put it down!'

"'That is an old stratagem, my friend,' I informed him contemptuously. 'A very old stratagem. Stand away from that telephone. I am about to call Scotland Yard and summon the Flying Squad, for I am De——'

"'I know what you are,' declared Dr. Gable, with a baffled malevolence beyond description. 'You're an escaped lunatic who's wandered in here somehow, and even if you're the whole Paramount Studios you're not going to spoil a jolly good rag on Greg Mannering.'

"Now although I should have been prepared for the movement he made, since a very similar incident occurs in the hand-book, the bitter fact remains that I was not. If I remember correctly I was standing on one of those small occasional rugs which are sometimes placed upon carpets. With a movement of Satanic quickness Dr. Gable had only to bend forward, seize the end of the rug, and exert a tremendous yank. . . .

"I am under the impression that, a moment after my heels went flying, I must have struck my head a violent buffet on the side of the desk just behind me. In my head I experienced a ringing and roaring noise: the

157

view of the room darkened slightly, expanding and contracting in vast ripples like an image beheld in water; and although I remained nebulously conscious of everything that was going on about me, still I lay partly upon my back quite unable to move.

"In this humiliating position, which the weak flesh could not conquer, I was (as I have remarked) quite aware of what went on. Thus I saw Dr. Gable lift an arm and address the ceiling in passionate entreaty, ejaculating the words, 'What am I going to do with this maniac?' I could even, with dispassionate dullness, follow his line of thought. He glanced at the lavatory, and then back at the lift—which, it now dimly entered my head, had on the outside an iron latch like a bar. What better temporary prison, buzzed my thought, what better temporary prison could there be than a steel-walled lift which was out of order and which could be locked from the outside? Even as I strove feebly to struggle, and mouthed inarticulate words, I felt myself being dragged backwards along the rug on my—dorsal quarters; whence, after Dr. Gable had opened the doors of the lift, I was twisted inside. When the doors slammed and were locked, I found my head clearing in the shock of that shameful position. I felt ill and dizzy, but I contrived to struggle to my feet: the pain I received from bruising my anklebone against an empty wooden box in the dark lift helping also to clear my aching head.

"In each door of the lift was a window, perhaps a foot square, of thick glass. By pressing my cheek against the glass, I had a good view of the room. If the worst came to the worst, I could endeavour to smash that thick glass with my fist, but for the time I thought it best to husband my energies until my nausea had passed off. So I watched. Dr. Gable's first movement after locking me in was to run to the hall door, which I had locked, and open it. There entered in some haste the light-haired young man with the spectacles, with whom Dr. Gable began an excited conversation, both of them several times pointing to the lift and making indecipherable gestures. Unfortunately the steel walls of the lift prevented me from hearing what they said. I could only rage impotently while I peered out from that humiliating place like some creature in a zoo. So far as I could gather, the spectacled young man seemed trying to persuade Dr. Gable to go out and speak with somebody in the hall. Then they both had started for the door when my inspiration reached me.

"In the rear wall of the lift—that is to say the wall which ran parallel with the hall outside—I had observed a brightness against the dark, and perceived that this came from a species of wired ventilator, or screen, running for some distance along the top of the lift. Ah, inspiration! If I could reach that ventilator I should have a full view of what went on in the hall outside, as well as being able to hear what went on there. Although I am a man of considerable stature, I was not quite tall enough to bring my eyes to its level; but the assistance of the wooden box to stand upon would have rendered the process simple to anyone.

"In a flash I was upon the box, with my nose pressed to the ventilator or screen, and by craning my neck slightly from side to side I had an admirable view of almost the entire hall."

Here Dr. Illingworth stopped, drawing his breath hard. For the first time since the old boy had started talking, his face had got a queer colour.

"And from that vantage-point, Sir Herbert," he told me, "I saw murder done."

12

View From A Lift: How Dr. Illingworth Played The Devil

Now at last—at last, at last—we were going straight to the point. Here was the crux of the infernal business. And I didn't want to cut short the old boy's narrative or tell him to be brief after all the verbiage before, because he had a knack of being thorough. Even he seemed to feel he had got into a different atmosphere, though I'm pretty sure it puzzled him to know why.

This wasn't a game; this was murder now. And the fact that Illingworth had expected it to be murder all along would let him memorise like a cinema film everything he saw and heard.

There he sat by my desk, with his cigar burnt down to a stump and gone out, still making motions of smoking it, but looking a little grey and tired. Still, on he went, as harsh and roopy as a crow.

"I am aware that you will wish me to be most precise at this particular juncture," says he, wiping his forehead, "and so I shall endeavour to be. From my vantage-point, the first objects discernible were the marble pillars which, set perhaps ten feet apart, ran down this side of the wall. Beyond them I could discern a large open space down the centre of the hall, then another line of pillars on the opposite side, and beyond them the line of coaches. Immediately to my right was the staircase at the rear of the hall; and by pressing my cheek to the ventilator and looking hard towards the left, I was even able to make out a portion of the bronze front doors. Near these front doors a group had assembled, speaking in whispers. These were Pruen, the treacherous caretaker, the plump young woman in the red dress whom I had seen before, and a slim, light-haired young woman whom I had not seen before—one of these must be the Miriam who would betray her lover to the knife, and the other the Harriet of whom Dr. Gable had spoken. Finally, with them stood the villain who was to impersonate a prince of the House of Mirhán, still in his stolen finery, and making savage gestures. Even their whispers roused echoes in this place, blue and white and pale with its manufactured moonlight, and inexpressibly terrible.

"The door of the curator's room opened; Dr. Gable and the fair-haired man came out, so that for the first time I could hear them speaking. The conversation struck me as incongruous, even bewildering; but I quote it verbatim, and I can testify to its accuracy, for I was scarcely a dozen feet away from the speakers.

"'—but he can't really be Illingworth!' Dr. Gable was protesting in a low voice, but with a species of yelp. 'Curse it all, Ron, I tell you this fellow's loopy! He said he was Wallace Beery of Scotland Yard, and reeled off a lot of verse about Scots wha hae wi' Wallace bled!' (I may add parenthetically, as an example of the curious tricks played by the human mind, that I have no recollection whatever of quoting aloud the ringing lines of Robert Burns.)

"'We're in the soup,' asseverated his companion, whom I had already selected as the double-dyed wretch Holmes: that secretary who betrayed his employer. 'You go up and talk to Pruen. Pruen's been at the doors all the time. He thought there was something very fishy about this chap when he walked in. Then, not ten minutes after Illingworth—if that's who it is—arrived here, in walked the *real* actor from the theatrical agency——!'

"Dr. Gable appeared distraught.

"'Well, why didn't Pruen warn us?' he demanded. 'And where's the real actor from the agency now? He didn't come in to see me. Where is he?'

"'I don't know! Nobody seems to know!' replied Holmes. 'Pruen didn't dare leave the front doors, in case Mannering should turn up unexpectedly; and the actor didn't get here until five minutes or so ago, and Pruen didn't tumble to it fully until he saw him. *Then* Pruen didn't dare leave the doors; I came downstairs just afterwards, and Pruen told me, and I came running back to see you. . . . Listen, Jerry, why are we waiting here? For God's sake, let's go back and pull Illingworth out of that lift, and apologise to him, and try to smooth him down! I wish we'd never gone in for this thing. If the old man ever hears of it I'll lose my job, and Sam will be laughed out of the legation—you know what old Abbsley is; and you'll be kicked out of the house, to say nothing of what will happen to Miriam. It's got to be hushed up somehow.'

"Truly you may well say an extraordinary speech to

162

hear from a member of this gang, delivered in such a tone of cool and cutting sanity that my brain wavered. Could this be one of the band less murderous than his fellows, or could there have been a mistake somewhere? But I had no time to speculate on the ramifications of this, for the Persian-clad Baxter had detached himself from the group near the front doors and was hurrying towards the two under my ventilator. On his way he was required to pass a line of display-cases wherein were exhibited a variety of weapons, and then his path led him past the five coaches or carriages drawn up on the opposite side of the room. As he passed a large and dark closed carriage of a type with which I am unfamiliar, he appeared to glance at the floor a little to the rear of it. He bent down, wound his way under the carriage and (since there was a pillar just there) disappeared from view for a few seconds; after which he reappeared carrying in the palm of his hand some small and darkish object which at that distance I could not positively identify, although I am gifted with unusual long sight. All this, as I say, had taken place while the two confederates were speaking together; nor, may I add, was the pain in my head or my smarting and humiliated spirit at all soothed by the tone Dr. Gable adopted with reference to me.

"'Yes, I suppose we'll have to call the whole thing off,' said Dr. Gable. 'It's just on eleven o'clock, we're completely disorganised, we've got a maniac shut up in the lift, and now the man from the Brainerd Agency seems to have walked in and—oh, Lord!'

"At this point the man called Baxter, in his blue embroidered tunic, came sputtering into the group. His face, I deduced, must have been artificially darkened (indeed he showed a tendency to touch it and run his hands over it in the fashion of the domestic house-cat),

163

and by the disarranged order of his hair I perceived that under the sheepskin hat he must be wearing a black wig. His speech, on a querulous note, was now involved in an interminable redundancy of 'I say's,' and 'Dash it all's.' A wave of wonder passed over me, I confess, for to add to the intrinsic terror of the situation the sanguinary conversation of these people had assumed a weird note like that of schoolboys.

"'No, we're not going to call it off,' snarled Baxter. 'Who said call it off? We don't back out now.' When Dr. Gable began to explain the situation, Baxter cut him short. 'You're talking like the women up there. Let this blighter, whoever he is, stop in the lift. Won't it make the story better? We can turn him loose at the right time and throttle him in front of Mannering to give added effect. . . . What I want to know is, where's that actor we hired? He came in here, Pruen says; he can't have vanished like a blasted spook, unless he walked out the back way. What sort of funny business is going on in this place, anyhow? Look here!'

"He held out in his palm the small object he seemed to have picked up and, by clinging precariously to my ledge under the screen, I saw that it was a segment of black hair or wool cut into the form of a false moustache.

"'I've been looking all over the place for this thing,' he said. 'Rinkey swore I ought to wear it. He's cracked on the subject of decking people out with hair. Now I find the thing on the floor. Furthermore, where's my dagger? I can't find that either. How the devil do you expect me to play my part if I don't have the dagger? It's the most important thing in the lot. Ron, you're the property-man for this show—where's my dagger?'

"'I haven't the slightest idea where your dagger is,' replied Holmes, speaking with his jaws closed just as my friend Mr. Murdoch does when he gives ventriloquial entertainments at the church festivals. 'I opened the case and put it on the stairs in sight for you. Will you try to get it through your head that there are things more important than finding your dagger? Just now—Sam!'

"Baxter, with a curse, had turned round and was hurrying again towards the front of the museum. The other two, talking rapidly, followed him, and I endeavoured also to follow their progress by craning about on my perch. How I overbalanced myself I cannot say; it has been observed of me (notably by my wife, who complains of certain insignificant breakages about the house) that when I am deep in thought my limbs possess erratic tendencies, although I cannot but think that the view is highly coloured. In any event, I was leaning too far, the box toppled from under me, and I was saved from a fall only by clutching at the ledge under the ventilator, whence I let myself down. Again, sir, I say it—the slipping of the box was providential. While I groped feverishly to set it up again, my fingers encountered a cold substance; they encountered, in brief, the blade of a hatchet lying on the floor of the lift. I could have shouted for joy when I touched it, since, with the pain of my bruises, my humiliations, and a certain nervous strain, I was fast reaching an extremity wherein my heart burst to grapple with these miscreants; and (I confesss it without shame) there were almost tears in my eyes. Armed with that hatchet, like some American Indian warrior of the Miami streets, I might bid defiance to my enemies and answer them in the same language of that defiant Seminole:

Blaze with your serried legions!—I *will not* bend
   the knee!
The shackles ne'er again shall bind the arm that
   now is free;
I've mailed it with the thunder when the tem-
   pest muttered low,
And where it falls ye well may dread the lightning of its blow!

"No, no, Sir Herbert, you need not urge me to keep
to the story. I defer it—I introduce these lines—because I do not like to think of the sight which I saw
when I climbed back upon that box. It was the climax
and the horror—believe me—but let me be as pro-
saic as possible when I describe it.

"I was looking, as I have told you, straight across the
hall at the line of coaches opposite. Opposite, at a
slight angle, but not so far to my left that I could not
have an uninterrupted view, stood the gigantic black
carriage of which I have told you. All the members of
the group I had previously seen had gathered together
in the upper far corner of the hall, near the door labelled 'Persian Gallery'; they were on the other side of
the line of coaches, at the head of it, and could not see
what I saw. I heard their voices twittering in muttered
silly echoes, but I did not listen to them. For the door
of the travelling-carriage was very slowly opening.

"The door of the carriage was opening, towards me,
under that bluish moonlight glow. It appeared to be
large enough for a man to stand up inside, and a man
was standing there, bent a little over and staring down
at some large lump at his feet while with his right
hand he pushed open the carriage door to get a better
light. This man was dressed in the uniform of an ordinary police-constable; my first thought was that the

police had arrived, until I remembered my host's description of a member of their gang in police uniform. Holding the door open with his foot, he bent down and with a powerful heave began to raise this hump from the floor. I then saw that the hump was the body of a man, with head lying in my direction; that the bogus policeman had caught this man by the shoulders and was pulling him up. Now holding the body with one hand, he took hold of the back of the head—apparently by the hair or the hat, a top-hat pressed tightly there—and pulled it up so that he could get a look at the face.

"It was a dead face, Sir Herbert, and it was looking straight across at me with wide-open eyes round which I could see a ring of white; although the neck lolled. It was the face of a bearded man whose mouth was open. As the dark overcoat swung open I saw protruding from his chest a whitish projection resembling ivory. And I knew.

"At that moment the voice of the light-haired girl came calling and screeching from the front of the museum, where she could not see the inside of the carriage or its grisly exhibit. She called out to the bogus constable, addressing him as 'darling'—the effect of that endearment echoing over a dead man in the vault was horrible—and asking him why he had 'gone about jumping into carriages at a time like this.'

"He acted quickly, and by his actions I knew he was guilty. Still partly propping up the body with one hand, he slid down from the carriage on my side; then with his other hand he slammed the door in the face of the dead man. I confess I winced at the booming noise of the door slammed, as it shut off the head of a corpse seeking to get out, and I winced still more at the sound of his hearty voice reverberating.

"'Nothing at all wrong,' he called out. 'I left my

truncheon in one of these coaches, that's all. No, there's nothing wrong—except that we've got to get out of here, and get out quick. The show seems to have busted, so why stay? But let's pack you gals off somewhere, and then Jerry and Sam and Ron and I ought to have a little conference.'

"Baxter came striding round into the main aisle down the middle.

"'What do you mean, get out?' he asked. 'There's nothing wrong, is there?'

"'No, no—!' the other was crying, with a cracked and spurious heartiness, when he turned round, lifting his eyes, and looked straight across the hall into my face.

"Although the perforated holes in the ventilator were set close together, it was, of course, impossible that he could have distinguished my features; but the vague sight of a head was enough. I shall not soon forget that blue-clad figure in its helmet, standing motionless on the white marble with a small bluish shadow at its feet, and the ghostly pillars around. Though the eyes were shaded by the helmet, they seemed to shift and gleam; and down the side of the face I saw the light gleam on a moving trickle of perspiration from under the helmet.

"'Who's in that lift?' he said.

"'That's the captive of Jerry's bow and spear,' chortled the light-haired girl. 'Why?'

"'I want to have a talk with him,' said the policeman.

"Before he had even started to speak, I acted in a species of madness which even now I cannot regret. Leaping down from the box, I drove my hatchet at the glass in the lift door. The first blow shattered it, the second and third cleared it nearly out of its frame, so that I was enabled to thrust my hand through the aperture and grope after the latch outside. Just as I did so I heard the voice of the agonised Holmes, apparently roused by the crash of glass, cry, 'He's getting out!' and shortly after it the heavier voice of the bogus constable bellowing: 'We'd better stop him, I'm warning you! You won't know why, and don't ask me, but there'll be bad trouble if he gets out and finds the police.'

"Those words inspired me to greater efforts, even with an obscure feeling of savage triumph, especially when I heard them come stampeding towards this room. Having got the lift doors open, I flung away my hatchet, for I had but one purpose now, and made a dash for the hall door to lock it before they could get in. And—I was triumphant. Even as a wave of clattering footsteps seemed to rise up against that door, I turned the key in the lock, and leaned against it with sight dimmed but still steady in resolve. These questions of personal dignity must be forgotten now. I walked with firm steps to the lavatory, where I found it perfectly possible to mount upon the wash-bowl (although the convex surface of smooth porcelain rendered one's foothold extremely precarious); thence to seat myself upon the windowledge and push outward the swinging window. The drop presented no great hazard, and, to facilitate my escape, just at the left of the window descended a strong rainspout or drainpipe of some terra-cotta material. For a weaker man than I would have been stimulated by the shouts I heard behind me.

"Though the door was still locked and no sound could penetrate there, I heard voices faintly through the ventilator when the lift doors were open.

"'He can't get out of there,' said the voice of Dr. Gable.

"'I tell you he can,' yelled the voice of the bogus policeman. 'He can get out the lavatory window. Don't argue; you people duck out and head him off by the back door, or there'll be the devil to pay. I'll cover the front.'

"No further stimulus was necessary to aid my frenzied descent. I found myself standing breathless in a back garden or yard surrounded by high walls, but the blessed moonlight illuminated it with chaste glory to show me an iron-railed gate in the rear wall. I ran towards it, and with hands of eager supplication sought my deliverance.

"The gate was locked.

"Behind me I discerned the sound of a rattle and click. Against the black silhouette of the museum a line of light slanted out along the path from an open door. With my oasis turned to cruel sand, I had no thought except to avoid that searching light, for now I must be penned in this yard before my pursuers. I doubled along the wall, without object or conscious seeking, just as my pursuers plunged down the path towards the rear gate. Finding myself at the front, I found something else when my outstretched hand groped along the wall: an iron rest or spike, a series of projecting spikes, ascending the wall in a sort of ladder.

"I have no recollection of climbing that ladder; only a feeling that freedom lay on the other side. And that did not endure. For no sooner did I find myself, with painful breath, seated astride the wall, than a light struck me in the eyes. I discerned below the hated form and helmet of a man whom I believed to be my enemy, the bogus policeman; my swimming wits took in some triumphant words he uttered, but I cannot recall what; for most distinctly I remembered his cry a few moments ago, 'I'll cover the front.'

"We are told that there is no fury like that of the constantly defeated. *I* was the constantly defeated, and the sealed bomb burst then. We were one against one; I would take the murderer single-handed, or I would die. Over subsequent events, when I madly hurled myself from that wall upon him, I pass hastily. One crowning bitterness remained to me just before the blow which sent me into real insensibility, and this bitterness was composed of two pieces of knowledge: That I was a minister of the Church, and that I had murderously assaulted the wrong man."

Dr. Illingworth put his head in his hands and remained silent for a good while. I put in my oar.

"But what happened then, doctor? That's not the end, is it?"

"So far as I can command myself or my faculties to outline a coherent story," he said, and shuddered, "it—in short, it is. Flashes, glimpses, nothing——"

"Still, in your letter you mentioned a coal-hole. . . ."

"A coal-hole!" says he, as though I had jabbed a pin into him. "Merciful heaven, a coal-hole! That I—! Well, I dare say, Sir Herbert, it is best that you should have what little information there is about that hazy interlude, between a little past eleven and half-past twelve, even though *I* can make nothing of it! If they were criminals, as nothing will convince me that they are not, why did they stay their hands and refrain from killing me when I was at their mercy? The fact is, I remember nothing of any coal-hole. Thus:

"The next conscious impression I can recall is of sitting up and being jolted from side to side in some motor-vehicle, with a head painful beyond endurance,

171

and a sensation of lights flickering in my eyes. So far as I could make out, the place was the dark interior of a taxi. I was sensible of pungent odour of spirits, emanating ostensibly from my own clothing, and a dark figure sat beside me holding a bottle to my lips.

"I asked weakly where I was.

"'Hammersmith Bridge,' said a distant voice. 'We've been as far as Slough, in the hour and something it's taken to pull you round. Thank the Lord you're better! Don't worry; it's all right. The taxi-driver thinks you're drunk.'

"Despite the mists of pain I had to struggle to sit upright at this, and fold my arms, for I knew that voice.

"'If you have any more killing to do tonight,' I heard myself muttering to the bogus policeman, 'get on with it. I am finished.'

"'Nobody wants to kill you, Dr. Illingworth!' said the man Butler, shouting in my ear with a painful loudness which made my head open and shut. 'Yes, I know your name; we found your visiting-cards in your pocket when we pulled you through the coal-hole. Dr. Illingworth! Can you hear me? We owe you an apology—on our knees we owe you an apology. There's been a terrible mistake, that's all. That's why I wanted to get you alone, and explain, and I persuaded the others to let me take you home. *They* don't know yet —what you and I know—about that body. . . .'

"Of what he said for a time I am uncertain, though he continued to speak volubly. The combination of the jolting cab, the flickering lights, and a general nausea made me inattentive of anything else; and at one point (you have asked for the humiliating truth, Sir Herbert) I can recall—you will excuse me—being violently ill out of the window. In one instance I did follow what he was telling me, since I felt a nebulous wonder as to what happened after my encounter with the policeman.

"'I had just got the front doors open about three inches, when I saw you sailing into the copper out there,' he informed me. 'There was no way to walk out and get you without blowing the gaff. Then down you went, right beside where I knew there was a coal-hole. If the copper went for assistance, I knew we could get you in. Sam and I went down into the cellar. The copper was just going away, and there you were almost on the edge; we got you through, and he couldn't see the place because you'd smashed his light. . . .'

"It went on interminably while we drove back into London. Once, I remember, I plucked up spirit and called him a murderer. He swore to me that he had nothing to do with that terrible business, but his argument was difficult for me to follow. It seemed to consist chiefly in an appeal to me to suppress the names of his confederates in the business, especially of the women. One tense remark returns to me from the welter.

"'Look here, I'll tell you what I'll do,' he said. 'It's all my fault for disliking that swine Mannering, and what he said about my friends. If you will give me your word as a preacher and a gentleman that you won't say anything about their being at the museum tonight, on my honour I'll go to Scotland Yard tomorrow and confess that I killed that fellow in the coach. There are reasons why none of them must be mixed up in this business.'

"I told him I could do nothing of the kind, and I remember his white face under the passing lights.

"'Then I'll have to fight it somehow,' he said. 'I'll have to take a walk somewhere and think.'

"You will understand, Sir Herbert, my bewilderment at this conduct, coming as it did after the events of the evening. When we reached my hotel, the Orkney in Kensington High Street, he eventually found in his pockets just enough money to pay an appalling cab-fare. He escorted me into the hotel, still impersonating an officer of the law; and, to account for my wildly disreputable state (the whiskers, thank heaven, having been removed), he told the hotel-clerk an imaginative tale of my having been involved in a riot while addressing a meeting. At the moment I had not the heart or the stomach to contradict it; but, ensconced once more in the soothing quiet of my room, after a night as lurid as any described in your police hand-book, I knew that I must take up my pen to indite the truth. All has now been revealed to you. The moment to judge the folly of my conduct has arrived. Sir Herbert——"

He waggled his hand in the air, hoarse as a man on the morning after, pulled in his chin, and stopped.

13

The Eleven Points

It was past lunch-time when I got rid of old Illingworth, but I wanted to sit down and stop up my ears and think. Of course I carried on something awful before Illingworth, because I'm a hard man—grrr!—and I believe in treating 'em rough. But I had to assure him, even when I was putting the fear of the Old Nick into him, that *he* wasn't likely to get into any trouble over the thing, and that he'd given us a few stray bits of information that might be valuable. My eye, but weren't they valuable! That's what I was afraid of. It was a hell of a mess, and I was afraid it couldn't be hushed up. So, when Illingworth had stalked out after a final upsetting of my wife's picture, I walked round the office kicking the furniture and generally relieving my feelings, and then I punched some buttons.

Popkins, my *aide-de-camp* that I was telling you about, who had been listening with his elephant-ear at the door, came in.

I said: "Sit down, fool. Aside from a shorthand reporter with writer's cramp, what have we got?"

He went through his usual motion of wrinkling up his forehead and scratching the back of his hairline. Then he said:

"We've got a very unusual gentleman, sir, with a complex for cross-breeding film-stars and thrillers. He'd have made a gr-rand actor himself. At any minute I expected him to strike an attitude and announce that he was Mickey Mouse of the *Sûreté*. I suppose he really is an honest man? He seems a little too good to be true?"

"Yes, I think he's an honest man. Have 'em check up, of course. Come to think of it, Carruthers' report says he told the finger-print man to go over that lift for prints. If Illingworth was in there—well, I should have asked him here if he'd mind having his prints taken, and, if he was in that lift, they'll match. . . . Dammit, I should have——!"

"I have already arranged for that, sir," said Popkins, looking so much like a police-force Jeeves that it was enough to drive a man crazy. "He will be stopped as he goes downstairs. We should have the prints for comparison in a few minutes."

"All right, all right," I said. "Now let's hear you give your celebrated imitation of intelligence and see what else you got out of that story."

Of course it never comes to anything, but I usually ask Popkins this; it stimulates me. Out came his notebook.

He said: "The main outline is easy enough to follow. Young Wade, Butler, Holmes, Baxter, Pruen, and the two girls were putting up this game on Mannering to see whether they could scare him after his tall bragging about his adventures. They had to do it cleverly, because Mannering really had been in the East, presumably knew some Arabic, and wouldn't have fallen for anything clumsy. The key-character in the business, of course, was 'Dr. Illingworth,' who was to do most of the tall talking—the question being which one of them should play the part? And none of them could do it adequately; because Holmes, the only one of them with the requisite knowledge of this subject, was barred from the part because Mannering knew him and would have spotted him. You see how it worked out. Young Wade had the gift of gab and some knowledge for Illingworth's part, but he had to play Jeff Wade because he looks so much like the old man that he was the only one who could do it convincingly. Mannering had never met the old man, but he might have seen a photograph. Baxter had the Arabic for Illingworth's part, but not the knowledge or the gift of gab. Butler had the gift of gab, but not the knowledge or the Arabic.

"So they were stumped, until they thought of ringing up a theatrical agency and asking whether they could get hold of anybody to play the part, with full qualifications; knowledge of the language, monuments——"

I said: "That's a hell of a tall order to give a theatrical agency. Anyhow, we know the name of the agency (Brainerd, ain't it?) and we can ring 'em up——"

"I have already done it," says Popkins, with that Jeeves-like nod, and out comes another note-book. "And the full details about Raymond Penderel are here." He stopped and looked hard at me. "It happened, I say it *happened*, that they knew of a man who would exactly fill the order. . . ."

I used some more wicked language. "'Happened.' So this is where the wavering waters unite and the star-destinies cross? Popkins, I don't like this."

"All the same, I like it. It's taking us straight to the point—excuse me; taking *you*. The Brainerd Agency specialises in supplying turns for private parties. If you want a dance orchestra for your daughter's reception, if you want a dozen chorus-girls for a bachelor party, if you want anything from a soprano to a troupe of performing fleas, you ring them up and they supply."

He opened the note-book.

"Raymond Penderel. Age 32. Born in Iraq, son of a British father and a Persian mother; hence a good British subject. Not too much education, but plenty of native talent. Came to England just four months ago, from Baghdad. . . ."

"Wow!"

"Yes, sir. To one of the people at the agency, whom he seems to have given a pain in the neck, he unburdened himself a good deal. I talked with the fellow ten minutes ago, and got some useful information. Penderel told him that he (Penderel, I mean) was the son of an English nobleman, a major—the depravity of majors is notorious—that he went to an English school when Great Britain took a mandate over the territory in 1919, and that he served as a tourists' guide—mark that, a guide—to the ancient wonders. When he was twenty-one he went to Paris; he did some singing in a musichall, as well as character impersonations. Mark that again: character impersonations. Also he was a professional dancing-partner. He seems to have got into trouble, on what he said was the false accusation of a woman that he had tried to extort money from her."

"My God, Popkins, I was afraid of that."

Here my faithful hound looked at me, as though he

were wondering what I had in mind, but he gave that hiss of his and went on.

"Then he came to London, and about four years ago went back to his native heath in Baghdad. That's about all, except that since he arrived here again four months ago he's been on his uppers. There wasn't much call for his singing or his character impersonations. But, when yesterday your Wade crowd phoned the agency for a man who would suit their needs naturally they thought of Penderel. . . ."

"Which one of 'em phoned?"

"Butler. He offered twenty guineas for a little impersonation, on a part that had to be swotted up in a hurry; it was just noon when he rang up. He told them to have the man meet him at a bar in Piccadilly at two o'clock in the afternoon to go over the details. So, when Carruthers last night sprang the information on that crowd that a man named Raymond Penderel had been murdered, it wasn't very surprising that the name meant nothing to them. They'd never heard the name; or, at least, most of them hadn't. . . ."

"Look here, you louse," I roared at him, "what are you insinuating about Jeff Wade's daughter?"

Popkins said: "Now, now, I'm not necessarily insinuating anything, sir. I'm outlining the probable course of events. Which is this:

"Penderel arranged to act the part, and hence we have an explanation of a lot of things. His false whiskers, tinged with grey; he was going to impersonate Dr. Illingworth, and both Butler and Jerry Wade seem to have been strong on scholars being decked out with whiskers. His eyeglasses on a black ribbon; very scholarly touch, like our friend Dr. Fell. His sedate top-hat and evening-clothes; the clothes of his gigolo days, if you'll remember the Paris label

Carruthers found in 'em. It all fits together, even if those crazy kids—well, not so crazy, one of them. Take it easy, now sir!

"Finally, if Illingworth heard things properly, Penderel must have arrived at the museum about ten minutes after Illingworth himself. Between then and eleven o'clock, somebody murdered him. Now, I don't have to point out to you that, while it's possible, still it's exceedingly improbable that an outsider sneaked in and did the business. We've got the whole cast of characters now under our—your—eyes. So?"

I had to admit Popkins was right. I chewed that over for a minute, and went across and looked out the window at the Embankment. Then I asked him if there was anything else. There was.

Popkins continued: "Now, with Dr. Illingworth's story, we have an explanation of most of the lunacy Carruthers walked into last night. Most of it! We can make a connected story. But there are a few points which the account doesn't explain. Some of them may be important, some of them not. You'll have to have a go at hauling those kids over the coals; and also notably the faithful Pruen, who may be your chief witness, since he was on guard at the doors all evening and had a clear view of the hall. Some of these points, consequently, you may get cleared up first shot. Some are likely to prove nasty.

"When that crowd switched off the lights and cleared out of the museum last night in such a devil of a hurry, just after they'd rescued the real Illingworth from Sergeant Hoskins, they did one thing. They made a pact together that, whatever happened, they wouldn't admit they had been at the museum that night. It was Illingworth they were afraid of; they didn't want him to tell Jeff Wade that they had been fooling about with Jeff's beloved museum and locking Illingworth up in lifts—they thought Butler might be able to smooth Illingworth down. . . . But, with two exceptions, they didn't know that a murder had been committed. Those two exceptions are Butler and the murderer; or Butler may *be* the murderer, for all I know. But the others—well, I doubt it."

Popkins likes the sound of his own voice.

I said: "Do you think I'm a fool? Of course they didn't know it. Otherwise Pruen wouldn't have been so cocky when Carruthers walked in. He wouldn't have been gleefully dancing about in the dark, admiring the spirit of the crowd, if he'd known there was a nice fresh corpse stuffed away in that carriage. Talk sense. Pruen's devoted to that girl, and to the whole gang as well. But——"

"But, as you say," Popkins got in as smooth as butter, "now that the murder's out, they'll have to talk. Hence I suggest that you concentrate on these points. Some of them, as I say, may be easily cleared up. I've made a list of the points which Dr. Illingworth's story does *not* explain. I've prepared a duplicate list for you," he shoved it across the desk, "and, with your permission, I'll go over it now. It's divided into sections I and II, first as to practical points, and then as to what we can call general philosophical points. Thus:

I

1. What about the coal-dust tracks just inside the front door of the museum, those indistinguishable smudges which Carruthers found on the floor?

    Comment: Since a coating of coal-dust was found on the soles of the murdered man's shoes, the tracks were presumably made by him. Where had he been then, just before he entered the museum, to leave traces on the white marble?

2. What about the typewritten note, beginning, "Dear G., There has got to be a corpse—a real corpse," etc., which was found in Mannering's pocket?

    Comment: This note, written on Holmes's typewriter, and, according to Mannering, found in Holmes's flat, does not exactly square with the story of the fake "murder" as Dr. Illingworth understood it.

3. What about the large lump of coal which Carruthers found had been thrown at the wall in the Gallery of the Bazaars, for no apparent reason?

    Comment: This is not mentioned by Dr. Illingworth, or anybody else, and does not seem to fit into the story. The proper persons to question are Pruen, who had a clear view of the hall all the time, and Baxter, who was in the Gallery of the Bazaars at (about) 10:35, when Dr. Illingworth arrived at the museum.

4. What were the adventures of the black false moustache?

    Comment: This moustache, meant to have been worn by Baxter, was—according to Holmes—placed by Holmes, along with the dagger, somewhere on the stairs in the main hall at an earlier time in the evening. Along with the dagger, it seems to have disappeared. It was found by Baxter on the floor of the museum later; then we lost sight of it, and Carruthers finds it inside a locked show-case in place of the dagger. Does this mean anything? Question Pruen, on duty there.

5. Why, after the party left the museum at some time after eleven o'clock, did Miriam Wade return to the museum?

   Comment: Shortly after Carruthers discovered the body at 12:25, Miriam Wade returned to the back gate in the wall. She had a key to this gate, which was locked. She took Carruthers for Ronald Holmes, and said, "I saw your light in there, but I didn't think you'd be here. I thought you'd gone on to your flat; I was just going there. Is anything wrong?" Where had she been in the meantime, and why did she return?

6. Why, when she did return and was told by Carruthers of the murder, did she telephone to Harriet Kirkton at Holmes's flat—in a disguised voice?

   Comment: If she merely wished to tell them and warn them about the murder, why not ask for anybody and blurt it out? There seems to be no reason for this.

7. (and last.) What about the cookery-book?
   Comment: unnecessary.

"That, I think," says Popkins, screwing up his face modestly, "takes care of a few points. Of course, these are intended only to tie up the story coherently. I omit the plain lines of questioning: where everybody was between (about) ten-forty-five, when Penderel entered the museum, and (about) eleven, when Butler found his body in the carriage. You understand that this document is only meant to go after odd points. But I'll respectfully suggest that when you've got the answers to all these you'll have the murderer."

"You're subtle, you are," I told him, for of course all this was plain without any hocus-pocus of fancy documents or ruled lines. Popkins is the kind of chap who likes to draw up a schedule for anything. Hah! "And," I said, "you're jumping far ahead of the business before we've questioned anybody."

Then he went on with a lot of nonsense about my being a member of the police department, and how it wouldn't do to have any preconceived notions. But I shut him up pretty curtly; I told him, if he had anything further to suggest to get on with it (as though *I*, I of all people, would have any prejudices!). Well, the second half of his document went like this. I simmered and simmered; I'm simmering yet.

II

8. What about the telegram which Dr. Illingworth received from Mr. Geoffrey Wade at five o'clock yesterday afternoon?
   Comment: This telegram, handed in at Southampton, invited Illingworth to come to the museum that night at half-past ten, and said that G. Wade would be able to return early. Apparently he did not; where was he, and what does it mean?

9. Why was Raymond Penderel, when he came to the museum last night, so very late?

Comment: This is an important point, though not as obvious as some others. Mannering, on whom the hoax was to have been played, had been invited to the museum at eleven o'clock. It must be assumed that Penderel must have been told to be there at a much earlier time, in order to go over the ground and rehearse the business with the others. This is only common sense. But he did not arrive until about 10:45, only fifteen minutes before the show was due to begin. In fact, we know that Illingworth—mistaken for Penderel when he arrived first—was rated for being very late by both Pruen and Jerry Wade.

10. Has any of the group ever been a medical student, or have special knowledge of anatomy or surgery?

Comment: See the testimony of Dr. Marsden, the divisional surgeon, who said that penetration of the heart with that curved blade was the result of a singular coincidence or of medical knowledge.

11. (and last.) What was Miriam Wade doing in the cellar, just as Dr. Illingworth entered the museum?

I cut him short here, before he could get in his prim little comment. Out of eleven points, three had directly concerned Miriam, and that made me mad. Now, I know that girl; if you want to know the bitter truth, I stood godfather to her. Jeff used to put people's backs up so much that nobody else would do it, but I understand his funny mentality, and I've never minded him. As for the girl, she might turn into a very refreshing little harlot—in fact, I wouldn't say she hasn't got tendencies that way, and I was thinking about it when Carruthers here gave his description— but she'd never be mixed up in anything like this."

Popkins said: "They're all mixed up in it. I didn't say anything about your god-daughter. I only asked, What was she doing in the cellar? And I only mentioned it because there's such an eternal flavour of coal-dust about this case that I thought it might be important."

"Yes, but *what* cellar? What's a blasted cellar got to do with her? Is there anything in the evidence about her having been in a cellar?"

"You believe Illingworth's story, don't you, sir?"

"Suppose I do? What about it?"

"Very well. He states—here it is in my note-book, and you can find it in the shorthand report—he states that, as he was going back to the curator's room, the door at the *left* of the staircase opened, and the girl in the red dress came out. Now look at Carruthers' report. That door leads to the cellar. It leads *only* to the cellar. Therefore she was in the cellar. Q. E. D. I don't say anything about the girl, I don't even say it's necessarily important; I only say she was there. . . . But the whole point is, it's now time to decide. What orders shall you give?"

I had a complete distaste for that man's face.

"We'll put Hadley officially in charge of it," I said, "and young Betts to help him. But just at this time *I'll* take charge, until I can get some sense out of it. Get me Jeff Wade on the telephone, and don't be put off by any excuses. Now hop it."

I was pretty busy, but just at the moment business would have to lump it. So I sat down and shut my ears and thought it over. In spite of what I'd said to Popkins, you can see how the business ran. I was sure Miriam had known this fellow Penderel, from a good many suggestions you'll have seen yourselves; but what made me so sure of it was a little clue whose importance Popkins' long nose hadn't sniffed, even though he had it in his outline. Why, when she learned about the murder and saw Penderel's body, did she telephone Harriet Kirkton in a disguised voice?

Now, I didn't know this Kirkton girl. In fact, I hadn't seen Miriam herself for three or four years, when she was just blossoming out as a comehither hellion and expressed her delight in anything by wrinkling up her face and saying, "EEE!" The only thing I'd always thought was that she had guts and nerve, which she'd shown in this instance. The Kirkton girl, by all accounts, was her best friend. She had been out in the waste country with Miriam during the eighteen months, she had travelled back on the boat with her, she probably knew what was going on. Penderel came to England from Baghdad; four months ago. Miriam came to England from Baghdad; one month ago, and by Jeff's orders was immediately shipped off to an aunt in Norfolk—the aunt being at the boat to make certain of prey—until Jeff himself arrived home to take charge. When you've been away from your friends and your home town for nearly two years, that's not done without good reason. Finally, a press-cutting about Miriam was found in Penderel's pocket; and Carruthers said that the one member of the crowd who definitely did seem to recognise the name "Raymond

Penderel" was Harriet Kirkton, just as Miriam seemed to recognise the face when she saw the dead man. All little, unprovable, out-of-court bits of evidence that did lead to the big one.

Now I don't know much about women, only having been married once, and anyway the only reason why people air their speculations about women is just to make an epigram. But I do know two things. I do know that I never met a woman who liked a bowler hat, and I never met a woman who could resist giving an alarm unless there was a crushingly personal reason against it. As soon as she could, last night, Miriam ducked in to telephone. The natural thing, of course; but if she had only been terrified by the fact that there was *a* corpse, and not *this particular* corpse, she would have called Holmes's flat where she knew they were all assembled, and blurted to the person who answered: "Stand by for squalls and get your stories ready; they've found a dead man in here." But that wasn't her first thought. No, no. The first thought was to talk privately, to warn privately, to tell this girl something which the others didn't know. Something that must be kept from the others. If she'd called up and said, "This is Miriam," she would have had to tell the ordinary news first, and that might have meant a delay which she couldn't afford before Carruthers caught her telephoning. What she wanted to say was not, "There's a dead man here, and we're all in trouble"; it was *"Penderel* is dead, so keep quiet about everything when you learn." And that, she considered, was worse trouble. Hence the disguised voice, which would have changed to her own when she spoke to Harriet.

D'ye follow me, my fatheads? In spite of Popkins'

nosing, one good fact stands and shines. Something was so important that she had to tell it to Harriet before she told the others about the murder. Something she'd just discovered; the identity of the corpse. It meant that she, or Kirkton, or both of them, had had dealings with Penderel.

Don't you think that her telephoning in that way is a good fact? I do. For the identity of the corpse had crowded the fact of the murder clean out of her mind. That's probably the act of a woman guilty of what they call "indiscretion." It's certainly not the act of a woman guilty of murder.

But it was still a mucky business, and I didn't feel much better when they told me Jeff Wade was on the wire. I set myself for a blast and a battle. When I said, "Hullo, Jeff," and he growled, "Hullo, Bert," that high, cracked, aggressive voice of his didn't come quavering and squeaking out of the phone so that you had to hold the receiver two feet away. There was another sign. When I said, "You know why I've called up," he didn't do what he usually does when you introduce a pertinent question at first. That is, he'll usually say, "Fine day, ain't it?" and pretend to go doddering off without understanding, until you say, "Look here, you blasted old jackass, wake up out of that and answer me." Then he says, "Ah, that's better," in a normal tone, and brightens up and gets to business.

It was a bit of a shock when I heard him mutter:

"Uh-huh. I sort of thought you'd be ringing up." There was so long a pause that I thought the wire had gone dead. "It's a dirty business, Bert. You busy?"

"I'm always busy."

"Well, I was only thinking—if you could come round here about two o'clock. . . . I'm at the museum.

189

The landlady of this fellow Penderel got in touch with me, and says she's got important information. It's bad, Bert. It's pretty bad."

And for the first time since I've known him, he sounded like an old man.

14

The Secret Of The Cookery-Book

It was past two o'clock when I got round to the museum. My lunch had disagreed with me, which it doesn't usually, and my shoes were too tight. Meantime, the only fresh news was the fact that Illingworth's finger-prints tallied with all those found inside the lift; the lift hadn't been used for some time, and they were the only prints there; so that part of the old boy's story was all right. I had put Hadley officially in charge of the case, and given him the reports. Also, June or no June, the day had gone rainy and raw as October.

The museum doors were shut, of course, but there was a black mushroom growth of umbrellas sprouting round 'em. I had the satisfaction of bashing a couple before I got through to the constable on duty; the doors were opened by Warburton—that's Jeff's day-attendant—who is as much of a dignified sergeant-major as Pruen isn't.

Although I had been inside the place a few times before, I knew it better from Carruthers' and Illingworth's descriptions than from anything I remembered on my own. It all had a queer familiar look with that moonlight effect on it, even to the way the shafts of the coaches stuck out and the green-and-white tiled roof was reflected in places on the glass cases down the middle; though I didn't suppose I had been wandering about it in a dream. They told me Jeff was back in the curator's room, alone.

It was pretty shadowy in the curator's room. Jeff hadn't turned on any lights, and the only light came through the window in the lavatory, where the rain was splashing because the window was open. But I could make out a big handsome room. Behind a mahogany desk, Jeff sat tilted back in a swivel-chair with his big heavy-leather boots propped on the edge. He was looking towards the window; he didn't move, and there was an inch of crooked ash standing out on the cigarette stuck under his white moustaches. The grey light showed the hollows in his temples and a queer blank look in his eyes. He didn't turn round; he only creaked his boots a little and nodded at a chair. With all his money, Jeff would never patronise anybody but the fifty-shilling tailors; not because he was mean, which he wasn't, but because he genuinely detested expensive clothes.

I sat down, and we listened to the rain splash for a minute or two.

"We've come a long way, Bert," says he.

And I remember nodding my head and saying, "Aye," exactly as though we'd been in Somerset years ago; although I hadn't thought of using that word for just as many years.

"I was just sittin' here thinking," muttered Jeff, in

192

an argumentative sort of way. "Beer used to be five-pence a quart, and you could get it warm, with nut-meg in it. *Haec olim* something or other. But now here're you Assistant-Commissioner of Police, with a title and all. . . . And you're no policeman, Bert."

"And you're no business man, if it comes to that," I said, "but you're a millionaire just the same."

"Ah," agreed Jeff, considering this.

He turned round a little, so that the ash spilled off his cigarette; he began brushing his hands up and down the hollows in his temples, and blinking as though he couldn't see very well. You know the bleary look which people accustomed to wearing glasses have when they take the glasses off? He had that look under his brushing hands.

"I suppose you know, or maybe you don't," I went on, "everything that happened in this place last night. A fellow by the name of William Augustus Illingworth dropped into my office this morning, and told me all about it."

"I know all about it too," grunted Jeff, cursing be-hind his teeth. "Miriam and Jerry told me this morn-ing. I suppose they decided they had to. They think they're going to get into a lot of trouble; and I rubbed it in when I told 'em they would."

"As a matter of fact, Jeff, they all will. The inquest will be held day after tomorrow, and the coroner is going to cut up rough when he hears about that fool masquerade. . . ."

Jeff sat up. Any mention of authority, especially po-lice authority, is to him like throwing a pail of water over a bad-tempered dog. He bristled again. I saw with a good deal of pleasure that he would probably take the side of these kids, and not bite them particu-larly hard, just to spite the police.

"Oh, he will, will he?" asked Jeff. "The coroner will cut up rough, will he? Who is the coroner? What's his name?"

"Never mind that for a minute. Have you got it through your head that one of that crowd in the museum last night killed this man Penderel?"

"Uh-huh. Yes," answered Jeff slowly, "I have. I don't suppose anything can be done to hush it up, can it? Under the circumstances. . . ."

"What circumstances?"

Again he brushed his hands slowly up and down the sides of his face, but he did not answer.

"Look here, Jeff: has it anything to do with Miriam?"

"Yes."

"Well? Did she know Penderel?"

"Yes. . . . In a few minutes there'll be somebody here who wants to see me. It's Penderel's landlady; or, from what I could understand, the woman who's been keeping him. I got her name and address. 'Mrs. Anna Reilly, Crown and Dragon public-house, Lant Street, Borough.' Then we'll see what we're goin' to see. . . . Also I told the whole crowd of the others, Miriam, Jerry, Holmes—damn him—Baxter, the Kirkton girl, her friend Butler, and Pruen (dash my buttons, Bert!" says Jeff, with the first squeaky roar of surprise I'd heard out of him, "dash my buttons, I didn't think old Pruen had it in him!); I've told 'em all to be here for you to talk to. You might go a little easy on 'em. . . . You know, dash my buttons, I'd have given half a crown to have seen Illingworth wearing these whiskers, I would for a fact. . . ."

"That's a little better," I told him. "Now about this Illingworth affair and your part in it. . . ."

"*My* part in it?"

"Look here, you old jackass, don't you realise it was

you who brought Illingworth walking into the middle of it and let the whole thing splash out? That's what's caused the trouble. If it's anybody's fault, it's yours. Yesterday afternoon you sent him a telegram from Southampton, didn't you?"

"Uh-huh. By George!" says Jeff, suddenly vibrating with all his arms and legs at once, exactly as though you'd pulled the string on a jumping-jack. "I believe I did, at that."

"You know damn well you did. All right. You sent him that telegram after Holmes had already phoned Illingworth's hotel not to come here last night, and *you* told him to be here at ten-thirty. All right. Where were you? What happened to you? Didn't you get back to town after all?"

Jeff reflected.

"Uh-huh. Oh, yes, I got back to town," he replied quite simply. "I was buyin' a restaurant."

If you knew him, boys, you'd know that this *non-sequitur* was entirely natural, but to have to live with or near a fellow like that for very long would drive strong men to the nearest public-house. Along different lines he and Illingworth were two of a kind. If they owned this museum together, half the exhibits would be broken and the other half wouldn't be here. It was always what worried the kids: they never knew which way he would turn, or whether he would be smiles or claws.

I said: "You were buying a restaurant. Excellent. And what do you think you want with a restaurant? Was it a sudden impulse to rush out and buy a restaurant, or did you just want to play a joke on Illingworth?"

He looked straight at me. "Bert," he says, "there's method in every bit of madness I ever had, or we wouldn't be sitting here right now. And buying that restaurant, I begin to feel, was a good bit of madness, though I didn't think of it just then. . . . I get funny ideas sometimes. And this was an impulse. You know. I was comin' back on the train from Southampton. At the last minute I decided not to ride with the van. It hurts my behind. And on the train I met an old friend of mine, chap named Shattu from the Zagros near Shíráz, and a Greek friend of his named Aguinopopolos. . . ."

"Restaurant-keepers?"

"Yes. They'd opened a place in Soho, featuring Asiatic cooking. But it was on its last legs because they said nobody knew artistry. Now I'm very fond of that kind of grub; I've been eatin' it for years. (You ever taste any Shíráz wines, or the port that the Jews and Armenians make at Ispahan? No, you wouldn't, you *bourgeois*.) So I said, 'Well, I'll patronise the place. . . . No, dash my buttons, look here!' I said, 'I'll buy the place or put up enough of the ready so's you can keep afloat.' I thought they'd go delirious. Shattu said, 'This must be celebrated. You come along to the restaurant tonight and with my own hands I cook you such a banquet—oi!' And I was hungry, Bert. . . ."

"You're telling me you forgot about Illingworth?"

"Uh-huh," responded Jeff, sniffing. "We got to Waterloo about nine o'clock and climbed into a cab, and they were singin' folk-songs—that made the goddam placid crowd jump, you can bet, to see somebody show real exuberance!" squeaked Jeff, with a whack of pleasure on the desk. "We went up to this restaurant. What with one thing and another, discussin' new plans and the like. . . . They'd named this place The Graeco-Persian Restaurant, or some such fool thing. BAH! I said, 'That's no way to do business,' I said. 'You take a great big electric sign, a whacking great thing as big as you can buy, with SHATTU OF SOHO on it, and you plaster it smack up over the place; and you get some snakes in glass jars and put 'em inside....'" He stopped, grunted, and blew his nose on a big handkerchief. "Ah, never mind. What with one thing and another, I didn't get home until two o'clock."

"So you can console yourself," I said, "that this business here is partly your fault."

He got up and walked round the room. He looked a little queer and drawn in the face, and the rain kept splashing outside.

"I could have had a lot of fun with that restaurant," said Jeff abruptly.

"What do you mean, you could have had?"

"Oh, nothing. I'll be goin' back East when this business blows over, and if Miriam—" He put his hands together, cracked the joints hard, and looked up. "Was there anything you wanted to ask, Bert? Anything important?"

"Maybe. For instance, what do you know about this fellow Mannering, who seems to be engaged to Miriam?"

He whirled round. "Why the hell have you got to keep harping on Miriam? *I* don't know anything about Mannering; I mean I haven't met him. Seems like a decent lad, in spite of his lying. I asked you if there was anything important."

Under cover of the desk I got out Popkins' infernal list and gave a quick look at it.

"There is one thing," I suggested. "Among the people who were here last night, is there anybody who is, or has been, a medical student?"

That took him a little off balance. Jeff hates anything he can't understand, and this got him. He stood moving his wrinkles and wrinkling his moustaches like some sort of freak.

"Eh?" he muttered. "Here, what's the game? Medical student! Not that I know of. Miriam never did anything except maybe get chucked out of posh schools. Jerry started in to study electrical engineering, because I told him he damn well *should*. Holmes is nothing but books through and through, books and politeness; he's been a schoolmaster, but never a medical student. Baxter was a no-good with too much money until Abbsley clamped down on him—ho, ho! Dick Butler writes a lot of fool adventure stuff that he don't know anything about. Hold on a bit!" He stopped. "I believe they have all got a friend, name of Gilbert Randall, who is a medical student somewhere, but I dunno anything much about him."

"What do you know about the Kirkton girl?"

He puffed out his cheeks.

"Not much. She's old Major Kirkton's brat, from out in the end of nowhere. Not a bad sort of girl," grunted Jeff, chuckling slyly and tapping the side of his nose. "She's got the devil in her and, my eye, does she like to drink! She's the only one who's got the gumption to sauce me to my face, and that's why I like her. She's stayin' at our place now." He brooded. "She's devilish fond of Butler, and he's not inclined to run from her; which is so-so."

There was a knock at the door, and Jeff jumped round with a kind of yell.

"A Mrs. Reilly is here, sir," said the voice of Warburton, the day-attendant. "She said she had an appointment."

"Send her in," said Jeff in a funny voice. He looked at me. "Sit tight, Bert, and give me a hand with this if I need any help. I don't think I will. But I warn you,

I'm not usin' any kid gloves."

He switched on the centre lights, which made me blink; then he sat down behind the desk, leaning forward with his hands folded on it. He looked like an old ghost, except that he was burnt lean and reddish; and every time his little black eyes winked they seemed to twitch his moustaches. And then in with a flourish came Mrs. Anna Reilly.

I never saw such a big fur-piece round any woman's neck. It was black, with a lot of tails, and it seemed to go up and circle her head round like one of those Elizabethan back-collars. She was a handsome but rather dumpy woman in the late thirties or early forties; her skin looked as hard as a prize-fighter's, and she swung when she tripped—if you understand me. She wore one of those brownish-yellow tailored suits, with bright flesh-coloured stockings and heels high enough for a toe-dance. There were three diamonds on her left hand, which looked scrubbed; maybe the diamonds were what gave her such a blaze all over. What you noticed was the face looking and wagging out of that neck-piece: square, brunette, painted like a circus poster and shooting out smiling magnetic rays all over the room.

That was what you noticed—the magnetic rays, which blended with gold gleams in her teeth. If it hadn't been for those gold gleams in her teeth I'd have thought her a devilish fine figure of a woman, for I like Juno types. And then there was her voice, which was so cultured it pained you.

"Mr. Wade?" she said, "I've called with reference to poor dear Raymond."

Having swept the room with magnetic rays as though she were fumigating it, and made the proper impression on Jeff, she pulled a sad face. She even got out a handkerchief from her bag and rubbed some mascara from the corner of her eye. But I noticed that she was looking very hard and thoughtfully at me.

"Siddown," says Jeff in his foggiest tone. "Rotten day, ain't it? Who's poor dear Raymond?"

"But surely you understand—oh, by the way, Mr. Wade," she broke off, shooting smiling rays at me, "I presume this is your solicitor?"

"Well, as it happens, he is," said Jeff. "But how'd you guess that? What made you think there'd be a solicitor here?"

She laughed—musically. She sat down in a chair with a gesture like a parachute coming to ground.

"Now we're all nice and comfy," said Mrs. Reilly, stripping off her gloves (and if there's one word in the world I hate and want to hit the person who uses, it's "comfy"!). "I think we all understand each other, don't we? Ha, ha, ha. But what a perfectly charming room!"

Jeff said: "Charming room be beggared. Who are you, and what do you want?"

That didn't jar her at all, though the rays hardened a little. "How odd!" she said. "I thought—I am Mrs. Reilly, of course. My late husband was the owner of The Crown and Dragon Inn, and I inherited the ownership from him."

"Pub, hey? It's a good business. You look prosperous."

"Looks are often deceptive, Mr. Wade. Even yours may be, about one thing or another. I was saying: I reside over the premises of The Crown and Dragon. And I believe I am the *only* person in London who knew Raymond Penderel, the poor lad who was killed in this perfectly fascinating museum last night. He has been residing at my home, as a paying guest, for three months or so . . ."

"Uh-huh. Did he pay?"

"He had a terrible time of it, poor fellow," she went on in a louder voice. "And he used to tell me all his troubles—so distangay, Raymond was! with such an air! So handsome, too!" The woman simpered; I swear she did. "Only last night, just before he came here, I helped him put on his costume and his make-up for what he was going to do here. Do you know, I believe the police have some of my property even now? Raymond borrowed a cookery-book from me."

It was plain that she hadn't hoped to ring a bull's-eye or produce any sensation with this remark, but she did.

"He borrowed—" I said, and got up. "A cookery-book. Why?"

"But didn't you know that?" asked Mrs. Reilly, with her merry little laugh, wagging her head round and raising and lowering her hands in her lap. "But how odd! I thought you would have known. . . . You see, Raymond was to have played the part of a very eeroo-dite gentleman, a professor, I believe. When Raymond went yesterday afternoon and met the other gentleman who was to have instructed him in his part —a Mr. Butler, I think—Mr. Butler told him that the professor was *never* seen anywhere without a certain book in his pocket or his hand. I've forgotten the book (something to do with Calcutta, I believe). But Raymond said to me, 'Come, acushla,' he said, 'I believe in realism. We haven't the money to buy any real book like that; but then I shan't have to open it, shall I?—so what have you here in your bookcase that would *look* like a book of that sort from the outside?' So we looked over my little bookcase and the only thing we could find was that cookery-book which my dear mother-in-law stoutly bound for me when I was married. . . ."

Stung.

I was not so much annoyed because I hadn't seen it before, although I should have seen it, as that the thing was so simple. Carruthers had described the rubbed calfskin of that book, the book that had been chosen because of its binding. When he saw it lying face down on the museum floor, he thought at first there were mysterious things inside, until he looked at the contents. That was what it was intended to convey. It was a dummy book, and it had made dummies of us. It meant nothing.

One more point could now be scratched off the list of questions Popkins had drawn up. I glanced over at Jeff, who was raising and lowering the fingers of his clenched hands.

"Uh-huh," he murmured vaguely. "You have to look at the outsides of things sometimes. That's what you fellows forget. Sometimes you have to stop grubbing the dustbin and go round to take a long, novel, refreshed squint at the front of the house. But what about it? Why waste my time, Mrs. Umum? Why not go to the police? *I'm* not interested in cookery-books. Why come here?"

Mrs. Reilly's eyes had assumed a hard, pleasant brilliance.

"My dear Mr. Wade! Of course not! But I told you a moment ago that Raymond was a paying guest, and you quite naturally asked, Did he pay? But that's just the point, you see. He didn't. He owes me—it's horrible to be so mercenary, isn't it? But then one must live!—he owes me nearly three months' board and lodgings."

"You don't say so now? You want me to pay his board and lodging?"

Her forehead clouded. She wiggled the toe of one shoe and studied it.

"Well—I thought you might be interested at least in claiming his belongings, considering the close family connexion. . . ."

"Close family connexion?"

"Yes. He—he married your daughter, didn't he?"

Jeff, who had been blinking across at the window, now turned on her such a broad and fishy and diabolical grin that I could be pretty sure that this at least wasn't true. Jeff cackled a little. She faced him with wide-open innocent eyes under the circus paint. But she seemed to breathe hard.

"So," said Jeff. "Mrs. Umph, I don't know where you picked up such ruddy rot. But you can take it from me, right here and now, that my daughter ain't married. And in any case she'd never have married anybody like Penderel, whoever he is."

Mrs. Reilly uprose with a little scream. Her breathing had quickened, and her eyes were bright.

"But—this is awful! Oh, how frightfully awful! I'm sure I never thought or I shouldn't have mentioned—You see, she had a child by him."

15

The Secret From Iraq

Jeff had left himself wide open for the punch. She had delayed it, and feinted, and then let him have one of the hardest jolts I ever saw a man take. He didn't move a muscle, except in his face, but I thought his face was going to burst. He was not used to self-control; still he sat there with his wrinkled eyelids moving up and down, and breathing slowly.

"I underestimated you," he said. "All right. You asked for it. You'll get it."

Mrs. Reilly leaned over.

'Stow your gab, grandpop," she said in a flat voice. "It's true, and you know it as well as I do. And it's *rather* a dark-skinned brat, you know."

She was a very hard hitter, but she left the rough-and-tumble tactics after just those words, thrown out in an undertone. Once again she became all gold-toothed smiles and magnetic rays of charm.

"But perhaps I'd better tell you. The child, a boy,

was born a little over six months ago—on the ninth of January, to be exact—at a very private nursing-home in Cairo. You knew about it; you had your daughter sent there because her health was bad, and you didn't dare have an abortion performed. It was awfully thoughtful of you.

"Poor Raymond wanted marriage; it was dreadful to break his heart like that, wasn't it? When you heard of it (I mean the prospective heir), which was rather late, you sent her from Iraq to Egypt, and you put about a false report that she had gone home. Raymond was frantic. He tried to get information from Miss Kirkton—whose company he had also enjoyed, though without such concrete results—but she had gone with your daughter. Naturally Raymond wanted to follow her to England, but he had no money. It took him a very long time to scrape up some, and I'm sure I don't know how the poor boy did it, because *I never* can," she smiled breathlessly, "and four months ago he did get here. To find what? That you had tricked him and that she wasn't here after all. Oh, my!"

Jeff was sitting bolt upright, looking steadily at her and smiling a little; it seemed to upset her. Her voice went up a couple of notes.

"*Now* are you interested, dear Mr. Wade?"

"I might be. Go on."

"And Raymond only learned the truth of the matter from a friend of his, and he couldn't write because he didn't know the address. But of course he would insist on seeing his son, and having him legitimatised!... Then he learned that his wife by the law of God," breathed Mrs. Reilly, lifting her hand piously and giving him a kind of giggling glare, "was really coming home. Oh, my—You didn't know Penderel was really in England, did you?"

205

"Didn't I?" said Jeff casually. "Who is this fellow Penderel? You're telling the story, such as it is."

"You didn't think so, but you were taking no chances."

"No?"

"No. First sending her to a relative for over two weeks—so that Raymond, the poor distracted husband, didn't know that address either—and then, when you'd come back, bringing her home not very long ago—fenced round—and fenced round—dear, dear, dear! You've got a very faithful butler, haven't you, who would ward off letters or phone-calls? But, really, it wasn't necessary. For, just before *she* got back to town from the relatives wasn't it *Raymond* who had to leave town on an engagement? And Raymond was a very wise lad, who didn't believe in letting the pennies slip when the pounds were sure if he waited for 'em. He didn't get back until the day before yesterday. So what did you and Miriam think? You thought he wasn't in London at all; now didn't you? Since, of course, if he had been, he'd have turned up to exercise his charm again or else to——"

"Or else to——?" prompted Jeff patiently. He was waiting.

"Confess, confess, confess!" cried Mrs. Reilly, as though she were playing a very arch cross-questioning game. It wasn't a pretty sight. "You let her walk free again because she was safe now. And she was so *very* anxious to forget nasty Cairo. Child with a nurse. All past. So very unpleasant, but all past now. . . . But you can't guard her petticoats, grandpop," snapped Mrs. Reilly, with sudden venom and a dart forward. "Does this deep experience affect her, and the tender touch of—Dear me, no! She really does forget when she sails

206

away from the East on the great big ship and meets another man. Completely."

Jeff got up slowly behind the desk.

"What did Penderel want? Money?"

"I'm really afraid he did," tittered Mrs. Reilly, assuming a shocked air. "He was an awful person at times. Wasn't it astonishing chance—almost Providence, you might say—that in the little game last night the one man in all London who wished to meet his wife-before-God should be picked to meet her?"

"And what do *you* want? Money?"

I had been waiting for this. I was aching to break loose and wipe the floor with her; but it wouldn't do to act too soon. She looked at us with wide-open eyes. Her shocked expression grew.

"Money? Good heavens and gracious, no! That would be blackmail, wouldn't it? Oh, no, no, no; you misunderstand me! Really, I don't want a penny. I don't threaten to tell anything or say anything. . . ."

"Good," said Jeff. "There's the door. Get out."

"With pleasure, grandpop," she giggled, beaming at him but breathing hard again. "You see, anything I say could be said before a whole bench of judges, as your solicitor will tell you. Really, all I wanted to do was make sure that you were the right person (or Miriam was) to hand over his luggage to, now that he's dead. But of course if the girl's not married to him and can show no claim——"

She was all patting and bustling in an eager preparing to leave while she went on:

"You see, the poor fellow never paid me a penny for his board and lodgings. A dozen people can tell you that; where are his receipts? So, as a result, his luggage—and everything in it—becomes my property until the bill is paid. You can't get around that. I believe—I'm not sure, but I believe—there are some letters in his suit-case written by our Miriam when she learned she was *on-sant*. I don't know and they don't interest me. But I do know that I shall be forced to keep his luggage until somebody pays his bill."

Jeff looked at her in a detached kind of way.

"You ought to go far," he announced, "before you land in gaol. . . . How much is his bill?"

"We-el, now," said Mrs. Reilly, pursing her very red lips and putting her head on one side, "it'll be rather high, I'm afraid. *Rather* high. Three months, you see, and Raymond was an awfully hearty eater. But I haven't quite totalled up the full sum, except that it'll be *rather* high. If you'd care to call round one day soon I'll have the accounting. Meantime, not the police or anybody else can take a single thing that belongs to him out of the house; that's the law, you know, and even the police have to respect it sometimes. Good day, gentlemen. *So* glad to have had the pleasure of your acquaintance."

"Mrs. Reilly," says Jeff, "did you ever hear of the Duke of Wellington? Do you know what he said in a case like this?"

"No, and I don't know what Gladstone said in 1876 either," says Mrs. Reilly coolly. "But I've heard of Waterloo, and this is yours."

"He said, 'Publish and be damned,'" answered Jeff, without batting an eyelid. "That's what I say to you now. And whether you've let yourself in for a blackmail charge or not, I'm going to institute one just the same. This is the Assistant-Commissioner of Police. Have a go at her, Bert."

I did have a go at her, and I put the fear of God into that woman. I beat her this way, I beat her that way (figuratively, that is), I beat her into every shape known to geometry. She collapsed in hysterics presently, but she was quite right about having made no blackmail threat—and she knew it. That was one thing she stuck to; it was a neat trick. But I didn't want to carry the business too far, because there was still a way out for us if she thought she was still keeping within the law.

Our people would simply "borrow," not take, the luggage for examination in a murder case. In case she had hidden the letters anywhere, a search-warrant would dig them out to be examined as part of his property. It would be a very long examination. Besides, though I'm not a lawyer, that part about her legal rights in the matter of the luggage struck me as a bit fishy. According to what she had trumpeted to everybody, Penderel had been a "paying guest," not a lodger. Therefore there was no signing of lodgers' book, no written agreement, no receipts; the person was a guest. Therefore the landlady couldn't hold the guest's baggage after his death—if the next of kin claimed it. Somebody had said that Penderel had a Persian mother in Iraq. While we hold the luggage for examination, Jeff gets in touch with a solicitor there, who gets in touch with the mother, and obtains authority to salvage poor son's possessions, appointing Jeff as representative. Jeff comes to us and presents his credentials. "Good," we say, "here you are." "But he owes me money!" screams Mrs. Reilly. "All right," says Jeff, "here's fifty pounds. If you think he owed you more, go to court and sue me for the value of a couple of suit-cases."

So I ended by speaking fairly soothing words to Mrs. Reilly, who went away in a tearfully hopeful mood. Then I shut the door and explained matters to Jeff, whose hands were shaking now and who was as dirty-pale as his own collar.

"Thank God for that," says Jeff. He had to sit down.
"You are useful sometimes. Yes, he's got a mother in
Iraq; I've heard of her. I was about at the end of my
rope, Bert, and I was bluffing. Do you think it'll
work?"

"We'll make it work. Brace up now and listen! Those
letters in themselves, if there are letters, don't amount
to two hoots . . ."

"Oh, don't you think so?" sneered Jeff. "As it happens, I do."

"Don't start that line of talk now. I mean they don't
matter, since this whole business is coming OUT. It'll
be splashed everywhere, it'll come out sooner or later
unless a miracle happens. Let's face the facts. Considered as a motive for killing Penderel, it's terrific. That
is——"

I thought Jeff was going to smash something, just to
get the hysteria off his chest. He was in one of those
cold moods when a man very deliberately tries to turn
a chair to matchwood.

"That is," I added, "if it's true. Is it?"

"Yes, of course it's true. I didn't know whether to
murder the wench or what to do. I—I still don't. You
see, I'm not broad-minded like people nowadays, but
still I wouldn't have minded if it had been anybody
else but this Penderel. You didn't know him, Bert. He
was the sort who calls a woman 'dear lady,' and makes
a flourish when he kisses her hand, and all the time
he's got his eye on her diamond rings. Uh-huh. I've
got all the sympathy in the world for two people who
can't keep away from each other, but this kind of
thing—especially when it's your own daughter—
Reilly was right about one thing. I didn't know the

man was within a thousand miles of London, and neither did Miriam."

"Now think! Here's the next and most important question. How many people know about the affair—the child, I mean?"

"That's what I don't know! Dammit, can't you get anything through your head? The Kirkton girl does, of course. So far as I know, nobody else. But as I say, you can't tell. I've spent thousands to hush it up, but these things leak out. I can never tell what the kids are thinking. . . ."

"Does Jerry know?"

"Humph. He might. But he was never very close to Miriam, and he wasn't out in the bad lands, so he didn't hear through me or her. I doubt it, but still he might have heard. They all may know there was *something* wrong. I doubt whether they knew about Penderel by name."

"Baxter or Mannering?"

Jeff grinned sourly. "I'd take a little bet that Mannering doesn't know, wouldn't you? Baxter. Humph. N-no, although he was in Cairo. Secret agents hidin' in a cellar weren't anything to the precautions I took. My God, Bert, but it's a mess! Out of the thousands of actors in London they had to pick the one——!"

"Well, it's not as queer as all that; their requirements were pretty unusual to give a theatrical agency. Still, the point is this: How many of those people, if they did find Penderel hanging about attempting blackmail, would have or might have killed him?"

Jeff gave a jeering cackle. "Don't you think I've been poundin' my head to powder to decide that? *I* would, for one. Jerry would. Baxter would. Mannering—I dunno; strong question. Miriam herself—h'm. Hard to tell about her. Sometimes guts, sometimes as weak as toast in water; funny wench. Dick Butler's allegiance wouldn't be as strong, because he's tied up with Harriet. How should I know?" He fiddled with his chin a minute. "Look here, Bert; you don't suppose they could ALL have been tied up in it, do you? Whole thing a frame-up and planned from the beginning like? I read a good story like that once. Thirteen people, and ALL of 'em had a crack at the dead man."

"Nonsense," I said with reason. "Or they wouldn't have gone about it in such a fool way. No. One person did that murder, and it's a mess whichever one it turns out to be."

Jeff walked drearily up and down, and the rain kept on splashing through the window.

He said: "All right. What do we do now? I s'pose it's no good asking whether you can hush it up altogether, but as much as you can——?"

The first thing was to go to work on the actual events between ten-forty-five and eleven, and see whether we could eliminate anybody. It was a question of going straight to the point, boys: the point being Pruen first of all. Pruen, according to Illingworth, had the whole stretch of the museum under his eye all the time. Right! Pruen had already arrived, ahead of the others; he was out in the hall talking to Warburton now. I decided that it wasn't best for Jeff to be present during the interview. That would only lead to trouble, and probably make Pruen lie even more than he was likely to do naturally. Also, we decided that as yet we wouldn't mention Mrs. Reilly to anybody, or try to find out whether anybody else knew what she knew: the epidemic of lying would become more feverish.

Before Pruen came in, I took out Popkins' infernal list, spread it out on the desk, and sat down to study it. Questions answered? Yes, a few. Of eleven points, we now had reasonably satisfactory answers to four of them: numbers 6, 7, 8, and 10. In 6 my theory, as to why Miriam had called up Harriet in a disguised voice after she saw the corpse had been pretty thunderingly verified. Number 7, about the possible meaning of the cookery-book, was now clear. So was number 8, the question about Jeff Wade's telegram from Southampton, and why he hadn't come to the museum. The reply to number 10—has anybody been a medical student?—was no. Which, as you will shrewdly point out, left us with 1 to 5, 9 and 11. Well?

I got up and shut that window in the lavatory, for the place was chilly. The bright lights were burning now, showing up all the frippery of rugs and Moorish fretwork, and particularly uninteresting framed photographs of ruins. Jeff likes plenty of colour about him, even to red leather chairs. There was no sign of last night's party except one pane of glass gone from the door in the lift and Green's *Practical Arabic Grammar* on the desk. I concealed my question-list in the grammar. Then Pruen came sidling in.

A snuffy-looking specimen Pruen was. I hadn't seen him for a long time; he was a little bonier than I remembered, his face more mottled and his eyes more watery behind the Woolworth glasses—he kept taking off the glasses to wipe his eyes—but it was the first time I had seen him out of uniform, and I never knew he had a bald head. Also, he kept snuffing. He was not at all hostile, for he was frightened to jumpiness. I got him into a chair, where his knees stuck out at angles and his head hung down.

Then I said: "Are you going to lie to me?"

"No, sir!" (He was as roopy as Illingworth, and I thought he was going to jump out of the chair.)

"I don't say anything about yourself, but you know the whole Wade family will be for it if you do lie?"

"You're 'is friend," says Pruen simply. "I'll tell you the truth."

"Who killed Penderel?"

"Strike me dead, I don't know!" says he, with a gesture like a high tragedian. "Strike me dead as I sit in this chair, I didn't even know 'e was dead until—you know, sir. That inspector came."

"Ever hear of Penderel before now? Do you know who he is?"

"No, sir. _I_ don't know the bleeder. _They_ don't know 'im. So why should anybody want to kill him? I ask you, sir?"

"You understand I know everything about the game you people were playing here last night. Mr. Wade told you, didn't he? You don't deny that part of it, do you?"

"Not likely," he answered candidly. There was the look of a far-off grin hanging about somewhere. "Spirit, I call it. Spirit!"

"Is it true that you were on guard at the front doors all last evening?"

He was emphatic. "All last evening, sir, including before the museum closed. After it closed, I was there from ten minutes past ten, or thereabouts, until just on eleven. Just on eleven was when that loopy old bloke—you know, sir; thought 'e was Wallace Beery; and, if you ask me, '_e's_ the one who done it—he came a-roaring out of the lift! Out 'e goes through the lavatory window. . . . Coo! You know the rest. We dragged him down the coal-hole. Then Mr. Holmes says, ''Ere! we've got to get out of this, in case the coppers come.' About the loony, of course. But first Mr. Baxter had to go outside and climb back in through that window"—

he pointed—"so they could unlock the door that old Colney Hatch had locked and get their coats and 'ats from the closet in this room."

He was breathing hard. I said:

"Never mind that for a minute. You start in and tell me everything that happened last night; everything, understand?"

"Right you are, sir. And 'ere it is." He drew a deep breath and plunged. "Last night, you see, I kept the doors open, seven to ten, doing business just as usual——"

"Wait. Why were you so conscientious about keeping it open last night, when the big doings were scheduled? Would it have mattered?"

"Would it have mattered?" demanded Pruen, with an offended yelp. "'Ere, sir! Don't you know 'ow *popular* this place of ours is, especially with the kids being taken round by their schools or their elders? I ask you: do you know a kid who could resist the Gallery of Bazaars, now? Or the Eight Paradises, that's a reconstruction of a sultan's palace? *Do* they eat it up?" (To tell you the truth, I hadn't thought much about this. I rather took it for granted that nobody went to museums, but I could see the force of this.) "This 'ere place," said Pruen, with dark pride, "ain't the National Gallery, you know. Popular? I ask you again, sir: do you think, knowing Mr. Wade, that 'e'd keep the place open one minute if it didn't draw people? Look at the Bazaars, or the Eight Paradises! Barnum and Bailey couldn't 'a' done it better. He's a real showman, Mr. Wade is. We wanted to get a big electric sign, and we'd 'a' done it if they'd let us. And a Hall of Mirrors too!—*I'd* have charged admission. Popular!"

"All right. How was business last night?"

"Lovely. Friday night, d'ye see, sir—no school next

day. Lovely! That's why we 'ad to keep open. One exception to the rule, of course. Usually three charladies come in every night, ten sharp, to clean up the place. Only not last night. They were told not to."

"Go on."

Another deep breath. "Well, sir, the others—Miss Miriam, Miss Kirkton, Mr. Jerry, and the rest—they come 'ere about," he threw back his head and wrinkled up his forehead in agonised thought; he was getting so excited that he forgot his fear, "they come 'ere about ten. Yes, just about ten. They come in by the back door, because Miss Miriam's got a key. Right! The ones who had to dress up for their parts, Mr. Baxter and Mr. Butler, they'd got dressed at Mr. 'olmes's flat. Mr. Jerry, who was just going to wear wig and moustache and whiskers (thought I was against him wearing the whiskers) wore his ordinary clothes and was going to put the whiskers on in 'ere. When they got 'ere, they came straight to this room and waited for me to close the museum."

"When did you close it?"

He reflected. "Ten minutes past ten, nearabouts. Bit difficult to get some of 'em out, d'ye see, sir. And then——"

"And then, what?"

He was squirming about in his chair, squeezing up his face and hammering softly on the arm of the chair.

"Cor, I've just thought of something! 'Ere, sir, this is new! Just you wait a bit, till I get it in order. . . .

"Now, then. Ten minutes past ten, I shut the doors and bolted 'em. Then I came down to this room—they was all in 'ere—and give 'em the wire that everything's clear. Mr. Butler was walking about pretty fierce. 'Where's that actor bloke from the agency?' he asks me. 'The rest of us has just been over our parts; where's that chap from the agency? Hasn't he turned up yet?' That's what Mr. Butler says to me."

"What time was the actor supposed to get here?"

"Which," replied Pruen, pointing at me triumphantly, "was the next thing Mr. Butler said. Mr. Butler said, 'I told him to be here as soon after ten as he could manage.' Then Mr. Holmes, who was sitting over there on the typewriter-desk and looking a bit uneasy-like—he was the luke-warmest of the lot—'e says, 'We shall look most awful fools if this doesn't come off right; where do you suppose the fellow is?'

"And Mr. Jerry, who was sitting with 'is feet up on the desk imitating Mr. Wade, says, 'Keep your shirts on; it's not quite fifteen minutes past ten yet. What about the coffin?'—I say, sir, do you want me to tell as *much* as this? As much of details, like?"

"Yes."

"Right you are," agreed Pruen, and sighed with something like pleasure. "As the coffin, you see, they were using a silver-chest from one of the big glass cases upstairs. They hadn't taken it out, or got it packed up in a packing-case yet, becos I didn't want 'em to disarrange the exhibits before the museum closed. . . . Of course, d'ye see, sir, they 'ad to sneak the Persian costume for Mr. Baxter in the afternoon, just to see whether it would fit him; fine business if it *wouldn't!* . . . But the coffin wasn't packed. I'd already, early in the evening, taken a packing-case upstairs for 'em. And a sackful of sawdust from Mr. Wade's workshop down in the cellar. And some sealing-wax to make it look posh.

"So they decided that while Mr. Jerry was putting on his whiskers and make-up, with Miss Miriam and

Miss Kirkton helping him, Mr. Butler and Mr. 'olmes should go upstairs and get the case ready. Mr. Sam Baxter, he wouldn't give a hand with that. He said 'e'd got in to fancy clothes and dyes on his face, and he wasn't going to go mucking 'em about with sawdust. So Mr. Baxter went into the Gallery of Bazaars, and walked up and down muttering lines to himself." Pruen winked. "Not such a good actor, Mr. Baxter ain't—cor! Only a few little bits to say, too—done better meself. . . .

"They all came out into the hall before they separated. Mr. 'olmes unlocked the glass case where the *khanjar* was—that dagger, sir—and then 'e takes a black false moustache out of his pocket, and tries to hand 'em both to Mr. Baxter. 'These are yours,' says he, 'take 'em, Sam, before you forget 'em.' But Mr. Baxter says, all in a loud voice, as though they'd bite him, 'Take 'em away!' says Mr. Baxter, 'I don't want 'em yet; I'm not a-going to walk about on a slippery floor with that thing stuck in my belt—not until the proper time. Take 'em away until the proper time.'

"So Mr. 'olmes takes the *khanjar* and the moustache, and walks back and puts them down on the lowest step of the staircase. 'There they are,' says he, 'where they can't be missed.'

"Then, as I say, they separated. Mr. Butler and Mr. Holmes went upstairs. The two young ladies went to help Mr. Jerry put his whiskers on. Mr. Baxter came up to the Gallery of Bazaars to walk about and mutter. And me? I walked straight down to the chair by the front doors, and I didn't stir from there the rest of the time. . . . The time then, sir, would 'a' been just about fifteen minutes past ten."

"Pruen," I said, "who stole that dagger? Who picked it up?"

He huddled himself together, took a deep breath and then looked up with wide-open eyes.

"Strike me dead, sir," says he, "but I haven't got the least idea."

16

First Appearance of An Actor

And there was that little blotched-face worm, leaning forward in the chair with his hands clasped; his head a little on one shoulder and his neck wrinkled round; a sort of frozen, ingratiating smirk on his features. You know how people look out of the advertisements in the magazines, urging you to buy something? That was it. But his eyes looked deadly serious—and scared.

"You bleary-eyed little gnome of hell," I said, with restraint, and reached across the desk and stuck my finger at his face. "You swore to tell the truth. Who stole that dagger?"

"'Ere, now!—" said Pruen in a hurt tone.

"*Who stole that dagger?*"

"No call to go and get apoplexy, sir," he complained. His voice had got to be a little thread, but he was holding on hard to that thread. "You will if you carry on like that. Listen, sir, 'arf a mo! All I want's a chance to explain. Listen!"

He gulped, and his speech steadied.

"Here's me on the chair—down at the doors. See? Near on a hundred (eighty, anyway) feet away is the staircase. That dagger's on the lowest step. Between me and the stairway is a line of glass cases that cuts off me view; now, don't it? Lights? Not so bright as moonlight. And, as you saw, I can't brag about excellent long eyesight. Now I ask you—people was passing and repassing between then and eleven o'clock. If one of 'em leans down quick, do I notice? Do I notice the dagger? I ask you: do I ever think about it? There! I say, why don't you let me tell the *'ole* story before you judge?"

There was some sense in this, but I was still convinced he was lying. Anyhow, I told him to go on.

"Starting with the time the man who was murdered walked in, of course," he said without guile, and cleared his throat. "Well——"

"Starting with where you left off. Quarter past ten. You've got half an hour before the corpse walks in. Get to it!"

Pruen conveyed that this was a complete waste of time, but he went on.

"I didn't notice much. Maybe a couple of minutes after I'd sat down (getting out me pipe, because we're not allowed to smoke on duty, of course), the door of the curator's room opens, and out comes Miss Miriam and Miss Kirkton. Just as they done so,"—the worm was now imitating a constable giving evidence before a magistrate—"Mr. Butler appears, frantic-like, from the Arabian Gallery upstairs, and runs down the steps.

His constable's uniform looked a barmy thing on 'im. Ho, ho!

"'Nails!' says he, waving the hammer I'd left upstairs for 'em. 'Nails! Where's the nails, Pruen?' he yells across the room. 'Terrible time we 'ad getting the chest out of that glass case without smashing anything, and the sawdust sack broke, and now you didn't put out any nails.'

"He was very excited-like, was Mr. Butler.

"I told him I was sorry. I told him there was plenty of nails in the pockets of Mr. Wade's jacket in the cellar—you see, sir, the governor's got a workshop, and working-clothes and everything 'e likes down there—so I said I'd hop down straightaway and get 'em. But Miss Miriam speaks up very quick and nice, and insists on getting the nails herself. She's always helpful. So, while Miss Kirkton goes upstairs with Mr. Butler, Miss Miriam goes down after the nails."

Pruen had leaned back. He was going on in a dead, casual voice, blinking round the room as though he were anxious to get this over with.

"You," I said.

"Sir?"

"Do you mean to tell me she went eagerly rushing down after nails into the cellar?"

"And very nice about it she was," he declared defiantly. His hands were shaking; and, instead of sweating, his eyes would water instead. "I've always said about Miss Miriam, I've said——"

"When did she come back again?"

He reflected. "Oh, maybe five, eight minutes. Something like that."

"Pruen, you lie in your teeth. Damn it all, can't you see you're only hurting everybody? I've heard

222

Dr. Illingworth's testimony, and I'll hear the testimony of all the others. Illingworth got to the museum at about twenty-five minutes to eleven. You say *she* went down in the cellar not much after a quarter past ten. . . . Do you want me to believe she was down there looking for nails for nearly twenty minutes? Because it's like this: When Illingworth walked to the rear of the hall, he saw Miriam just coming up out of the cellar. Twenty minutes! And that's not all. Just as she was coming up, and just as Illingworth walked back there, he heard from upstairs a sound of somebody hammering nails. What about it? When Illingworth got here at twenty-five minutes to eleven, did he see her just coming upstairs?"

"Yes, 'e did," returned Pruen. He was snarling now. "Yes, 'e did. And why not? That was the second time she went down there."

"The *second* time she went down to the cellar?"

"Yessir, on my Bible oath! Not that it's got anything to do with the business. Not it! But you look 'ere, and let me tell it."

He reached out and tapped his finger into his palm. I don't want to indulge in the usual fool talk about atmosphere; but there was now about him an atmosphere of truth. A lessening of strain, an eagerness, the usual eagerness to spread himself in talk. He did not mind talking now, because he had got past the danger-point. What danger-point? Yes: the stealing of the dagger. It was a creepy, ugly feeling to feel what I knew clear inside my bones as a conviction—that the dagger had been stolen just then, and that Miriam Wade had stolen it.

"She went down after them nails," he pursued, with a hoarsely confidential air, "and she come upstairs with

223

'em after about five, eight—N-no, say nearer five minutes. Mr. Butler was coming downstairs again, to see what 'appened to her, when up she came, and gave him the nails."

"That would be between twenty-five and thirty minutes past ten?" (The other question stuck in my throat. I couldn't ask it just then.)

"Yessir. She gave him the nails, and he went back upstairs. Then she walked about in front of the staircase a little—idling, you might say—and then she walked up quick towards the front of the hall, towards me. But she only nodded and smiled at me. She went in the Persian Gallery——"

"That's on the left-hand side of the hall, isn't it, looking towards the back?"

"Yessir. There wasn't no lights on in there; I'd turned 'em out when I got rid of the visitors at ten o'clock. And so I says, 'Shall I turn the lights on for you?' But she says, No not to mind. So everything settled down for a few minutes. Quiet, it was. I could 'ear Mr. Baxter walking up and down in the Gallery of Bazaars a little way down, muttering 'Googly-ook' or something to himself in Arabic or the like. And I was getting a bit worried why that actor chap didn't show up. Then out comes Miss Miriam from the Persian Gallery, and walks down the 'all again—and blowed if she don't open the door to the cellar and go down again!"

"Have you got a good view of the door to the cellar?"

"Oh, yessir. Straight in my line of heye, as you might say, when I'm sitting in the chair—or a good half of it, anyway. Well, I didn't 'ave much time to think about that, for just afterwards the door-buzzer buzzed. . . . Hah, and that was a relief! Actor chap at

224

last, thinks I! I don't expect they 'eard it upstairs—I mean Mr. Butler and Mr. Holmes and Miss Kirkton —for I could hear the banging going on where they was nailing up the case. Ow, but I was relieved! I opens the doors, and in walks this loony. . . .

"Now, I ask you," yelped Pruen, "'ow could I tell this wasn't the chap from the agency? He looked the part to the life, except he'd got no whiskers! Comicallest solemn air you ever saw (and that top-'at, I say!); long face, chin tucked in, big horn-rimmed glasses like a Yank and his beetle-squashers was number elevens or I'm a Dutchman. But even then, sir, I thought there was something fishy about it. Because when I started a bit o' fun, like, out 'e comes with a card that says, 'William Augustus Illingworth, D.D.' on it, and shoves a book with Arabic writing under me nose, and walk off in a huff.

"I think to meself, ''Ere! that's real enough,' and I begun to get a bit worried. But then maybe it was all right—look at the pains they take in the films, to get everything just so! He stops down by the door to the Gallery of Bazaars, and must have seen Mr. Baxter, for 'e unreels a couple of yards of some language. Back comes Mr. Baxter with some more of it. Then the loony walks down the hall. Miss Miriam comes up through the cellar door again, looks at him, and goes upstairs without saying nothing. Then the door to this room opens, and out comes Mr. Jerry in a rage, and says, 'You're late; come on in 'ere,' or words to that effect."

"Time?" I interrupted him.

"Just turned twenty-five minutes to eleven," Pruen replied, positively. "I'd just looked at me ticker, to see how late the chap really *was*. Half an hour late! Er! I ask you! The loony and Mr. Jerry come into this room, and I was still a bit worried—but I didn't have much time to think about that. It might 'a' been three or five minutes later, when all of a sudden: *Bang!*"

"Don't jump like that!" I yelled at him. He had given a hop and cracked his palms together, and I hate nervy people. "What do you mean, bang?"

He seemed genuinely perplexed.

"I dunno. It was kind of a crash, sir, like as if something had fallen and busted. And it come from down in the direction of the Gallery of Bazaars, right inside, like. I called out, 'Mr. Baxter!' because I thought 'e might have busted something, and then would I catch it from Mr. Wade. So down I went hurrying to see——"

"Stop a bit!" (This looked like business.) "I thought you said you didn't leave the doors all the time?"

He seemed again genuinely startled. "Cor, sir, I never thought of that! Yes, I left 'em then; not for long, though. You couldn't count that, quite, because it isn't as though I went far away..." A new, agreeable, and startling idea appeared to paralyse him. "That's it! I see what you mean, sir! You mean anybody might 'a' sneaked out and pinched that dagger from the step while my back was turned?"

I hadn't thought that, but it was a suggestion.

"How long were you away from the front doors?"

He reflected. "Two or three minutes, maybe, sir. It was like this. I goes down to see what was 'appening in there; then, when I looks in, Mr. Baxter ain't there and I wonder what's gone wrong, because I don't see no signs of anything 'aving been smashed. Then I *do* see it! Bits of coal on the floor, and a big, messy place on the wall where somebody's stood there and chucked a lump of coal bang at the wall."

"Who?"

"That's what I dunno, sir, because nobody'd gone in there except Mr. Baxter, and now I couldn't see 'im either. I called out, and then 'e come barging through the streets. He said he'd been in the Gallery of the Eight Paradises—that's next door, and there's a communicating door so you don't have to go out in the hall—and he says, ''Ere, what the devil's the matter?' I said, 'Mr. Baxter, sir, did you throw that coal?' He said, 'What damn nonsense are you talking? Coal? What coal?' And, when I pointed it out, he only said *he* didn't have time to go mucking about with coal, and walked out as though I'd offended him, and across the hall and into the Persian Gallery opposite.

"But, straight, sir, I began to get a queer feeling—creepy, like. Just that little bang brought it on. I thought: 'Ere, there's some very rummy business going on in this place. And you do get a creepy feeling in there sometimes."

"Steady. While you were in the Bazaars, and before Mr. Baxter went across to the Persian Gallery, did you hear any sounds out in the hall? Footsteps, or anything like that?"

The jump he gave, and the gleaming look of recollection, might have been a lie or it might have been imagination. But it looked real to me.

"Yes, I did! Now you mention it—I didn't think much at the time, because there's always a lot of echoes 'ere. But I did, strike me dead, I did 'ear a noise like footsteps out there! That's when the dagger was stolen, you take my word for it. I swear I——"

"When did you hear these footsteps?"

Again he squeezed up his face in a physical lunge to remember.

"Well—just after I'd poked me nose in to look at the Bazaars, I think. Yes! Just about then. Quick, rappy steps they was. Quick and rappy. I remember now."

Boys, I'm not an imaginative person, but the idea of those quick and rappy footsteps prowling out there tended to give me the creeps as well. I said:

"Where were all the others at this time?"

"'M, now. So far as I know, Mr. Jerry was down in this room with the loony that I still thought was the actor; and the others, except Mr. Baxter, was all upstairs. I know about their being upstairs because, after quarter past ten until twenty-five minutes to eleven—when the loony arrived—every once in a while, at intervals, one of 'em would pop out at the top of the stairs and sing out to me, 'Has 'e got here yet?' Meaning the actor, of course. I can't give you times for all that sir. I didn't remember. Just one after the other, at times. Miss Kirkton, Mr. 'olmes, or Mr. Butler would. Oh, yes! The last time somebody sung out was just after the loony had gone into this room with Mr. Jerry, and Miss Miriam had come up from the cellar for the second time. Yes! Mr. 'olmes come out on the gallery that runs round up there, and sings down to me, 'Not 'ere *yet*, Pruen?' (He looked a bit funny from worrying.) I calls back cheerful, 'Just arrived, sir, and with Mr. Jerry now.' Yes, I'd forgot that. I remembered it distinctly because I wondered at the time why Miss Miriam, who'd seen the loony come in, hadn't told 'em up there that the actor had arrived."

"This was before you heard the coal smash in the Bazaars?"

"Yessir, a couple of minutes before. Not very long, anyhow. But to go back to somebody chucking coal at the wall . . . I 'eard it go bang, and I've told you what happened then. And I got the funny feeling, and heard the footsteps out in the 'all. . . ."

I was writing all this down, in the form that Popkins would have approved of; I could imagine his spectral applause right beside me. Also, I was getting nearly as excited as Pruen.

"Stop a bit," I told him. "We've got you in the Gallery of the Bazaars; Baxter having gone across the hall to the Persian Gallery opposite; Jerry and the—Dr. Illingworth in this room here; and the others upstairs. The time must have been close on a quarter to eleven. Now, then. Is there any other way to get downstairs (from the floor above this, I mean) except by the staircase at the end of the hall? Any other staircase but that marble one? Could anybody have come down to this floor without being seen by you?"

He didn't answer for a second. He was studying me hard; his bony hands had gone creeping and plucking round his collar; and I heard his breath whistling. He'd got a curious expression as though his pale-blue eyes were expanding and contracting.

"Way down," he repeated. Then he seemed to remember the question. "Just one, sir."

"What's that?"

"Stairway over in one corner of the Persian Gallery, on this floor. Persian Gallery—you can go out and look at it now, if you like. It goes up to the room where all the shawls is exhibited, just up above. Sort of privatish kind of stair. Circular iron thing; you know."

"And that's the only way down?"

"Yessir. Except the lift, but that's dead as St. Paul and anyway Mr. Jerry and the loony was sitting right outside it."

"You say the Persian Gallery was dark?"

"That's it."

I had to fight to keep my head above water in this confusion, because I'm a business man and not a detective, but I thought I had it straight.

"Right. Now take up the story from the time you went into the Bazaars and found the coal smashed on the floor."

He drew a whistling breath. "I looks about, and pokes about—now we're a-coming to it—and I was just going to search to see whether there might be somebody 'iding there—lots of places to 'ide, you can see for yourself, with all them tents and things—when, *Brrr!* The door-bell buzzes again.

"Cor, I nearly jumped out of me skin! I drags me watch out, because I thought it couldn't be Mr. Mannering so soon, and them all unprepared. Sure enough, it was too early. Just quarter to eleven. But I thought, Maybe 'e's early. . . . No, I thought, not that; they yelled and yelled at 'im—or Miss Miriam did—not to get there before eleven. Then I started to wonder whether the loony I let in might 'a' been the wrong man. Oh, I was in a rare state of mind, I can tell you! But there wasn't nothing to do but find out, and warn the others if it was Mr. Mannering. To tell you the truth, sir, what most pumped the breeze up me was thinking that maybe, just maybe, it might have been old Mr. Wade suddenly come back all unexpected. . . .

"Well, there's a bit of a panel in that door (just a little thing) you can open on a knob to take a dekko outside. I goes to the front door and opens the panel. And there was the chap you found dead afterwards——"

The sweat was coming out on his forehead. He wiped it with his sleeve, jabbing it in sharp little gestures like a woman putting on powder. He swallowed.

"But 'ow the 'ell, I ask you, sir, should I know who the chap was? A bit darkish skinned, kind of, with a black beard, and yellowish kind of glasses, with a ribbon, and 'is collar turned up—a sort of sneering at me. It's a rum kind of face to be poked at you, all of a sudden, through a hole in the door; like as if it had jumped out of the bronze.

"I said, 'Who are you?' and he said, with a queerish kind of—of——"

"Intonation?"

"Yessir, if you like. And with 'is teeth just about on the lower edge of the panel. Cor, what a sight! 'E looked wildish, if you understand me. He said, 'I'm from Brainerd's, you fool. Open the door.' Then I did 'ave a sickish feeling—funny, but I believed 'im, and I knew I'd made a mistake about the other chap.

"As I opened the door he says, still in a funny kind of voice, 'Where's Miss Wade?'—that's what 'e said. I said, 'She's upstairs, along with the others; but never you mind that. There's somebody here that I thought was from Brainerd's.'

"He got inside past me. He says: 'Upstairs, with the others. Right. You stop where you are,' says he, as I made a move; 'I want to see somebody.' Cor, but 'adn't he got a way with him! Down he goes walking with quick mincy steps; old top-'at and all, and a leather-bound book under his arm; before I could move or get a word out of me throat.

"Now follow me close in this part, sir. I dreamed about it last night. 'Twasn't pleasant to dream about; I always seemed to see that face all of a sudden stuck through the bronze wall at me. . . . But he walks down, and just as he gets in a line with that big black travelling-carriage, there was a noise.

"Somebody went, *Ssss-t!* Just like that," said Pruen, making a hissing stop through his teeth. "Sss-t! Like when you want to attract somebody's notice. Understand? Maybe not loud, but with all them echoes and sounds that get round in a place like this, the fellow jumped. 'E jumped, and turned 'is head round to the left—to look towards the coaches. Somebody was standing there going, Sss-t! The actor chap stopped and just stood a-looking for a second. He didn't say anything. 'E just nodded his head and ducked very quick down under the shafts of the carriage—which was stuck in this direction—and over to the other side of the carriage where I couldn't see anything at all. Somebody was standing on the far side of the line of carriages where I couldn't see."

I interrupted the recital, because Pruen's voice was going up shrilly a note at a time.

"You mean," I said, "sitting where you were, you couldn't see on the other side?"

"Sir, strike me dead if I could! You go out and sit down in my chair and try. 'Ere's me chair—like this. I looks straight down past that line of doors on this side of the coaches, with the cellar door at the end. That line of coaches is on the left. Right! There's a line of pillars, and the coaches is strung along between the pillars and the left-hand wall; they don't much more than fit in, with a little aisle between them and the wall on the other side. The light's not awful bright, as you know, and there's 'eavy shadows from the coaches.

"So I started to go down there, to find out what was what. Then I realised that Mr. Mannering might turn up at any minute, and I couldn't leave the doors; becos the time was getting on. . . . I say, I didn't know *what* to do. Still, I went a little way down, and called, 'Ullo! Where are you? What are you doing in among them coaches? Who's there?'

"And there wasn't any answer.

"No, sir, I wasn't what you'd call scared; I wasn't scared till after that inspector 'ad found the body in the carriage. Not me. I was annoyed, like. Like what you feel when you've expected something pleasant and it all goes wrong. But, then——!"

Pruen leaned forward. He had a light of inspiration about him now, like a fluttering gas-globe.

"Then I saw something that I only understand now, because I remember things, and put 'em together. As I looked back to the front doors, and went to close the panel, I saw some marks on the floor just inside the doors. Those marks hadn't been there a minute ago. They were dirty, smudgy tracks on the marble, like dark dust, made by that chap's boots——"

"Penderel's boots? The actor?"

"Yessir, the chap that just came in. The marks trailed on a bit down the hall, and then faded out. I thought, Where's that chap been to get so much dirt on his boots? And then, sir, I remembered something. As that chap went walking down the 'all past the coaches, there was something about his *back*—and his top-'at—something about his *back* that was familiar. And this is what it was:

"He got here, as I told you, at a quarter to eleven. That's not all of it. For that same chap had been in the museum earlier in the evening, a little before ten o'clock."

Pruen sat back triumphantly.

Eleven Points, Eleven Suspects

"He had been in the museum," I repeated, after a pause, "a little earlier, before ten o'clock. You mean he came in, looked about, and went out again?"

Again Pruen was having a hard time arranging his ideas.

"I dunno just what I do mean, so help me! But I'll try to tell you what I remember. It's all mixed up in— what do I mean——?"

"Impressions?"

"'M," grunted Pruen, rather suspiciously. "It was like this. In my profession, sir, you get to observing people who comes into the museum; their little ways and how they act when they first come in. Now, as I told you, there was a crowd last night. Two parties of kids under schoolmasters. An old lady and gent. Two sets of spooners: you can tell the spooners a mile off, and they make for the Gallery of Bazaars like ruddy 'oming-pigeons. A family party from out of town. I don't know just 'ow many; there was more. *But* there was only one gent in a top-'at and black coat. I noticed him a bit, because as a rule people in top-'ats don't come in here of nights—why, I dunno, but as a rule they don't. . . . I didn't get a good look at this 'un, because he came in behind the family-party at maybe quarter to ten. I only saw the gent's back (that is, I thinks of him as a gent just then; only it was this actor). Well!

"Now, then, I noticed him for another reason. It has to do with the way people act when they come in, usually. Ten to one, sir, when a person comes in, 'e'll stand looking about a bit undecided-like, just inside the doors. Then, ten to one, 'e'll turn round and look at *me*. Why, I dunno. I dare say they're all wondering whether to ask me something. Sometimes they do, and sometimes they don't, but as a rule they look at me whether they asks anything or not. You'd be surprised at the rum questions I do get asked, sir! Most want to know whether there's an admission-fee, and some whether there's a torture-chamber, and some where's the lavatory; and all the time I've got to keep a sharp look-out on the basement door—I do it automatic—and on the door at the other side of the stairway, to me own quarters, just to see they don't walk in in spite of the doors being marked private. Well!

"When this man comes in the first time, before ten o'clock, 'e don't ask anything or look round. He just goes a-strolling straight down the 'all. And I thought, 'You're looking for a lavatory, and I'll keep an eye on you to see whether you don't open one of them doors at the back.' Then was when I noticed the top-'at and coat. But he didn't. No, he stopped by the coaches—then he goes between 'em like as if

236

he was going into the Egyptian Gallery. The Egyptian Gallery is the second room down on the left-hand side.

"Then I forgot him altogether, because some kids came up and asked questions. When it came time for closing up, I'd got a bit of a hazy idea I hadn't seen 'im go out. That's why I 'ad a look round, as I told you, to see everybody was cleared out. When you asked me about it a while ago, I remembered the chap."

"Had he gone out?" I demanded.

Pruen hesitated.

"Well, sir, I didn't find 'im when I looked round, and 'e certainly *did* come in again at a quarter to eleven—near on an hour later. I dare say he must have gone out, don't you, if he came back in again?"

There was no jeer in this. Pruen was doubtful himself; but I wasn't doubtful, because I was beginning to see the explanation. I said:

"Think now! Was this before the others—Miriam and Jerry and the whole crowd—had arrived here?"

"Yes, sir. Some minutes before that."

"Would it have been possible for Penderel (don't pretend you don't know who Penderel was!) would it have been possible for him to have sneaked down into the cellar when he came here the first time?"

Pruen's expression was that of somebody looking for a trap, and just on the verge of putting his feet on the spring.

"Not till the museum closed, so 'elp me! Sir, there was only two times the whole evening I 'ad me eyes off that cellar door: that I'll swear. The first was when I went about looking round after I'd turned everybody out at ten o'clock. The second was when somebody smashed the coal in the Gallery of Bazaars. So——"

"But," I said, "he could have come into the museum and hidden himself; couldn't he? Then, when you went round turning people out, he could have ducked down into the cellar. Answer me! Couldn't he?"

And I had to juggle this a bit before it escaped me: there were too many things to keep in the air at once. Still, I could see blazing clear the explanation of that coal on Penderel's shoes, the coal that made the smudges on the floor when he entered the museum the *second time*.

He enters first at about ten minutes to ten: ahead of time. For some reason he hides, and then ducks down into the cellar; the reason probably being that he wanted to waylay Miriam Wade and remain in hiding until he could find out how to waylay her alone. All right! The others arrive shortly after he does, but for some little time they are all together in the curator's room while Pruen is closing up. Then—why, blast it, then Miriam Wade goes down into the cellar after nails!

Ergo, my fatheads, she must have met Penderel there. Was the meeting arranged? No, no, no; couldn't have been! Besides thinking that Penderel was not within a thousand miles of London, he was the last person in the world she would have wanted to meet. But she did meet him. What happens? We don't know. We do know that she came up from the cellar a little more than five minutes later. After walking up and down a few times in front of the staircase, she then walked past Pruen into the dark Persian Gallery. She remained there for a short time, and then returned to the cellar. On this occasion she was gone a fairly brief time, before she hurried up again once more. What happened in those two interviews?

The only thing we knew was what Penderel *did*, which is the only thing he could have done to fit the evidence. He went to the front of the basement into the coal-cellar. There he had piled up a couple of boxes (which Carruthers later found) in order to climb up through the coal-hole into the street outside. Hence the coating of coal-dust on the soles of his shoes, which was not greatly worn off in the few steps he must take across the pavement to reach the front doors again. When he returns to the museum, *he is in a furious temper and asking for Miss Wade.* What happened, let's ask again, at those two interviews? One thing is certain: he had decided to appear at the museum to play his part in the charade, just as though he had not been hiding there before.

And, boys, he walks into a trap. Somebody was waiting for him, out of sight behind the line of coaches.

Yes, it was a nasty business; and I'm not ashamed to admit, like old Illingworth, that it was giving me the horrors. All this stuff was circling in my head like a cloudy roundabout, with Pruen's face sticking out of the middle of it and gabbling.

I said to Pruen: "You heard somebody making a noise like Sss-t! back behind the coaches. You called out but there was no answer, and you didn't like to leave the front doors after Penderel had gone to join this— unknown person. Did you take any sort of look at all?"

Now he was cradling his hands in his sleeves like a Chinaman, and moving them up and down his arms. He looked pretty miserable.

"A bit of a one, sir. I ran over very quick to the door of the Persian Gallery. As you stand there, you can look in a straight line down the *other* side of the coaches: the aisle, I mean, between them and the wall."

"Did you see anything?"

"Nothing, so 'elp me! Not 'ide nor trace of them two. But, you understand, I didn't have reason to think there was anything—you know, criminal. I thought it was a bit of a rum go, that's all."

"Where could they have gone? Climbed into the travelling-carriage before you looked round on that side?"

"I s'pose so," he said drearily.

'Was the door of the carriage open or shut on that side?"

"Shut, sir," he answered after a pause. "That is, if it'd been open I'd 'a' noticed it, and I didn't notice nothing."

"Did you hear any noises—talk, footsteps, anything like that, after the two disappeared?"

His fright increased. "Cor, now you mention it—I thought I did catch some footsteps! Yes, and strike me dead, they was the same quick, rappy footsteps I'd 'eard out in the hall before, when the coal was smashed. That's it! The quick, rappy ones. . . ."

"Where? Where did the sounds come from?"

"I dunno, sir. They seem to be all about in the air; it's the echoes. You can't place a sound to spot it, like. And there wasn't many steps that I 'eard. Just a few. . . . It was maybe two or three minutes after the actor-chap had ducked under the shafts of the carriage to the other side. But it's a bit difficult to fix times when you had no reason to remember 'em."

"Were these steps you heard the sound of somebody running away?"

He turned on me. "Won'tcher shut it, sir?" he

screamed. "I'm windy enough as it is thinking 'ow I
enjoyed meself so much, even though the game
went bust—dancin' round that packing-case afterwards—and all the time the body of that bloke—
and me with only me *lantern!* God!" He began to
flap his open palms up and down on the arms of the
chair. "I'm windy enough—without that. Only me
lantern, all alone in the place with that thing. Cor,
I'll dream about it! And now you asks me about
steps a-running away. . . . They were! They were a-
running, and that's what I know now."

I let this blast go up and collapse before I got after
him again.

"Take it easy, dammit!" I had to tell him. "We've
got this. When the murderer gets hold of Penderel,
he acts like lightning. He either gets him into the
coach, stabs him, eases the door shut—and runs. Or
else he stabs Penderel in the aisle behind the
coaches, opens the door of the most enclosed one
where the body won't be found for some time,
shoves Penderel inside—and runs. You said you
heard only a few steps running. A few steps. . . .
Then the murderer couldn't have run across the hall
or up the stairs, or anything like that, I suppose? Or
you'd have heard him."

"And seen 'im! Becos I only took a quick look, and
then went back to the front doors. No, sir."

"Where could he have gone, then?"

"In to the Egyptian Gallery, sir. That's the only
place. D'ye see, the door to that gallery is down along
that aisle, between two of the coaches. It's in line
along o' the Persian Gallery—just like the Bazaars and
Eight Paradises is, connected with each other, on the
other side of the hall."

"Connected with each other," says I. (You can see

241

what I was thinking about, can't you?) "The Persian and Egyptian ones were connected. The Persian one was dark, you've said. What about the other?"

"That was dark too. D'ye see, sir, we wasn't going to use either of them for the game last night. And, for instance, we didn't want Mr. Mannering maybe wandering into the Persian Gallery and seeing we'd pinched Mr. Baxter's Persian suit out of a case."

My notes were all skew-wiff and unreadable by this time, but I kept battering away, shoving down fragments of what he said even if I was uncertain about it myself. Also this yanked me back to something I'd forgotten.

"Here!" I said, "let's get our people straightened out. Baxter! You said Baxter had wandered over to the dark Persian Gallery just after somebody fired the coal at the wall. Was he there all this time? What was he doing? Didn't he step out and say something when Penderel arrived?"

Pruen rubbed his cheek.

"Why, I suppose 'e must have gone upstairs with the others. I mean, using that iron staircase in the Persian Gallery. No, 'e didn't come out until afterwards. That's what I was going to tell you. We've been plodding about with it, and going backwards and forwards on the evidence—but reely, between the time the actor walked in the front doors and the time I 'eard the footsteps running away it was only a short time. So! Not knowing what to do, I goes back to the front doors and shouts for somebody. I shouts 'Mr. Butler! Mr. 'olmes!' just to see what was being done, for I was pretty near up the pole by that time . . ."

"Well?"

"Just after I'd stirred up the echoes I heard footsteps

over in the Persian Gallery. Mr. Holmes came hurrying out, waving his hands for me to keep quiet and looking even more palish than he'd done earlier. 'E says to me, 'What's all this row about?' (He'd come down that iron stairway from the rooms up above, d'ye see.) 'What's all the row about?' he asks me. Then I tell him about the two blokes: first the loony who come in, and now this one who disappeared. And he went on something awful.

"'Where is he?' says Mr. Holmes. 'Why didn't you tell me?'

"'Sir,' I says, becos I didn't like his tone, 'you told me yourself not to leave me post. And the other chap's down in the room with Mr. Jerry—the thin one in the glasses that came first is—and Mr. Jerry seems to think he's all right, so why shouldn't I? Besides, if I may say so,' I says, standing right up to him, 'why do all of *you* 'ave to take a good thirty minutes just nailing up a footling little packing-case?'

"What it turned out, I found later on, was that the lead top of that silver-chest 'ad been so corroded that they'd got to work on it a long time before they could get it open. But I didn't know that. I was a bit flustered at being left so long on my own. But Mr. 'olmes just stands there with his fists pressed against his forehead, and he says:

"'*My God*, it reely must have been Illingworth after all!'

"He leaves me in a rush and goes rushing down towards the curator's room—towards this room where we are now. Just then, Mr. Butler and Mr. Baxter appear at the top of the marble stairs, pulling and trundling the packing-case, and start to bump it downstairs. Mr. 'olmes put his finger on his lips in a savage sort of way, and makes a gesture at 'em to keep quiet. Then he points up at me, and very softly starts to open the door of the curator's room to look inside . . .

"They get the case downstairs while Mr. 'olmes has his head half-way through the door, listening and looking in 'ere. Then Mr. Baxter, with Miss Miriam and Miss Kirkton, come running up to me to find what it's all about—but Mr. Butler snaps his fingers and runs back upstairs again like as if he'd forgotten something.

"And just then—wack! The door of the curator's room slams in Mr. Holmes's face with one 'ell of a crash, and we all nearly jumped out of our skins again. That's where the loony begun 'is work, only we didn't know it just at the moment. . . ."

Which, boys, was the end of evidence that was new to me. In Illingworth's statement, I had a sure means now of proving or disproving Pruen's tale. And it fitted together exactly. Thus:

Pruen's account wasn't quite so flowery, but it had all the facts. Up near the door of the Persian Gallery, a little group consisting of Pruen, Miriam, Harriet, and Sam Baxter had listened while Pruen poured out his story. Holmes was pounding on the door of the curator's room demanding to know what was going on. Butler had gone upstairs, announcing that he had mislaid his truncheon. Then the door of the curator's room was opened by Jerry, after his victorious hauling of Illingworth into the lift, and Holmes had gone inside. He and Jerry had come out after a minute or two, arguing volubly. Then Baxter had run down to them, finding the black false moustache on the floor; and, after some argument, the three of them had joined the group near the Persian Gallery. While Jerry was telling his experiences with

Illingworth, they heard Butler come down the marble staircase. He had gone along beside the coaches, looking into each, and had opened the door of the travelling-carriage. . . .

Then Butler had jumped down, slamming the door of the carriage. Nobody had been able to see inside, of course, because they were on the far side of the line of coaches. But Butler had caught sight of Illingworth's head, silhouetted up against the ventilator, and thus began the wild business of first pursuing Illingworth and then dragging him down the coal-hole.

"And," concluded Pruen excitedly, "we didn't know —any of us—about the dead man." (He seemed still unaware of Butler's premature discovery.) "All that scared us was the copper coming back with reinforcements, to find out what was going on. So they all decided to 'op it—quick. Mr. Butler 'ad already gone first; 'e was hauling old loony, still in a stupor, and insisting on taking loony home; seemed quite scared, Mr. Butler did, which surprised me. Also, 'e made 'em all swear to meet him in Mr. 'olmes's flat later that night. Funny, now; I wonder——"

He reflected, with a startled look but went on again:

"Miss Miriam left when Mr. Butler did. She—well, she wasn't well, sir; you know her health had been bad." He looked at me sharply. "She said she wanted to do a bit of driving about to feel better. 'Er car was parked back in Palmer Yard. Miss Kirkton offered to go along, but Miss Miriam wouldn't 'ear of it She said she'd join 'em in Mr. Holmes's flat later, if she felt better, and out she hurried. . . ."

"Alone?"

He eagerly jumped at something else. "That reminds me. Did you wonder why Miss Miriam, if she was in the game, 'ad come *back* to the museum later last night, when the inspector was 'ere? That's it. She'd gone for a bit of a drive. Then she'd returned and parked her car in Palmer Yard where she usually does —and saw a light in this room. So she thought they was still here, and came in to see.

"But they wasn't, though Mr. 'olmes 'ad wanted to stay coppers or no coppers. 'E kept saying, 'What's happened to the actor-chap? Where is he? Where's 'e gone?' He was pretty worried; but Mr. Baxter only said, 'Damn the actor; he's walked out on us, don't you see; and *I'm* not sticking here in this infernal rig-out.' Then Mr. 'olmes, who's awful conscientious-like, says, 'There's a devil of a mess in this place; we shall have to clean it up.'

"'Don't you worry about that, sir,' I says to him. 'I'll clean it up, and there's all night in front of me.'

"'Yes,' says Mr. 'olmes, 'but you can't unpack that silver-chest and lift it out and carry four 'undred-weight of lead up to the glass case upstairs; now, can you?'

"But Mr. Jerry says, 'That's easy enough, you fat-heads. We'll skip out now and wait till any row has died down; if there is one, which I doubt. Then we'll all come back and clean the place up. We can go over to Ron's flat in the meantime. We'll 'ave to return any-way, because Sam will 'ave to put that Persian costume back.'

"And Miss Kirkton said that was the best idea; she was a-crying, Hurry, hurry, hurry! It was a rum busi-ness, because we'd switched out all the lights in the whole place and we was just a-standing there with only my lantern in the 'all. But Mr. 'olmes wasn't to be flurried. 'E puts my lantern on top of the glass case where the dagger 'ad been, and says:

"'Well, anyway,' says he, 'we'll put the *khanjar* back, becos that's a valuable piece.' And 'e takes out his keys and unlocks the case again. 'Where's the *khanjar*, Sam? Hand it over.'

"And Mr. Baxter, who's a temperamental sort of gent, gives a howl:

"'*I* ain't got it!' he yells. 'I been asking *you* all night what you done with it, and yet all I could find was this 'ere ruddy false moustache lying over there on the floor. The moustache and the dagger was together; where's the dagger now? Right now, I don't give two hoots *where* it is, myself; all I want you to do is come along and get out of 'ere before——'

"The door-bell gives a couple of long buzzes.

"Wow! Sir, you should 'a' seen how they jumped when that bell buzzed! There was all their faces in the lantern-light; the only ones who wasn't scared was Mr. Jerry and me, and we grinned at each other. Of course, who it actually was pressing the bell—we know that now—was Mr. Mannering! But Mr. Baxter thought it was the coppers; and 'e was afraid of being found in that silly-ass suit and being made such a fool of that 'e'd have to leave the Diplomatic Service or whatever it is. Cor, he almost 'it the roof! And Mr. 'olmes wasn't much better.

"'We're getting out of here,' yells Mr. Baxter. 'E takes that black false moustache, and stuffs it away in the first place 'e could see: which was right inside the case. Then 'e yanks Mr. 'olmes's key from Mr. 'olmes and as quick as a wink 'e locks that case up again. And then they all stampeded for the back door. The only one who stopped a second was Miss Kirkton. She puts her hands on my shoulders—cor! with them big blue eyes a-shining and scared and with tears in 'em,

though I couldn't for the life of me understand why—
and she says to me:

"'You promise me this,' she says. 'Whatever happens if St. Paul's falls on you or if the dead gets up out of their graves, promise me you'll never let on any of us was 'ere tonight.'"

Pruen stopped, drawing a long breath and straightening his shoulders. He looked at me. His eyes were shining with pride.

"And, by God, sir," says he, "even when that blinking corpse did tumble out of its grave, your inspector can bear witness that I kept me promise."

There was a long silence, while the rain still splashed on the window and Pruen sat straight in the red leather chair. I looked him up and down. From Pruen and Illingworth, two people about as different as you could very well find, we had now the two halves of the story.

"Yes, you're a fool," I said, "but let that pass now. Look here: there are just two things about this 'game' that was being put up on Mannering which aren't clear in my mind yet. . . ."

"Yessir?" he prompted, and grinned.

"This joke on Mannering was got up in a devil of a quick time, wasn't it?—that is, you didn't know until the forenoon of yesterday that Jeff Wade was going to be away last night. How did you make your arrangements with everybody so quickly and smoothly? Lines written and everything?"

He chortled. "Oh, it's been talked about and arranged for a week, sir. All that 'adn't been decided was the date. It was to be some time soon; whenever a good opportunity popped up. And this was a rare good opportunity—because, d'ye see, the real Dr. Illingworth reely was in London, as Mr. Sheik Mannering could see by the papers, and that would 'elp make him believe it. Oh, lots of plans for the stunt 'ad been thought out."

He leaned over confidentially.

"Why, would you believe it, the first scheme we 'ad—the original one, which we 'ad to discard—was to stage a *murder*. I mean, a full murder with a real corpse and everything. Of course, sir, I mean a corpse from a medical school—what are you a-jumping for?"

My brain was giving way. I said: "Look here, that was my next question. Did you say a corpse from a medical school? Did one of that gang write on Wednesday, a note beginning: '*Dear G., There has got to be a corpse—a* real *corpse. The means of death doesn't matter, but there has got to be a corpse. I'll manage the murder—that ivory-handled* khanjar *will do the trick, or strangling if it seems preferred....*' Did somebody write that?"

Pruen nodded shamefacedly. "That's right, sir. Nobody dared own up last night, or—well, you know how it was. Did the old governor tell you that Mr. Jerry's got a friend, name of Gilbert Randall, who's at medical school? They'd got an idea he might be able to get 'em a corpse from the dissecting-room; the 'means of death,' that is, 'ow the corpse really had died, didn't matter so long as they could get a corpse to use. They wanted it for a dummy. So Mr. Jerry sat down and started to type a note on the machine in this room. But Mr. 'olmes interrupted 'im and said, 'For cat's sake, you fathead, don't *write* anything like that; see Randall, if you've got to do it at all; 'cos if the letter goes astray it'll look awful funny.' So Mr. Jerry 'e shoves the note in his pocket, and it fell out afterwards in Mr. 'olmes's flat. Of course, when Mr. Jerry saw Mr. Randall, 'e found out they couldn't possibly get a real corpse; so they 'ad to abandon the idea." Pruen gave a gleeful chuckle. "You wasn't 'ere last night, but when Inspector Carruthers springs that note, solemn and terrible-like, it caused a sensation. Mr. 'olmes was scared to death. So scared that you'll find it recorded if Inspector Carruthers left you any notes on the interview. . . . Mr. Jerry was gong to chip in and explain when Mr. 'olmes stopped him. But, lummy, sir, it *did* fall into the wrong 'ands, and it *did* look awful funny."

Stung again.

I sat back in a kind of daze. From Illingworth and Pruen we had the whole story. And we had—what? It was enough to make a man wild. With great pains and scrabbling, we had gone grubbing about to pick up the pieces of the most scattered jig-saw puzzle that ever littered the floor of Scotland Yard. We had fitted them together so that the picture was complete. And what did we see? We saw the picture of somebody sticking out his tongue at us. Even with the bits joined, we were no nearer knowing who killed Penderel than we had been before.

That cursed fact was the reason for my coming to a decision. Pruen looked at me hopefully while I clawed at what remains of a once fine head of hair.

He said, "Now, sir, what are you going to do? That's the truth I've been telling you, as I hope to answer for it to Gabriel. You can test it! Ask any of 'em! Ask all of 'em! Mr. Wade told me you were going to have a go at all the others——"

I said firmly: "Pruen, my lad, I am not going to have a go at the others."

He goggled at me, and I told him then what I tell

you others now. I felt so much better at making the decision that I gave him a cigar.

"Pruen," I told him, "my purpose in sticking my nose into this case was to find how the wind blew (any reference to scrambled metaphors will be treated with contempt); to see how bad things were, and to give Jeff Wade whatever help I could. I have discovered how bad things are, and How. I am still ready to give all the help I can, without going to clink for corrupting my office. But the rest of it is out of my line. In this museum on the night of June 14 were eight people: Miriam, Harriet, Jerry, Baxter, Holmes, Butler, Illingworth, and yourself. If we except Illingworth, any one of seven *might* have killed Penderel. Outside this museum there were at least two others—Mannering and Jeff—who might have killed him if they'd got the chance. Throwing in Illingworth just for cussedness or because it completes the roster of everybody in the case, we have ten——"

"Excuse me, sir," interrupted Pruen, "but ain't you forgetting that lady, hard-faced party who was in 'ere a while ago and made some sort of row? I didn't 'ear what she said, but I gathered from what you was telling her when she left that she'd got some connexion with Penderel. . . ."

"Right!" I said. "Mrs. Anna Reilly. Yes, she must go in. Therefore we have eleven suspects, possible or impossible, probable or improbable. I repeat, my son: I am an organiser and director, not a detective. This pinning the tail on the donkey must be done by somebody who's used to working blindfolded, which I am not. Therefore——"

"Um," says Pruen thoughtfully.

"Therefore I feel it is now time to turn loose that

251

celebrated bloodhound, Superintendent Hadley. My son: Popkins correctly defined my position. I am a gather-upper of odd bits; not to say crazy bits and busted bits. I am a sweep, in one sense or many. Popkins made out a list of eleven points for me to clear up. Eleven points, eleven suspects; so everything tallies. Popkins said: 'I omit the obvious lines of questioning; these are only odd points.' He was undoubtedly right about that. But Popkins also said: 'I suggest that when you've got the answer to all those you'll have the murderer.' To which *I* can only suggest that Popkins was a cock-eyed liar.

"Each one of those points has been answered; some fully, some in part; and the whole issue has become, if anything, slightly more crazy and incomprehensible than before. And my contribution to this case, my only contribution and my last floral tribute to insanity, will be this, and this alone. I turn his guns on him."

While Pruen wondered what in blazes I was gassing about, I spread out Popkins' list of eleven points on the desk, and took a large red pencil from the pen-tray. Across it I printed the final question:

Who killed Raymond Penderel?

Part III

The Scotsman in the Arabian Nights:
Statement of Superintendent
David Hadley

18

The Veil Is Taken From The Nights, But Not From The Murderer

Who killed Raymond Penderel? I can tell you. It is a person you might not at first have suspected; but I am certain of it, the Director of Public Prosecutions is certain of it, the Home Secretary is certain of it, even Sir Herbert is certain of it. Except for a perversion of justice, Penderel's murderer would now have been—I won't say hanged, because neither police nor juries are inclined to be cut up about the death of blackmailing gigolos, but at least given a sentence.

That is the trouble. Whether or not I am the celebrated bloodhound Sir Herbert describes, I am willing to admit I was never overly keen about baying this trail. If the whole business had ended in a natural fiasco, the D. P. P. would have been inclined to let it sleep and go down as unsolved. But nothing like that happened. We were greeted with a deliberate nose-thumbing and upsetting of justice, which made it impossible for us even to say, "Tut, tut" to the murderer. Now that sort of thing cannot be allowed, and we have got to find a way out even if only to nail a perjurer. The Home Secretary is intent on it, though for once *I* am not the person to get it in the neck. And if the personal is bound to enter into it sooner or later, I should like to see our case vindicated because it was the best bit of work I ever did.

Since this seems to have developed into a story-telling contest, I must admit that I can't lay claim either to Carruthers' polished irony or Sir Herbert's garrulous ease. Or, for that matter, to Illingworth's lurid and polysyllabic vividness: the auld meenister, it seems to me, has captured the story-telling honours so far. I believe in a clear, straightforward, logical narrative, with an accent on all three; Sir Herbert's examination of Pruen, for instance, resulted in a slightly muddled story which must be straightened out if we are to appreciate its significance. *Clarté, clarté, clarté*. The only writer I can read and reread constantly is Lord Macaulay, because there is never a sentence which needs to be read a second time in order to make out the meaning. Dr. Fell will tell you that I like drama and ringing phrase (as Macaulay did), but these must be subordinate to clearness and logic.

There was never a case, I believe, in which you find so much opportunity to exercise pure logic as in this one. That's because there are so many oddities. Logic, gentlemen, is not lost among oddities; it is at its best there. For an *ordinary* circumstance or puzzle, there may be a dozen explanations, so that the detective may choose the wrong one and throw his whole case off at the start. But for a very outlandish circumstance there is usually only one possible explanation; the odder the circumstance may be, the more narrow becomes the list of motives which produced it. For example, take the case of the cookery-book, which was explained so easily, and yet caused so much puzzling before it was explained. Logic would have shown that there could have been only one explanation, the simple one. But it was missed because of our natural human tendency to leave logic and go star-gazing for an answer; when the problem is so queer, we feel the solution must be queer as well.

So I propose to take you step by step towards the answer to this whole series of events. I was put in charge of the case on Saturday, as Sir Herbert has told you, but I didn't begin any actual investigation or questioning until the following Monday. But I read over every available report, and had a two-hour conference with Carruthers, in which certain very suggestive facts struck me. For the moment I won't tell you what inferences I made, except that they concerned the dead man's shoes and eyeglasses; but I was interested in the case, violently interested, and I wished Fell had been at hand to argue them over, instead of skylarking in the South of France. Late on Saturday afternoon Sir Herbert sent for me. He had come back from the Wade Museum, having heard what he has just told you. Also he gave me his list of odd points. The invaluable Popkins (a bit of a strait-laced ass, but a sound man) had brought it up to date. And it was beginning strongly to confirm the first suggestion in Carruthers' report.

Still, my middle name is Caution, and I said nothing whatever as yet. Instead I tried to get in touch with the various people concerned. In spite of Geoffrey Wade's boast about hauling them all together by the scruff of the neck for questioning, they seemed disorganised. Miriam Wade was at the old man's house in Hyde Park Gardens, suffering from nervous shock; in any case, there were two doctors who said she must have quiet for twenty-four hours. Harriet Kirkton, the doctors said, was little better. Young Baxter was at his flat in Duke Street, dead drunk. The others seemed to have taken matters more lightly, but there had been developments. Jerry Wade, who talked to me when I rang up the old man's house, told me about the newest.

There had been another row (which, believe it or not, seemed to have ended up amicably) between Butler and Mannering. You remember Carruthers telling how Mannering, the night before, had landed one under Butler's jaw and knocked him cold? Bright and early on Saturday morning Butler was waiting down in the foyer of Mannering's chambers when Mannering came downstairs. No sooner had Mannering stepped out of the lift than Butler walked up to him and said: "Good morning. Did anybody ever tell you that you don't hit a man when his hands are in his pockets?" Mannering looked him over for a second and said: "Are your hands in your pockets now?"—and without any more ceremony hauled off again. This time Butler was ready for it, and he gave Mannering a staggerer straight in the mouth. Then there was one hell of a row, all over the floor of the place, with the hall-porter too interested even to interfere. When the fracas began to draw attention, and the porter had to make some show of interfering, both of them had taken a good deal of punishment. Butler looked at Mannering, and then at himself, and started to laugh; after a minute Mannering himself achieved a grin, and said, "Come on upstairs and have a drink." Butler said, "Right," and up they went. They seemed to have patched things up and decided that neither was such a bad sort after all; though I should have thought Mannering had about as much sense of humour as this brief-case.

The incident might mean anything or nothing, but I filed it away when I decided to postpone real work over Sunday while I again went carefully over all the evidence. So I spent Sunday at home, locked myself in my study, lit my pipe, and studied the facts from every possible angle. I paid particular attention to Popkins' list, now amended and brought up to date. It contains many of the really valuable suggestions leading to the truth, and I call it to your attention in its amended form.

I

1. What about the coal-dust tracks just inside the front doors of the museum, those indistinguishable smudges which Carruthers found on the floor?

   Comment: Since a coating of coal-dust was found on the soles of the murdered man's shoes, the tracks were presumably made by him. Where had he been then, just before he entered the museum, to leave traces on the white marble?

   Answer: He had been in the basement and the coal-cellar. Entering the museum at about 9:50, he had concealed himself and, at some time between 10:00 and 10:10, when Pruen did not have the cellar door under observation, Penderel went down into the cellar. At 10:15 the other group separated—Butler and

Holmes went upstairs, Baxter went to the Gallery of the Bazaars, and the two women went to the curator's room with Jerry Wade.

At 10:18 or slightly later (the times are approximate), the two women came out of the curator's room, just as Butler came downstairs demanding nails. Although Pruen, who would know exactly where to find the nails, offered to go and get them, Miriam Wade insisted on going herself into the cellar. She did so, while Harriet Kirkton went upstairs with Butler.

Miriam Wade came up from the cellar at about 10:25 or later; and Butler was just coming down the marble stairs again to find out what had been delaying her. Miriam Wade wandered about for some minutes, and went into the Persian Gallery; then she descended into the cellar for the second time, and was there for a very brief space. She came upstairs at 10:35, when Dr. Illingworth arrived at the museum. She then went to the floor above to join Holmes, Butler and Harriet.

During all this time Penderel was still in the cellar. At some time shortly before 10:45, he must have gone into the coal-cellar, climbed up through the coal-hole into the street, and presented himself at the museum door as though he had never been there before.

That gives us a time-schedule as well as an answer. If I followed Popkins' method, however, I should add a comment on the reply. This comment would simply be: Why? Why did Penderel make his escape via the coal-hole and return to the museum? You may answer, if you like, that he did so because Miriam had persuaded him to pretend he had never known her; had persuaded him not to be found there in the cellar with her, but to leave the museum secretly and return as though it were his first visit. For the moment I do not contest the point.

Point 2 in the list, the problem of the note beginning, "Dear G., There has got to be a corpse," etc., is fully explained and for present consideration can be set aside. We go on to:

3. What about the large lump of coal which Carruthers found had been thrown at the wall in the Gallery of the Bazaars, for no apparent reason?

   Comment: This is not mentioned by Dr. Illingworth or anybody else, and does not seem to fit into the story. The proper persons to question are Pruen, who had a clear view of the hall all the time, and Baxter, who was in the Gallery of the Bazaars at (about) 10:35, when Dr. Illingworth arrived at the museum.

   Answer: It is mentioned by Pruen, and it still does not fit into the story. The smashing of the coal fits next into the time-schedule after the arrival of Dr. Illingworth. Pruen says he heard the crash "three to five minutes" after Illingworth's arrival; let us take round numbers and say that the crash occurred at 10:40.

Pruen heard the noise from the Gallery of the Bazaars. But, though the door to this gallery was under his eye all the time, he had seen nobody go in—except Baxter, who had been in there since 10:15.

Pruen went immediately to investigate, and found nobody at all in the gallery. Just after he did go in to look round, he heard footsteps (which he describes as "quick and rappy") out in the hall behind him. Pruen then saw the traces of the smashed coal. While he was looking at them, Baxter appeared from among the stalls or tents in the gallery. Baxter stated that he had been in the adjoining room, called the Gallery of the Eight Paradises, and knew nothing of any coal. Then Baxter left Pruen, crossed the hall, and went into the Persian Gallery.

Finally, Pruen was still looking for traces in the Gallery of the Bazaars when the door-bell rang at 10:45, and Penderel was admitted.

Between 10:40 and 10:45, where were all the others? Baxter has been accounted for, or apparently accounted for. Holmes, Butler, Harriet and Miriam were upstairs together, so far as we know. Jerry Wade was with Illingworth.

Who threw the coal, and why was it thrown?

For:

It is a significant point that, in the half-hour between 10:15 and 10:45, the only time when Pruen did not have the whole hall under his observation was when he went to investigate that noise in the Gallery of the Bazaars.

Thus the admirable Popkins, who would get everything on paper even if he did not understand it. I call your attention to his full remarks, however, without shortening them; because I think they contain the key to the whole affair. Popkins evidently thought so himself, for he now passes on quite logically to expand his next point thus.

4. What were the adventures of the black false moustache?

Comment: This moustache, meant to have been worn by Baxter, was—according to Holmes—placed by Holmes, along with the dagger, somewhere on the stairs in the main hall at an earlier time in the evening. Along with the dagger, it seems to have disappeared. It was found by Baxter on the floor of the museum later; then we lose sight of it, and Carruthers finds it inside a locked show-case in place of the dagger. Does this mean anything? Question Pruen, on duty there.

Answer: Pruen has been questioned, and we have now traced all the movements of the moustache except the important ones. Holmes's statement, overheard by Dr. Illingworth, is confirmed: He placed the dagger and the moustache on the lowest step of the staircase at about 10:15, when Baxter refused to take them.

Which leads to the questions:

(a) When did the dagger and the moustache disappear?

(b) Why were *both* of them stolen?

Baxter seems to have noticed their absence, but we do not yet know when he first noticed it. The first actual mention he made of it was shortly before eleven o'clock, when Illingworth had been locked up in the lift and the whole place was in confusion. Illingworth saw Baxter pick up the moustache from the floor near the travelling-carriage; and heard him ask Holmes what had happened to the dagger. Subsequently Baxter, in a moment of panic, thrust it into the glass case to get rid of it and locked the case with Holmes's key. But between 10:15 and 11:00 we are on questionable ground.

We must presume, however, that dagger and moustache were not stolen *after* the arrival of Penderel at 10:45, since the murder took place so quickly. Therefore they must have been stolen between 10:15 and 10:45, an interval of half an hour.

There are two alternatives:

Either they were stolen between 10:15 and 10:40 in which case it must have been done under Pruen's eyes, so that Pruen knows who stole them and is de-

> liberately lying. Or they were stolen be-
> tween 10:40 and 10:45, and the smashing
> of coal on the wall was a ruse to draw
> Pruen's attention away and give a clear
> field to the thief-murderer.
>
> But we have still no clue as to why
> both were taken.

That last, friend Popkins (I thought) is carrying matters a little too far; because my idea as to why both
were stolen was crystallising. But I told myself that I
must not go too fast, because I had questioned none of
the suspects about the fifteen minutes between a
quarter to eleven and eleven o'clock.

Naturally, those were the vitally important minutes
to my case; though not, I warn you, in the way you
may perhaps think. According to Pruen's story, where
were all these people between the time Penderel
enters the museum at 10:45, and the time his body is
prematurely discovered by Butler at 11:00? Again according to Pruen, Penderel walked down the hall, was
hailed by somebody from the shadow of the coaches,
and disappeared. After a short time, while Pruen does
not understand what is happening, and no reply comes
back to his call as to who was there, he began to get
the wind up. He heard those "quick and rappy" footsteps again. He ran over to look down the other side of
the coaches, and saw nothing.

When he bellowed for somebody to come to him,
Holmes presently came out of the Persian Gallery.
After a consultation, Holmes went down to the curator's room to investigate Illingworth—and had the
door slammed in his face when Illingworth suddenly
towers in his role of Detective-Inspector Wallace
Beery. At this time Baxter and Butler were just carry-

ing the packing-case downstairs, followed by Miriam and Harriet.

Now I was aware, of course, that unless we got another corporate alibi, any one of the group upstairs might have had the opportunity to kill Penderel. There were several galleries upstairs. From one of these, an iron stairway led down into the *dark* Persian Gallery. Somebody could have come down that stairway, gone into the communicating Egyptian Gallery— also dark, you remember—come out of the Egyptian Gallery by its door into the hall obscured from sight by the coaches, and waited for Penderel without having been seen from Pruen's position. Which one?

But I have dwelt on the three points from Popkins' list because, along with Inspector Carruthers' report, they gave me the suggestions which led me to definite proof against the murderer. You can glance down the rest of the list if you like, but all the others are fully answered. As the story broadened, only one thing was made more convincingly clear from them, and that has already been touched on by Sir Herbert: Whoever else might have committed the murder, Miriam Wade did not commit it.

Take points 5 and 6, for instance: the questions as to why she returned to the museum after the murder, and why she telephoned Harriet in a disguised voice. She returned to the museum because she had left it before the others, had gone for a drive because she was genuinely upset, and, on coming back to park her car in its usual place, had seen a light there: so she assumed the others had not yet left. As Sir Herbert has pointed out, her behaviour on the finding of the body—when she telephoned to the other girl, and disguised her voice so that she could speak to Harriet alone about a mutual secret—was not that of a woman guilty of murder. But the important fact about those two points is one whose significance seems to have been overlooked by everybody. I wonder, Fell, if you see the significance now. The fact is this: She had a key to the back gate of the museum.

Mull that over while I conclude this interlude. It was just as well that I had that quiet Sunday in Croydon. For events began to run fast and dark on Monday morning.

When I got to my office at nine o'clock, I was told that Harriet Kirkton was waiting for me, and had to speak to me.

19

The Person Who Stole The Dagger

The weather was still raw and rainy, and a fire had been lighted in my office. Those brown-distempered walls are never very cheerful; they looked less so with the rain whipping the windows. I let the girl wait on a bench outside while I ran through my correspondence. Then I turned on the light over my desk, another light as well, and rolled over a chair near it. I've never believed in that nonsense about having the light on people's faces, but I do believe in putting witnesses in a chair slightly lower than your own. The effect of their having to look up while they answer you is usually good. Then I had them bring her in.

I took a thorough inventory of Harriet Kirkton while she was trying to make conversational openings. Carruthers had been quite right in saying that she had a face like the Soul's Awakening or an Easter-card angel, but she was not at all the sort called fluffy. She struck me as a girl who ordinarily would be light-headed in small things and very long-headed in large ones. Slender, on the athletic side—you know the lines: like a long racing dog—she had a few freckles round her nose, and a pair of the largest and most expressive blue eyes I have ever seen. She wore a rain-coat and a wet felt hat under which you could see ends of her blonde hair; and she sat forward with her fist twitching on the edge of my desk. When a woman is nervous, she doesn't gasp or stammer; you do not notice it at all except in the look of strain and the way her voice shakes a little when she runs off into one irrelevant conversational opening after another. This girl was so thoroughly nervous that she came to the point at once. Her eyes had a real shine and gleam about them.

"I had to see you," she said.

I poked at the edge of the desk-blotter with a pencil and said, "Yes?"

"And I came on behalf of Miriam," she went on, with the big eyes still fixed on me. "She's not well enough to come out. Mr. Hadley—I've come to find out how much you know. Wait!" She held up her hand, although, as a matter of fact, I said nothing. "I know people aren't supposed to ask the police that, but this is a different case, and you've got to tell me. . . ."

"Yes?"

"It's like this. I know there's been nothing in the papers about—about *that*. But yesterday a horrible woman named Reilly rang up the house, and said she wanted to speak to Miriam on something very important about 'R. P.' I took the call. It seems she's got some—belongings, suit-cases or something." She stopped. She had been speaking very low and rapidly, with her eyes looking at a corner of the desk, but she choked over that word "belongings" as a person would choke on a fish-bone. "And she also said that she had spoken to the Assistant-Commissioner, and he knew all about it. Do you understand what I'm talking about, Mr. Hadley?"

"Yes, I understand."

"Well, then, *has* it got to come out?" she cried, with a kind of pounce even when she would not look me in the eye. "Has it got to come out? *Has* it? Oh, for God's sake don't tell me we've got to be hounded any more!"

This is the sort of thing that makes you feel acutely uncomfortable. There was colour in her cheeks as bright as a strawberry-mark; otherwise she had a waxy sort of pallor. The girl wanted fattening up. She wanted more sleep, and fewer drinks, but she had been having a few whiskies that morning.

"Nobody is going to hound you, Miss Kirkton," I said. "Listen to me, and I'll be frank with you. We are human beings. We don't like scandal any more than you do. But whether we like it or not we are bound to go after a murderer, and the difficulty is just this: it's almost certain that this murder was committed directly because of Miss Wade—or because of you."

She remained very still for a little while, breathing slowly.

"So you know about that too," she stated rather than asked, towards the corner of the desk.

"Just a minute, Miss Kirkton. You understand that you don't have to tell me anything unless you wish to. . . . Now *we* don't want publicity, either; it only interferes with our case in any event; until we have completed a case against somebody. But then it is inevitable, unless we have not enough evidence for an arrest. But don't build too much on that hope. Unfortunately, there is the coroner to consider. Most coroners will string along with us, play our game, and give us help in keeping dark the things we want kept dark. But some coroners are officious asses who like to stand in the limelight and dig up all they can, even if they ruin the case. And Willerton—that's the man who will handle this, worse luck—is one of them. It's only fair to warn you of that."

It is a foolish thing to take a high hand with a witness in this frame of mind. If you speak quietly and and slowly, as though you were explaining something to a child, you usually discover what you want to know. This girl was so hurt that she was only bewildered now.

"But," she said, as though she could understand nothing, "but—in that case, what is Miriam going to *do?* This Mrs. Reilly..."

"Don't let that part of it worry you. We'll take care of Mrs. Reilly. If you want to put yourself—yourselves—entirely in my hands, I'll see what can be done about the rest of it. But that means utter and complete frankness. Do you understand that, Miss Kirkton?"

She shivered, but she nodded her head.

"It's a matter for your own choice," I went on. "And you people have all put yourselves in a bad light already by lying about what was going on at the museum on Friday night...."

She struck the desk. "And that means more trouble, I suppose," she said drearily.

"Oh, you'll get a few acid remarks from the coroner. But they needn't worry you if you are absolutely frank with us."

"I'll tell you everything you want to know," she answered in a quiet, steady, colourless voice not much above a whisper. "Anything and everything, so help me God." The voice grew reckless. "Yes, I'll trust you. You look—solid. Yes. What do you want to know?"

"Very well. We'll leave Miss Wade out of it for the moment, and cut right into it. You were this man Penderel's mistress, weren't you?"

"Yes. No. No, mistress isn't the right word. I mean, that sounds like—a long time, do you understand? Do you? I spent one week-end with him. I couldn't stick him!" She composed her face deliberately, and with an angry nervous snap opened her hand-bag to take out a compact. Her hands were shaking. "I say, why am I making so much fuss about this? I mean: we all do it at one time or another, don't we? I suppose it's because he was so—greasy. Do you understand?"

"Did he ever try to get money from you?"

"No. He knew I hadn't any."

"How many people knew about the affair?"

"My affair, you mean? Miriam did. *He* told her. You see, he knew me before he knew Miriam; and neither of us—Miriam nor I—knew the other knew him at all. I know I'm getting horribly mixed up, but do you understand? Then when Miriam discovered—discovered she was pregnant, and told him to go away and that she never wanted to see him again, he laughed and said she would see him all right. Just to add point to the joke he told her about me."

"Is she still—fond of him?"

"Miriam?" She gave a short, contemptuous breathing sound like the beginning of a laugh; a sort of "Huh!" and twitched her shoulders as though she had got rid of an insect. "Miriam? Not likely."

"Now a personal question. Are you in love with Richard Butler?"

"Yes."

"Does he know about you and Penderel?"

"Yes."

"Since when?"

272

"Since this morning. I told him." She looked at me curiously, with widening eyes; and then tottered on the edge of real hysterical laughter. "Oh, Lord! You don't think—you don't think Rink would have killed him, do you? Oh, look here! You must be horribly old-fashioned. He might think things like Penderel were an excrescence on the face of humanity, but he wouldn't go to the extent of killing him. You don't think that, do you?"

I did not tell her what I thought, as I do not tell you others now. She continued to look at me, now with a growing triumph.

"And I'll tell you something more, Mr. Hadley. Whoever might have wanted to kill Penderel, I can tell you who didn't and couldn't have killed him. There were four of us—four of us!—who were together all the time upstairs in the museum. Rink— Rink told me about his discovering the body before—you know—at eleven o'clock,"—she was breathing hard—"but he couldn't have done it, and you know that perfectly well. I mean, he couldn't have killed him. Rink and Ron Holmes and I were all upstairs from about twenty past ten until eleven o'clock. Miriam joined us a good deal before a quarter to eleven, and we were all together until eleven. Four of us together. What do you think of that?"

Again I did not tell her what I thought, but she looked me in the eye with a bursting kind of sincerity or defiance; I could not quite tell which. I said to her:

"Can I depend on that, or is this just another corporate alibi?"

"You can depend on it, Mr. Hadley. It's true, I swear it's true!"

I opened my desk drawer and got out the rough plan of the museum which Carruthers had drawn.

"Here is a map of the ground floor. Show me in which one of the upstairs rooms you were, with reference to which room it was *over* on the ground floor plan. Understand that?"

"Yes. Certainly. Here! You see, there are four main galleries upstairs, just like the downstairs ones. There's a sort of balcony running round outside them. We were in the Arabian Gallery, and that's directly over this one; over the one marked Egyptian Gallery."

"And next door to the Arabian Gallery is what?"

"What they call the Shawl Room."

"That's directly over the Persian Gallery downstairs?"

"Yes, of course."

"And you know that in one corner of the Shawl Room there is a circular iron stairway leading down to the Persian Gallery?" As she nodded, still looking at me fixedly, I went on: "Let's get this straight, then. You are willing to swear that between, say ten-thirty-five, when Miss Wade came up to join you, you and she and Holmes and Butler were all in the Arabian Gallery and never out of each other's sight—until when?"

"Until about five minutes to eleven," she replied, positively. "Then Rink and Ron had got the chest all packed up. Sam Baxter had just come up to join us from downstairs; *he* came up by the little stairway in the Shawl Room. Then Rink and Sam, who were the strongest, started to cart the packing-case downstairs. Ron—yes, Ron heard Pruen yelling downstairs. So Ron dashed down the little stairway, to see what was the matter, and Rink and Sam carried the chest down the main staircase. I don't know if you know everything that happened. . . ."

She had grown from a too-reluctant witness into a

too-voluble witness, and I diverted her as quietly as I could.

"Let's ask that again, Miss Kirkton. You are positive that from about ten-thirty-five to ten-fifty-five you, Miss Wade, Holmes, and Butler were never out of each other's sight?"

Mere repetition will often do the trick; not necessarily to make a witness change a statement, but to bring out facts that have been buried. Harriet Kirkton was no fool. She had been plucking at the edge of the desk, evidently in a fever to see where she might have made a mistake. Now she nodded, but her flushed face did not alter.

"Yes, I see what you mean," she announced slowly. "You've been talking to Pruen, haven't you? You mean that that comic old Dr. Illingworth got to the museum about the same time that Miriam came upstairs to join us; that would have been about ten-thirty-five, wouldn't it? I hadn't thought of that. And just afterwards Ron Holmes went out on the balcony to yell down to Pruen and ask him whether the actor had got there. . . . Was that what you meant?"

"Well?"

She shut her lips. "Ron was gone from the room about twenty seconds. He was only outside the door. We heard his footsteps, we heard him sing out, and we heard him come back. For all practical purposes, that means that he wasn't out of our sight, doesn't it?"

For all practical purposes, it did, admittedly.

"Just one little point in connexion with that, Miss Kirkton," I pursued. "Illingworth, who was mistaken by everybody for the actor from the agency, met Miriam in the hall as she was coming up from the cellar. . . ."

I said this casually, because I did not wish her to

think I attached any importance to the cellar.

". . . and directly afterwards she came up to join you people. Yet shortly after that Holmes comes out in a fever to ask Pruen whether the actor has arrived. Didn't Miriam say anything about having met him downstairs in the hall?"

It seemed to me that she had not been prepared for this question, and that she had never even thought of it.

"No, she didn't, come to think of it! She didn't say anything at all."

"How was her manner when she came upstairs? Nervous? Worried? Upset?"

"She was very nervous and very upset," replied Harriet Kirkton in an even voice. "You asked me to tell you the truth, and I am doing it."

That girl was assuming a position many people take when they pass through a duty that is lightly—not bitterly, but lightly—dangerous; she was holding herself physically rigid. So do people walk past a vicious-looking dog which has just faintly begun to growl.

"Do you know why she was upset?"

"No, Mr. Hadley, I do not."

I let the thought of that sink in. I got up from my desk, walked over to the window, and stood looking out at the rain while I jingled coins in my pockets. But I caught a glimpse of her from the corner of my eye when I passed the circle of light. Since I dislike over-statement, I do not wish to pitch this too strongly; but it seemed to me that when my eye was turned away there was a sudden relaxing and then horrible tighten-ing of muscles, a slight throwing back of the head to show convulsive wrinkles in the throat, a flutter of waxy eyelids in that bedraggled Burne-Jones figure with its pink-and-white prettiness. But she only took a cigarette-case out of the pocket of her rain-coat, and remained looking quietly at the floor. Then I turned back.

"Miss Kirkton, if your statements can be proved, you have provided an alibi—apparently—for four people. You realise, don't you, that this puts two people in a very bad light. Under your conditions, the only persons who could have committed the murder are Baxter or Jerry Wade."

Which startled her considerably.

"But that's impossible! No! *No!* Oh, it's completely absurd. Wait! The Gaffer was with Illingworth, wasn't he? Besides, he would never— And as for Sam— *Sam!*" Her voice rose to a pitch where the sentence could only be completed by a gesture; words failed to express Sam's shining inadequacy as a murderer. "Sam—oh, my *hat!* Just look at him! Just talk to him! I mean, he's a thoroughly good fellow, of course, but to think of him as a murderer——!"

"Well, it isn't precisely a compliment to be called a murderer. You don't say anything against him if you maintain he isn't."

"Oh, you know what I mean!" She was so violent that tears came into her eyes. "At any other time I'd give you as good as you send but I can't now. I don't want to joke. I don't want to do anything but crawl off in a corner and have a fit of the jim-jams. That is, Sam with his red hair and his wicked past (which just consisted as a rule in getting very drunk) and his new-found dignity and his—just talk to him for a while! As I say, he's a very good fellow, but he's the kind who would propose to a woman by winding up every sentence with, 'if you know what I mean?' Besides, come to think of it, he came up with us in the Arabian Gallery before eleven o'clock. . . ."

"At what time? Do you remember that?"

"Oh, I don't know. I've been all over it with Rink, a dozen times, trying to decide what took place when! I should say he was up there by ten minutes to eleven, anyway. Probably earlier. And if——"

Clarke knocked on the door of the ante-room, and came in with a folded note which he put on my desk; his own elaborate means of private communication, when it would be much easier to use the telephone. I opened the note, which said, "Two men downstairs who accompanied lady in car waiting outside. Names Butler and Wade. Thought you might want to see them."

So I said to Clarke, "Yes, I'll tell you when."

I turned back to the girl and went on.

"Suppose, Miss Kirkton, we get a sketch of this affair from the beginning. Now, about this game that was to be put up on Mr. Mannering?"

"*That's* what makes me feel worst of all!" she burst out. "It's a funny thing, but it does. Greg Mannering's certainly turned the tables on us, hasn't he? We set out to make a fool of him, and he's made the most awful fools of us. I can just picture him laughing—and everybody else—when they tell that story in front of the coroner. And it's made us look so unpleasant as well, don't you see? But we never meant any harm. We just wanted to see him break down when the Fiend was threatening to cut out his liver. It's his insufferable conceit; if you knew him, you'd understand."

"He is in love with Miss Wade?"

She looked thoughtful. "Yes, I think he really and truly is."

"And she with him?"

"It's odd, isn't it," she told me in a queer voice,

"that I should be so sure of him and not of her? It's a bit difficult to tell about Miriam, even when you know her as well as I do. I don't think she is, so terribly much." Harriet grinned. "I know she was most enormously impressed by that police-inspector—what's his name? Carruthers—the other night. But she's talked Greg Mannering, and boasted about Greg Mannering, and fluttered so much over Greg Mannering, that she's got to keep it up in pure self-defence. And there's one thing. If she'd been really so fond of him, I doubt whether she'd have let us put up that game. I mean: suppose it had been Rink Butler; I know I'd jolly well never have let a trick like that be put up on him, just in case he didn't behave too well."

"And what do you think of Mannering? In general, that is?"

She considered a long time, an unlighted cigarette in her fingers.

"I've thought a lot about that. I think he's a *poseur* who really is solid underneath. That is, he might do some wild deed of heroism in the Himalayan jungles, or wherever it is, out of pure vanity; but the point is, he'd do it."

I poked the pencil against the edge of the desk-blotter for a little while. "Very well. Start as I say, at the beginning, and tell me everything that happened on Friday night—from about ten o'clock, when, I understand, your party arrived at the museum. There's just one little point there that nobody seems to have mentioned. . . ."

She was on her guard again, but she nodded enquiringly.

"On Friday night, or rather at a little past one on Saturday morning, Carruthers went round to Holmes's flat to rout you out after he had discovered the body.

The boy at the telephone switchboard said all of you had been upstairs since nine o'clock. That was arranged, I suppose?"

"Yes, it was arranged when we all came flying back from the museum after the fiasco; when we really and truly didn't know there'd been any murder, but we thought there might be a little trouble about our rag. Jerry gave the boy a whacking tip and told him to say that. The boy won't get into trouble, will he?"

"No, not now."

"And, you see, your Inspector Carruthers wouldn't have been allowed to go upstairs at all, except for a ghastly mistake. We were waiting for Rinkey—Rinkey had gone home with old Illingworth, and he made us swear to wait for him at Ron's flat. He hadn't broken the news about the murder yet. Well, so that Rink could come upstairs but nobody else could, Ron said to the boy, 'There'll be a man round here shortly disguised as a police-officer; let him come straight up.' And then up comes your real inspector, and laughs and says to the boy, 'Don't announce me; I'm going to knock on the door and say I'm a police-officer.' So naturally, the boy thought——"

"I see. But he had received no instructions *earlier* in the evening, before you came back from the museum, to say there was a party going on upstairs?"

"No, certainly not. I say, what are you thinking? Why do you sit there like a Sphinx, and never say anything?" She began to pound her fist on the edge of the desk. "What do you think? What is it?"

"Steady, Miss Kirkton. Let's start at ten o'clock, when all of you arrived at the museum. Go on from there."

"You seem to know everything already," she told me drearily. "It was to have been such a grand time, but it wasn't. After Pruen locked up, Rink and Ron Holmes went upstairs to get the chest ready; Sam went away somewhere to say over his part; and Miriam and I started to help Jerry put on his whiskers. . . ."

"Just one moment. There was something between, I understand. Is it correct that, just before then, Holmes took the ivory-handled dagger out of the glass case? And that he put it along with a black false moustache, on the lowest step of the staircase?"

"Yes, that's right."

"Miss Kirkton, I want you to understand that if you do not answer the next question truthfully, I shall know it, and things will go very hard with you. Who took that dagger off the staircase?"

She seemed to brace herself.

"Miriam did," she replied evenly.

20

The Arrow-Headed Key

"Don't misunderstand me!" she cried, and held up her hand again, although still I had said nothing. "I don't mean there was anything—anything *furtive* about it, or that she stole them. Why, both Rinkey and I saw her do it, and old Pruen as well; yes, and she put them back again. She didn't keep them, I tell you! I wish I knew what you were thinking about." She studied me. "But just the same, I've got an idea that that startled you a good deal.

"It was like this. After the party separated, as I told you, Miriam and I were helping Jerry put on his whiskers, and Miriam said, 'I say, Gaffer, you ought to have the right clothes——!'"

"Clothes?"

"Yes. You see, the Gaffer was just wearing his ordinary ones. 'But,' Miriam said, 'there are a couple of papa's old jackets hanging up down in the cellar. You ought to have one. I'll go down and get one, shall I?

Let me go down and get you one!' The Gaffer was cursing the whiskers, which are pretty hard to get exact and not stuck on anyhow, and he didn't pay much attention. But Miriam was enthusiastic about the idea. So Miriam and I went into the hall, and Miriam was going to go down after the jacket. . . ."

"Would she let you go along with her?"

"Yes, of course! I was going. But just then Rink came storming downstairs, calling thirstily for nails, so Miriam said, 'I'll get them, I'll get them!' By the way, Rink nearly tripped over that dagger on the stairs as it was. Rink said to me, 'You come along upstairs with us, my wench. You can do the sealing-wax if you can't do anything else.' We went upstairs; and just as we got up to the top, and were turning round the gallery to the side, I happened to look down. Miriam was just picking up the dagger, and as I looked at her she reached out and touched the false moustache too. Now, listen to me," the girl commanded violently, "because this is absolute truth, I swear! Miriam smiled up at us and said, 'Somebody's going to fall over this dagger if we're not careful. I'll give it to Sam safely.'"

"Did Butler see her, and hear her say that?"

"I—yes, I think so, but I'm not sure. He was in a hurry, and going into the Arabian Room ahead of me, so I couldn't swear he heard it, but he must have."

"What about Pruen? He must have seen and heard, mustn't he?"

"I don't know about hearing, because that's a long hall. But I think he certainly should have seen her, unless the glass cases were in the way. Don't you believe me? Don't you?"

"Take it easy, Miss Kirkton. Here, have a light." She was twisting the cigarette in her fingers; I struck a match and lit it for her. The strawberry marks were showing in her cheeks again, and her eyes were brilliant. "Do you know what she did with the dagger?"

"She—she put it down somewhere else."

"Do you know that for certain? Did you see her?"

"No, but I asked her afterwards—after the business had been found out. I asked her yesterday, because I was horribly afraid; but she told me it wouldn't make the least difference, and certainly to tell the police if anybody asked me. There!"

"How was her manner when she picked it up?"

The girl wore a pale, jeering smile. "Still looking for guilty wretches wringing their horrid hands, Mr. Hadley? She looked perfectly normal; a little excited and surprised, but perfectly normal."

"Surprised? Surprised at what?"

"I don't know."

"Go on."

"But that's all, don't you see? That's absolutely all I can tell you. I went upstairs with Rink and Ron Holmes. Then there was all the delay. First it took them ages to wriggle that chest out of the glass case without smashing any of the pottery round it. And the sack with the sawdust in it had broken. And then we discovered that the lid of the chest was so corroded that it couldn't be opened without using a hammer and chisel on it very carefully. Miriam came up to join us, as I've told you; or rather as you tell me, about twenty-five minutes to eleven. . . ."

"When, I think you said, her manner *was* nervous and upset?"

"We all were, for that matter. All that delay, and the time getting closer and closer! You see, they'd got the chest out, and sealing-wax stuck on it, and started to nail it up in the packing-case before somebody discovered that the lid wouldn't open anyway. Things always happen like that when you're in a hurry. Yes, we were all a bit—you know. So that means nothing. But it completes everything I can tell you. For we were all in the Arabian Gallery until five minutes to eleven o'clock."

I picked up my desk-phone, and said to Clarke in the outer room:

"Send them in."

She made no sound or movement, except to raise the cigarette mechanically to her lips. I should have said that she was exhausted and incurious. Even when Richard Butler and Jerry Wade came rather sheepishly into the room under the guidance of Pierce, she only smiled in an odd sort of fashion, and said to them: "So they nabbed you, did they? Come in and join the party."

"We thought we'd barge in," observed Butler. "Your blandishments may work very well, but we thought you might need backing. How de do, superintendent?"

From Carruthers and Illingworth we had received two different impressions of Richard Butler: from Carruthers that of brilliant mountebank, and from Illingworth, not unnaturally, that of a large devil in a policeman's uniform. I should have judged him in calm appraisal to be nearer the former than the latter, but not a great deal of either except under some great emotional strain. He was large, he had a pleasant face undistinguished except for very intelligent greyish eyes, and his carefully brushed black hair was thinning on top; in after life he would be the sort of person who grows fat and sits chuckling in clubs. He had got a tooth knocked out, as I saw when he smiled rather nervously, and there was a cut over one eye. Infinitely more shrewd and determined, if less placid, looked the sharp-eyed little youth standing beside him after the fashion of an organ-grinder's monkey in a bowler hat. Both of them wore waterproofs, both dripped with rain, and both were nervous: Jerry Wade much the more so. When he sat down, he flopped straight down on the edge of a chair, which is a painful and jarring process.

"I don't know whether you know me, superintendent," he remarked, steadying his voice. "I am the lewd and terrible Dr. Gable of old Illingworth's narrative. Illingworth went round to see my old man yesterday, and I listened to the history of my villainies outside the library door. This is Mr. Butler."

I looked him over. "The Mr. Butler," I said, "who can be charged with being accessory after the fact in Penderel's murder. Who found the body in the carriage, but concealed information——"

"I ask you, Mr. Hadley; what would you have done?" enquired Butler simply. "Blurt it out and start a panic right there in the museum? I was going to tell them afterwards, of course, when I had ridden Illingworth round in a taxi. But your officer got there ahead of me; and, when they had all already sworn they weren't at the museum, I couldn't very well go back on them and spring the surprise then. If there's any bad medicine to swallow, I'm willing to take it; but don't make my offence any worse than it was. . . .For the matter of that, so did old Illingworth see the body in the carriage, but I presume you're not going to say he accessed after the fact as well."

He smiled again, with an air of being broadly at his ease, and dropped his hat.

"Sit down, both of you," I said. "Smoke if you like. You realise, Mr. Butler, that you're in a very nasty position?"

"Quite, thanks."

I leaned round, "And you, Mr. Wade; you know that, unless Dr. Illingworth's narrative is completely believed—and he's rather an erratic gentleman—you may be arrested for murder?"

"Ouch! Jesus!" said the Gaffer, and burnt his fingers with a match. "Here, wait a bit! *Me?* Why?"

"Because all the others, with the possible exception of Mr. Butler, have alibis which do not depend on the testimony of erratic old clergymen who might say anything."

"Well, believe it or not, I didn't do it," he said. "But it's something I hadn't thought of. It's quite true, as I can tell you for my sins, that old Metro-Goldwyn-Mayer suffers from delusions. Stap my vitals, *I* don't know what's the matter with him!—unless the constant reading of thrillers has turned his brain. When he showed up at the house yesterday afternoon to see the old man, he was armed not only with a book called *The Dagger of Doom,* but also with what seems to be a sequel to it, called *The Return of Dr. Chianti,* which somebody at Selfridge's handed him in an unguarded moment. If anybody ever presents him with a Wild-West story, they had better look out for squalls in Edinburgh. All the same," he wiped his forehead, "he may have delusions, but—hang it!—I mean, we really were in there. . . ."

I cut his protestations short. "By the way, Mr. Butler; it really is true, is it, that four of you have a complete alibi? Miss Wade, Miss Kirkton, Mr. Holmes, and yourself?"

You will see that it was useless setting any traps in this respect. Whether they told the truth or whether they lied, they would already have determined on this. I adopted a policy of straightforward frankness.

Butler studied me under the heavy lids of his eyes, twiddled his thumbs, glanced over enquiringly at Harriet (who was smoking placidly), and adopted the same straightforward air.

"I suppose you'd call it that," he acknowledged in a wry tone. "We were certainly upstairs when the—the fellow arrived. At a quarter to eleven, wasn't it? Yes. But, look here, why leave out poor old Sam?"

"Was Mr. Baxter up there with you?"

"He certainly was. That is, he got there just on a quarter to eleven."

"You kept an eye on your watch enough to notice that?"

He laughed boisterously. "No. But there's a clock up in the Arabian Gallery where we were; an exhibit clock, but it's running and it keeps good time. Naturally I was keeping an eye on it. We all were, to see how close to eleven it was getting. It was just a second or two before a quarter to eleven that Sam stuck his head in."

"You will swear to that, of course?"

What appeared to disconcert Butler was the tame way in which I took this, merely recording the statement as though it were a casual fact. Despite himself he stared at me. (I was examining my clasped hands.) He glanced at Harriet, and then at Jerry; and, when he moved his shoes back and forth along the floor, Butler seemed to be feeling for a trap.

"Swear?" he repeated. "Ah! Oh, yes. Of course. The—er—the fact is, I thought you were going to call me a liar."

"Why?"

"Why? Well, the police do, don't they? That's your business, in a way. Where would you be if nobody ever lied?"

"That," I said, "is true enough. Now let's take up your own part in this, Mr. Butler. We might talk about Raymond Penderel."

A stir went round that group. The girl threw her cigarette at the fire and pressed herself with her back flat against the back of the chair. Jerry Wade fished a mouth-organ out of his pocket.

"Did you ever hear the name Raymond Penderel before Friday, Mr. Butler?"

"No," said Butler, very firmly. "What's more, I never even heard it then until Inspector Carruthers mentioned it after he had discovered the body."

"You phoned the Brainerd Agency for an actor, didn't you?"

"Yes."

"You met Penderel at a bar in Piccadilly on Friday afternoon, to tell him about his part, didn't you?"

"Yes," agreed Butler, and laughed again. "What you don't understand is this. I rang them up, explained our wants, and they said, 'Why, as it happens, we've got the very man: Mr. Umph-umph.' I paid no attention to the name; I don't know that I even heard it. Let me ask you this: how many people are there whom you meet in social—not professional—life, whose names you can immediately repeat as soon as they're introduced to you? We don't remember names, unless we have reason to. How much less would I remember this name that was just mumbled off in a telephone, about somebody as abstract as X in the problem; even if I heard the name at all? That's absolutely true, superintendent. I didn't know the name. I said, 'Well, tell him to meet me in the Caliban Bar at two o'clock this afternoon, and ask for me there.' I met him. I didn't like the swine's looks even then. But he seemed capable enough. When I did ask him his name, he said,

'Oh, never mind that; my name will be Illingworth for tonight.' I thought he was acting a bit oddly, and chuckling like a villain in a melodrama—"

"Just one moment. If you knew nothing about him, why do you say that you 'didn't like the swine's looks even then'? Do you know something about him now?"

Butler stopped. He said to Jerry: "I knew we should have brought that damned solicitor along."

"It's no good, Rink," said Harriet, and her cheeks were flaming. "He knows all about it. That is, he knows about me and he knows Miriam had an affair with Penderel."

She very slightly stressed the word "affair." We were at last walking up a path inevitable from the first, and I had long ago decided what course to take. "Affair," and a serious affair, was deep enough motivation in this business. Unless it became absolutely necessary there was no need to bring in the child. I said, spacing the words so that there should be no mistake:

"Yes, there was an affair. During this affair Miss Wade became Penderel's mistress. That is all I officially know, and, if all of you keep your heads, all that anybody need ever know."

There was a silence. They were loyal friends. Harriet Kirkton had tears in her eyes. Jerry Wade's head was lowered, and his mouth was clamped hard on the mouth-organ.

"That—" muttered Harriet. "That's—all right," she added with a queer weakness of phrase. "But what about this terrible coroner of yours?"

"Get a good man to hold a watching brief for all of you. Don't lose your heads, and don't be bamboozled. You'll come through. But remember: don't lie to me. I'll ask you again. Has anybody lied about anything?"

"No," said Jerry Wade, quietly. He looked up. His

face was suffused with blood, and he had not quite recovered his mask of amiable cynicism. "And— thanks. Nobody will lie to you, now."

"Did you know about your sister and Penderel, Mr. Wade?"

"No, I didn't. That is, I didn't know about it until last night. Then she told me. *I had* heard Penderel's name mentioned, though: mentioned in writing. A very long time ago Miriam wrote me about a 'terribly charming' person she had met by that name, but she was always doing that. I remembered the name because it sounded like somebody in a Michael Arlen story." He blew a few sour notes of cynicism into the mouth-organ. "What am I supposed to do? 'Sir, I will horsewhip you on the steps of this club!' I wish I had known, though. I might have proved useful for something. But not very much. Ah, me eye! The devil!"

He blew a long blast and then shut his eyes.

I turned back to Butler. "Now, then, suppose we have your account of Friday night. Why, for instance, were you so anxious to make a fool of Mr. Mannering?"

Butler seemed puzzled. "Frankly, I don't know. It was the reports I'd heard of him, I suppose, or probably just my usual desire to stage a show of some kind. Actually he's not a half-bad sort when you come to know him." He pointed to his missing tooth. "I don't think I could ever be a close friend of his, but then— well, you have an easier time in life if you let things go smoothly. I don't know whether you heard, but we had a bit of a dust-up. All of a sudden, while we were in the middle of it, it struck me as so damned funny that two people should be banging each other all over the place, just for the amusement or admiration of others, that I couldn't help roaring. I achieved something like a philosophy in that minute. It was like walking into poison-gas and finding that it was laughing-gas. I question whether there would be very many wars if that state of mind could become universal. But the show— well, as I say, put it down to general theatricals."

His own account of the evening was so exactly like the other accounts in every particular that I will not go over it. I stopped him in only one place. He was telling the usual story about Miriam Wade going down into the cellar after nails, while he and Harriet went upstairs to the Arabian Gallery.

"You went upstairs," I interposed. "Now, when Miss Wade picked up the dagger off the staircase, what did she say?"

Butler stopped as though he had tripped over something. Then he looked at me.

"Here!" he cried, in the manner of one who has been hit below the belt. "Here, damn it, I say——!"

Harriet spoke curtly: "I'm sorry if I have put my foot in it. It doesn't make the slightest difference, as I've insisted a dozen times, but we ought to play fair with Mr. Hadley as we've promised. Rink, I didn't know whether you would have seen, but I thought certainly you would have heard. Miriam did pick it up off the stairs; she put it back, of course, and it can't do her the slightest harm, because she certainly was upstairs with us all the time. . . . Don't *look* at me like that!"

"I'm not looking at you like that," protested Butler in an aggrieved tone. He got out a handkerchief and mopped his forehead. "Come to think of it, I certainly did hear her say something like, 'give it to Sam safely.' Yes, by George! She did! But this is the first time anybody's mentioned it. . . ."

"Miriam and I discussed it together," the girl snapped. "And, since we'd agreed to be frank—well, there it is."

"Well, what the devil did she do with it?" he demanded. "Did she give it to Sam? I didn't see it sticking in his belt any time. But I can't remember when I did see the cursed thing last. The only thing I do remember is that it definitely wasn't on the stairs when Sam and I brought the coffin downstairs at eleven o'clock, because I was looking for it. For the love of Mike, where did she put it?"

I stopped him. "According to what Miss Kirkton says, we have now no more information than that she 'put it down' somewhere. But that can wait. Since her alibi is good, it's not necessarily damaging. Let's come to the last act in the affair. . . . Your discovery of the body."

They all went quiet. For the first time Butler looked genuinely uneasy instead of merely nervous.

"Oh, yes," he said. "That. As you've heard, Sam and I brought the 'coffin' downstairs at just before eleven o'clock. I didn't hear what they were gabbling about at the front of the museum. All I could think of was that it was not yet eleven, Mannering hadn't come, and we could still work the trick. Then I thought I remembered having left my truncheon upstairs. . . ."

"Why the truncheon? You were got up as a point-duty man."

"Was I?" he asked hazily. "Yes. It came with the uniform, and besides it was very necessary. You see, I was the policeman and a very important figure. You'd realised, hadn't you, that there had to be an *ending* for this little farce of ours? That is: as soon as Sam Baxter was to be bending over Mannering, threatening him with the knife, it wouldn't stop there or peter out as an obvious joke whether we scared Mannering or whether we didn't. No, no, no. Bad dramatic unities, and we wanted to keep the business for future reference. Just as Sam bends over with the knife, while the actor in the role of Illingworth covers the rest of them with a gun, Harriet was to break loose and run screaming. At this moment I charge in. 'Illingworth' (the devilish Mohammedan in disguise) fires at me point-blank. I crumple up, breaking a red-ink pellet inside my tunic; but I am still full of fire even if I pretend to lie doggo. When he approaches to fire again, I paralyse his wrist with the truncheon and grab his gun. Then I have got both Prince Abú 'Obiad of Táif and the treacherous Illingworth where I want them. Mouthing curses, they are taken and locked in the curator's room. Then I, badly wounded, urge Mannering to take the gun and stand guard over these desperate characters. Either he funks it, or he agrees. If he agrees I say: 'You have the courage to take them to Scotland Yard?' 'Yes, yes!' cries the dauntless Mannering. 'Lead me to them!' While he holds his pistol with grim determination, I say hoarsely, 'Get ready!' —and fling open the door. Gritting his teeth, he rushes in.

"On either side of the desk, their wigs and whiskers laid aside, their feet propped up on the desk, and smoking cigars with relish, Sam Baxter and the actor sit comfortably with a bottle of whiskey between them.

"'Allow me,' say I with a great bow, 'allow me to present Dr. William Augustus Illingworth and Prince Abú 'Obiad of Táif.'"

I said: "I am very glad, of course, to hear the final instalment of the serial. But——"

Butler made a savage gesture.

"Oh, I know it sounds plain damn silly told here and now," he snapped. "Anything would, in this place. But we all thought it was a thundering good idea, and that a camera-study of his face at the moment would be interesting. It's important, very important, because I had to have that truncheon. Don't you see? You can't stage a really convincing fight-scene, but a blow across a padded arm—! So, when I discovered that the time was near and I couldn't find the truncheon, I went roaring round to find it. Then I remembered that, when I came in, I had slung it into one of the coaches to get it out of the way.

"While the others were at the front of the hall, on the other side of that thing, I opened the door of the travelling-carriage on the hall side. I don't know why I chose that one. Maybe because it was the most imposing-looking. . . . And there was that hellish thing lying on its face on the floor just below the level of my eyes.

"My first idea was that it was some loony sort of joke on me. So I didn't swear, or say anything. I just hauled myself into the carriage, and pulled the thing upright so that I could get a look at it."

"You recognised him?"

Again Butler was swabbing his face with the handkerchief. "Yes, of course. The whiskers were coming off his cheeks; I knew him in a second. So I just held him half upright, jumped down, and slammed the door in his face. . . . The next couple of minutes are about the worst I ever remember; or don't remember. Everybody seemed to be yelling at me, but I couldn't see things clearly. Otherwise it's a bit hazy. I came to myself when I happened to glance across the hall and saw the faint silhouette of a head sticking up behind the ventilator in the lift. There was nothing intrinsically horrible about that head, but it was horrible to me."

He drew a deep breath.

"Now then. There's one thing Illingworth didn't see, if I heard his story rightly from old man Wade. He tumbled off his perch in there; he didn't see me go to the carriage, and the first thing he did see was me opening the door wide while I stood inside, to get more light.

"When I first opened the door, something fell out. It must have been on him or beside him, and had rolled against the door. I caught it; I couldn't help catching it. I must have put it in my pocket, although I don't remember doing any such thing. The next time I found it—in fact, the next time I even *thought* of it— was this morning, when I was going through the uniform before I took it back to the people I had hired it from. I haven't mentioned this to anybody yet, and I don't know what it means. But I came here to give it to you, and here it is."

The others had jumped up, and I had a difficult time to keep a wooden face. He laid on my desk a steel key of rather curious shape. It had a long, narrow shaft, with a narrow hole at the head, and four even little flanges in an end shaped something like an arrow.

"Why, hang it—" said Jerry, and stopped.

"Yes?"

"I know what it is. It's one of the special design the governor likes. That looks like a key to the back gate in the wall of the museum."

I stood up abruptly.

"That's all," I said. "You can go now, all of you."

21

The Print On The Mirror

There were, however, a few more things settled before I let them go. So far as I could ascertain, only three people had keys to the back gate of the museum: Ronald Holmes, old Geoffrey Wade, and Miriam. Jerry did not know that Miriam had possessed a key at all, but Harriet remembered it. Miriam had told her the night before that she (Miriam) had procured one from Holmes. Nevertheless, Harriet stated that the key Butler found in the travelling-carriage could not be Miriam's, since the latter key was still in her friend's possession and she had seen it the night before. The key Butler found was a new and shining one; it had recently been cut, and, what was better, the cutter's firm-name was engraved on it. *Bolton, Arundel Street, Strand*.

Finally, I asked whether any of them would object to having his fingerprints taken. Most people refuse, as is their right. But these three seemed interested in the idea and Butler even insisted on it.

"I want to get this clear, because *I* touched that knife," he admitted freely. "I didn't grip it or handle it, you understand. I only touched it—I think in a hazy kind of way to make sure the thing was real. How do we go about it?"

When they had gone, I sat down to study and tabulate all the reports before I went on to have a look at the Wade Museum. The various prints found on the dagger, as I discovered by going over the photographs, were so confused and smudged as to be almost meaningless. We should never get a conviction on evidence like that. But there were other leads which gave me a good deal of satisfaction. I sent Sergeant Betts to Bolton's with the key. I rang up Carruthers at Vine Street, asking him to do a bit of off-duty and investigate a certain affair for me at Prince-Regent Court, Pall Mall Place; and then to join me at the museum. It was nearly lunch-time before I set out for the museum myself.

The drizzle was clearing off, but it was still raw and gusty. And, even if Carruthers' fanciful ideas about such a solid-looking place as the museum were too highly coloured, I was bound to agree with him about its desolate appearance. There were no loungers round the place today, and it remained closed to the public. The doors were opened by the day-attendant who gave his name as Warburton. Only one cornice of lights had been turned on in the main hall, and the place was half in darkness. Again I am bound to admit that it struck me as quite an ordinary-looking hall, very much like that of any other museum. Poetical values are all very well in their way, but I do not find them an efficient substitute for a tape-measure and good eyesight.

Somebody was coming towards me from the famous "Gallery of the Bazaars," which was my first point of interest. (You see why?) The person who walked up and spoke to me in the half-darkness was, from his description, Mr. Ronald Holmes. I was very favourably impressed by him; he struck me as a capable, energetic and quiet young man who could look you in the eye and was not to be hoodwinked by nonsense. Though he seemed under a strain, his manner was without nervousness and he spoke straightforwardly.

"Yes, sir," he said. "Sir Herbert told us to expect you. Mr. Wade is down in the curator's room now, along with Dr. Illingworth, going over some of the newest acquisitions. If you'd like to go there——?"

"Never mind the curator's room," I said. "I should like to have a look at the cellar. But something else first. Will you have all the lights turned on in the hall?"

He looked at me curiously, but he made no comment when he went out to speak to Warburton. In the meantime, I went to the obliquely-jutting wall of the exhibit at which the coal had been thrown; its mark was still visible on the reddish-yellow roughened plaster high over my head. It was—as you have heard— just above a curtained booth displaying brasswares (a dusty germ-trap if I ever saw one). I put myself with my back to the entrance to this booth, and measured off a line of vision as to what I could see from there through the very broad, high archway into the hall. The lights were turned on. From this position I could barely see a segment of the archway to the Persian Gallery just across the hall. But I had a clear oblique view of all the five coaches in a line, of part of the archway giving on the Egyptian Gallery, and of the cellar door at the end. Since the Gallery of the Bazaars was dark, that part of the hall glowed before me like an illuminated stage, and there was no possibility of a mistake.

I was whistling "John Peel" in a pretty satisfied way when I noted all this. (You see why?) Then I beckoned to Holmes, for he might be able to give valuable information, and went to the cellar. Holmes was studying me with an intent expression, and I wondered if he had any idea of what I was thinking about. But he said nothing.

Carruthers has already given you a partial description of the cellar. Beyond the door, you descend a flight of concrete stairs. These stairs face the rear wall of the whole museum. To your right, as you descend, is a board partition cutting off this long narrow segment from the rest of the cellar. To your left is a coal-bin, enclosed. The rear wall, facing you from ten feet away as you stand on the stairs, is pierced by three high basement windows half below the level of the ground outside. The cellar has a stone floor and whitewashed walls comparatively clean. Do I make myself clear?

All this I saw when Holmes switched on the electric light. Perhaps you remember that Carruthers, in his story, mentioned this fact: when he climbed down through the coal-hole on the night of the murder, and came through to the rear of the cellar here, he felt a draught. Added to what I already knew, it was a suggestion. Over against the coal-bin I found a decrepit kitchen chair. Climbing up on this, I tested each of the windows in turn, and found exactly what I knew I should find. The middle window was unlocked.

Then I turned back to Holmes, who was standing just under the hanging electric bulb. It gave his glasses an opaque reflection, and threw shadows down his face. He stood with his hands in his pockets, whistling a tune between his teeth.

"At the time," I said, "let's pass over your story of events on Friday night. I've accounts from several people, which seem to tally. I want to ask you about the gate in the rear wall round the yard of this place. Is it always kept locked?"

He was clearly surprised. "Always, sir. The gate in the wall, you mean? Yes, always, by Mr. Wade's orders. We have sufficient protection against burglary, of course, but Mr. Wade wants no tramps sleeping in the yard. Yes, you can even find tramps in the neighbourhood of St. James's. Er—" He hesitated, and rubbed the back of his hand across his forehead. "May I ask why you want to know that?"

"I have been told that there are just three keys to that gate. You have one, Mr. Wade senior has one, and Miss Wade has one. Is that correct?"

"Not quite, sir. There are only two keys."

"Two?"

"Yes. You see, Miss Wade borrowed mine. And so, when Mr. Wade went away on Friday morning, I had to borrow *his*. Besides, it was a good scheme." He smiled. "By his time you know all about that idiotic show. I was fool enough to consent, so there it is. Since I did consent, I thought it was as well to do the thing thoroughly and take no chances of Mr. Wade's coming home unexpectedly and breaking in on us through the rear gate."

"So Mr. Wade has had no key to the gate since Friday morning?"

"That's right. By the way, here is the key, if you want to see it." He was eager to do the conscientious thing. He took from his pocket an exact duplicate of the key Butler had found in the travelling-carriage, except that this one was old and discoloured. "I shall have to give this back to him. He's kicking up enough row as it is. When Miriam came down here on Friday night to rummage after nails, apparently she messed up and disturbed his beloved workshop in there." Holmes nodded toward the board partition. "She threw about his working-gloves and screw-drivers and whatnot, just as he does himself. If I hadn't known better, I would have sworn that the old man had been working there himself."

I considered matters for a second or two, and then examined the key.

"The other key," I said, "the one Miss Wade has now—is it an old one too?"

"Old?"

"It hasn't been recently cut?"

"Good Lord, no!" He was growing more perplexed, though he remained courteous and watchful. "We've had them for a couple of years, at least."

"Do you know what she wanted with the key?"

"Haven't the faintest idea. That's what I asked her. But Miriam's a strange girl, superintendent." His smile became a little grim, and it made his face appear older. "Whims, you know! She'll always give you that answer. 'Oh, come, now; don't ask questions!—indulge a whim of mine!' *I* don't refuse her anything. Look here, not to be unduly curious, but just what the devil is all this about?"

"Thanks. Will you go upstairs for a little while?" I suggested. "There's some work to be done down here on my own..."

He shrugged his shoulders. "Just as you like, sir. Shall I tell Mr. Wade that——"

"No. I shall not want to talk to Mr. Wade until after I have seen Miss Wade. Leave me a clear coast to get out of here quietly. If Inspector Carruthers shows up here, send him to me. There is just one point I want to get clear. On Friday night, when Dr. Illingworth got loose and you people dragged him down through the coal-hole, were you one of the people who pulled him down?"

You have seen people's faces completely freeze up. His did. To his mind (and perhaps he was not far from wrong) the tomfoolery was nearly as bad as the murder.

"I was down here, yes. Mr. Richard Butler pulled him through the hole, with Baxter helping. I'm quite aware, sir, that the whole thing was quite indefensible . . . !"

"Yes, of course. When you came down here, and went to the coal-cellar, were there already packing-cases piled up so that it was easy to get up into the street? A sort of natural bridge?" He nodded, his eyes narrowing, and I went on: "So that no member of the party got coal-dust on the soles of his shoes? Is that true?"

"I suppose so. I didn't notice any traces, certainly, but I was hardly interested in anything like that."

"And, except for the actual coal-cellar, is there any place down here where coal is kept, aside from that bin over there?" I pointed.

"No. No, that's the only place."

"Finally, to clear up the point, Mr. Holmes: Is there a looking-glass anywhere in this cellar?"

He was so surprised that his intelligent face looked rather witless. One side of his face wrinkled up; he pulled at his collar, moved his neck about, and finally exploded into laughter.

"Excuse me, superintendent, but this is fictional-detective stuff with a vengeance! You sound like the anecdotes I hear about that friend of yours, Dr. Fell. That's his method, isn't it?"

"Never mind that," I said curtly. "Answer the question." (This was the first piece of real damned cheek I had heard that day.)

"Looking-glass!" he repeated, and grinned again. "It's about the last thing you would usually find in a cellar. But, as a matter of fact, there are a couple. Mr. Wade at one time had some great showman's idea of a Hall of Mirrors—like Madame Tussaud's, only we managed to dissuade him. He bought a couple of those big distorted glasses, you know; he used to keep them down here and stand in front of them roaring with laughter. But they've never been used, and they were stacked over there beside the coal-bin."

"That's all," I said; and Holmes, a grave sort of smile on his face, backed away from me slowly—watching me steadily—until the back of his heel kicked the stairs. Then he went up, still smiling. If I had not known better I should have thought he disliked the idea of those mirrors being found.

I discovered them leaning against the far wall beyond the coal-bin, where the light was very dim. They were pier-glasses, the topmost one facing outwards and so grey with dust that only a hazy image was discernible. Its surface consisted of a series of bulging ridges—you know the sort—which distort the human figure out of the shape God gave it, and present a show considered humorous by those people who must laugh at a monkey-house even if they have to laugh at themselves. I got out my electric torch, flashed it on the mirror, and for one second I got a devil of a turn. On a blank surface of dust, a face looked straight out at me: broad and flattened beyond nightmares, with a long moustache and a row of teeth like a wolf. It was only my own face, of course. But nothing in this case was so charged with nightmare as that flattened monstrosity thrust out at me from the dust in the quiet and dark of the cellar.

But I was not interested in that. I could see my face, and nothing else, because the surface of the mirror had been wiped clean in one patch. I bent over to examine this clean patch, and found that godsend which even criminal investigators sometimes receive. Just on the edge of the dust, smeared down from the top but firm where it stopped, there was one clean finger-print.

I had got the murderer. There needed to be issued only a few more instructions—an examination of that coal-bin, for instance, in a light stronger than my flash-lamp—then an interview with Miriam Wade; and I had the murderer. I wasn't especially pleased about it; I was even a little dispirited. But I had to go through with it, which is the curse of having a conscience.

The door up at the head of the stairs opened, and I switched off my flashlight.

"—but if some miscreant has indeed purloined gloves from your desk," rose up a measured, loud, argumentative voice, "I can suggest an immediate connotation, gleaned from——"

"—and screw-driver!" squeaked another voice. "Dash my buttons, they pinched my little screw-driver to open that damn Arabian silver-chest, and where's the big one? Watch your step. The *Bab-el-Tilsim* imitation ain't been unpacked yet, but it's back in my workshop and we'll have a go at it if— Hullo!"

Their feet, especially those belonging to the tall, lean man whom I spotted as Dr. Illingworth, made a great clatter even on concrete stairs. Old Geoffrey Wade bustled down ahead; even his long moustaches seemed to bustle. Behind him, jerking his shoulders forward at every step, doddered the other figure with its big goggles and long wrinkled chin shoved into the collar. There was enough light for old Wade to see me standing in the corner. At the foot of the stairs he stopped so abruptly that Illingworth bumped into him.

"Hullo!" he crowed. "Who's that? Hey? Who's that over there?"

I switched on my light and explained. He stopped a little way in front of me, a ruffled turkey-cock, his head slightly on one side and the little black eye with a completely unreadable expression gleaming like a bit of glass. While I explained, that eye roved. There was something in the air. He was preparing for something.

"Ho?" he said, jingling coins in his pockets while he expanded his chest. "Hadley, eh? Yes, yes, yes. Bert Armstrong told me. Well, but you don't have to come sneaking in like that." Then he threw back his head and crowed with mirth. "Mucking about!— Still, you interested in my funny mirrors? Here, let's have a good look!"

His spring was so quick that I did not have time to move. He was past me, swabbing at the mirror with his sleeve, before I could catch his arm and spin him away. But then the damage was done. There was no longer a finger-print.

There was a silence you could hear in that cellar instead. Then he crowed with angry, giggling mirth. "Here, what the hell you doin'?" he demanded. "What's the idea of——"

Fell, I think you will admit I am a pretty even-tempered sort of fellow. I try to mind my own business, and it's a weak kind of man who likes to threaten. But I think it was that inane, cracked laugh of his, thrown in my face like water—and dirty water at that

—which did it. And it was not the last time that feeling came to me in this case, or the last time it happened.

"Do you know what you've done?" I said in a voice that sounded queer to myself.

"Done? Done? What do you mean, done? You take that expression off your face——"

"Go upstairs," I said, and sounded easier this time.

"Oh-ho?" said Wade, putting his head on one side and his fists on his hips. "Now that's it, is it? You'd have the blasted nerve, would you, to try to order *me* about in my own——"

"You get out of this," I said, "and get out of it now. I've tried to do the best I could for your family in this thing. I don't care whether you're Geoffrey Wade or the Cham of Tartary; but, by God, you'll go upstairs when I tell you or you'll go to gaol and stay there. Which do you want it to be?"

He was going to have my hide, of course, but presently he went. The business was made no more soothing by Illingworth, who kept enquiring in a pleasant solicitous way whether anything was wrong. When they had gone, I walked up and down the cellar a few times to get things in perspective. There must be some sort of internal combustion when you are boiling mad and still you don't let your voice get above normal—anyhow, it has a bad effect afterwards. That long-moustached tyrant, who had never had a thorough taking-down in his life, jeered at me from the staircase and threatened what would happen when his influence got to work.

My best cure was to go quietly to work and see whether there were any other evidences which had not been destroyed. I discovered something else smudged on the whitewash, which might or might not be a finger-print. But it was dubious. When Carruthers here arrived some minutes later I was still looking.

"You were quite right, sir," he told me. "I've just come from Prince-Regent Court. And—what you told me to ask—you were right."

I gave him certain instructions, among them to stay there until I had phoned to the Yard for Betts and Preston to excavate that coal, as well as for the fingerprint outfit. Then I left. As I went out through the upper hall, Holmes was in the open gallery which ran round the place above. He was leaning his arms on the marble balustrade, not far above the top of the big black travelling-carriage. He stood there motionless, in his spectacles a kind of miniature and younger Illingworth against the bluish-white light. And, though he nodded courteously, I wondered whether it was an accident or whether he had tipped off old Jeff to go down into the cellar. There were many things yet to be investigated at that museum, but I had to see Miriam Wade first.

After a few breaths of the rainy air outside, I felt cooler. From a telephone-box in St. James's Street, I sent word to the Yard, and then I drove in the police-car through the crush of noon traffic out to Hyde Park Gardens. From the outside Geoffrey Wade's house was no more pretentious than the other dun-coloured stone houses which blocked up the street; and no different, except that it was larger.

But it was pretentious inside. I am no authority on these matters, being myself inordinately proud of my six-room place in East Croydon, with the garden and all; still I do know, if only from police work, when a butler really acts like a butler and when he acts like one in a drawing-room comedy. This one gave me the hump. He took me through a big hall where many plush horses were stabled, and into a little room furnished in what they call Renaissance style. Then, carrying my card delicately, he went to find out whether Miss Wade could see me.

I had not long to wait. There was a rustling and whispering in the hall outside, dominated by a decisive voice proclaiming, "I will deal with him." Then the *portières* were whirled aside, with a gesture like Cyrano de Bergerac, and I was confronted with the calm sneer of Mr. Gregory Mannering.

"Yes, my good man?" said he. "Yes?"

22

Why Miriam Wade Visited The Cellar

I knew it must be Mannering, because it could be nobody else. He walked into the room with a casual sort of air, flicking his fingers against my card; and behind that air of his there was hate—why, I couldn't tell. But I studied him fairly closely. He was a good height, very broad of shoulder and narrow of waist, which his light grey suit showed without emphasising. Everything about his clothes was in what Fell might call frantic good taste. He had his head held back, but not too far back; he had his craggy sunburned good looks oiled over with a kind of humorous contemptuousness; his black hair was sharply brushed; and from under those "tangled brows" of which Carruthers had spoken—whatever that may mean—he looked me over. Of that "likeable brag and bounce of excitability repressed," also mentioned by Carruthers, there was no sign. I should not have called him likeable. But there was undoubtedly a power about him. He came shouldering in, lit by the long windows and appropriately set off against those Renaissance furnishings which looked bogus but were probably genuine.

And he smiled.

"My good sir," he said with heavy gentleness, "do you know anything about police work?"

This was not merely impudence; it was a kind of lunacy. In his own way he was quite serious. For the first time that day I felt inclined to laugh; and I almost laughed in his face. He saw me suppress it by keeping my jaws together, and that curious hatred grew.

"Well," I said, "I'm a superintendent of the Criminal Investigation Department, but I suppose that depends on the way you look at it. Aren't you the young man who solves thug murder mysteries in India?"

He came over to the table.

"Do you know the country north of Hyderabad?" he enquired politely.

"No."

"Or the upper Jumna?"

"Never heard of it."

"Then do you think," he said, "that in your ignorance you are quite qualified to talk like that?"

However reason might argue against it, to say that this fellow was not putting my back up would be a lie. All the same, I wanted to forget personalities and get to business, when he went on:

"I asked you, Mr.—" he made a feint of looking at the card, found that too much trouble, and changed it to: "I asked you whether you knew anything about police work. The reason was this. You wish to see Miss Wade. If you know something of the law, you will know that she is not compelled to answer any questions, and even then she may demand the presence of a solicitor."

"Yes, I knew that. That's why I want to know if she will see me."

"I'm making that point, you understand, because you over-stepped badly this morning. You got three people into your office and pestered them with questions you had no right to ask; and they were weak enough to answer them. Good God!" He opened his mouth and laughed snortingly. "They went against my advice. I told them, if they must go, to take a solicitor. . . . As I say, what your silly little traps may have been, or what your bluster may have done, I don't know. But——"

There was a flurry at the *portières* and Harriet Kirkton ran in. She was followed more lumberingly by a stoutening young man whose violent red hair placed him at once. Sam Baxter wore a morning-coat which sat cumbrously on him, and carried a whiskey-and-soda in his hand. His heavy brown eyes were pinched down under reddish lids; and his expression, as he regarded Mannering, was of a dislike which startled his easygoing nature so much that he could not quite believe in its intensity.

"Greg, don't be a fool," said Harriet in a voice of sharp common sense. "He's our friend. He knows the truth——"

"The truth," repeated Mannering, and smiled and made a sound out of his nostrils. "Yes, I know the truth too, you see. That's why I'm trying to conceal it."

Baxter made a gesture with the glass and spoke in a protesting voice, "But hang it all, she *wants* to see him! She's going to see him anyway. Here, superintendent, I'd have been round to see you myself this morning, only I was recovering from a binge. Ask me anything you like. I was Prince Abú, you know"——

Mannering's grin broadened at this point—"and maybe I can help."

"The point is," I said, "whether Mr. Mannering is willing to answer any questions."

"I am not, of course," replied Mannering.

"Why not?"

"Because I don't have to and I don't choose to," he informed me, with a cool smile.

"Would you rather answer me or answer the coroner?"

He laughed. "The old question, the old story, the eternal threat of the police! My good Mr. Hadley, do you think you can subpoena me to this inquest?"

"My good Mr. Mannering," I said, for this business was beginning to get under my skin considerably, "they could subpoena the Archbishop of Canterbury if they thought he had any connexion with it. Particularly if they could prove that, in one respect at least, His Grace was a liar."

I thought that was going to take him on the side of the jaw; but it had only a faint effect. I saw for the first time that business of drawing his eyebrows together so that he looked half cross-eyed; but his contempt was so queer and utter and complete that he opened his mouth square like a Greek mask and grinned palely again.

"Am I indeed?" he said, indulgently. "The old story and the old bluff. In point of fact, I don't lie. I don't bother to lie, that's all."

"In point of fact, I don't bother to bluff. It's not entirely necessary to question you, because you have already made some statements to Inspector Carruthers, which are now on record. What I *was* wondering was whether you would stick to those statements."

"What statements?"

"I see. Then you are willing to answer questions after all?"

"That's a pretty poor quibble, you know. I'll answer them if I choose; and if I don't choose I won't, of course."

"Fair enough. Not even a guilty person could say more, could he? All right. You told Inspector Carruthers on Friday night that you called at Prince-Regent Court, in Pall Mall Place, at twenty minutes to eleven. The switchboard boy told you that there was a party going on upstairs; but you beat him into submission and went up just the same."

I put no inflection of a question into that, but merely read it from my note-book. He lifted one shoulder, slightly, looked steadily at me, and said nothing.

"That is quoted," I explained, "not to call you a liar, but because it is the choice between deciding whether you told the truth or all the others told the truth. Miss Kirkton told me in my office this morning that the boy had not been told to say there was a party going on upstairs until after they had all returned from the museum at considerably past eleven o'clock. Until then, the boy had no orders to say anything at all; he knew they had all gone out, and that was all he knew. Now then: is the whole church singing wrong except you? —by the way, that was what you said, wasn't it, Miss Kirkton?"

The girl sat down in a high-backed chair, and her eyes moved round uneasily.

"I don't know whether it's what she said," observed Baxter with violent inspiration, "but it's true. I mean to say, I remember that! The kid got a couple of quid to say we'd been up there all evening."

Mannering's laughter was beginning to grow monotonous, a sort of talkie of those endless reels the kids show on their toy motion-picture machines. But it jarred and jarred, and it was evidently worrying Harriet.

"Is that all you've got, my friend?" he enquired with amusement.

"No, not all. For instance, at what time did you really go to the place; at what time did you really arrive there?"

That touched him. "Oh? So you doubt I went there? Very unfortunate. Because, you see, I did."

He was on safe ground here, and he knew it, but he evidently took the whole world for a kennel of fools.

"I don't doubt you went there. I was only asking: at what time? It was not at twenty minutes to eleven anyhow. The boy says you didn't. Inspector Carruthers talked to him not half an hour ago."

Mannering, hitching his shoulders a little, walked round the table and took up a position with his back to the light. He seemed to be considering. His self-assurance was so complete that he elbowed me aside as he strolled past.

"Now that is very clever of you, *monsieur l'inspecteur*," he said. "As a matter of fact, the boy would not have seen me in any case, since I went up the back way and by the back staircase so that I should be unobserved. Do you care to know why I wished to be unobserved, and why I wished to pay a visit to the flat of the good Mr. Holmes? My good sir, you will learn in the proper time, but you will not learn from me, because I like to keep you on tenterhooks and therefore I do not choose to answer. Ah, well! *Lahm elkhanzeer yuhfaz muddah izâ mullih!* Allow me to spell that out, my excellent rattle-twister, so that you can write it in your note-book. It means that pork keeps a long time if it is salted; and I recommend the treatment to you. Meantime, you are not going to see Miss Wade."

A woman's voice said: "Why not?"

I had not seen her come in. She stood with her hands on the back of a chair, and now at last I saw Miriam Wade. What is the rational viewpoint, the practical and common-sense viewpoint, from which to look at that girl?

She was undoubtedly good-looking, and, except for a strain round the eyes, she also seemed in the pink of health. What Mrs. Hadley would have thought of her I can guess, but that has no place in my own testimony. I say pink of health, because that was the first thing which struck me: she was wearing a pink dressing-gown or négligé or the like; and, although I have always considered pink an unholy colour, it suited her proportions admirably. She made you conscious of it, if you understand what I mean; Carruthers will. And, to a certain extent, I can understand what made everybody follow her—even though she was not beautiful, not posed, and (God knows) not clever. The whole atmosphere of the room changed when she came in. No, no, Fell, I am not an old satyr and I am not indulging in poetic flights; I am simply a practical man stating facts. She stood there with her hands on the back of the dark chair; dark-haired, dark-eyed; and I am convinced that to have seen any other woman in London walk into a reception-room, in négligé, at one o'clock in the afternoon, would have been a staggerer. You were not conscious of anything like this, but only felt guilty for noticing what you did notice. Do I make *that* clear?

She spoke, rather snappishly: "Why isn't he going to see me?"

316

"He wants to send you to the gallows, that's all," answered Mannering coolly. "If that means nothing to you——"

"Rubbish!" cried Miriam with a grinning gusto, and threw up one hand. "Where's that other police-officer, the nice one? Gallows! Oh, I say, what awful *bilge!*"

Mannering whirled round.

"I am simply warning you, my dear," he told her in the same cool tone, "that if you do what I've told you not to do—well, we must break it off, mustn't we? And where would you get another husband after this business comes out?"

She went white, but she did not speak. I have never seen on any stage the cool poise and power with which Mannering carried that off; he was marble, he was a maniac, but he spoke that sentence—which, uttered by any other man to any woman or in front of anybody else, would have turned loose thunders—he spoke it in such a way that nobody spoke or questioned him. He turned, nodded to me with a casual twinkle in his eye, and without a word more strolled out of the room.

And what I saw in Miriam Wade's eyes was fear. She moved over a little, slid down in the chair, and suddenly started to cry.

Hum! I see that in remembering the scene, and in sketching it out completely so that Fell may understand, I have possibly overstepped the limits of a practical man. Nevertheless, there it is. I shepherded the others out of the room, telling them that I wished to question Miriam alone. Then I closed the *portières*. But I felt that, unless I played very cautiously now, I was beaten.

She had gone over and sat down near one of the high windows, in a settee sort of affair with a stamped leather back and brass nail-heads. She was leaning forward, with the faint light falling down one side of her face and throat, the pink négligé drawn round her; leaning forward with her big eyes fixed on me; leaning forward, though I am willing to swear without conscious intent, in such a manner that any jury of women would have hanged her simply on her appearance. All the same, I sat down in a chair at a discreet distance and explained who I was.

"And," I concluded decisively, "you must not let him frighten you."

There was a silence. But I could not quite read her expression. She was studying the carpet.

"Oh, he doesn't frighten me. That is—I don't know what I do mean. I can't make him out! He—he called me a dirty little trollop this morning."

"Does he know what the rest of us know?"

"I don't know," she answered with flat candour, and looked at me. "*I* didn't tell him, and I don't see how anybody else could have. Maybe it's just as well. Sometimes I like him, and sometimes he gives me the creeps. I—" She stopped.

"Miss Kirkton, when she came to my office this morning, was very much worried for fear the whole affair—you know what I mean—would become public. How do you feel about it?"

Again she looked at me, with an indecipherable expression; one of those naked looks which are a little embarrassing, and in which there might have been weariness or even humour. Then she put her head on one side as though considering, and spoke with the same flat candour.

"We-el, to tell you the truth—provided they don't bring it out about the baby; provided *that*, of course; that would be horrible—then, to tell you the truth, I

318

shouldn't mind so very much. I can't understand why Harriet should be upset. Of course if it hadn't been known before, I should be terribly afraid of my father; but since he knows already, he won't do anything to me—and that's all that could worry me. As for the rest of it, the publicity or anything of the sort, I don't see why *that* should worry me, do you?" She opened her eyes wide, with a rollicking expression, and smiled. "Let's be frank, shall we?"

This was a bit staggering, but I did not show it.

"Then," I said, "there is no reason why you shouldn't tell me the whole truth, is there?"

"I don't know!" she cried, and clenched her hands.

"What do you mean, you don't know?"

She said pettishly: "Just what I say. What did you want to ask me?"

"First of all! On Friday night, at about eighteen minutes past ten, you and Miss Kirkton came out of the curator's room at the museum. And you went down into the cellar—apparently to get nails. Is that true?"

"Yes."

"And in the cellar you met Raymond Penderel. That's also true, isn't it?"

She went white. I had tried to talk as casually as though all this were understood, but it scared her half to death.

"Yes! That's n-nothing against me, is it? Yes! How did you know that?"

"Just a moment. Did you meet him by appointment?"

"By—oh, my God, *no! No!*" She rose up and sat down again, with an earnestness as shattering as her candour. "No. Believe me, I didn't know he was in London at all. Neither my father nor I knew it. It was

319

the most horrible shock I ever had. I walked down, and there he was, standing under the electric-light and bowing to me. For a second I didn't know who it was, because he had a black beard on, and tinted eye-glasses that altered his appearance, and he looked older. But he came close to me, and took off the eye-glasses and said, 'Good evening, darling. Don't you know me?' " She shuddered. "And now he's dead."

"Go on. What happened then?"

"I said, 'How did you get here?'—meaning in London, but he said, 'I came in before the museum closed, darling, and crept down here like a little mouse when the keeper wasn't looking.' Then he said, 'How is our—?' " She stopped and went on in a rush: "This is what I wanted to ask you, Mr. Hadley. When they ask me about it, *must* I tell about the baby? That's the point. Harriet said you told her it wasn't necessary. Can't I just say he wanted money for the rest of it, and all?"

"If you like. Did he tell you he was the actor from the agency?"

"No! He just went on talking: horrible things. He wanted money—ten thousand pounds. I was frantic. I said, 'You'd better get out of here, because—' " Again she stopped in mid-flight.

"Because?"

"Because," she obviously altered with a wrench what she had intended to say before, "because I said I'd call the others and have him thrown . . . He laughed and said he thought I wouldn't do that. What I was thinking was, 'Oh, my God, if I don't get those nails and go back upstairs again, they'll all be down.' I hurried over in the big workshop and got the nails, and ran back again, and all the time he was following me, talking. He followed me back to the stairs again; I'll

320

never forget that black beard of his, and the top-hat, and his face, bobbing up and down just over my shoulder like something in a dream.

"Then I screamed at him to get out. I said 'Get out now, anyway; if you must see me, come when I'm alone; not here. There's a window,' I said, 'get out!' And I rushed and ran up the stairs. I thought he was going to follow me, but he didn't. When I got upstairs I gave Rinkey the nails—he was just coming after them—and then I walked up and down for a little while in front of the main staircase, in case he should come up from the cellar. He didn't, and I wanted to go somewhere and think. You can understand how I felt. So I went down to the Persian Gallery, where it was dark and nobody should see me. But I kept thinking, 'Suppose he does come up, or, oh, Lord, suppose—!' " Again she checked herself. "Never mind what I thought, except I decided I'd better go down and see whether he *had* gone after all. So down I went again—and, sure enough, the cellar was empty, though the light was still on. I could feel a draught blowing from a window right opposite. So I thought, 'Well, anyway, he's gone for the minute; that's something'; and I thought, 'Ugh! He's grown whiskers!'

"But I was still horribly upset, as you can imagine, and I ran upstairs again. Just as I got to the top of the stairs I came face to face with some man I thought was the actor from the agency. But I went on up to join the others, as Harriet told you. . . ."

The whole case was unfolding now, coming together slowly but inevitably into one compact pattern, as I knew it must from the beginning. I could not help feeling that kind of excitement which occurs when a thousand meaningless bits come together in a whole.

"When I saw him dead afterwards, in that carriage,

or lying on the floor outside it—well, what was I going to *think?*" she demanded. "I tried to phone Harriet, and ask what to do or say, because Harriet's clever; but——"

"Just a minute again, Miss Wade. We've forgotten a few matters that will clear it all up. . . . When you went down into the cellar the first time, you took along the dagger and the false moustache, didn't you? Please don't deny it. Miss Kirkton said you had no objection to anybody knowing. Why did you take those things down there?"

She remained staring at me, and her eyes grew wider.

"I say—" a new thought struck and startled her. "*I* didn't kill him! Dear God, I didn't do it! Is that what you're thinking? Is it?"

"No. Not at all. Easy, now! Maybe I can help you answer why you took them down. But if you won't answer that for a second, let me ask you this: What did you do with them afterwards?"

"But I don't know! That's just it! I can't remember. I clean forgot about them; forgot them altogether! I don't have the slightest recollection of what happened to them after I went to the cellar. The shock of seeing *him* down there . . . I only remembered them long afterwards, and though I thought and thought and thought, still I couldn't re——"

"In fact, Miss Wade, you left them in the cellar, didn't you?"

"I must have," she said wearily, "because I don't remember having them when I came up."

I leaned forward: "Finally, then! Didn't Mr. Mannering really know, all the time, of the game you people were going to put up on him that night?"

"No!"

"Think again, please. Isn't it true that you tipped him off in advance, so that he should be prepared for it and not by any chance make a fool of himself? Isn't it true that you wanted to make certain of saving his face, because you had bragged so much about him?

"Isn't it true that you didn't know, and weren't to know, the full details of the scheme until Friday night? In case anything new turned up, isn't it true that you told him to meet you in the cellar of the museum just before the stunt was due to start, so that you could have a conference? Wasn't it for this purpose that you borrowed a key to the back gate from Holmes, the gate always kept locked? Didn't he have a duplicate of this key made at Bolton's in Arundel Street? Didn't you tell him to come in by the back gate—*and to speak to you through the basement window of the museum?* Isn't that why you were so infernally anxious to rush down into that cellar after coats or nails, and not let anybody else do it for you?

"Isn't it true that, as you were going down to the cellar, you saw the dagger on the stairs, and you thought you would have a laugh over showing him what they were going to 'kill' him with? Isn't this why you picked up the dagger? When you looked up and saw Miss Kirkton was watching you, didn't you say something about 'giving the things to Sam'; and, to make everything look in order to her, didn't you pick up the false moustache as well as the dagger? Didn't you take them both down there with you? And there, instead, you met Penderel.

"Isn't it true that you left both those things there and forgot them? Finally, and inevitably, isn't it true that—by the details of your own plan—Gregory Mannering must have heard every word of your conversation with Penderel just outside the window of the cellar. Isn't it?"

After a long silence in which you could hear the house creak, she put her face in her hands like a small girl, and began to cry.

"Yes," she said.

Two days later, after the sensational but fruitless inquest; after a certain flat had been searched, certain evidence found, and every strand of the net woven; two days later I applied—with the full step-by-step analysis of the crime which I next propose to show you—for a warrant to arrest Gregory Mannering on a charge of murder.

23

The Case For The Crown

On Wednesday afternoon, by appointment, I met the Chief-Commissioner, the Director of Public Prosecutions, and Sir Herbert here, in Sir Herbert's office. There I first outlined my case to them step by step, just as I intend to do it now, as logically and concisely as I can.

I therefore ask you, for the purpose of complete clearness, to forget the testimony of Miriam Wade; to forget that you now know any supporting evidence; and review with me the facts as they have been presented to us from the beginning. I do not ask you to concentrate on any person or any thing, but merely to follow the straight narration of the evidence.

The first actor to appear on the scene that night, whose questions and answers have been recorded, is Gregory Mannering. About the apparent lunatic who jumped off the wall and attacked Sergeant Hoskins, we do not as yet know anything whatever. We do know something about Mannering.

At ten minutes past eleven on Friday night, after the lunatic has disappeared and the sergeant has gone, Mannering presents himself at the Wade Museum before the eyes of P. C. Jameson, and makes an extensive row over a somewhat trivial business. We do not yet say that it was an unnecessary row; we merely record the fact. When Jameson asks him to come along to the police-station to answer some questions about a "*disappearance*," he comes along; he is then described as making no fuss, but looking "very queer," and several times attempting to question Jameson about it.

Carruthers has given us a description of him then. He is a little over six feet tall, with broad shoulders and a narrow waist; he has a tanned face, black hair, and blue eyes; he is in evening-clothes, with a black overcoat, a top-hat, and a stick. He appears to be under some nervous agitation when he tells his story: that Miriam Wade phoned him that afternoon asking him to come to the museum for a private view, at which they were going to "rob a grave," but that the museum was unaccountably closed when he did arrive. However, nothing remarkable develops until Carruthers uses the following words:

"Do ghosts wear false whiskers? This particular ghost was lying very quietly, and then he disappeared right under the sergeant's eyes; *he was moved.*"

And, unaccountably, Mannering fainted.

Still we only record it as an odd circumstance, since Carruthers was referring to the lunatic in the white whiskers. Carruthers then goes to the museum, where his first discovery after a conversation with Pruen is a set of smudged tracks in coal-dust. These tracks stretch away some feet from the front doors of the museum, and then fade out; but, since no clear footprint has been made, they are useless for purposes of identification.

Carruthers next finds a body in the travelling-carriage, which has been propped facing the door and tumbles out when the door is opened. When he examines the body, he notices a fact which does not appear to have impressed him, but which is of such vital importance that it cannot be stressed too strongly. It is this:

Not only is there a coating of coal-dust all over the soles of the murdered man's shoes, but it is a *thick* coating.

I ask you carefully to consider that. Someone, with coal-dust on the soles of his shoes, has walked into the museum—tracking the white marble floor until there is no longer enough coal-dust on them to make smudges, and, consequently, the tracks fade out. But in the travelling-carriage lies a body whose soles are thickly coated with coal-dust. Therefore we know that, whoever walked into the museum and left those tracks on the floor, it could not conceivably have been the murdered man. This is the natural and even very obvious point at which we must begin to reason.

A man with a thick and undisturbed layer of coal-dust on the soles of his shoes is lying inside a closed travelling-carriage. How did that man get there, alive or dead? He could not possibly have walked there, since around him on every side stretches a great expanse of white marble which would unquestionably have showed traces if he had stepped on it anywhere. But nowhere in the museum are there any tracks in coal-dust except those which come in for half a dozen steps from the front door. Very well; in some fashion the dead man was conveyed or carried to where he was found.

327

Conveyed from where? Since the museum is centrally heated, and since there are no fires or coal-containers anywhere else, he must have been carried from the cellar.

We examine the body. The man has a real black moustache, but is wearing black false whiskers. I say "wearing"; but this is not literally true. Though his chin and cheeks glisten with spirit-gum, and a sort of lint which demonstrates that they *had been* completely affixed, still they now hang down by no more than a spot the size of a sixpence along his jaw. They were not forcibly torn off in a struggle, since there are no signs of the tearing, nor any roughness or abrasion which must have been caused if they had been violently yanked away. Their removal has been careful, but they have been left hanging there by one small patch.

Who almost completely removed them in this fashion? It seems clear that it could not have been the dead man. This is a good-sized heavy set of whiskers; even in the event that the man chose to walk about in life with the whiskers dangling by a sixpence spot under his jaw, it is more than improbable that they could have been held there by so tiny a patch of gum. Coupled with our belief that he was carried to the coach, it is clear that someone else—the murderer— must have done this bit of work after the victim was dead.

Why?

Now, as to what the murderer did, we have two alternatives. Either the murderer (1) carefully removed the whiskers from the face, all except that one tiny bit, and allowed them to hang as they were thus found; or (2) he removed them altogether, and afterwards stuck them so hastily back on the face that they adhered only by that one small spot.

Leaving out two alternatives for a moment, we go on to other evidence. Round the dead man's neck, on a black ribbon, we find hung a pair of tinted eyeglasses. But this ribbon is placed round the neck *on the outside of the overcoat collar.* Again, gentlemen, consider that carefully. People who wear eyeglasses do not wear them with the ribbon draped round the overcoat collar. Even in the event that a man forgets his glasses, and only hangs them round his neck after he had put on his overcoat, he will not have that broad ribbon getting in his way like a clergyman's stole; he will tuck it down inside the overcoat and even the jacket, where it belongs. Therefore it seems clear that the glasses on the dead man must have been put there by somebody else, and draped hastily round his neck after he was dead.

But this becomes nonsense if we accept the first alternative: *viz.,* that the whiskers were carefully detached except for that little bit on the jaw. For in that case we have an inexplicable murderer who both adds and subtracts. He puts a pair of glasses round the neck, but he detaches the whiskers even though he leaves them hanging there. However, we have a completely rational explanation if we accept the second alternative: that the whiskers were first altogether removed, and then subsequently put back so hastily that they were stuck only by that patch. For now we see that the same thing must have happened with the eyeglasses. They also had been removed from the dead man—and afterwards put back hastily round the outside of his overcoat.

Our conclusions amount to this. A man has been murdered in the cellar, and his body has been conveyed from there to the travelling-carriage. The man, while he was alive, has worn a pair of tinted eyeglasses and black false whiskers; these have been removed from his face, and then put back again. Finally, *some other person* has at one time that night walked into the museum with coal-dust on his shoes.

Now, at this point in the analysis it would be too big a step, and logically unwarranted, to say that this second man is the murderer. On the other hand, considering that these two people *alone* have coal-dust on the soles of their shoes, it is possible to connect them and to say that the second man probably knows something of the crime. Of all the conclusions to which we have come so far, only one presents a challenging puzzle, which is this: Why should the murderer have removed both the whiskers and the eyeglasses from the dead man, and then put them back? We could go stargazing for an answer, but the straightest and most logical answer would be this: that he wanted them for himself, that he wanted them as a disguise (which a bush of whiskers and tinted eyeglasses almost theatrically suggest). But if he wanted them for himself, why was it necessary to return them to the dead man? Again we have the not very complicated reply: Because it must be assumed that they had never been removed from the dead man. Taken together, these points (1) that he wanted the properties to disguise himself, but (2) that nevertheless nobody must think they had left the dead man at any time, we come to the simple conclusion that he wished to disguise himself *as* the dead man. He wished to impersonate a man who was dead.

Leaving this situation for a moment, we advance. After Carruthers' evidence, we hear on the following day the stories of Dr. Illingworth and Pruen. These supply us with an almost complete set of facts, as regards external circumstances, to pursue our logical line.

And immediately we learn some significant facts about this "other man," the second man, the man who made the smudges on the floor. This man, *professing himself to be Penderel*, has appeared at the museum at a quarter to eleven and been admitted. And here is a verification of our reasoning: here is an impostor disguised as Penderel in the latter's glasses and whiskers. Since he wears those, we must assume that Penderel is already dead; that he was killed at some time previous to a quarter to eleven.

Before discussing who this impostor might be, let us try to decide when Penderel was really murdered. Pruen states that he arrived at the museum "for the first time" about ten minutes to ten. We have reason to believe that he hid himself in the cellar, and this has now to support it our belief that he was murdered in the cellar. He could not have been murdered before 10:15, since at 10:15 the dagger was placed on the staircase in full view of everyone and had not yet been stolen. He could not have been murdered after 10:45, since then the impostor arrived at the front door wearing the properties. Can we narrow down that half-hour in any way to decide?

We can. If he was murdered in the cellar between 10:15 and 10:45, when was his body carried to the travelling-carriage? It was discovered in the carriage by Butler a minute or two before eleven o'clock. Very well. Now, it is inconceivable that the masquerading murderer, dressed up as Penderel, could have carried the body upstairs between 10:45 and 11:00. For, to do this, he would have to walk to the back of the museum, descend the cellar stairs under Pruen's eye, pick up the body of his victim, carry that immense weight—Penderel was a six-footer—upstairs and through the door directly under Pruen's eye, place the body in the carriage, and make his escape. This tissue of improbabilities we may disregard at once. Consequently, we have eliminated fifteen minutes; we now know that Penderel must have been murdered AND his body placed in the carriage between 10:15 and 10:45.

But if a man carrying that immense burden up through the cellar door would necessarily have been seen between 10:45 and 11:00, he would also have been seen by Pruen at any of the previous times— when Pruen was also on guard with a full view of the hall. He would have been seen by Pruen at any time *except* during that five minutes, between 10:40 and 10:45, when Pruen's attention was completely distracted from the hall. This was the only time when Pruen was not on guard; and the only time when the body could have been carried up unseen and placed in the carriage.

For what happened? Pruen hears a crash from the Gallery of the Bazaars; he runs down to investigate, and discovers that a lump of coal has been smashed high up on the wall there. Pruen wastes five minutes in fruitless search. And he overlooks something which others appear to have overlooked, though it would seem clear enough. The general assumption seems to have been that the coal must have been thrown by someone who was actually *in* the Gallery of the Bazaars. But Pruen states that nobody entered the Gallery at any time except Baxter; and, if Baxter threw it, where did Baxter get hold of a lump of coal—since he had not visited the cellar all evening? In fact, the very choice of that missile must lead us in only one direction. It leads us first to the assumption that the coal must have been thrown *from a distance,* and thrown from the direction of the cellar door. Now if you visit the museum—or even glance at the plan here—you will see something which makes this certain. The coal smashed flat on that wall: flung in a straight line. If you stand with your back to the wall against which it struck, you will see that there is only one straight line on which it could have travelled: an oblique line to the cellar door. Had it come from any other door, it must have described a circle or a half-circle like a boomerang.

In addition, the cellar door is just half hid from Pruen by the nearest coach. There is a roomy space between that door and the nearest coach, and (finally) the door opens outwards towards the left-hand wall as you face the rear. Therefore someone must have opened that door a crack, slipped out while bending low, straightened up, and thrown; a distance not more than twenty feet longer than an ordinary cricket-pitch. When Pruen went to investigate, the murderer carried his burden upstairs—choosing the travelling-carriage because it was the only completely closed one—hid the body, and returned to the cellar for—for what? Let us see.

The body, then, was placed in the carriage at 10:40. We have eliminated another five minutes in discovering the time of death. We can carry it further. If the ivory-handled dagger was sticking in Penderel's chest at 10:40, when and how did it get to the cellar? The only person in the museum who went down into the cellar *at all* (since Pruen was on guard at every other time) was Miriam Wade. Therefore, innocently or guiltily, she must have taken the dagger down. Since Pruen—in Sir Herbert's examination of him—persistently hemmed, hawed, and evaded at only one point:

333

viz., the girl's first visit to the cellar, it was probable that the dagger had been stolen on her first visit there, round about 10:18. So Penderel was killed between 10:20 and 10:40, and already our formidable three-quarters of an hour can be narrowed down to twenty minutes.

Very well. Does this look very bad for Miriam Wade, since incontestably she stole the dagger? Now, if she killed Penderel, she most certainly had an accomplice; the impostor who disguised himself as Penderel and came into the museum at 10:45. What is more, this accomplice must have been an outsider, since the presence of every person in the museum can be accounted for during the critical times. But, forgetting that for a moment, ask yourself this: Why, when she went down into the cellar, did she take the dagger? Did she know that Penderel was waiting there, and take it to kill him? Aside from the fact that we have not one shred of evidence for thinking she knew Penderel was within a thousand miles of London, there are serious objections to the theory. If she went down there expecting to meet Penderel or expecting to have a use for the dagger, then we can only say that she must have been stark, raving mad. For she calls attention to the fact that she is going to the cellar; she makes an uproar of insisting on going for the nails; and in full view of Pruen—as well as others, we are later to learn—she *openly* picks up the dagger from the stairs. You do not plan a murder and then take such enormous pains to call attention to it in a light-hearted, laughing way. No, we can only assume that she carried the dagger downstairs in all innocence—innocence of murder, at least.

But why did she take the dagger with her, and why was she so eager to visit the cellar? Was it to meet somebody? For instantly we remember the impostor who appeared later, and took the part of Penderel. An outsider; well, let us see if we can build up a description of this outsider.

Penderel, the real Penderel, has been described by Carruthers. Penderel is six feet tall, with broad shoulders and narrow hips; he has black hair, a slightly dark complexion, brown eyes, and a black moustache; he wears evening-clothes, a top-hat, and a black overcoat. Is there anybody in this case, who—concealed. behind a brush of whiskers, and with tinted eyeglasses hiding the colour of his eyes—could pass as Penderel before the weak and watery eyes of Pruen? Pruen, of course, has never seen Penderel before; it is only necessary to convince him that this is the man when the body is discovered *later*. And in the whole case there is only one person who fills the description: Gregory Mannering. The proper costume, the proper height, the proper hair, the proper tan to pass for dark complexion; for the eyes are concealed by glasses and half the face by whiskers. There is at first glance only one difficulty: Penderel wore a real black moustache. If Mannering by any chance took and wore the beard, how would the moustache be supplied? And we have an immediate answer in that elusive and inexplicable black moustache which has been so difficult to trace in its movements, and has *seemed* to have no part in the picture.

Disregarding the moustache for a moment, let us see how this physical description of Mannering would accord with the picture we are building up. Miriam goes to meet someone in the cellar—is it reasonable to suppose that this outsider might be Mannering? It is most decidedly. To meet him; why? The inference is so clear that I need scarcely indicate it. A game was being put up on Mannering, and Miriam Wade, who had boasted so much about him that she must see he did not act badly in it, had tipped him off; she had, moreover, arranged to meet him in the cellar to give him any final details. Does this inference accord with the physical evidence? It does: for the cellar is the only place she could have met him in secret which also has accessible windows to afford him entrance. And, in support of this, we have Carruthers' statement that, while he was telling the story of the night to Miriam Wade after the body was found, she muttered the words, *"cellar window."* Could Mannering have entered the museum grounds to gain access to these windows? Yes, since we know that Miriam Wade has a key to the back gate. She therefore took the dagger down to show him what they were to "kill" him with; probably a humorous impulse when she saw the dagger lying on the stairs; and she picked up the false moustache as well.

The next question is: Have these two arranged to meet in the cellar, with the purpose of together killing Penderel? That must be ruled out, for the same reason which applied to Miriam alone: she would not have called such attention to her conduct. Everything indicates that the whole crime was not premeditated, but that Penderel appeared in the cellar where he was least expected.

Arranging our facts and conclusions in consecutive order, we now have a pattern something like this:

Miriam, with no thought of murder, has arranged to meet Mannering in the cellar. Penderel appears at the museum without anyone's knowledge, and conceals himself in the cellar. At 10:18 or 10:20 Miriam goes down into the cellar, taking with her the dagger and the moustache. Between five and seven minutes later, she comes up from the cellar. More than five minutes later than that, she goes down into the cellar again; reappearing almost immediatley, at 10:35, and going on upstairs. At 10:40 a lump of coal is thrown—almost certainly by Mannering—to distract Pruen's attention. The body is brought up to the coach, Mannering returns to the cellar, climbs up through the coal-hole into the street, rings the museum-bell, and performs his impersonation. He must return the whiskers and glasses to the dead man. He walks down the hall; and, with his back turned to Pruen, makes himself the noise of, "Sss-t!" By stopping and looking towards the coaches, he gives Pruen the impression that this noise has been made by somebody else. Dodging under the carriage, he opens the door on the other side—where the body is still lying—but can only thrust back the beard in a hurry, put the cookery-book into the dead hand, and the glasses round the neck. And, finally, he gets rid of his false moustache, later found under the carriage. This takes only a few seconds; then Pruen hears the rappy footsteps of Mannering again. In the subsequent confusion, he can get down into the cellar, and escape by way of the window and the back gate.

Why was it necessary to perform this impersonation?

That is the crux of the problem. In deciding the actual murderer we have two alternatives, which are:

1. That, though the crime was not premeditated, still Miriam Wade and Gregory Mannering committed it in collusion when they found Penderel in the cellar. Either Miriam or Mannering stabbed Penderel with the dagger. Then Mannering, in order that Miriam should have a cast-iron alibi, performed the impersonation—while

she went up and was careful to establish her presence among her friends.

2. Both the murder and the impersonation were done by Mannering, and Miriam knew nothing of either.

At first glance, the probabilities seem almost overwhelmingly in favour of the first alternative. To support it can be put forward such powerful and convincing reasons that it seems beyond a doubt, *since it provides ostensibly the only good reason why the imposture should have been performed at all*. Miriam knew that she had been seen openly going to the cellar, carrying the dagger. She was the only one who did go into the cellar. Therefore the body must not be found there to point so clearly to her guilt. To risk such a dangerous piece of mummery as that impersonation, there must have been only an incentive as strong as that; since otherwise Mannering runs his head unnecessarily into a noose.

But study the matter again. I have stressed the necessity of looking for the most natural explanation; but, if this is the most natural explanation so far, surely it proceeds farther on in the most unnatural way ever taken—or ever likely to be taken—by two conspirators. Thoroughly credible so far, it next becomes insane. For:

If Miriam stabbed Penderel, or Miriam and Mannering together stabbed him, this could only have been done during the first five-to-seven minutes when Miriam went to the cellar for the first time. If she had a guilty part in the affair, she took it then. It is not reasonable to think that she went down to the cellar carrying the dagger; met Penderel, had a talk with him; came upstairs again to think it over, either still carrying the dagger or having left it there; went downstairs again after some thought—under the eyes of Pruen—stabbed Penderel then, in a few brief moments she was downstairs; said, "Carry on," to a waiting Mannering, and then ran up again.

Very well. If she had anything to do with killing Penderel, it was between 10:18 and 10:25. Penderel, in the course of a wild row, was murdered then. She says to Mannering, who has either overseen it or come in afterwards, "You have got to help me"; and one or the other of them (probably Mannering, even in this hypothesis) thinks of impersonation. First of all, the body must be conveyed upstairs unseen.

That, of course, is the most dangerous part of the plan; even more dangerous than the impersonation. Pruen's attention must be diverted while the body is disposed of. *If these two are acting in collusion,* there is only one natural and even inevitable thing they will do; any other course would be mad. Miriam must distract his attention while Mannering does the work. Not only would this be a very simple course for her, since Pruen worships her; but it would also provide her with the alibi she is apparently seeking. To take him into the Bazaars, or the Persian Gallery, anywhere so that the hall is cleared for a minute or two. . . .

But what does she do? She comes upstairs at a little after 10:25, idles about, goes to the Persian Gallery, comes back, descends the stairs, and comes up again— to join her friends upstairs. Are they still preparing for the imposture? If so, why does she not distract Pruen's attention *at any time?* It is not tenable to argue that she lost her nerve, for she had no hesitation in making a second visit to the cellar; she did not lose her nerve in any other respect that night; and, finally, where was the risk in merely talking to Pruen? Nor would she have deserted Mannering, since it was her own neck which was in danger all the time.

As a last consideration, we have the second danger-point of the scheme: the entrance of the impostor, his returning the beard and glasses, and his disappearing again. Suppose Pruen had insisted on following him? Suppose Pruen had made a row of some sort, or called the others? Mannering would have been undone. It is no very far-fetched belief to think, that, if there had been a conspiracy, the second conspirator would have been on hand to see that things went smoothly; to keep Pruen in the right frame of mind; and again to distract his attention while the impostor got away; and again there would not have been the least grain of danger in it for Miriam. On the contrary, it would still provide her with an excellent alibi.

To this point, gentlemen, I had come on the Sunday after comparing all the records. Examine the case as I would, I could find no point anywhere—anywhere at all—which was consistent with a belief in Miriam's complicity. The murder seemed to me the work of a single hand; a strong, theatrical, daring man of inordinate vanity. In my own analysis, the course of events must have gone thus:

Miriam went to the cellar, and unexpectedly met Penderel there. Mannering had arrived outside the window, and heard it; but he did not make his presence known. Very few men, hearing such revelations as he must have heard, would immediately have appeared. Miriam, ordering Penderel to go and afraid that at any moment the others must come down to find out why she has not got the nails, runs upstairs leaving the dagger and the moustache behind. Then Mannering got through the window—and acted. He has spent much time in the East, and would know the handling of an Eastern weapon so as to reach the heart. Why did he act? I say to you that whether out of genuine love, vanity, a desire to crush the future, or all three; still a man of Mannering's type, suddenly thrown into one of his familiar furies by the revelation of a story which hurt him and whipped his vanity to the bone, would inevitably have confronted Penderel and (let us take our one effort of imagination, which I deprecate) and "slain the Eastern dog with his own Eastern blade." For concealment, in case somebody should come down, he would drag the body into the only possible place of concealment: the high-walled coal-bin near by. His glow of heroism would still be very strong. And then—he heard somebody coming downstairs. It was Miriam, who took one look round the empty cellar, thought that Penderel had gone, and hurried upstairs herself.

Give the man his due. I do not like him, I may even say that I hate his guts; but there can be no denying that he showed guts. He realised, when he saw Miriam for the second time, that she must inevitably be accused of this murder. She had brought the dagger down, she was known to have been there, Penderel had been her lover. Whether or not he was genuinely in love with her, Mannering knew that a *fiancée* accused of murder would place him in an awkward position. He determined on one of those spectacular and theatrical stunts which are a part of his life. Only Mannering could have conceived such a wild and yet successful plan, only Mannering would have the strength to carry the body upstairs, only Mannering could have passed himself off as the dead man. To transfer the properties to his own face, he needed one thing: a mirror. Otherwise, did he have sufficient knowledge of the museum to have known exactly how to proceed? Yes, because we have testimony to prove that he had been shown round by Holmes, "even all over the cellars." And on the floor is his deliverance to complete the disguise: a black false moustache to imitate Penderel's real one. What of his fainting-fit afterwards at the police-station? Have we not been told of a similar fainting-fit, which overtook Mannering some days before, *about half an hour after he had carried an immensely heavy trunk upstairs?* On Friday night, the reaction of his heart was from the reaction of carrying an immensely heavy body.

On Sunday, as I say, I had come to these conclusions, and on Monday I began to test them out. Since my middle name is Caution, I would not finally discard the complete possibility of Miriam Wade's complicity; but determined that if she answered my questions fully and freely, making no secret of her carrying the dagger to the cellar or seeing Penderel there, we could exclude her as my reasoning demanded we should. You know the result, up to that point.

There remains to be put before you only the physical evidence of Mannering's guilt which we collected for evidence at a trial; and which on Wednesday I placed before the Chief-Commissioner and the Director of Public Prosecutions. The coal-bin in the cellar was turned out and examined, with the result that a good many blood-stains were found there; going to show not only that the murder had been committed in the cellar, but that the dead man's body had first been propped against the wall in a squatting position like a Buddha, so that there was thick dust on the shoes but little on the clothes. A search-warrant was obtained for Mannering's flat in Bury Street. In the flat we found a pair of white kid gloves—the gloves he had worn with his evening-clothes on the night of the murder—which gloves were coated with coal-dust and had blood-stains on the tips of the fingers. There was also a photograph of him in Persian native costume, wearing in his belt a dagger precisely similar to the one with which the crime was committed.

The key, found by Butler in the carriage, was discovered to have been obtained by him from Bolton's in Arundel Street; a copy having been made of Miriam Wade's key.

Our one clear finger-print, as I told you, had been effaced from the mirror in the cellar by Geoffrey Wade; we found one other, a dubious one which might entail trouble in an examination of experts, but was strong enough to put into court. Finally, Mannering's alibi was shot to blazes. We had the testimony of two switchboard-boys at Prince-Regent Court to show that not only had he not come there at 10:40 on Friday night, but that he had not been there all evening. Mannering, of course, had said that he had gone up the back way, but this could not be proved. If anything, it could be proved to our advantage; since the porter of the flats thought that the back door had been locked all evening. But we were willing to concede the point of his visit, since it was plain that he did not go there between 10:30 and 11:00, the crucial times of our investigation.

Having put this evidence on the table in Sir Herbert's office, I sat back and let the Director of Public Prosecutions and the Chief-Comissioner decide. I am not likely to forget that afternoon, because of the startling interruption which came immediately afterwards.

The D. P. P. spoke first after my story.

"I think it'll do," he said, in that usually grudging way of his. "I could use more actual exhibits—more stuff to fire right at 'em—but I think it'll do. Eh?"

The Chief-Commissioner grunted. He said:

"Damn shame Jeff Wade messed up that finger-print; we ought to be able to do something about it, but of course we can't. But I haven't got a doubt that Mannering's guilty. Eh, Armstrong?"

Sir Herbert here didn't say anything. I am not going to rake up any old suggestions or old rows, especially with my chief in the department; I should be a damned fool if I did. But just as the D. P. P. was gathering up his papers, and we were squashing out our cigars, the Invaluable Popkins came hurrying in. He looked worried.

"Excuse me, gentlemen," said he, "but there's"— He changed that. "Mr. Geoffrey Wade is here, with Mr. Mannering, and he would like to see you. He says he's got absolute proof that Mr. Mannering is innocent."

24

Alibi

Again I am not likely to forget that scene, or the faces round our council table. It was a bright June afternoon, with the sun shining on the luxury that is permitted to Assistant-Commissioners, and a haze of smoke in spite of the open windows. The D. P. P. was annoyed at the interruption, because he was going off for golf.

But there was no time to plead engagements. In swaggered—swaggered is the word—old Jeff himself. He was decked out in a loud suit with a grey bowler hat, and had a flower in his buttonhole. He was in a savage good humour, with his white moustaches bristling; squeaky but absolutely assured of himself. Behind him came Mannering, as suave as a film star. Geoffrey Wade walked over, pushed the papers into a scramble at one side of the table, and sat down on its edge.

"Fine day, ain't it?" he said amiably. "In case you

don't know it, I'm Jeff Wade. *The* Jeff Wade. I wanted to have a little talk with all of you."

"Did you, indeed?" asked the Chief-Commissioner, with about as much acid as the sentence would hold. "Well?"

The other cackled with mirth. Then he put his neck down in his collar and looked across the table.

"You think you've got a case against young Mannering, don't you?" he enquired.

"Well?"

That withered old devil was enjoying himself. He put his hands into the breast pocket of his coat, and pulled out a wallet. From that wallet he took out what I had never seen before, and did not believe existed. It was a five-thousand-pound note, and he spread it out on the desk.

"Put down a sixpence," he said.

"Great—God—Almighty," muttered the D. P. P., as though he could not believe his eyes. "Are you trying to——"

"No, gentlemen," interposed Mannering in a smooth voice, and very courteously. "It is not bribery, or my father-in-law-to-be would not go so far; I dare say it would be possible to buy any of you for less. Put down a sixpence."

Nobody said anything, for the thing went even beyond anger. Old Wade leaned across the table, and tapped the five-thousand-pound note.

"Nobody want to risk a sixpence?" he asked. "Surely you ain't all as close as that? I want to bet you this little piece of paper to a tanner that you don't have a case against Mannering, and that if you try to prove one you won't even get it past the Grand Jury. What about it?"

"Jeff," said Sir Herbert here, after a pause, "this is

going too far. I'll string along with you a certain distance; but for consummate and complete and unadulterated gall, this goes beyond anything you've ever done or are likely to do. Out you go, and go now."

"Just one moment," said the Chief-Commissioner. "Why are you so certain no case can be made out?—Here, what's that row about?"

Popkins intervened, for there was a good deal of noise coming from the other side of the door.

"I believe it is some of Mr. Wade's party, sir," he informed us suavely. "They are here in considerable force."

"It's witnesses," announced Wade coolly. "Thirteen of 'em. It's witnesses to prove that on that night of Friday, June 14th, from nine o'clock until a quarter to eleven, Mannering was sitting with me in The Graeco-Persian Restaurant in Dean Street (now named 'Shattu of Soho'). There's the two proprietors, Messrs. Shattu and Aguinopopolos. There's four waiters, a cloakroom attendant, and a porter. There's four independent witnesses who were eatin' dinner there, finally——"

"That," said the Chief-Commissioner calmly, "is only twelve."

"Oh, there's a thirteenth for something else," replied the old man, with a curious grin. "You wait. They're all good British subjects, and acceptable to a British jury. On testimony like that, I could prove that a fish never had a drink of water. That's what you call an alibi. Can you bust it? Try? The witnesses are all here; go ahead and try. You take that to court, and I'll move and get a dismissal of the indictment the moment the judge wobbles out on the bench. But you'll never get it so far, because I'm making a small bet that the Grand Jury throws out the bill. So that's why I warn you: you'd better drop this business right now, or you'll drop yourselves into a whole lot of hot water."

Sir Herbert said: "Damn you, you bought that restau——"

"Prove it," said the old man, and grinned at him. "You keep out of this, Bert. You've been useful, and I don't want to turn on you."

"I suppose it's permissible to enquire whether you bought anything else with the restaurant?" enquired the D. P. P., without moving a muscle.

"You try asking it," said Wade, and leaned across and wagged his head at him, "and you'll have the finest slander suit on your hands you ever saw. Ho, won't you, though? There's the man I'm going to get dead to rights." He stabbed his finger towards me. "I think you'll find, Mr. Superintendent What's-your-name, that it's never very healthy to try threatening me."

"Isn't it?" I said. "Let's see what Mr. Mannering has to say. Mr. Mannering, you say that you were in this restaurant between nine o'clock and ten-forty-five on Friday night?"

Mannering nodded, with an expression of grave courtesy and smug complacence combined. He smiled pleasantly.

"I was."

"Even though you stated to Inspector Carruthers, and later to me, that you visited Prince-Regent Court at twenty minutes to eleven?"

"Pardon me," suggested Mannering, still gravely, "I do not think you could quite have understood me. Of course when I spoke to Inspector Carruthers on Friday night, certain overwrought feelings you will readily understand made me not quite responsible on that occasion. I am not sure what I said then; and the inspector cannot testify to it either, since I did not sign or initial any testimony. In fact, I am almost sure that I told him what I told you on Monday: namely that, while I had indeed visited Prince-Regent Court on Friday evening, I did not propose to tell you *when* I visited it. I stated only that I went by the back way, and very rightly refused you any more information. Er—can you deny that?"

"No, that's what you said to me."

He made a slight gesture of magnanimity. "However," said this triumphant thunderer, "I am now prepared to tell you what really did happen on Friday night, just to prevent your making one of your customary foolish mistakes. I have said nothing hitherto, because I did not wish to embarrass Mr. Wade.

"You see, I happened to meet Mr. Wade when he was coming from Waterloo Station, with his two—er —restaurant-keeping friends, at nine o'clock, and accepted his invitation to dine. Afterwards we were to go on to the museum, as it had been arranged; Mr. Wade informed me that he had sent a telegram to Dr. Illingworth asking him to meet us there at ten-thirty. Unfortunately, Mr. Wade became so interested in talking about Persia with M. Shattu, that he decided—let's be blunt about it, gentlemen—he decided to give Dr. Illingworth the go-by. But he didn't wish to hurt the good doctor's feelings. So he asked me whether I would go to the museum, where Dr. Illingworth would be waiting, and make some plausible excuse. It was just a quarter to eleven when I left the restaurant. One of the proprietors, M. Aguinopopolos, garages his car in the mews behind Pall Mall Place; he was going home at that moment, and offered to drive me. On the way, however, it suddenly occurred to me that there had been a mistake. Our original intention, as you know, was to have held the gathering at the museum

at eleven o'clock. Not only had Mr. Wade sent a telegram to Dr. Illingworth altering the hour—but he had
even neglected to inform the others that there was to
be a gathering after all, having called it off in the
morning. *They* had received no telegram, and consequently the museum would be deserted. I could not
get in, nor could Dr. Illingworth, who must now be
waiting on the doorstep. Still, I remembered that Mr.
Holmes lived in Pall Mall Place. I told M. Aguinopopolos to drive his car by the back way into the mews,
where he usually leaves it, and that I would go to find
Mr. Holmes. As I got out I was passing the back of
Prince-Regent Court, and at the back door (giving instructions to someone) I met Mr. George Dennison,
the manager of the flats. . . ."

At this point Sir Herbert Armstrong struck the
table.

"Long live perjury!" he roared. "Jeff, you own that
block of flats as well as the restaurant! Pruen said to
Carruthers——"

"Prove it," said Wade coolly. "I'm warning you
again, Bert: keep out of this. Go on, young fella."

Mannering's suave aloofness returned. "Yes, of
course. Well, Mr. Dennison—that's the thirteenth
witness Mr. Wade mentioned—let me in, and walked
up with me by the back way to Mr. Holmes's flat.
However, there was nobody there, and I saw certain
evidences which led me to believe that the whole
group must have gone to the museum after all. This
would have been about eleven o'clock. I went downstairs again, spoke with Mr. Dennison, and pursued
my way on foot to the museum. It was dark. I felt that
the others must be inside after all, so I rang steadily.
While doing this, I was interrupted by a policeman.

When he misinterpreted my efforts, naturally I could not explain Mr. Wade's—excuse me, sir—Mr. Wade's bad manners towards a distinguished guest, Dr. Illingworth, and thereby excuse myself."

Mannering smiled again, but his eyebrows were drawn together and he stared with a politeness that was like a jeer.

"I think that's all. By the way—would you care to arrest me now?"

"It is a formality," said the Chief-Commissioner, looking at him curiously, "which will give me a good deal of pleasure."

The old man leaned forward with a gleeful expression.

"You goin' to do it?" he demanded. "Good! Well—anybody like to take my bet, gentlemen?"

Again that inane giggle was like dirty water thrown over us. And he could afford to laugh.

Three weeks later the Grand Jury threw out the bill.

And that, Fell, brings me nearly to the end of my narrative. You will understand now the statements I made at the beginning. Nobody would be apt to beat his breast in agony over the injustice or the deep damnation of Penderel's taking off, though some of us might consider that murder is rather a strong reproof to anyone who took advantage of Miriam Wade's tendencies towards amusement. But the whole affair was a straight punch in the eye which could not be passed over. You see our position.

We cannot bring Mannering to trial for murder, or Wade to trial for perjury. We are convinced that the whole story of Mannering's being at the restaurant was a manufactured lie from beginning to end. We are convinced of it—and I see by your nod that you are convinced of it too. Yet our strongest efforts could not break down the testimony of a single witness. (That, by the way, was when Jeff instituted his charge that we were using third-degree methods, including the loaded rubber hose. It was not true, but it was the only time in my life when I have strongly wanted to use a rubber hose.) With a whole regiment of solicitors at his elbow to see that he made no slip, the old man intimated to newspapermen that it was only our crooked wish to secure a conviction and cover our incompetence which made us think we had a case at all.

For what could we do? With Mannering out of it, we could not swing round and try to make out a case against the girl, even if we had believed in it; Mannering was the prop of the whole business, whoever was guilty. It had us licked—and the old man knew it. That crowing charlatan, who has never had a taking-down in his life, had simply outguessed and out-manœuvred us. Even Sir Herbert here, his old friend, is not too happy about it.

That is why we have taken up a whole night talking. Not that we care two hoots about sternly bringing the murderer of Penderel to justice, although Penderel was at least a ticking, breathing human. But that old devil openly boasts that he has got the law by the short hairs, and it's causing trouble. As a last resort—and probably without any success—it is being put up to you. You, like ourselves, must be convinced that Mannering committed murder and Wade committed perjury. But is there any way to snare 'em?

That was more than three months ago, and there are only a few things to add by way of conclusion. We kept a pretty close eye on everybody, and we know what has gone on. This may interest you. A month after the Grand Jury failed to return a true bill, and all the uproar had died down, Miriam and Mannering broke up: apparently with mutual consent. Mannering has gone to China, but he is a richer man. Through private and discreet channels, we have learned that, before he went, the old man placed to his account a cheque for a cool twenty thousand pounds. Does that mean anything to you?

As for the others, they are in much the same position. We settled Mrs. Reilly's hash, though it did not please us too much to assist the old man. The Wade Museum is more crowded that Madame Tussaud's; Pruen remains as night-attendant and Holmes as assistant-curator. Baxter had to retire from the legation because of the outburst at the inquest; but their little crowd seems to have come the more closely together for all that. Jerry, Butler, and Harriet Kirkton are much as we left them. Illingworth—well, Illingworth became rather a hero for a time.

With regard to Miriam, I can only tell you that I saw her a month ago and any social ostracism she may have suffered rests very lightly on her. In fact, she seems to be having rather a better time than she did before. I met her in a bar, where I had gone to pick up somebody for forgery, and she was sitting on a high stool in a brilliant outfit, looking more beautiful than ever. I voiced a discreet question about Mannering, and she said she had not heard from him in some time. And, as I got up to go, I said:

"Tell me frankly. Just between ourselves what did you really think of Mannering?"

She looked at the mirror behind the bar, and smiled in a dreamy sort of way. "I think," she answered, "what the character said in the Shaw play: 'How splendid! How wonderful! How magnificent! And, oh, what an escape!' By the way, if you see that nice young police-officer, tell him it's all right for Thursday night."

So we end, as we began, with Carruthers.

Epilogue

"Hullo!" said Carruthers. "It's daylight."

The windows in the big book-lined room were grey, and the electric light over the table looked harsh and unreal. Despite steady replenishments, the fire had gone again to a big heap of embers in the great stone gateway under the mantelpiece. Stale smoke bleared the eyes of all the rather bedraggled-looking people round the table, who shifted or turned creakily in the slight surprise of discovering dawn. It was cold and stuffy in the room. The Assistant-Commissioner opened his eyes.

"This was a fool stunt," growled Sir Herbert Armstrong, always inclined to be testy at this hour. "Sittin' up all night. Bah!" He reached into his pocket, and in a hazy sort of way examined a pocket-diary. "Seventeenth Sunday after Trinity. Sun rises 6:20 A.M. We've been hearing so many times scrambled together tonight that you might as well know that one. I am also in a position to inform you that your Michaelmas Fire Insurance, if any, ceases tomorrow. Any of you lazy blighters going to church? Carruthers, you ought to be ashamed to. 'If you see that nice young police-officer——' "

"Sorry, sir," answered Carruthers, with suspicious humility. "*I* didn't say anything. The superintendent——"

Hadley alone looked fresh and unruffled, and pulled at his dead pipe.

"I merely put that in," he explained, with suspicious gravity, "to round off the story. The point is, now that we have wasted a night going over the facts again, what does the oracle say? What does Fell finally think of the whole aff— God damn it, he's asleep! FELL!"

Dr. Fell, enthroned in his largest, most comfortable and most decrepit leather chair, had been sitting slumped down in it; his eyeglasses dangling down and his hands pressed over his eyes. Now one irritable eye appeared behind the fingers.

"I am not asleep," he returned with dignity. "Your language pains and surprises me. Harrumph." He wheezed for a moment, rubbing his hands up and down his temples. He looked at the moment not like the vast Ghost of the Christmas Present, but rather tired and old. "I was only asking myself," continued the doctor, clearing his throat, "for the umpty-umph time the same question I ask myself at the end of every case: what is justice? Time, like jesting Pilate, will not stay for an answer. Harrumph, never mind. What you people need at this hour of the morning is some strong black tea, well laced with brandy. Stop a minute."

He hauled himself upright, wheezing, and lumbered on his two canes over the fireplace. Behind a pile of folios on a small stable was concealed a gas-ring. Dr. Fell plucked out a kettle, which he shook to assure himself that there was water inside. He lit the gas, whose bright yellow and blue flames made a faint hissing roar, and showed the only light in that dusky room. For a moment Dr. Fell remained bending over the flare, like an alchemist in a medieval tale. The light caught out of darkness his several chins, his great mop of grey-streaked hair, his bandit's moustache and owlish eyeglasses with the black ribbon dangling.

Then he shook his head.

"First, Hadley," he rumbled meditatively, "I want to congratulate you on a brilliant piece of work. You go from point to point as inevitably as one of those drawings built up out of figures, which produce a picture when you connect the lines."

"Never mind that," said Hadley in some suspicion. "The question is, do you agree? Do you think it's correct?"

Dr. Fell nodded.

"Yes," he said; "yes, I think it's quite correct, as far as it goes."

Sir Herbert Armstrong dropped his diary and sat up with a start. "As far as it goes?" he roared. "Don't tell me there's another layer to this business! I couldn't bear it. Whoa, now! We find a puzzle-box all decorated with mysterious characters. We open that, and there's another puzzle-box inside. We open *that* and—look here, the magician has fired his gun and the dove has flown out at last. There's nothing else, is there?"

"Stop a minute, sir," said Hadley, punctilious as ever. "Let's hear it, Fell. No blasted jokes at this hour! What do you mean?"

The doctor shrugged his shoulders with something like the effect of a slow earthquake. He sat down in a big chair beside the gas-fire, and got out his pipe. For a time he remained blinking at it, and there was no sound except the thin roaring under the kettle. Then he spoke abruptly:

"To my own humble way of thinking, gents, you will never convict Gregory Mannering of murder, and you will never convict Jeff Wade of perjury. If it's any consolation to you, I believe I can see a way of putting the fear of God into the old man and winning your game; which is what you seem to want. But as for the wisdom of the course——"

Again he rubbed his hands up and down his temples.

"Yes, Hadley, you've done fine work. Now, there is a good old English phrase to describe ME, and the phrase, in its literal sense, is scatterbrain. These old wits really do scatter all over the place. I am like the cross-eyed hunter who fired all over the landscape and left no game for anybody else. I am the man in the old wheeze who searched diligently in Piccadilly for a shilling lost in Regent Street, on the grounds that there was more light to see by in the former place. But there is often a great deal to be said in favour of looking for a clue in the place where you know it isn't. You see things you would never have noticed otherwise.

"You, gents, have set yourselves a problem and sharply defined it. You have done brilliantly; but you have given a complete answer to your problem without quite knowing what a part of the problem was. One part of the problem I do not think you saw: let me call it the puzzle of the Unnecessary Alibi. I don't think there can be any doubt in our minds that Mannering's alibi was faked. Jeff Wade, with a spaciousness worthy of the Count of Monte Cristo, threatened or bribed thirteen witnesses to give him a tale beyond tarnish. Twelve of those witnesses really were necessary; that is to say, the tale they told was very necessary, even though it was not essential to produce so many of them to tell it. But the thirteenth was an excrescence. The thirteenth was not even consistent with perjury on a large scale; he was an outsider, to obtain whose lying statement Jeff must have had considerable trouble—for no reason whatever, if we accept Hadley's analysis altogether.

"Now let me say what I do believe. I think Hadley's reconstruction of the crime was quite correct, except in one small and possibly trifling detail. That detail was that Gregory did not, in fact, kill Penderel.

"To me it seems clear that the real murderer was young Jerry Wade; but I doubt whether you will ever have enough real evidence against him."

"—I'm afraid I startled you," continued Dr. Fell, after a long silence during which there was only one lurid oath from Hadley. The doctor, sitting back in the gloom with only the light of the gas touching his face, wheezed meditatively, and nodded. "In telling you about this, let me take my own twisted way and begin at the end of the case in order to emphasise something. Also, let me begin with an analogy.

"Let us suppose that Carruthers here is accused of murdering his grandmother at Islington between the hours of eleven o'clock and midnight. You, Hadley, and Sir Herbert and I get together to fake him an alibi for the hour between eleven and twelve. We get hold of the manager of the Dorchester Hotel (which miscreant is in our pay) and his partner; we get hold of seven attendants and three outsiders (also our hirelings) whom we will call D. Lloyd-George, S. Baldwin, and N. Chamberlain, and who were having dinner there. All these swear that Carruthers was in the dining-room between eleven and twelve, leaving at twelve.

"Now this clears him completely. Nobody cares where he was after twelve, since he could not conceivably have killed his grandmother afterwards; and, anyway, it would have taken him so long to go from Park Lane to Islington after midnight that this gives ample leeway to emphasise the alibi. Therefore we do not need to run any thundering risk by bribing still another witness to prove that he dropped in at the Savoy at twelve-fifteen for a chat with the manager. It is altogether outside the most scrupulous alibi. If we put this in, it must be because there is a very strong reason for it.

"So with Mannering in this case. Jeff proved that Mannering did not leave The Persian Restaurant until a quarter to eleven—precisely the time when the masquerader was stepping into the Wade Museum. That was quite enough. Why, then, was the thing so elaborately planned that Mannering must be driven round to Prince-Regent Court by Aguinopopolos, that he must meet the manager of the flats, and go upstairs the back way? Echo answers: Because it was vitally necessary to back up Mannering's statement that he had paid a visit to the flats that night.

"But why was it so necessary? You people didn't give two hoots, as Hadley said, about the mere fact that he had visited the place, so long as you could prove he did not come in the front door at twenty minutes to eleven. You were not even going to press him on it: you, Hadley, told him as much when you talked to him at Wade's house. Still, it must be plain to you that—to Mannering—the assertion that he *had* visited the flats

360

at some time or another was the most burningly important thing of which he tried to convince you.

"If there is one thing which strikes us with regard to his behaviour, it is that tireless and almost fanatical insistence on the point that he *had* visited the place. He throws it in your face even when you do not doubt it, from the time that he first talks to Carruthers up to the time he produces his witnesses in Sir Herbert's office. It is natural for him to wish his story verified in all particulars, but it seems rather a curious monomania on a point having nothing to do with the crime. Now, just what the devil *did* he do at Prince-Regent Court, according to his testimony? He went upstairs, found the door of Holmes's flat open, poked about, *and picked up from the hearth a folded letter, unfinished, written by Jerry Wade....*

"There, gentlemen, is the whole secret. He picked up from the hearth a note (he says) which had tumbled out of somebody's pocket. He only explains that he found it there when it tumbles out of his own pocket at the police-station, and he must find an explanation for it.

"Now we know that Mannering is a liar; we know that he did not go to Prince-Regent Court at all. Where, then, did he really get that note, and why was it so necessary for him to scream insistently that he found it at the flats? When we see that the thing is grimy all over one side with coal-dust, we know that he must have found it on the scene of the crime. For Mannering—to account for that coal-dust—made the whacking error of saying he found it on the hearth in Holmes's flat by a coal fire. Carruthers visited that flat; visited both rooms; he saw no fire at all, either coal or wood. You chaps should realise that those service-flats have only those electric log-fires which are such a disgrace to our civilisation.

"I'm afraid that not enough attention was paid to that little note: 'Dear G., There has got to be a corpse—a real corpse,' simply because it really did have to do with a hoax. As a hoax it was explained; and forgotten. But that was not the important point in connexion with it. The important point was that, though its contents had no significance, its whereabouts had. It made no difference that Jerry Wade had written to a medical student asking for a corpse. It did make rather a large difference whether the note was dropped beside a coal fire which didn't exist in Holmes's flat, or dropped beside a corpse in the cellar of the Wade Museum. It explains a good deal that has been obscure. It explains why Jeff Wade was at such pains to exonerate Mannering; for he was exonerating his own son. I think it even explains that little twenty-thousand-pound cheque which will aid Mannering to stronger and tastier adventures in the Orient.

"With what Hadley calls my own particular brand of cussedness, I have given you the ending first. Still, it did seem to be pretty certain, as the story progressed, that Jerry Wade must have killed Penderel. . . .

"You've been talking about obvious suspects. You've been saying that, since Miriam Wade was absolutely the only person who went down into that cellar, and there was no other way down except by the cellar door, then the murderer must have been either Miriam or somebody who came through a window. The trouble is, there *was* another way down into the cellar. There was a whacking great lift. It may be my own congenital disinclination to avoid stairs, but in my own mind that lift stood out in colours of fire. Wherever you turn in this case, you fall over it or bump into it.

The lift sings and rattles in the brain. And the first thing we hear about that lift is—that it is out of order.

"Carruthers hears this first from Pruen on the night of the murder, when he goes in and finds evidence of Illingworth's hilarious escape from same. Pruen, by the way, makes on that occasion a remark which (like some of his others) should command your attention. Pruen says that the old man swears somebody put it out of commission deliberately, because the old man had a violent habit of using it casually and nearly beheaded himself a couple of times.

"Who could have put the thing wonky, I wondered? Well: Jerry Wade, according to what his old man told Armstrong here, was an electrical engineer. . . .

"I want you to take a long look at that lift and its history during the events of Friday night. Illingworth is very enlightening about it. I think I first began to have my eye on Jerry from the moment of Illingworth's entrance into the museum. This was at ten-thirty-five, and Miriam was just coming up from the cellar. (She had gone down for her second visit, found the cellar apparently empty, thought Penderel had gone, and had run upstairs again.) Illingworth passed her, and turned to the curator's room. Just then the door was flung open; out, in a glory of whiskers and nervousness, strides Jerry Wade. He says to Illingworth that the old doctor musn't waste time out there *talking;* why does Illingworth wish to hang about *talking?* This is what Jerry Wade says.

"There occurs here a little point to which, again, not enough attention has been directed. We have heard from Illingworth a bushel of pertinent facts about the curator's room and the lift. The door, it has been repeated, is steel-bound; nothing can be heard beyond it. The doors of the lift are so thick that Illingworth, imprisoned there, cannot hear what Jerry and Holmes are saying in the curator's room. Any conversation taking place in the hall—agreed?—could be heard *only when the lift doors were open*. Then it could be heard through the big ventilator screen, but otherwise not a syllable is audible.

"When Illingworth had come into the museum, he spoke to Pruen at the far end of the hall, and spoke to Baxter not much farther on. How, then, did Jerry Wade hear him? How, in fact, did Jerry Wade know the man was there at all if he were thus shut into a sightless and soundless room? We come to the not very staggering belief that he must have been in the lift. There's no other way of doing the trick. He must have been in the lift, and standing up on that box to peer out.

"Very rummy about this, at the beginning. For, when Illingworth came into the curator's room, he observed—he mentions it when he is thinking of breaking out—that the lift doors are fast closed and on them is carefully hung a sign, "OUT OF ORDER." If Jerry was in the lift, why trouble to conceal it? But, Lord, gents!—he concealed it even more than this. Take a grand leap to the next day, and hear what the finger-print men say about that lift when they want to make sure old Illingworth was really in the lift. Illingworth was in the lift; they found his finger-prints. The odd circumstance was not that. The odd circumstance was that they found no other finger-prints whatsoever.

"No other prints. Humph, Jerry must have been in the lift, he must have touched it somewhere, but there is not a digital mark in the whole place. This could only have happened if they had been carefully wiped away. Why does a man wipe off his finger-prints? Why does he conceal that he has been in that lift? The letter beginning 'Dear G.,—' which he dropped in the cellar when he killed Penderel, will give you the answer.

"D'ye see, I wasn't satisfied with any of his behaviour on that night. I wasn't satisfied with his tame acceptance of Dr. Illingworth as the actor from the agency. I said to myself: There is probably no living human being on earth who could talk to Illingworth for half an hour and really believe that he came from a theatrical agency. Jerry Wade was not gullible enough for that. He pretended to believe in Illingworth, he put up a grand show for Illingworth's benefit, because for the sake of his own skin he had better pretend he thought Illingworth came from the agency. It would not do to drop a hint of his knowledge that the real actor was lying dead in the cellar. I submit that the amateur actor put on a very good performance for Illingworth's benefit, just after he had stabbed the professional.

"Hadley, fit your conception of the crime over mine now, and see how the two come together like a stencil-drawing: exactly right. I'll try, in my own muddled way, to outline it. For we have another remarkable clue in the scrap of conversation which you yourself overheard on Monday afternoon, when Jeff Wade and Illingworth were coming down into the cellar just before Jeff Wade rubbed out the finger-print on the mirror. . . ."

Hadley got up stiffly from his chair and stared across the table. He pointed at Dr. Fell.

"You mean," he said, "what Illingworth was repeating to the old man? Illingworth said something like, 'If some miscreant has indeed purloined gloves from your desk,' to which Jeff answered, 'Yes, and a screwdriver——' "

Dr. Fell nodded.

"Humph. Exactly, my boy. Somebody had stolen gloves and a screw-driver from Jeff's desk upstairs. What does that suggest? Our wandering thoughts go straight back to that alleged broken lift, which somebody might have been putting right. . . .

"Jerry Wade was alone in the curator's room from eighteen minutes past ten, when Miriam and Harriet left him, until twenty-five minutes to eleven. He was alone for something more than fifteen minutes. He had been putting on his whiskers, no very lengthy job, since Harriet stated it was nearly finished by the time she and Miriam left him. Miriam had gone out, saying that she was going to get him—what? One of the old man's coats from the cellar, to complete his impersonation. I'll tell you what occurred to him, Hadley, as surely as though I had been there. 'The old man's away; good. No chance of him murdering himself with that lift. The crowd upstairs will be wanting to bring that big lead coffin downstairs shortly; let's make it easy for them, since we're going to have the coffin in here. Let's repair the lift—only take a second or two, for I've put it wrong myself.' He gets a screw-driver out of the old man's desk, and takes a pair of gloves in case the job should be oily. He gets into the lift. 'Got it! Perfectly simple. Try her out. Where shall I go? Here, dash it all, let's send the lift down to the cellar, and I'll pick out one of the old man's coats for myself. . . .'

"Down he goes, and steps out of the lift in the boarded-off part of the cellar, where the old man's workshop is. And he hears voices.

"Miriam, having taken the dagger and the moustache, has gone down there to meet Mannering. But she has met Penderel instead. And Jerry, there in the dark, hears the whole story. . . .

366

"You have seen that young fellow with his cynical mask laid off, Hadley; you have seen it several times. We have heard them jeer at him for his ineffectiveness: a voice rings and strikes and hurts, 'Shut up, you over-grown gnome!' We have heard him jeer at himself, and torture himself there in the background, because he is only 'good old Jerry' who wouldn't even exclaim a certain monosyllable to a goose. But you have also seen his face in your office when you announced that you would not make it public about Miriam's child. That good-natured little goblin could change into a worse goblin than ever leaped out of the dark. And he did leap out of the dark—at Penderel. . . .

"Miriam, screaming at Penderel to keep back, has run upstairs. Penderel, more or less satisfied, waits and wonders what to do. And out steps Jerry from the other side of the board partition. I can see that whole scene under the swinging electric-light. There is the dagger, lying on the floor. Maybe it is only, 'Now, damn you,' and the ineffective brother leaps with the same quickness in this deadly business as later he leaped in his mere dummy show with Illingworth to call attention to the fact that he had an alibi. In that stroke with the dagger he may have pierced the heart by accident, or he may have learned something about the use of such things from his friend Randall; it was accident, I suspect. But down goes Penderel as dead as Haroun al Raschid. 'Got to get this body out of the way, in case somebody comes down. Drag it—to the coal-bin.' Don't you think he'd have had the strength? He had the strength when he hauled Illingworth, as big and as heavy a man, to the lift. What's the time! Just on ten-thirty. 'Got to get out of here. . . .'

"Back he goes into the workshop, hiding the gloves

and screw-driver away. 'Got to get back upstairs; got to pretend that the lift hasn't been repaired yet.' He runs it upstairs, and starts to make sure he has left no finger-prints inside. He must make a good job of this, and also put the lift out of commission again. As he does so, he hears voices in the hall. With the box in the lift, placed endways, he can see out. Illingworth. Who the devil is it? He can't decide, but he had better pretend this is the actor from the agency. He closes up the lift again, gets out, and has the cool nerve to meet Illingworth at the door a minute or two later. . . ."

Dr. Fell pulled wheezily at his dead pipe.

"But downstairs? Mannering has seen the whole thing through the window. He has seen Miriam go down for the second time—just after Jerry has come up—and he has seen *her* go away. . . .

"Mannering's thoughts? Behold! The brother has committed the crime, and the sister will probably be suspected of it. Read your own interpretation of his motive into it but mine is this. With one heroic sweep, by playing a dangerous and fat-headed part that night, he can cast out the devil of mockery and force this brother who has jeered at him into such a position that, if it had not been for Mannering's dexterity and guts, sister and brother would alike be up for murder. That is the form which Mannering's unquenchable vanity took. Eat their words? He will make everybody eat words and cram them down their throats! Then he will say to Miriam, 'Thank you. I've shown you, and now good day.' Remember the tale of the chap who jumped down into the lion's arena and picked up the lady's glove, only to throw it in her face afterwards? In startling colours, and to be sound of fatuous bugles, Mannering saw himself in that position. He gloried in it. He did—what you said he did. And he picked up from the floor in the coal-bin, where it had fallen from Jerry's pocket, that damning note which is the last evidence that Jerry Wade committed the murder.

"Of course Mannering got the wind up afterwards. Hence old Jeff's assistance. That, I think, will have much to do with explaining the twenty thousand pounds from the grateful father. To the end there remains a puzzle. Was Mannering a gallant noble-heart, even though inspired and whipped and driven by pure vanity; or was he in his own way as thorough a blackguard as Penderel? I don't know. I rather question whether he knows himself, to the last day when he climbs the highest peak in the Himalayas or swims the Hellespont pursued by sharks. He is always the wise man who can tell us anything about a chap like Mannering; and, if we read the last riddle, we still should not know."

The grey was lightening outside the windows. Dr. Fell got up, in the midst of an absolute silence, and stumped over to open one of them and breathe the cool morning air.

"But there's not any evidence—" said Hadley suddenly.

"Of course there's no evidence now," agreed Dr. Fell cheerfully. "Otherwise I shouldn't have told you all this. I don't want you to arrest the young lad. There's been enough fuss and uproar as it is. Give Jeff Wade a scare if you like—but (to coin a metaphor which makes my gorge rise) let the dove which flies out of the final box at the magician's pistol carry an olive-branch and drop it on your consciences."

They all looked at each other, and presently Hadley began to laugh.

"Suits me," said Sir Herbert, and scratched the back of his head. "I am silent."

"And Lord knows I am too, sir," agreed Carruthers.

Dr. Fell, with a broad beam, turned round and stumped back to the gas-ring by the fireplace. "You'll always wonder whether I am right," he told them, "and so—just between ourselves—shall I. But this kettle's been boiling long enough."

He switched off the gas. There was a sharp pop, and the kettle ceased to sizzle. Then, with an untroubled appetite, all of them prepared for breakfast.

There's an epidemic with 27 million victims. And no visible symptoms.

It's an epidemic of people who can't read.

Believe it or not, 27 million Americans are functionally illiterate, about one adult in five.

The solution to this problem is you... when you join the fight against illiteracy. So call the Coalition for Literacy at toll-free **1-800-228-8813** and volunteer.

**Volunteer
Against Illiteracy.
The only degree you need
is a degree of caring.**

Ad Council Coalition for Literacy

THIS AD PRODUCED BY MARTIN LITHOGRAPHERS
A MARTIN COMMUNICATIONS COMPANY